Kill Zone

DAMIR SALKOVIC
KILL ZONE

❥❥❥❥

Gypsy Shadow Publishing

Kill Zone

by

Damir Salkovic

Gypsy Shadow Publishing, LLC.
Lockhart, TX
www.gypsyshadow.com

Library of Congress Control Number: 2020939963

eBook ISBN: 978-1-61950-615-2
Print ISBN: 978-1-61950-617-6

Published in the United States of America

First eBook Edition: May 22, 2020
First Print Edition: June 10, 2020

Dedication

For Riley, who was patient and encouraging,
and Bootsy, who kept me in my seat until the writing was
done.

One

They left the trenches right after the sirens and made their way through collapsed houses and wreckage. Progress was slow; the men cursed and groaned as they clambered over broken beams and piles of junked machinery.

Dawn was just breaking, a thin white line on the edge of the flat, featureless horizon. Watery light trickled through the smoke and dust, across the bombed-out buildings and courtyards, but the rutted streets under the shattered skyline were still awash in shadows. Already the air was heating up, promising another blistering day.

Clayton hung at the rear of the infantry column, keeping his eyes on the back of the man in front of him, placing each foot as carefully as he could, feeling grit and ash crunch under the soles of his boots in the dark. He supposed he had been lucky so far. In the first episode of the show, his assault company had alighted on the killing beach long after the worst of the massacre was over, encountering only sporadic enemy fire. Days later, as they hunkered down in the remains of a razed village during the push inland, a soldier from another unit had told them that thousands had died during the landing, many of them never making it off the barges. The body count exceeded all network estimates and the advertising revenue was nearly double. *Ninety-two percent up from last quarter,* the man had shouted over the dull thump of explosions, like he was reading a corporate propaganda piece. The feverish shine in his eyes, the pride in a job well done, had made Clayton sick to his stomach.

Death was everywhere. Death in the lenses of hidden cameras, playing on high-definition screens, over and over, to the cheers of a faraway crowd. Sooner or later it would be his turn.

But he was still breathing, still walking. He wasn't a corpse.

The squad moved out of the ruins, into the open space of a rubble-strewn square. The sound of running water reached Clayton's ears over the stomping of boots and the thump of distant explosions. Lieutenant Hall called a halt and the platoon crouched behind a low wall. On the other side of the wall was a concrete embankment, dark water rushing and swirling below.

Clayton saw a narrow bridge leading across the river, to a small stone dock and a row of low, square tenements. It was light enough now to see the tattered flags hanging from empty windows. Enemy forces had held the near side of the river until late afternoon the previous day, when they had been forced across under concentrated artillery fire. There had been no response so far from their own guns, entrenched in the earthworks on the single hill behind town. Command, faceless and cryptic, reported the enemy was digging in to make a stand. What this meant was anyone's guess, but Clayton expected a massacre, and to judge by the whey faces around him the rest of the unit shared his sentiment.

Hunched over to avoid the attention of snipers, the lieutenant moved along the ranks, barking commands. Prescott and Zielinsky hopped over the wall and moved forward, bent over low and clutching their rifles, using the crumbling bridge balustrade as cover. The assault platoon waited in heavy, tense silence, broken only by coughs and muffled whispers. Kintner started to light a cigarette and Sergeant Bennings knocked it out of his hands.

The purpose of luck, Prescott had said in the early days of the war, was to eventually run out. He had delivered this pearl of wisdom while the squad was sitting in a farmhouse cellar on the edge of one of the cleared villages, drinking wine from bottles made to look dusty and sharing cigarettes. To Clayton the proclamation had sounded trite, the type of dime store philosophy without substance or meaning that could sound insightful only to a mind fogged with tranks and spent adrenaline. Lately he found himself going back to the words, turning them over in his sleepless nights. He had thought that by enlisting he would leave his entire life behind, find a degree of resigned tranquility, if not peace, in the senseless, tumultuous grind of the war machine. But some ghosts refused to be stilled. They came to him in the blackest depths of night, in the small, still hours just before dawn. No matter how hard he tried, they always caught him unprepared.

He raised himself and looked over the wall. On the bridge, Zielinsky stopped and stood on tiptoe to inspect an empty sandbag emplacement. Prescott hunkered a few steps back, scanning the pocked façades of the tenement buildings. Zielinsky glanced over his shoulder. Lieutenant Hall waved him forward. The two men started to climb.

As if on cue, hell broke loose.

The machine gun opened up as soon as Zielinsky's boots touched the other side of the barrier, the bullets tearing through flesh and canvas alike. Clayton saw the scout crumple backward, saw Prescott leap down from the sandbag wall and flatten himself against the set stones of the bridge. Two more guns joined in, followed by scattered small-arms fire. A cloud of dust and sand enveloped the emplacement. Bullets whined and chipped the wall behind which the soldiers were crouching. *Panicking,* he thought, surprised by his ability to think clearly and rationally. *They're panicking.* He glanced at the dirty faces around him, white and strained with fear. Eyes rolling like those of cattle being led to slaughter. He repressed a terrible urge to laugh.

Lieutenant Hall leaped over the wall and motioned the unit forward. Clayton could see the man's mouth opening and closing, but the crash of gunfire drowned out all sound save for the roar of blood in his ears, the triphammer beat of his heart. Invisible guns poured scorching fire from every direction. Several men went down, but those only grazed hobbled and shoved ahead, and the platoon charged on, a huge, bellowing animal frightened into a frenzy. Nothing would stop it now.

Machine guns stitched the embankment, but dust and smoke covered all, and for the time being the enemy was firing blind. Clayton's mind had retreated completely in terror. The thinking part of him embraced death; the beast in him wanted to live. Bullets spat at him from the smoke, ripped through flesh, cracked off the stone of the bridge. He watched his hands shove a dead soldier aside, his feet scramble over sandbags and bodies and into the killing field beyond.

3

He stumbled through a shell crater, found cover, and knelt. Some of the soldiers had taken cover behind the stone parapet and were returning fire. The long concrete terrace between the bridge and the block of houses was littered with dead bodies. He fired like an automaton, aiming at muzzle flashes, pausing only to insert a fresh clip into his rifle. Through the settling dust, he could make out a shape crawling slowly toward the entrance of the nearest building, halting as the firing subsided, faster when it picked up again. Under the first floor windows, out of sight of the defenders, it raised itself to its knees; Prescott, white as a ghost with dust, pulling a grenade off his belt and yanking the pin with deliberate, unhurried movements.

Turning away, he closed his eyes, clapped his palms to his ears and counted the explosions. When he looked back, smoke was pouring out of the destroyed doorway and two lower-floor windows, and the men of the assault platoon were pouring in. Shots lit up the darkness within. The machine guns were no longer firing. He saw a soldier in enemy uniform climb out on the sill of a second-floor window, dangle by his arms for a moment, then drop the remaining distance. The man grimaced as he got up and limped into the shadows between the buildings. His uniform was dark and stuck to his side with blood, and he left a thin scarlet trail behind him. Clayton shouldered his rifle, lined up the shot and squeezed the trigger. The soldier's head snapped to the side; he fell to his knees and tumbled forward.

The sun had come out above the rooftops, hot and fierce. Distant detonations shook the ground, the advancing guns hammering enemy artillery positions. Clayton removed his helmet and wiped at the sweat coursing down his stubbly cheeks. His eyes searched the scarred walls until they found the camera. Machinery stirred at his presence, concealed optics drawing back for wide-angle shots, zooming in close on his face. Nothing human behind them; every move automatic, programmed to find and lock on him, to record every step he took.

He cocked his finger at it like a gun and pretended to shoot. The black, glistening eye stared at him with dead indifference. His hand where it touched his face was sticky and red and his uniform collar was wet. A piece of his earlobe was missing. There was no pain, only a faint ringing in his skull.

A piece of him left for the Scavenger teams to collect.

There was no stopping the laughter now; it bubbled up from some deep, black well inside him, a harsh, awful sound that threatened to tear him apart. The rest of his platoon walked past him, giving him a wide berth and averting their eyes. Clayton leaned against the wall and laughed until the sirens began to wail.

Two

Cigarette smoke coiled and drifted toward the black-ened ceiling. Clayton lay on his back on the bedroll, the talk and laughter of the others a faraway susurration, like the lapping of the tide. Closing his eyes, he summoned a memory; the three of them taking a trip east, to the edge of the city's boundless sprawl, where the water began.

It had been his first time riding the high-speed rail, seeing the world he lived in from the elevated track. The ugly square rises of gray, identical housing blocks stretched as far as the eye could see, blending with each other until they met a dull, orange sky. He had lived all his life inside one of them, packed tight alongside swarming millions, and still his brain balked at the disorientation, the unspeakable ugliness of it all. Half-flooded slums at the foot of colossal dams whose gates and locks kept the swelling ocean at bay. Above the sprawl, the glass-and-steel Aventus Spire burned bright, a beacon in the gloaming.

Other images intruded unbidden, unwanted: Josh's small, pale hand on the train window, his eyes bright with excitement. Linda laughing at their expressions, father and son both struck dumb as the Atlantic came into view. The seething black surface of the ocean going on and on forever, shuddering and falling. The boom and hiss of the waves on the beach.

Nothing could exist on the other side, Clayton had thought, looking at the immensity of dark water. It was the end of the world, the rim of the universe itself. He'd fallen asleep with his arms around his son, and while they slept his wife had pulled a blanket over them and when he woke it had been wet with her tears.

He remembered another beach, this one plowed by bombardment and stained red with blood. But there were no dead or wounded in sight, either in the landing zone or between the squat pillboxes and empty machine gun emplacements. This was an army that left no bodies behind on the battlefield. This was a war that would never end.

After the beach, death had hounded their every step; artillery barrages from a clear sky, snipers lurking in ruined bell towers of churches and behind mill chimneys, the incessant chatter of heavy machine and anti-tank guns. The men had marched across bleak landscape into hailstorms of gunfire, stormed concrete bunkers and fought hand-to-hand in a maze of trenches. Waves of soldiers had crashed into each other, smoke and fire spuming like surf on a stormy shore. Men shot and dismembered by shells, falling without a sound or dying screaming and writhing in the mud and dirt, clawing at ragged wounds and spilling coils of steaming intestines, eyes wide open and staring at the indifferent sky.

Death had become a familiar presence that ceased to frighten him, but the thought of becoming a corpse still filled him with horror. Corpses belonged to the machines. The sound of the meat-transport sirens after a battle was worse than all the shots and explosions and screams put together. When the sirens came, you crawled out of the trenches and laid down your weapon and headed for the nearest containment area. You sat down and clamped your arms over your head. Tried not to look, tried not to listen. Some of the men had been alive when the meat transports descended, when the removal teams started their grisly work.

There had once been a time when the dead were buried, each body laid in a neat plot of soil, a stone marker placed at its head. Huge swathes of fertile land used to lay corpses to rest, covered in green grass and trees. A time before methane cyclers and bioprotein factories, before the industrial badlands that spread between crowded conurbations in leprous patches. He found it hard to imagine that such a time had ever existed outside of old books and movies. But in his dreams the earth split open under his feet, spewing out gouts of blood and the remains of the rag-and-bone dead, cold hands reaching for him, pulling him down into the darkness.

Clayton grunted, started out of a doze. All around him men lay scattered through the gloom, sweating in the oppressive heat of the day. Some were sitting with their backs against the crumbling walls of the ruin, hoping to find relief in the coolness of the stone. Cigarette butts and empty ration cans covered the floor, the stench of stale smoke and unwashed bodies like a tangible presence in the room. There was nothing to do but wait for orders.

He propped himself up on his elbows and immediately regretted it. His skull felt like a balloon filled with blood. The bandage wrapped around his head was crusty and the wound beneath it throbbed like an infected tooth.

"You think we'll get some air support?" Alvarez asked no one in particular. A nerve twitched in his dark, sunburnt cheek. His eyes, flat and black, stared into nothing.

"There's no air support," O'Rourke said, without lifting his eyes from his work. He was stripped to the waist, sitting in the rectangle of sunlight that came in through the blown-out window casement, meticulously stripping and cleaning his rifle. Sweat glistened on his pale, freckled shoulders and back, already starting to peel from the sun.

"How do you know that?" Popovich's voice piped up from the other side of the room. "How the fuck do you know that? We got good ratings." He drummed his feet on the floor and glanced around the room for encouragement. Finding none, he hung his head. The feet continued their patter, as if of their own accord. "We got good ratings. You don't know nothing."

The room had gone quiet, the men drawn out of their listless stupor by the promise of violence. Fights broke out often and over nothing—a half-smoked cigarette, a couple of squares of toilet paper, an inane remark—and no one bothered to stop them or discipline those involved. O'Rourke was a head taller and at least twenty pounds heavier than Popovich, but it was a widely held belief among the men that the latter had reached the end of his rope.

Yet O'Rourke either didn't hear or chose to ignore the taunt. Nothing ever bothered O'Rourke. Beads of sweat dripped from his furrowed brow as his fingers, long and elegant and dexterous, at odds with his slouched, ungainly frame, oiled and caressed the parts of the weapon.

Clayton stared up at the ceiling and tried to doze off again. The squabbling held no interest for him; O'Rourke was cracking up, his manic obsession with his gun the first

8

step in the race to insanity, and Popovich already had the finish line in sight. They would both be dead soon, along with everyone else in the room. He felt nothing but indifference toward the other men, except Prescott, for whom he was beginning to harbor an active dislike. There was no room for camaraderie in the platoon. Faces changed, soldiers died, new ones were brought in to replace them. Like himself, the new arrivals were asocials, tribals, labor gang dodgers, credit rejects. The unwanted dregs of society, men with nothing to lose, resigned to death.

Footsteps crunched in the grit, and Lieutenant Hall appeared in the doorway. No one tried to get up or salute. A shadow darkened the officer's sharp features. Hall was new, both to the unit and to the war, and still believed the garbage he'd been fed at the two-week officer training course. Most of the officers were corpmerc rejects or aspiring security consultants, milking a temporary gig between two rounds of interviews, hoping for a second chance with the conglomerates. They worked for a percentage of gross, a sliding scale based on rank and contract clauses. In combat, their role was largely promotional. Tactics were scripted, troop numbers and movement predetermined, casualty rates estimated within a margin of a few percentage points. All an officer had to do was relay orders, make sure the squads went out on schedule and try not to get himself killed. Hall was cut from another cloth; he kept faith in his training and expected obedience and respect from the men under his command, both on the battlefield and off it. Every now and then, the studio's aptitude screening failed to keep out one of those: a true believer in outdated field manuals, a fanatic who saw rank and uniform as something more than colorful screen props.

"I need three volunteers," Hall said.

No one answered. Cold, hostile eyes met the lieutenant's gaze. Private Spinelli flicked a cigarette butt in his direction and turned to face the wall. Flustered, Hall squared his shoulders, did his best to retain the appearance of control. "It's for a special assignment. Network special. Point-three percent bonus cred, a week's worth of extra rations. Any takers?"

Clayton's arm shot up at the same time as Prescott's. Within a moment, Alvarez made it three. Emboldened by their response, the lieutenant laid out the operation. Heavy armor was on the way, two tank companies pushing west. The road to the north was mined, so Command had ordered the tanks to move through the town, roll up the hill and blast the enemy's gun emplacements from behind. Anticipating this, the enemy had mined the bridge on the hill road and set up a roadblock around it. With their viewer rankings dwindling, supplies would be cut. The hostiles knew that and had dug in with fanatical stubbornness. Their main force had pulled out of town, but a small group had been left behind to man the roadblock, which consisted of two machine guns and an armored car. Intelligence reports, really an exchange of notes between the two commands, indicated that the hostiles were waiting for their own armor reinforcements and that the soldiers on the bridge were a suicide rearguard, ordered to hold off the tank advance for as long as possible and blow up the bridge when overwhelmed.

The Lieutenant's finger moved down the production board, from strip to strip. As far as primetime television went, the script was a gamble, but a necessary one. The ratings were falling, and the networks were out for blood. The studio execs had decreed that the show needed a shot in the arm. Mass-scale battle scenes, which had netted the creators several major industry awards in previous years, were no longer in vogue. Surveys indicated that a segment on individual heroism might be just the thing; sacrifice and resolve, dramatic tension heightened by a split-screen montage of the tanks rumbling through the ruined streets, heading for the climactic battle on the bridge. Still, enthusiasm for the new pitch was tepid, the returns doubtful. Tristar-Paramount, the show's parent network, had issued assurances to the other participating cable monopolies. New writers had been brought in, promising buckets of gore, enough to sate the appetites of the most bloodthirsty audience.

"One of the sappers from Bravo Company will sneak up to the bridge," Hall said, tracing the line of attack. "His job is to defuse the charges. If the sentries see him, your job is to draw enemy fire. Best scenario, hostiles don't spot you and everyone walks away alive."

10

"What if they see him anyway?" Alvarez said. The Lieutenant shrugged.

"Then the hostiles blow up the bridge and we're left holding our dicks in our hands. That bridge is the only place our tanks can cross the river. Studio calls advantage for the other side and we get bombed into oblivion."

It was a hopeless mission, to be conducted in broad daylight. Hall finally seemed to be learning his lesson, Clayton mused; men had to die, and the lieutenant's job was to make sure it happened in a way that boosted the ratings. He realized that he hated the lieutenant more than he'd hated anyone before. The depth of this emotion took him by surprise. But it felt good, a long-dormant part of him waking up, asserting itself. He gritted his teeth, felt the tiny muscles around his eyes and mouth contract in a grin.

Hall mistook his grimace and smiled back, clapping Clayton on the shoulder. "You men did a hell of a job on the bridge. Word is that the numbers are through the roof. Top slot on all the networks. If this tank attack succeeds, we'll be set. Extra leave days, enough tranks to go around. Maybe even an air strike on the enemy."

Blackness stirred inside Clayton, something he could not put a name to; his chest tightened until he found it hard to breathe. He saw himself driving his fist into that broad, smiling face, obliterating every shred of expression, all resemblance to humanity. Grinning himself, he took a step forward.

Hall looked up at Clayton, and whatever he saw in there made his smile die on his lips. The moment hung in the balance; the silence in the room was suffocating. Clayton could feel animal eyes on him, heard the gnashing of teeth.

Prescott stepped in between him and Hall. "When do you want us to go, sir?"

"Right now." Hall backed away, keeping his gaze on Clayton. He seemed to have regained his composure, but the quaver in his voice gave him away. "Captain Gallard of Bravo Company called a few minutes ago. He's sending his man over as we speak. A Private Miller." He pulled out a map from his pocket and indicated their present location and the bridge, handed it over to Prescott. "Good luck, men. We're all depending on you."

"Why did you volunteer for this, Clayton?"

His mind had been wandering and the question took him aback. "Same reason as you," he said, an edge creeping into his voice.

Prescott seemed to contemplate the response for a moment. "No," he said calmly, without turning to look at Clayton. "No, you didn't. But that's all right. You can't tell me because you don't know yourself."

"But I suppose you're going to tell me." Clayton clenched his hand in his pocket, felt the rictus tug at the corners of his mouth. More than ever, he wanted to wipe the smug look off Prescott's face with his fist or with the butt of his rifle. "Because you know everything, don't you? You know better than anyone, and you're going to win the war for us and be a network hero."

"Cut it out, you two," Alvarez said. The big man was breathing heavily, sweat tracking lines down his dirty cheeks. His eyes danced like the inside of his head was on fire. Here in the street, his facial twitches were worse than ever. As if with a mind of their own, his fingers twirled the pendant of leather and carved bone that hung around his thick neck. "I don't need this shit. Not right now."

"You're in a bad way, Clayton." Prescott blew smoke through his nose and went on as if Alvarez hadn't said anything. "Don't get me wrong. We all are. Half of us can't shoot straight because our hands are shaking, and the other half sees things that aren't there. You grow up in a housing block, you develop a fear of open spaces. Look at Alvarez. He's been in the open for all of five minutes now, and he's already hyperventilating. But with you it's different." His gray eyes fixed Clayton with a long, considering look. "There's something in you that goes beyond the madness of this place. Like a piece is missing, and sooner or later the whole thing will fall apart. When it does, it won't be pretty."

They were sitting on a fallen wall, smoking and waiting for the sapper, Miller, to arrive. Fires from the night's bombing flickered amid the piles of brick. Nothing but props; the entire town was a prop, a stage element in the theater of war, carefully placed for long shots and closeup frames, for mathematically optimized carnage. Blank, featureless walls sprayed with chroma-key microcrystals, a canvas for more elaborate scenery to be draped over in postproduction, for false skylines of broken spires and bombed church-towers to be edited in. A maze for rats—struggling, frightened, gnawing each other to death.

The sound of distant gunfire drifted in from the north; heavy fighting was going on between the advancing armor and enemy anti-tank units holed up in two strategic buildings overlooking the entrance to town. Across the street was a ruined courtyard paved with smooth river stones. Clayton felt lightheaded, hot with rage. In his mind's eye, he saw his hand clutching one of the stones, rising and falling, Prescott's face disappearing into a mass of blood and pulped bone. The unacknowledged suspicion that Prescott might be right only made it worse. "You want to shut up now," he said, "if you know what's good for you."

"I saw what you were going to do to Hall," Prescott said, unperturbed. "That would've been an extra four months added to your contract. Six if you'd done some real damage. Keep that up, and you'll end up like Spinelli. In the zone for the rest of your life." He watched the glow of the cigarette, turning the lighter in one hand. "Then again, maybe that's been part of your plan all along. You're like a rabid dog that doesn't care if he lives or dies, as long as he gets to sink his teeth into someone's throat."

"That's enough," Alvarez said, getting up and slinging the Browning Automatic Rifle, his BAR, over his shoulder. "From both of you. Want to kill each other, it's no skin off my nose. Hell, I may help you out myself. But do it after."

A small, wiry soldier was heading their way up the decimated street. Private Miller looked very young, a child in an oversized uniform. He greeted them nervously and asked to see the map. "Command sent us a plan of the bridge," he said. "There are storage chambers built into the supports and both sides of the bank, used for construction equipment and material. That's where the explosives have to be. Drums or artillery shells and detonator wires, if I had to guess." He traced a route on the map with a fingertip. "We loop around east, come in from the side."

"On the map it looks like going down the main road is quicker," Alvarez said.

"It is. But it also puts us in the line of fire of the machine guns." He pointed to an area downriver. "Due east is the factory district. There's an abandoned chemical plant a block or two that way. Waste pipes run from underneath it almost all the way to the bridge. That way I can get to the supports without them seeing me, climb up and cut the cabling to the charges."

"What about us?" Prescott asked.

"You can take the embankment. Makes it harder for them to see you that way."

"It'll also make it harder for us to lay cover fire for you if they see you."

"They won't see me," the sapper said.

"It's your funeral." Alvarez shrugged and scratched himself. "Once they see us, it's all up. We don't stand a chance against those guns. You better be a fast climber."

They walked in silence for a while, moving into the shadows of the ruined town, jagged walls looming above them. Prescott's eyes kept darting toward the slight figure in front. "How the hell did you end up here, Miller?"

"I enlisted," came the reply. "Just like everyone else."

"No, I mean why? They must have told you the odds before you put your name on that contract. You're still a kid. Things can't be that bad for you yet."

"I got married last summer." The sapper's grin made him look even younger than he was. "We applied for a permit from the Demos, but our credit was too low. The advance took care of that, and now we got royalties coming."

Clayton didn't say anything, but the familiar pang of guilt and loss sliced through his gut. Prescott's sardonic expression crumbled; for a moment, it was as if a stranger were staring out of his face.

"You're a goddam fool, boy." Alvarez stared at Miller wide-eyed. "You signed away your life for a kiddie permit? You won't live long enough to use it."

"Already did." Miller picked up the pace, almost swaggering. He seemed somehow taller, his chest expanding with the firm, brash confidence of youth. "Three weeks ago. A girl. My wife sent me a picture in her last letter. Sent me a holovid too, but we don't have a rig in camp."

Alvarez shook his head and swore heavily. "Another hungry mouth in the world. Another human rat in the cage."

"My girl will never go hungry." Miller shrugged and didn't seem to take offense. "No matter what happens to me.

14

She'll have all the advantages Carrie and I never had. With my enlistment credit, we could get into the best eugenics clinic, get her into an advanced education plan. She'll have a chance to become someone important. Make something of herself."

Before Prescott could reply, Clayton broke in. "What's her name?"

"Angeline." The young sapper's face lit up. "We named her Angeline, after Carrie's Grandma."

"That's a pretty name," Clayton said, feeling foolish. Prescott glanced at him curiously. He kept his head down and walked on.

The factory was a gutted ruin, rising vast and stark from an open battleground cratered by bombs. Shattered smokestacks thrust up into the gray sky over heaps of bricks and great twisted iron girders, surrounded by the remains of barricades and abandoned trenches and breastworks. Miller pointed out their position on the map, then the bridge. "The embankment is on the other side of the factory yard. Just follow the wire fence and you'll see it. Give me fifteen minutes, then come on down." Another grin and a jaunty wink. "If you hear them shooting, come on down fast."

They watched him cross the devastated ground and vanish into the gaping black hole of a doorway.

"Brave little bastard," Prescott said, with open admiration.

"He'll get killed." Something was happening to Alvarez; he had gone very pale under his sunburn and his breath came in short, ragged gasps. One of his hands clutched at a steel fencepost, the knuckles white with tension. "He'll get us all killed." His voice broke on the last word, trailed off to a half-whisper.

The other two men felt it too, their bodies sensing the change before their conscious minds could catch up.

The guns to the north had gone silent.

From that direction now came the faint, keening peal of sirens.

All three of them looked up as one. A low, chopping rumble filled the air, something between a hum and a roar. Dirt and dust whirled around them. Clayton tried to run, found that his legs had turned to stone. Prescott's mouth was opening and closing, but whatever he was trying to say was lost in the sudden, deafening noise of aircraft engines.

The noise was the whole world.

The tiltjets swept in low over the charred, roofless houses; two gunships at the front, the huge squat shape of a transport thundering behind them, a third gunship bringing up the rear of the formation. A storm of grit trailed in the wake of the downblast.

The shattered street swam away from Clayton, the shadows growing longer, becoming monstrous. Above his head, the gray sky gaped like a hungry mouth, the walls of the ruins crowding in like jagged teeth.

Panic swelled inside him, closed his throat. Shuddering spasms shook his arms and legs. An iron band tightened around Clayton's chest, crushing the breath from his lungs. The space was too open, too vast. The burned shells of buildings stared down at him with hundreds of empty sockets. Under his feet, an abyss beckoned.

"Take it." Someone was shaking him roughly, pressing something small and solid into his hand. A yellow, oblong lozenge, a trank, already dissolving in the sweat of his palm. He gulped it down, felt it stick in his throat.

"Easy. Easy." Arms held him, tilting the neck of a canteen toward his lips. He managed one swallow, then another. The flash fire of panic was subsiding; remembering his basic training, he bent over and took deep, slow breaths.

When his vision cleared, he stood up straight. The mad shadows had dispersed. Prescott was standing next to Alvarez, forcing another yellow tablet between the big man's tightly clenched teeth. Nausea rolled through Clayton like a wave. He swallowed hard and fought the urge to throw up.

"Better keep that down, Clayton," Prescott said, slapping Alvarez lightly across the cheeks. "It's the last of my supply." The other man was swaying from side to side, still clutching the wire fence. His eyes were glassy, aimed at the empty sky, but his breathing was evening out and some color had returned to his face.

Clayton felt drained and weak, but the warm glow of the trank was already spreading through his bloodstream, bringing with it clarity and calm, a sharpness of focus. The slight tremor in his hands—which he was so accustomed to that he no longer noticed it—was gone for now.

He glanced over at Prescott, seeing him with new eyes. Tranks were a rare reward, a propaganda message from the program's corporate sponsors. The last time the platoon had received an allotment was after the bloody landing at the beach, which had broken all broadcasting records. Was Prescott a thief, or a plant, an agent for one of the networks? There was no time to think of that.

"We good to go?" Prescott asked. Alvarez unlimbered his BAR and nodded. Under his eyes, dark bruises stood out in the chalky pallor of his face and his massive chest heaved up and down.

Clayton took his helmet off and wiped the sweat off his face with the crook of his elbow. An ominous stillness had settled over the town in the wake of the sirens and the aircraft. To the north, a column of dust was approaching, the tanks heading for the bridge. Prescott tipped his head at a three-story concrete structure in the corner of the factory yard. One entire wall of the structure was missing, collapsed into rubble, exposing stairwells and corridors. "Miller said fifteen minutes. We don't want to be late to the party. I'll be on point."

Weapons in hand, they tunneled into the wreckage of the factory district.

Merciless sun beat down on the three figures crawling through the rubble. Burning sweat streamed down their filthy faces as they pulled themselves forward. The growl of the tanks was getting closer. Soon the front of the armor column would clear the corner of the ruined boulevard and head for the bridge.

Ahead, Prescott signaled for the other two to stop. Clayton trained the binoculars on the enemy roadblock. Two machine guns nested behind sandbags, each crewed by two hostiles. A soldier with a light anti-tank gun sat on the top of the armored car. Seven men with rifles peered over a high revetment in the back, two more from behind the car; these two held backpacks from which long black cables snaked over the side of the bridge. Clayton took these to be the detonators. If Miller was discovered, the three of them would have to be very fast.

Beneath the roadblock, silty dark water lapped the base of the supports.

Miller was nowhere to be seen.

"How's it look?"

"Not good," he said. "They'll blow it up as soon as they see the first tank. Unless their armor shows up first."

"So much for Command's master plan." Alvarez spat in the dust and took a long pull from his canteen. "We better head back and get ready to swim."

"Wait." A flicker of movement in the darkness under the bridge caught Clayton's eye. He moved the binoculars back down. A small shape crept along one of the massive girders, closer and closer to a dangling wire. In a few quick motions, the severed end of the cable dropped into the river below. Clayton inhaled deeply, realizing that he had forgotten to breathe. "That's him. The charges in the embankment. He's going after them first."

"I knew he'd come through." Prescott grinned through his mask of sweat-caked dirt. "We should get closer so we can cover him."

They crawled on. Clayton took one more look through the field glasses. The men on the bridge were silent and tense, listening to the sound of the approaching tanks. Strained faces looked out from under coal-scuttle helmets. But for the luck of the draw, it could have been him behind the roadblock. He wondered what had made them volunteer. A chance to become heroes, an extra ration of tranks. None of it made sense; this was a suicide mission. No one would be coming back. Under their feet, Miller was bent to his work, as calm and methodical as if he were sitting in his own home, thousands of miles away from the war zone. Clayton wondered if Miller would live to see his daughter grow up. The odds were against that, almost nonexistent.

He wondered if he would have made the same decision if Josh had lived.

He wondered what was happening to him, or if it had already happened.

From their new position, they had a clear line of fire on the bridge and the sun was behind them, shining into the eyes of the soldiers on the roadblock.

"Shit." Prescott gripped his rifle tighter. "They're getting ready to blow it up." There was sudden commotion on the bridge. One of the men with the detonators got up from the cover of the armored car and moved toward the stone railing. Any moment now Miller would be discovered. He'd be a sitting duck down on the supports.

Before Clayton and Alvarez could react, Prescott was up and running in a crouch, exposing himself to enemy fire. A shout rang out and rifle shots cracked from the barricade. Alvarez popped up from cover and fired from the shoulder. Clayton joined in, firing at the soldiers behind the revetment to force them to keep their heads down. The machine guns roared. A scouring plume of dust and powdered cement engulfed the running figure.

"Get down," Alvarez shouted. Something hot buzzed past Clayton's face, hammering into the brickwork inches behind him. The machine guns swiveled in their direction. He ducked down and pushed his face into the rubble. The wreckage around him erupted skyward. Fragments of brick and stone showered down.

Powerful arms tugged him up. Alvarez was half-crawling over a heap of broken masonry. Through the haze of dust, Clayton could see the anti-tank gun pivoting toward him, the bore of the barrel gaping like a tunnel. Without thinking, he turned and ran.

A split second later, the ground rocked beneath him. A vast, invisible hand lifted him into the air and hurled him forward with irresistible force. He landed on his shoulder and tumbled head over heels, scraping his arms and back. Burning steel rained everywhere. Blackness washed over the edges of his consciousness. His hands and feet felt caked with lead.

Alvarez was on his knees next to him, firing short bursts at the bridge. The response stitched a line of geysers in the rubble, pinning them down. Clayton sank lower and gazed through a gap in the debris. His shoulder burned and his sleeve was stiff with blood. Behind the barriers, a thousand miles away, the soldier with the detonators was leaning over the railing. Up on the armored car, the gunner was adjusting his aim. There was nowhere to go. It had all been for nothing. He slouched down, closed his eyes and waited for dissolution.

The sharp crack of a Garand rifle flew over his head and the soldier on the bridge jerked back in a spray of red and fell over the railing, still clutching the backpack with the detonators.

The machine guns stopped firing. One of the men on the revetment yelped and fell backward, shot through the throat, the report rolling across the killing field a moment later.

Clayton looked up. A puff of smoke trickled from a window three floors above him. Prescott was alive, shooting down at the roadblock.

"Come on," Alvarez shouted as he hauled himself out into the open and broke into a lumbering run. Clayton's legs lifted him from behind cover. Black exhilaration surged through him; he screamed and rushed forward, gun blazing, the butt of the Garand thumping into his bad shoulder. Bullets spat around him, whistled off the debris. A second machine gunner slumped over his weapon. His comrade dropped the ammo belt and tried to pull him away. Clayton shot him in the chest and kept running.

A few feet ahead of him, Alvarez ripped a grenade off his belt, pulled the pin with his teeth and lobbed it into the other machine gun nest. The blast tore the crew to pieces and knocked back one of the men behind the revetment. Clayton looked over the sandbags as he ran. The anti-tank gun tracked across the killing field, pointed at the window from which the shots were coming. Halfway across the bridge, the second demolitions man was walking backward, paying out the detonator cables.

Just as he reached the first line of sandbags, the armored car exploded with a roaring crash. He flung himself down and felt the shock wave of the blast wash over his back. Stunned, he lay for a few seconds, trying to get his limbs to move. The advance was coming. One of the tanks must have scored a direct hit.

With tremendous effort, he dragged himself up, gulped at the air. Oily smoke stung his eyes and throat. The armored car was ablaze, the space between the sandbag walls a carnage pit of mangled bodies and blood. He glanced over his shoulder. The tanks were already rolling into the clearing, heading for the bridge.

He staggered over to the railing. Far below, Miller was balancing on a maintenance ladder, working on the fuses. Further down the bridge, almost on the other side, the enemy sapper was groaning and picking himself up, dazed by the explosion. The backpack had been knocked from his hands and lay several paces away, trailing wires.

Clayton pushed off the railing and reached for his bayonet.

The hostile saw him coming and dove for the backpack. Clayton lunged and grabbed the soldier's leg. A booted foot slammed into the side of his head. Holding on with desperate strength, he stabbed upward. The blade skidded off the man's lower ribs and slipped from his fingers. The soldier caught him with an elbow and tried to throw him off.

They rolled on the ground, swinging and kicking. The hostile got the upper hand, straddled Clayton's chest and slammed his head against the stones, trying to pin his arms down. Hands closed around his throat. The soldier's face was a blur.

Black spots exploded in Clayton's vision. He clawed at the man's shirt, pushed his thumb into the open bayonet wound. There was a scream and the pressure on his windpipe lessened. Clayton thrust up and heaved the soldier off, felt around for his blade.

Two things happened at once. Clayton threw himself at the soldier and drove the bayonet into the back of his neck. The soldier made a terrible gurgling sound and sank to his knees, his hands closing around the detonators.

A vast shudder went through the bridge, followed by a dull roar and a mass of smoke. Clayton covered his head with his arms and curled himself into a ball. The echo of the explosion rolled along the banks of the river like the whisper of an angry god. He wanted to get up, but his body refused to obey.

On his hands and knees, he crawled to the stone railing and looked down into the drifting mist. Miller lay broken on the concrete, like a toy twisted and thrown aside by an angry child. But the bridge was still standing. The supports were intact.

Prescott was climbing down the slope of the embankment, waving his arms. Clayton waved back, sat down heavily. He was tired, so very tired.

The tanks had come to a halt in front of the bridge. What were they waiting for? Dust and grit whirled around him; the paving stones thrummed under his buttocks and palms. Above and around, shadows descended in utter silence. He knew it all meant something, but he could not say what.

Flying dirt stung his eyes. Two steel birds landed not twenty paces away from him, their railguns swiveling from side to side. Boots crackled on the rubble. A massive head in a black reflective-visor helmet bent over him and spoke in a distorted voice. The body it was attached to was clad in black armor reinforced with cerametal plates. One gloved hand gripped a riot shock-stick. The garbled phrase was repeated, a command. He caught his own reflection in the visor, a dirt-streaked apparition with a skull smile and black pits for eyes.

Behind the steel birds a transport touched down, its bulk filling the width of the bridge. A door slid open in its belly, sending out a gust of chill air and a group of figures in olive-green protective suits and masks. He tried to speak, but his thoughts were disjointed, and the words would not come. The armored figure took a half-step back, raising the shock-stick.

Someone seized him under his arms and lifted him to his feet. The scene—the bridge, the river, the devastation, another steel bird circling overhead—spun in slow, sickening circles. Blood running everywhere, slick runnels smeared on the stones. Clayton was dragged back, past the smoldering wreck of the armored car. He tried to stand and walk, but his legs wouldn't hold him up.

A voice shouted in his good ear, telling him to walk. Masked heads and biohazard suits swarmed over the bodies, cutting them out of the uniforms, rolling them into plastic bags.

A big, sunburnt man in a uniform like Clayton's own, his stomach torn open by bullets, was trying to get up. Cursing and shaking his head, slipping in his own gore. Alvarez. One hand, black with dried blood, clutched the pendant around his neck. A black-armored shape stood over him. The bolt-gin hissed and cracked. The big man sprawled back into the dirt.

He found his feet, pitched forward, like a drunk, steadied himself against Prescott. Coming toward them was another armored Scavenger, bolt gun in one gloved hand. Dim, animal terror froze him, tangled his legs.

"He's fine," he heard Prescott say. He pushed one foot in front of the other, kept his eyes on the ground. Any moment an armored glove would fall on his shoulder and he'd find himself staring into the reinforced glass of the visor. Then he'd be shoved to his knees, hear the tread of approaching boots, wait for the bolt.

But nothing happened. They made it off the bridge and among the tanks. Prescott was saying something, but he couldn't make out what it was. By the time the aircraft thundered off into the sky, he was beyond seeing, beyond hearing.

Three

The episode was played that evening in the makeshift mess hall, right after the day's Newscan and corporate propaganda message. A huge hi-res video screen was wheeled into a clearing in the ruins and placed next to one of the standing walls. Hidden speakers blasted the audio track in digital surround sound and the gunfire and explosions were more vivid and lifelike than the real thing had been only hours before.

The men clapped and cheered as the cameras panned to Prescott kneeling behind an empty window casement, sighting down the barrel of the Garand with lethal calm. Clayton didn't understand what they were cheering for. The assault had resolved nothing, changed nothing; all it meant was the chance to move on to the next scenario, the next staged battle. The script was little more than a rough outline, frequently altered and rewritten by the network writers for maximum dramatic effect. Had it failed, the armies would have met in some other location, on some other killing field. The footage would have ended up as cuttings on the editing room floor.

He tried to picture the scene playing in an elegant boardroom, deep inside a corporate arcology, studio execs huddled in front of the screen, holding their breath, waiting for the early numbers to come in. Accountants grumbling over the cost of digital postproduction—less real blood and guts meant more attention had to be paid to the stage setting and fine detail. Producers wringing their hands over test-screening numbers and back-end costs. Teams of analysts weighing viewer numbers and advertising revenues against projected quarterlies and the rising prime rates of banking conglomerates. Speculators smelling blood and circling like hungry sharks.

He looked around for Prescott but couldn't see him anywhere. For a man who jumped at every opportunity to play hero, to be the first into the breach, Prescott didn't seem to care much for the limelight and shunned the sponsored award ceremonies. To the teams of faceless network producers, none of that mattered. There was plenty of stock footage to make up for his absence, enough individual storylines to pursue.

On the screen, an immense, digitally enhanced Clayton raised his rifle and charged into the maw of the enemy. Over the chatter of guns, Alvarez bellowed, "Forward!" and let loose with his BAR. The big man was airbrushed to heroic proportions, bulging, rounded muscles straining the sleeves of his uniform, his slightly crossed eyes rendered a blazing green. Details had been added to the scenery, small touches to breathe life into the empty concrete stage setting; broken children's toys in the rubble, smoke rising from the few intact chimneys, a clothesline strung across a balcony in the background. The camera shot them from behind and slightly above, scrolled to a long shot of the enemy sapper walking backward across the bridge, preparing to set off the detonator.

In the opening sequences, a short montage had been devoted to the defenders of the bridge—the feverish building of sandbag revetments, the writing of last letters to loved ones, the stern face of the commanding officer speaking about honor and duty and the ultimate sacrifice. False, like everything else: the barricade had been put up by the scenery crew, the actor playing the officer had delivered the speech from almost a thousand miles away, and the condemned soldiers' final act was to eat a good meal with a double dose of stimulants for dessert. There would be no other mention of them, tonight or ever. Background segments ate up profitable advertising airtime, and multiple focus groups had confirmed that the audiences didn't care much for the episode's losers.

Sudden gunfire made him flinch. A machine gun burst cut Alvarez in half, but not before he'd thrown a grenade over the sandbags to silence it forever. Frames flashed by in a clever montage; Clayton firing on the other gun, a tank half-hidden behind a crumbling wall taking out the armored car, a soot-blackened spotter smiling from the turret and giving the thumbs-up sign. Two camera angles shown in split screen—one of Miller hanging from a maintenance ladder, working to dismantle the last charge, the other of Clayton and the enemy sapper grappling on top of the bridge.

A reverential hush fell on the audience. Even in the pale glow of the screen, Clayton could see the glassy eyes of the men behind him, their slack mouths. Before the evening meal, a package from the sponsors had been passed around, a yellow wooden box bearing the red-and-black logo of Tristar-Paramount. Inside the velvet-lined box were small glass ampules, one for each man; a mammoth dose of pharma-grade Synthazine, courtesy of Glasser-Kamada Pharmaceuticals, one of the war's biggest sponsors. It was the second time the unit had been singled out for extraordinary valor and meritorious conduct, and every last one of them was stoned out of his gourd.

Miller had almost made it: unable to reach the wire, he'd opened the metal door of the storage chamber and clawed the charge out moments before the explosion. The shock wave had torn him off the ladder. He was dead by the time his body hit the concrete below. The episode closed with the tanks rolling over the bridge into a false-color sunset, a panoramic shot of the hill above town, bristling with enemy artillery. The screen faded to black to the cadence of marching music. The faces of Clayton and Prescott, huge and rendered in perfect detail, sank into the fadeout. In their place came the image of an infantryman in generic uniform seated on an ammunition box, smiling and raising a tin cup of Nutramax Three-In-One bioprotein extract at the camera.

The scene cut to the Tristar-Paramount studio in the northeastern section of the megasprawl, where a tall, chisel-jawed host with swept-back platinum hair stood in full parade uniform, a solemn look on his tanned face. After saying a few stock phrases about duty and sacrifice, he waded into the studio audience amid cries and frantic applause. The cameras tracked his every move, zooming in on individual spectators as the host singled them out for comment, panning out to capture the pressure-cooker atmosphere inside the auditorium.

"Doug Prescott is my favorite hero," said a fat young man in a camouflage sweatshirt, his jowly face flushed with excitement and glistening in the bright lights. Cords stood out in his neck as he shouted over the screaming crowd. He pumped a fist in the air and grinned.

"Do you have a message for your boys on the front?"

The response was swallowed by the rising din. The host's head bobbed up and down and he moved on, brilliant smile in place. "What was your favorite part?" he asked a pretty young girl in a clinging, sleeveless turquoise dress. She blushed from head to toe and tried to look away from the tracking camera.

"When Frank Clayton stabbed the guy on the bridge," she said in a breathy voice, blushing deeper. "Blood everywhere. It was so, like, *raw!* I loved it." Her eyes were unfocused, her expression half-terror and half-sexual. The host leered and winked at the screen.

"Do you have a message for Frank?"

She leaned forward, giving the camera an ample view down the plunging neckline of her dress, and pressed her lips to the lens. The on-screen audience went wild, as did the men of the platoon. Hands clapped Clayton on the back and shoulders; feet stamped in unison. The host was already speaking to the next audience member, a thin, wizened old woman in a pink GIVE 'EM HELL tee-shirt.

Something hot and bitter welled up inside him, burning through the Synthazine haze. He got up and walked away from the screen, into the deeper darkness of the camp.

The drugs he'd taken on an empty stomach and the silvery moonlight turned the blasted ruins into an ethereal landscape of shadows and open spaces. Fires burned like flares on the black bulk of the hill. An unfamiliar feeling came over him, a sense of burdens removed, of letting go. It was contentment, he decided, however fleeting it might prove to be. For all its horrors, the war zone was the last place on the planet where a man could have privacy, where he could be left alone with his thoughts. Something long forgotten in the overcrowded world outside, in the monstrous conurbations blighted by hunger and disease and riots, where the weight of the blind, teeming humanity pressed from all sides, threatening to bury him. Life on the outside was a sordid litany of survival, violence and betrayal, petty evils and debased urges, lust and vicissitude. The noise of human despair, of smoldering anger and helplessness, was a constant low thrum at the back of the mind, driving you closer to madness with every second of every day.

Out here there was blessed quiet and solitude once the day's killing was done, once the guns had fired their last.

Out here, surrounded by death and insanity, a man could still pretend he was sane.

He was asleep the moment his head touched the bed-roll, sinking into a leaden, bottomless sea, the silence closing over him... only to surface in total darkness, sweating and disoriented, his mouth dry and his heart pounding.

He'd dreamed of being lost in the night, of hearing the tiltjets come down, their blades scything through the air. Powerful spotlights froze him where he stood, cold and naked and shivering. The belly of the behemoth split open and his son was standing in the light, reaching for him, blue veins showing under his pale, translucent skin. He tried to scream, but his throat was clogged with dirt.

In the carbon black of the ruin, he heard the walls scrape forward, closing in on him. He got up, pulled on his boots and trousers, and groped his way toward the exit, tripping over sleeping, moaning shapes, into the oppressive wet heat of the night. The putrid smell of the bunks dissipated. Thin clouds trailed across the huge bloated face of the moon. He struck a match and lit a cigarette, sucked greedily on the harsh, bitter smoke. Beneath the flavor of cheap tobacco, the rancid aftertaste of the dream filled his mouth.

"Can't sleep?" someone said behind him, making him jump. A red pinpoint glowed in the dark between two ruined walls. Prescott walked into a shaft of moonlight and tossed the butt away. "Me neither. Nerves, I guess. Once they get going, all the tranks in the world don't help."

Clayton didn't feel like company, but Prescott had saved his life on the bridge. He muttered something about bad dreams and stared out into the night. Prescott sat down on an empty ammo crate and leaned on his elbows. Clayton offered him the pack, but he waved it away.

"I had a nightmare too." He spoke with an urgency Clayton had never heard in his voice before. "It's those things. The Scavs. I've never seen them up close before. Never wanted to, either. Always kept my head down when I heard the sirens." He paused and looked up expectantly.

Clayton said nothing. "Alvarez was alive when they showed up. He was alive and they shot him like a dog."

"Alvarez was a tribal," Clayton said, without turning to him. "You saw that thing around his neck. He didn't deserve any better."

"He bled the same as the rest of us."

"He got what was coming to him." The flare of anger caught Clayton unaware, shook him fully awake. "It's a war. People die. I couldn't give two shits about some dirty tribal."

"You've let it get under your skin," Prescott said. "Let it get to you. All that free-market propaganda about asocials and freeloaders living off the hard work of others. The citizen-consumer and his rights and choices. To hell with everyone else. Even out here. Even after everything you've seen."

"You're one to talk." Clayton shook his head, sneered. "Big war hero. Always at the front of the line, a camera in your face."

"Why not? The war zone is the best of all possible worlds." A dry smile creased Prescott's face. "Unlike those poor bastards on the outside, every man here is guaranteed rations. Three meals a day, two thousand calories and sixty grams of crude bioprotein. Something the average citizen-consumer can only dream about. You ever stop to think where those sixty grams are coming from? What the secret ingredient in your ham-and-beans really is?"

"That's no secret." Clayton paused to light another cigarette. Prescott was still looking up at him. "No one made us do anything," he said, feeling like he had to explain himself without knowing why. His anger had collapsed; a sick, hollow feeling came in its place. "We all chose to enlist."

"Why did you?"

"We had a boy. He got sick." He probed the edges of the old wound, surprised at how little he felt. The pain was all but gone; it might have been something he'd heard about, something that had happened to someone else. "You got kids?"

"Never felt the urge." Prescott's eyes softened. "What was wrong with him?"

"He was diagnosed with blood cancer." Clayton's voice was steady, without a trace of tremor. "Rare these days, but it happens. When it does, when it's a terminal illness, the Demos and the Eugenics Board give you two options. One, you can agree to euthanize and have your permit canceled and reissued at no additional cost. Two, you can opt for treatment, which only works some of the time, but which is always expensive. Very expensive."

"Did it work?"

"He died." Clayton spat into the darkness and was silent for a while. "What about you?"

"Not much to say." Even in the dark, he could tell that Prescott was shaken. "I suppose I did this to myself. Tired old story about drink and drugs and running around with the wrong crowd. I've put my youthful indiscretions behind me, but not before they thoroughly wrecked my credit. Enlisting was the only way out."

"There's always a way out." He wiped his hand across his eyes and saw that it was wet. "We don't have to make the choices we make, but we have to live with their consequences."

"I don't believe you had a choice," Prescott said, "and I don't think you do either." He rose and stretched his arms over his head. "I'm sorry about your boy, Clayton."

Clayton tried to think of an appropriate response and came up short. Prescott halted at the entrance and chuckled. "You know what? That sonofabitch O'Rourke has it all figured out. Those who put us here taught us to do one thing and do it well. Kill others without caring that much."

"O'Rourke is crazy."

"Like a shithouse rat. But that doesn't mean a thing. Out here, everyone's crazy. All we need is a little push in the right direction, and off we go." Prescott laughed a little, but his eyes were hard. He seemed to want to say more and to reconsider. "I'll see you in the morning."

Four

Lieutenant Hall stuck his head over the lip of the trench and swept his binoculars across the slope. The covering barrage had been delayed over an hour, and the platoon waited for its turn to move. Command had decided to change the marching order, he informed Sergeant Bennings, moving them from reserve to first. Bennings gave him a dirty look, but otherwise didn't respond. Hall didn't have to be here, in the thick of the fighting, but always insisted on leading his platoon from the front, which only made the men loathe him even more.

At the top of the hill, the tank columns were attacking the enemy gun emplacements. A huge tumultuous roar hung in the air; the whistle and thunderclap of exploding shells, the crashing of cannon and tank guns, the crump of mortar fire. With every pounding strike, dirt pattered on the men sitting at the bottom of the trench. Some of them were smoking, others were wolfing down rations. O'Rourke was taking his rifle apart and inspecting each piece with great care, unfazed by the goings-on around him. Kintner and Avetisian were playing cards for the last chocolate bar. Popovich was shuffling along the trench, his arms wrapped around himself, muttering incoherent strings of curses mixed with religious verse. Spinelli lay on his back, his eyes closed and his fingers steepled on his chest. Prescott was wadding cotton into his ears.

Clayton sat between two of the new men who had joined the squad to make up the numbers. His senses barely registered the explosions. The exchange with Prescott had left him seething and confused. He had enlisted out of hopelessness and spite, with the understanding that he was coming here to die. Part of it had been a desire to hurt Linda, to provoke a reaction from her, any reaction. It hadn't worked. The other part was hate. It came from somewhere deep inside him, a hard pit of pain and rage, unfocused and irrational but no weaker for it. He hated himself for outliving Josh, but he didn't want to die. But what was it he *did* want?

There's something in you that goes beyond the madness of this place, Prescott had said. Something that had been building up since Josh's death, something huge and malevolent that wanted to lash out, to destroy in a blind frenzy. They had done everything by the book, he and Linda, brought their son into the world and did their best to raise and protect him, only to have him taken away. Perhaps that was all there was to it. Perhaps there was nothing to understand.

The man to his right opened a meat-ration can and started shoveling the chunks into his mouth using his fingers and a handful of dry crackers. Clayton's stomach turned at the smell. He tried not to think about the machines, the figures in protective suits collecting the dead, the blast of cold air from the insides of the transport. The man saw him flinch and grinned, revealing white even teeth specked with the remains of the meal.

"Can't stand the smell?" The newcomer's name was Salvesen, and the rest of the men avoided him like a disease. He leaned closer with a jeering expression, enjoying Clayton's discomfort. "Me, I love it. Smells a lot better than anything you can get to eat on the outside, I'll tell you that. Tastes better too." He leaned in with a leer. "Best part is, there's plenty more where it came from. Just look around you."

"Don't listen to him," said the man on the other side of Clayton. He was middle-aged and pudgy, with large, frightened eyes. Each time an explosion sounded close he winced and dipped his head into his shoulders. "He's asocial. Got his credit frozen for running an illegal flophouse in Southwest. Everybody knows about it." His face collapsed into a pathetic grimace of self-pity and revulsion. "I've had to put up with him since basic training. It's a goddamn disgrace. Psychotics like him don't belong with the rest of us."

"Fighting in a war is what's psychotic." Salvesen shrugged and pulled his helmet down over his ears. "I'll take your ration, if you don't want it," he said to Clayton and patted his belly. When there was no answer he sighed and hugged his knees, looking wistful. "When it's my turn to become mystery meat, I hope I get stuck in some bastard's throat. I hope he chokes to death on me." He winked at the pudgy man. "Maybe old Dawes and I will end up in the same can. Wouldn't that be something, Dawes?"

"There he goes again," Dawes said in a wheedling voice. "I didn't sign up for this. Back on the outside, I was someone, you know. I used to work—"

"Shut up down there," Sergeant Bennings shouted. The barrage thinned out and stopped. The reports of the guns sounded closer now. Shells screamed over the trench and exploded further up the slope. Hall glanced down from the firing step, beaming. "Those are ours, boys. Get ready and wait for the signal."

The men hunkered down and waited. The sky filled with the rush of shells; the earth bucked and heaved with blasts of thunder. A wall of smoke rolled into the trench and stung Clayton's eyes. A hand grabbed his arm. Prescott was next to him, shouting into his ear. "Follow O'Rourke," he thought he heard, before another wave of explosions deafened him. He gritted his teeth and lowered his head.

Silence, sudden and total. Grimy faces tensed, waiting. The asocial, Salvesen, was staring at Prescott with a strange, unreadable expression.

From the other end of the trench came the shrilling of the whistle. The assault company spilled over the edge of the trench, into the inferno beyond.

Prescott reached the top of the hill first and threw himself into a shell hole. Clayton and O'Rourke plunged in after him, landing on top of each other just as machine gun fire raked over their heads. The attackers were swarming up the slope, firing at the sandbagged, log-reinforced bunkers and trenches. The rattling guns cut them mercilessly down and mortar barrages swept across the open ground.

Within moments of the whistle signal, the charge had broken down into a mad dash for the top, the slope strewn with dying, screaming men. Clayton had rushed headlong into the smoke and bullets, the explosions all around him, great gouts of earth and stone showering down. He had been dimly aware that he too was screaming, that his teeth were chattering hard enough to hurt. The man running next to him—Dawes, the pudgy newcomer—had fallen flat and bounced like a rag doll. Clayton had fired and reloaded without looking, the bullets digging dirt spouts at his feet, his throat raw with smoke and terror.

Prescott had found him in the chaos and carnage and pulled him to the side, pointing through the billows of smoke. A short distance up the slope, O'Rourke was kneeling, oblivious to enemy fire, picking up a satchel charge dropped by a fallen soldier. Prescott and Clayton had followed the tall, rawboned figure up the hill, staying low to the ground and heading straight for the bunker on the eastern side of the hill.

Clayton's body had acted faster than his brain; there had been no time to think about the maneuver, or what O'Rourke was doing. Now he clung to the wet earth at the bottom of the hole, face buried into his arms. The machine gun was firing over their heads. O'Rourke was crazy, and so was Prescott. He couldn't move, couldn't breathe. There was nothing left to do but be killed.

O'Rourke scrabbled up the side of the shell hole, Prescott close behind him. Clayton lay frozen for a split second, then pushed up and started across the edge. The machine gun fire had shifted to the other side of the bunker. Men went down in a tangle of blood and thrashing bodies. Before the line of fire could sweep back, he covered the last stretch of open ground and crouched behind the logs of the bunker entrance.

Prescott motioned them quiet and peered around the timber beam. The space on the other side was dark and smelled of pine and dirt and cordite. He took a grenade and peeled the yellow tape off the pin. Clayton and O'Rourke shoved fresh clips into their Thompsons and took cover on either side of the entrance. Prescott jerked the pin free and tossed the grenade into the bunker.

The blast was muffled, but Clayton could feel the impact through the ground. He leveled his Thompson at the entrance, waited for the first dazed and bloodied defenders to stagger out and pressed the trigger. O'Rourke and Prescott opened up from the other side, cutting down the enemy soldiers as they came out. Bodies piled up under the hail of bullets. Some tried to crawl back into cover or run forward into the open. Clayton kept firing until the submachine gun clicked empty. His head throbbed, his heartbeat pounding in his temples.

It was over in seconds. Prescott stepped over the bodies and into the bunker. Clayton and O'Rourke followed. The interior was thick with an acrid haze and cluttered with maps, ration cans and splintered cots. The dirt walls glistened wet. Soldiers were climbing through the abandoned firing ports, shooting at the defenders fleeing the trenches. The tanks were rolling over the earthworks and barbed wire, turrets swiveling to fire into the gun pits. Clayton started toward the trenches, but Prescott held him back.

"Over there," he mouthed, holding out a pair of binoculars. Clayton pressed the eyepieces against a gun slit in the back of the bunker. He saw a long row of tanks advancing down the road, a cratered rockscape scattered with the burning hulks of destroyed armor, a gray, barren plain stretching below the ridge of the hill. In the distance, a dark line snaking across the wasteland, vanished toward the far horizon.

Bit by bit, the smoke and explosions cleared, and the image gained clarity, the line resolving itself into a high barrier.

The wall of the war zone.

He stepped back from the slit and lowered the binoculars. Prescott was carefully folding a map into his trouser pocket. O'Rourke hefted his pack and smiled a cryptic smile. Clayton felt like he was on the brink of a great realization; a cog slipping into place, parts of his mind coming together and engaging. The connection was still beyond his grasp, but that didn't matter. It would come to him in time.

When the sirens began their banshee wail, he stood at the firing port and watched everything.

Five

They were given four days to rest for the final push, the returns had come in, and the drink and drugs flowed freely. Rumors were already circulating about the setting of the last act; a soldier from Alpha Company claimed to have seen plans of a great city with soaring cathedrals and domes, while two men from the quartermaster unit had it on good authority that the network was constructing an island fortress off the southern coast of the zone, a nightmare of craggy rock, caves and underground tunnels. Projected casualties ran into the thousands—a fitting finale to one of the most spectacular broadcasting events in history—and extras were being flown in from the outside day and night. Massive video screens played and replayed the highlights of the campaign to build up morale. Great projected shapes bellowed and rampaged through the ruins, their reflections dancing and rippling across the slack, drooling faces of the drugged-up veterans, across the lost, terrified countenances of the new arrivals.

Tempers frayed in the heat. Shellshock and fatigue exacted a heavy toll. Popovich took his bayonet to one of the newcomers over a trivial argument and had three months added to his never-ending contract. Two drunk, belligerent infantrymen with a profound dislike for asocials decided to put Salvesen in his place and ended up with broken jaws and concussions. Punishments were relatively mild; command believed in keeping the men's aggressiveness and fighting spirits high, and the behind-the-scenes footage would provide bonus material for the downtime between network runs.

Clayton wanted to speak to Prescott about what he'd seen on the ridge, but the other man seemed to be avoiding him. O'Rourke kept to himself even more than usual and spent most of his waking hours dismantling the fuse of the satchel charge. The presence of an explosive device a few feet from his bunk was something Clayton did not find reassuring at all, but getting blown to pieces in his sleep was no worse than getting blown to pieces charging a gun emplacement. He didn't know exactly what he expected to happen, but he decided to bide his time until Prescott made a move or gave him a sign.

He was given the sign he'd been waiting for on the night before they were to leave. Clayton had wandered into the ruins for a smoke, leaving the blaring screens and rowdy men behind. He sat under a block of crumbling masonry and gazed upward. A tiny sliver of moon hung in an enormous sky studded with stars. It occurred to him that he hadn't seen a rain cloud since he enlisted. From what he vaguely remembered, the war zones were built in arid wastelands. Dead land inhabited by dead men. Every square foot of precious fertile land was used to grow crops for the billions in the sprawling cities. With each passing day, the world on the outside grew less substantial, less real, like a dream dreamed by someone else.

A shadow blocked his view. Prescott stood over him, holding out an open ration can. Clayton pushed the can away.

"You have to eat." Prescott lowered himself onto a toppled section of stone. "God knows it's not easy. Half the time it's all I can do not to throw the stuff back up right away. But then I hear the machines in my head, coming for me. It's easier if you pretend it all comes down to eating or being eaten."

"That's not pretending," Clayton said. "We all get eaten in the end." *Except the corporations and execs,* he thought. *They always survive.*

"Suit yourself. Want a smoke?"

"No."

The glow of the match lit up Prescott's face long enough to reveal deep furrows around his mouth. He looked weary almost to death. "I was hoping they'd send us to the island. But that doesn't seem to be in the cards. I heard Hall talking to the sergeants. Tomorrow we'll march to a depot in the east of the zone. From there we'll be loaded on trains to the next set."

"Why?"

"Why what?"

"Why the island?"

"There's water all around it. Easy to disappear in the confusion, and there's no wall keeping you in. Easy to stay hidden. The city is dead in the middle of the zone—you have miles of empty space to cover just to get to the wall."

"I hate the water," Clayton said in an absent tone. During the beach landing, the black depths beneath the thin metal of his barge had frightened him more than all the gun and cannon fire put together. Then the full implication of the other man's words sank in. Prescott was talking about escape. "You can't be serious."

"It's been done before." Prescott took his helmet off and wiped his brow. "More than once. The networks never show that, of course. Not the sort of thing the investors like to see."

"I thought you were just as crazy as O'Rourke, but I was wrong. You're far crazier than he will ever be."

"Maybe, but what do you have to lose?" Prescott picked up a piece of brick and drew a rough circle on the dusty concrete. "This," he said, chalking an x-mark on the perimeter, "is the southern edge of the zone, where the beach landing was staged. Where we came in." He made two more marks, each a few inches closer to the center. "Here is the village we fought in after the beach, and here is where we are now. At this point you can still see the wall if you have enough elevation, like we did up on the hill. But tomorrow we head straight for the center." He traced a ragged arrow to the middle of the circle. "Two or three days by train. More than seven hundred miles from the wall. This is the closest we'll get. We'll never get a chance like this again."

"It's impossible," Clayton said, shaking his head. "Even if you could pull it off, you'd be worse than dead on the outside. Remember why we ended up here in the first place? There's nowhere to go, nothing to eat. The network would hunt you down in a day or two, or you'd turn yourself in again. Without credit, you might as well not exist."

"Maybe there's a way." Prescott's eyes gleamed in the darkness. Again Clayton had a sensation of tumblers turning, of what was left unspoken falling into place.

"What way would that be?"

They jumped back from the voice, startled. Clayton's bayonet was in his hand before he had any conscious awareness of what had happened. Salvesen was standing at the corner of the ruined wall, looking at them with wry amusement.

"Get the hell out of here." Prescott signaled with his eyes. Clayton took a step to the side, standing at an angle that hid the bayonet from view. He didn't know how much Salvesen had heard, but his grip on the hilt tightened. With chilling clarity, he realized that he was prepared to kill the newcomer to make sure word didn't get out. *Us against them,* he thought, *and I haven't even said yes. Already it's us against them. Just like they trained us.*

"Not before you tell me what you two are whispering about." Hands in his pockets, Salvesen came toward them and squatted over the drawing. "Now what do we have here? Not bad at all. Didn't know you had an artistic bent, Prescott."

Slowly, Clayton moved to put the man between himself and Prescott, within reach of the blade. The network had taught him how to kill with it; hand over the mouth, twist the head to the left to expose the neck, a deep thrust into the carotid and a slash sideways. Work the blade across. They had shown him how to throw a hand grenade, how to use rimfire pistols and rifles: old weapons, obsolete save for the screen, but they still did the job. After a few times, it became routine. Men died all the time in the kill zone; no one would wonder what happened to an asocial.

"You shouldn't have come out here," Prescott said, his fists clenching. His eyes found Clayton's and his head dipped in a nod. Clayton shifted his weight to his front foot and tensed his shoulders, the blade poised to strike.

"Miss out on a chance to learn from the best? I don't think so." Salvesen straightened. His gaze dropped to the blade, but his smile didn't falter. "Ever wonder how come our war hero knows everything he knows?" he asked Clayton. "What the zone looks like, what's in the middle and what's on the outside, what direction the train will be going in? Why he's always in the right place? They don't teach this sort of thing in basic training. We all know that much."

Before Clayton's brain could process the words, Prescott was on his feet and swinging. The first blow caught

Salvesen under the ear, and he went down as if shot. He tried to raise his hands, but Prescott was already on him, pummeling his unprotected face with both fists. Salvesen's head bounced from side to side; his cheeks shone wet and black in the moonlight. Kneeling over him, Prescott grabbed a chunk of concrete and raised it overhead. Before he could bring it down on his opponent's head, the cold steel of Clayton's blade was at his neck.

"Let go of him."

Prescott's shoulders slumped. The chunk of concrete fell to the ground. Salvesen crawled out from under him and rolled away, panting. Blood trickled from his broken nose and a gash above his eye. Prescott sat down and ran his hands through his sweat-matted hair. His knuckles were bruised and raw.

Clayton stood over him and pointed the blade at Salvesen. "Tell me what he's talking about."

"Go ahead, tell him, Prescott." The newcomer snorted back blood and barked a harsh laugh. "It's only the biggest story of the year. Or would be, if the networks let the word get out. It's all over the pirate broadcasts. The sole scion to the Prescott media empire, slumming it with asocials and debt slaves in the killing zone. Sending the studio profits soaring. The wealthy and powerful of Aventus sacrificing their own young on the altar of Mammon."

Clayton stood frozen with anger, arms hanging at his sides. Prescott watched him closely. When he spoke, his voice was even. "It has nothing to do with money. Scum like him can't understand that."

"Damn right I can't understand." Salvesen tilted his head back and gingerly moved his jaw back and forth. "The conurbations are hell on earth itself. Riots, crime, food shortages, disease. Millions piled on top of millions inside huge concrete mausoleums. Every breath you take has already been fouled by lungs of another human being, or a dozen of them. But I'd go back in a heartbeat if I could." The bleeding had all but stopped. He gave a cautious sniff. "You, on the other hand, have been programmed for privilege since before birth. Real food, fresh water, untainted air. Space—all the space you could ever need. Unthinkable luxuries for the rest of us. But you chose to come here and be slaughtered for the entertainment of the masses. I don't understand it, and I don't think I ever will."

"I've got my reasons."

"Sure you do," Clayton said. Infinite hatred and contempt made it hard to speak. He took a step forward, squeezing the hilt of the bayonet so hard his hand was trembling. Even here, having already taken his life, they were trying to deceive him. All his life he had been lied to, tricked into believing in individual freedom and the right of choice, when the deck was stacked against him, the system rigged, every decision he had ever made playing right into their hands. He had been manipulated, changed into something he no longer recognized by the faceless masters of his fate.

Only they weren't faceless now. One of them was right in front of him, helpless and within the reach of his blade. "Your kind always have reasons. You're a network plant. I should have known it the minute I saw your trank stash."

"No." Prescott was talking fast, eyes fixed on the glimmering point of the blade. "Believe what you want, but that's not true. I hate the networks more than you do. The pills I saved because I don't need them. Unlike the rest of you, I don't have agoraphobia, or any other paranoid conditions." He backed away on all fours until his shoulders touched the wall. "I can't change who I am, or where I come from. But I can choose what I do. I don't know why I'm here, what I wanted. Revenge, at first. My father to see his only son and heir die in primetime, killed by his goddamned show. Maybe that was it. To know that his dynasty dream would go to the grave with him, that he had exploited and murdered for nothing. But I was wrong," he said, as if to himself. "People like my father care about nothing but themselves and keeping their shareholders happy. There's only one thing that will make them start paying attention."

"Cutting your throat would be a start."

"You have to think bigger than that." All fear had left Prescott's eyes, replaced by defiance. "Remember what I told you on the way to the bridge. You think you want to kill yourself, but deep down you know that's not all of it. I saw it in your eyes. That's why I chose you for this. Why I want to get out. There are better uses for what they taught you to do."

"Chose me for what?"

41

"What if there was a way to strike for the heart? Get close and take as many of them out as you could?"

Clayton hesitated. *Those who put us here taught us to do one thing.* Prescott didn't just want to escape the zone, he wanted to take the war to the enemy. The real enemy, the only enemy, not the grimy, emaciated men wearing the other color of uniform. Unless he was lying, unless this was all part of some greater game, even less comprehensible. "You better start making sense," he finally said, slipping the blade back into his belt.

"First, we have to get out of here." Prescott got up and went over to the circle he'd drawn on the concrete. "O'Rourke has a plan."

"O'Rourke is part of this?"

Prescott glanced suspiciously at Salvesen. Clayton laid his palm on the bayonet and nodded. "Go on. He's part of it now, too. He's got nothing to gain by turning us in."

Salvesen raised a hand in acquiescence. In the gloom, it was hard to see his face. "If you're thinking about running, I'm coming with you."

"Forget it," Prescott said to Clayton. "We're not taking him."

"I can help," Salvesen said. "There are more like me out there. Others who can provide food and shelter, medical help, even guns. We know how to stay off the grid and we trust each other. That's how we stay alive." He spoke with assurance, as if he'd prepared his speech in advance. "You were right about me being part of it. In here I'm a marked man, more hated than any hostile. Can't fall asleep for fear of some psycho cutting my throat. I'd rather take my chances on getting out."

Prescott glanced from one man to the other, turned away with an angry motion.

"He's got a point," Clayton said. "But we'll be keeping an eye on him. If he so much as opens his mouth, he's as good as dead."

"O'Rourke will make that call."

"Then let him make it," Clayton said. "What's your plan?"

"O'Rourke has worked out the whole thing," Prescott said. "He told me. People think he's crazy, which is exactly

what he wants them to think. His idea is to derail the train
and blow a hole in the wall."

"Blow a hole with what?"

"The satchel charge he picked up on the hill. He's been
thinking ahead."

"That won't work," Clayton said. "All our weapons have
failsafe switches. They wouldn't have given you a rifle if you
could use it against them. As we board that train, the network flips the switch. Then the guns can't shoot, the bombs
don't go off. They showed us how it works in basic training."

"I'm not forgetting anything. O'Rourke removed the
failsafe from the charge detonator. Add one live charge to
a train car full of disabled ones, and you got a very big explosion. Big enough to punch through that wall like paper."

"He took off the failsafe?"

"He did the same with his rifle," Prescott said. "In case
the Scavs come after us. Quite the tinkerer, our friend O'Rourke. Before coming here, he worked for Global Technics
as a senior engineer." He picked the piece of brick up and
scratched a second arrow outside the circle. "Once we're
out, we head east toward the coast. There's a slum colony
forty miles in that direction, people living in the locks and
dikes at the foot of a dam. The recovery teams won't follow
us there, and if they do, we'll lose them without much trouble. From there on, we make our way north through the
city."

"Suppose we make it that far," Clayton said. "What
happens then?"

"Like I said, we should think big." A cold smile flickered on Prescott's face. "I know my way around Aventus.
The layout, the routines, the security. As a resident, I had
access to the biolocks and retinal scanners, the terminals
that feed into the arcology's central computer. There's a
way to get inside. A handful of determined men can cause
a lot of damage."

"There's no getting inside." Salvesen nodded at the circle Prescott had scratched into the concrete. "An arcology is
like a medieval keep, surrounded by corporate gated com-
munities. Paranoid and heavily policed. Residential permits
only. It's impossible for one of us to even get close."

"Not Aventus," Prescott replied. "They built it on top of
the eastern seaboard dam complex, overlooking the sea and

the flooded relief zones. It stands where once the world's biggest trading floor stood, the heart and brain of the free market before the Collapse. They designed it as a testament to the rise of the transnationals, to the triumph of free will over nature. They've turned it into a fortress, but every fortress has its weaknesses, places for an insider to slip through."

"We'll need credit for that sort of thing," Clayton said. "Lots of it."

"I've taken care of that. Before I came here, I set up several false identities, each with its own set of papers and consumer profiles. There's a man in East Central, a lawyer, who arranges the necessary paperwork for me."

"How?"

"It's easy to do, as long as you pay the bills on time and you have an elite credit rating. You make a few credit transfers through bogus investment companies, buy and sell goods to yourself. Back when the government collected taxes, the rich had it down to a science."

"You're really serious about this," Salvesen said, his broken nose apparently forgotten. He was staring at the other man with rapt attention, absorbing every word.

"I've had some time to think about it. A direct intrusion is the last thing the corporates expect. They are protected by the police, by private militias, by state-of-the-art security systems. People have been brainwashed to believe there's no other way. Eat what the transnationals tell you to eat, breed when they let you breed. A good citizen-consumer would never dream of raising a hand against those who keep the shelves stocked, who keep the television on and entertainment streaming." Prescott spoke with the easy, heedless confidence of a man accustomed to getting his way. "By the time they realize what's happening, it will be too late to stop us."

"It won't change anything," Clayton said. "When I was a boy, we lived across from one of the refugee camps. I watched them come in from the south, from across the sea, swarming without end. Entire families, entire cities. Kept them like animals—hundreds to a room, razor wire all around. The centers for disease control used to transport corpses by the truckload and bury them in mass graves. When they ran out of space, they started to burn them in piles. Crop failures had become the norm by then. Food was already scarce, and it got worse. The refugees often broke out of the camps. There were riots, lootings, killings. The army—back then there was a real army, run by the government—bombed the camp to the ground. Razed half of our neighborhood along with it."

He paused, grasping for words. "Now we store food in vaults, shoot illegals and napalm rioters. Fight the tribals in the slums. We keep the population down by recreating old wars for amusement. That's all we learned from that experience. How to lay claim to what's ours and mark our territory. How to eat our own dead. I guess what I'm saying is that things are the way they are because we are the way we are. We're a dying species, waiting for extinction, and on some level, we've already made peace with this."

"I don't want to change anything," Prescott said. His voice was flat and void of inflection. "Matter of fact is, I'm not thinking about the consequences, or about what comes after that. Being here gives you a whole new perspective on life. There are no grand statements to be made, no right and wrong. Things seem to have gone beyond that point. All I want to do is hurt them and hurt them good."

Clayton could think of nothing to say to that. There was a way out. It didn't have to end here. The notion of it swept all other thoughts from his mind. It was a wild hope, but it was a hope where before there had been none.

He had a sudden vision of Josh playing on the strip of sand under the great wall of the dam, thin, pale limbs gleaming in the sun like bone. Linda had begun to cry, and he'd held her and told her everything would be all right. That night he'd waited for them to fall asleep and gone down to the beach to watch the play of lights at the top of the wall. He'd lain in the sand and started to sob, ragged, rending shakes that wracked his entire body, the tempest inside him a steady, senseless counterpoint to the roar of the sea.

The faces of the other two men floated out of the night. He looked from one to the other and realized that this was it. There was no turning back.

"Tomorrow," he said. "We get on the train and wait for you and O'Rourke to make a move."

"You'll know when it's time." Prescott rubbed out the drawing with the sole of his boot. Salvesen watched them and said nothing. "Don't talk to anyone. Keep your knives ready and watch your backs. Let O'Rourke handle the rest."

They took separate paths back into camp. Clayton flopped down on his bunk in the darkness, deaf to the sounds of drunken revelry coming from outside. Maybe there was a reckoning coming, maybe not. But he could do something other than die. He lay staring into the dark, wound too tight to sleep, nursing the thought deep inside, playing it over with bitter exultation.

Six

Josh looked up at him and smiled. One small hand gripped the arm of a ratty stuffed animal that had once been either a bear or a lion. His favorite toy. The other hand disappeared into his father's. They were standing on a patch of pristine lawn, surrounded by trimmed flower bushes and decorative trees. In front of them was a wide building of white marble, a company logo displayed above the colonnaded entrance. The dark glass doors beneath the logo swung out, revealing a tasteful interior in somber gray and pastel hues.

Clayton looked around, but Linda wasn't with them. She was ill, it came to him; he had a flash of her screaming and struggling against two burly men in white coats, a woman in a gray uniform pressing a drug injector against her neck. The uniform bore the same logo as the sign plate above the entrance, and that was supposed to mean something. His thoughts floated in disarray; he knew he had brought Josh to the white building, but he could not remember why. The reason was within his reach, flickering at the borders of his consciousness, but his mind recoiled from it and veered away.

A man and a woman in uniform came out of the door and stood at a respectful distance from the father and son. Their faces were set in identical expressions of professional condolence. A bolt of pure terror stabbed its way through the muddle of Clayton's thoughts. He didn't know why, but the sight of those identical faces frightened him more than anything else.

The uniformed man took a step forward and held his arms out to Josh. Numb with terror, Clayton pulled his son closer. Instead of thin shoulders, his fingers closed around something that felt like a bundle of sticks wrapped in cloth. He glanced down. A small pile of rags and bone lay in his arms, the skull huge and grinning, empty sockets turned up toward his face.

Clayton moaned and woke up. His eyes were gummed up and salt tracks cracked down his cheeks. An enormous weight pressed on his chest, and when he tried to lift his hands nothing happened. Something warm and sticky pooled under his head and neck, seeped into his shirt. Panic stole over him; trembling with effort, he lifted a hand and rubbed his eyelids.

With the movement, the darkness shrank around him and pain rolled in like a long, slow tide. Sunlight slanted through gaps in crumpled sheet metal walls. Heat burned up through the floor, down from the rusted ceiling. The train car was on its side, he realized, but he couldn't remember why. He was on his back, pinned under a steel ammo box. His skin prickled as feeling returned to his extremities. All around him broken forms groaned and sobbed. The sweet, heavy smell of blood filled his nose and mouth.

He shoved the box off his chest and pushed himself up on quivering limbs, struggling to find balance on the slick, tilted floor. He had to get out of here. Every muscle in his body screamed in agony, but adrenaline pushed him forward. A hand clutched at his pants cuff and a hoarse voice rasped for help. He tore free and nearly lost his footing, wheeled his arms. Mangled, shattered flesh filled the front end of the car. Blood dripped, pattered against the metal sides, a loud, steady sound.

It had gone wrong; it wasn't supposed to end like this. Pieces of memory fell into place. The conversation with Prescott in the ruins. Boarding the train under the blazing sun, thousands of feet trampling the dust. The long track shimmering in the morning heat. O'Rourke standing by the connecting door, swaying with the motion of the train.

He put his face against a crack in the twisted metal, cupped his hands to cut off the glare. On the other side was a long sweep of cracked desert, the wall of the zone rising above it, an eighty-foot ferroconcrete cliff bristling with automated gun turrets and communication relays, going on into infinity.

The strength went out of Clayton's legs and he sat down hard into wetness. Beneath the cries of the wounded and dying, he could hear distant thunder. The sound of rotor blades and wingtip engines, growing steadier and more pronounced, drawing closer.

He had failed, and now the machines were coming.

The train had pulled out of the depot not long before and was rattling across the boundless sun-cracked desert. The men sat on curled-up legs or lay back against the walls, smoking or dozing in the swelter of the car, their boots off and their shirts dark with sweat. An unbearable stench rose from the covered waste buckets and hung in the stillness.

Prescott glanced over at the others and gave a small nod. Clayton laid his rifle on the floor and felt for the blade in his sleeve. Across from him, Salvesen did the same. Following their cue, O'Rourke got up and walked to the metal connecting door at the end of the car. Several faces turned in the half-darkness, but most dozed on, lulled by the heat and the rocking motion of the train.

"Sit down, O'Rourke," Sergeant Bennings said, more out of reflex than real interest. Prescott picked his way through the listless soldiers and took up O'Rourke's rifle. Bennings sat up on his blanket roll and scowled. "You too, Prescott. That's an order."

Prescott raised the rifle without pointing it at anyone and checked the clip. The train clacked around a slight curve and he leaned back, bracing himself against the wall of the car. Already florid from the heat, Bennings flushed a deeper red. "Goddammit, son. You'd better put down that gun and sit your ass down. Don't make me tell you twice."

"Sergeant, will you please control your men?" Hall's voice came from the other end of the car. Bennings opened his mouth to speak, then thought better of it. O'Rourke was bent over the lock, hidden by the shadows. Prescott was staring into the sergeant's eyes, his finger curled around the trigger.

Heavy silence in the car, the men holding their breath, watching. Bennings suddenly looked uncertain, as if he'd sensed something wrong.

"Sergeant?" Hall came forward, his shirt unbuttoned and his helmet under his arm. His voice was even and authoritative and his dripping face shone in the slats of light. "What are these men doing? Get away from that door," he said to O'Rourke, who gave no indication of having heard.

The barrel of the rifle pointed at Hall. "Sit down and shut up," Prescott said in a calm, pleasant tone, "or I'll blow your brains out."

Behind Hall's back, Clayton eased up into a half-crouch and drew his bayonet.

The Lieutenant's face contorted in angry disbelief, then relaxed into a sneer. "You just earned yourself three months, Private. Keep it up and you'll double it. Now put the gun down. It doesn't work in here."

"Everybody listen up." Prescott kept the rifle leveled on Hall. "In about ten minutes, this train will be making an unscheduled stop for some of us to get off." An excited murmur went around the car. "We're leaving the zone. Come with us if you want. If not, make sure you stay out of our way."

Hall's sneer vanished. He took a step forward until the muzzle of the gun pressed into his chest. "Go ahead, you dumb sonofabitch. Pull the trigger. You'll never get out of here."

A shadow peeled itself from the wall and advanced on the officer, rocking with the rhythm of the train, holding its rifle in both hands, like a club. Prescott's brow creased in confusion. Hall saw the frown and tried to turn, but it was too late. Spinelli swung the butt of the rifle into the back of his knees and the lieutenant went down with a surprised grunt.

No one moved. The men in the car sat frozen in tableau, watching the scene as if hypnotized. Hall raised himself on one elbow, a look of bewilderment and anger on his face. Bennings turned to the wall and clasped his knees. Spinelli planted his feet apart and drove the rifle butt down again, ramming it into the middle of the officer's back. Hall screamed in pain and horror, frantic eyes searching the faces around him in a mute plea. His attacker kicked him over onto his back, raised the weapon and hammered it down into his face.

Hall's skull split against the floor with a mushy crack, the face replaced by a shallow, bloody cavity filled with meat and gristle and shattered fragments of bone and teeth. His feet jerked and his hands made a futile grasping motion, then were still.

Chaos erupted in the steamy, stinking car. Soldiers were scrambling to their feet, turning on each other with bayonets and rifle butts. A scuffle had broken out at the back of the car and one of the men went down, spilling a waste bucket. Spinelli stood over the lieutenant's corpse, his trousers and hands spattered with blood and flecks of bone and gray matter. He had dropped the bloody rifle and was wiping his hands on his shirt. His face was distant and abstracted, almost dreamy.

Clayton and Salvesen moved closer to Prescott, shielding him from the fray. A man lunged at him from behind, teeth bared and eyes rimmed white in bloodlust or fear. Prescott smashed his elbow into the other's face, but the man grabbed the rifle with both hands and held on. Clayton tried to reach around Prescott with his bayonet. Rough hands pulled him back, clawed at his eyes.

He flailed and snapped his head back, felt the crunch of cartilage, felt the grip on him loosen. He broke free and slashed wildly, all coherent thought swallowed by a burst of wild panic. Through the press of bodies, he saw Salvesen go down in a flurry of fists and feet, a trench knife flash in the dim light.

The rifle in Prescott's hands roared, deafening in the closed space of the car. The man who had lost the tug staggered backward, a dark stain spreading across his chest. Around them the melee parted. Salvesen was on the floor, cursing and clutching at his middle, his hands stained red. Prescott was shouting at the others to stay back.

He was obeyed, but reluctantly. In the eyes of the men Clayton saw a blank madness which had carried them beyond fear. By standing out, by threatening them, Prescott had given them a focus for their frenzy. They no longer cared who they killed, as long as they got to spill blood. The rifle was now the only thing standing between the escapees and a train car full of psychotics, and there were only seven bullets left in the clip.

Clayton knelt at Salvesen's side and held his head. Salvesen was breathing in shallow gulps and his eyes were turning glassy. Blood washed over Clayton's hands, too much blood. The wounded man was beyond saving. The knife had gone in deep, nicked his spleen, or a major vessel. His pale lips were moving, but nothing was coming out. Clayton leaned closer.

"It doesn't have... to be that way." Salvesen's voice was barely above a whisper. His breath stank of warm iron. "What he said. Killing for the sake of killing. If you get out—" He paused to gulp at the hot, reeking air. "If you get out, you'll have a chance. Go to Canaveral City. Try to get off world. Look for the orbitals."

He trailed off into silent coughs. Blood bubbled on his lips, down his chin. His eyes burned like flames. Holding him, Clayton felt the shivers race through the man's body. Emboldened by the smell of death, the mob moved forward with the slow, irresistible force of an avalanche. At the front, Popovich was shifting the trench knife from hand to hand, humming under his breath. The tip of the knife dripped dark red.

"We have to move," Prescott called behind his back, stepping backward over the body of the man he'd shot. O'Rourke had gotten the door open and was squatting on the connecting platform between cars, hammering on the coupling. Baking heat and whorls of dust gusted through the opening. Tracks flashed past below the train. His eyes on the advancing crowd, Clayton got up and followed. His right foot squelched inside his boot, soaked through with blood. On the floor, Salvesen murmured something unintelligible and closed his eyes.

"They're gonna kill ya." Kintner was sitting cross-legged by the door, naked to the waist. His sparse chest hair was plastered to his scrawny body with sweat. "They're gonna kill the lot of us dead," he said in a lilting, singsong voice and closed his eyes. "Get us all with the camera. We'll be on the tee-vee."

Swaying between the cars, O'Rourke took his pack off and set it down behind him, on the floor of the car. Inside the men were snarling, stringy muscles tensed, jaws grinding—animals gathering the courage to attack. One mind with a hundred anonymous limbs, a boiling structure of hatred made flesh. The air was sour with the odor of sweat and desperation, of psychotic, pent-up anger.

"Take the gun," Prescott said. "I'll go outside and help."

His foot caught in the strap of the backpack, tipped it over. Clayton heard a deep, sharp intake of breath.

"He's got a live charge," Bennings shouted from the gloom of the car. "He's gonna blow us all up!"

Bodies surged forward, sweeping Clayton off his feet. He slashed blindly, felt a jolt of pain slam into his temple. The bayonet slipped from his hand; the bloody floor came up hard. Feet trampled over him, pushing him deeper into the stinking bowels of the train.

Somewhere above his head, the Garand fired. Once. Twice.

The world turned red and black, careened madly into spinning darkness. He flinched and consciousness ceased.

He remembered.

The long line of soldiers wound from the concrete depot building to the train, shuffling forward in the blistering heat. Clayton stared down at his booted feet, at the imprints they left in the ochre dust. An odd sense of finality had settled in, a heavy, leaden resignation. Something inside him felt frayed and raw, turned in his heart like a rusty key. He reached out and tapped Prescott on the shoulder.

"I didn't tell you," he began, suddenly unsure. Prescott was looking at him in wonder. The words came out wrong. "About my boy. The one who died."

"I know. He got sick and he died."

"No. I didn't tell you all of it." He wanted to tell Prescott about the trip to the beach, about a white building set in a well-maintained garden. If only he could unburden himself, it would all make sense. Something great and empty and incomplete would be made whole, click together. But the words eluded him. He felt a tightening in his throat and a warm, liquid hitching in his chest, like the beginnings of a sob. "He got sick and I—we—and Linda—"

Prescott grabbed him by the arm. "You told me everything there was to tell. There's no choosing in it. There never was. Your son got sick and he died. It wasn't your fault. It was theirs. Remember that. It's all anyone needs to know."

Clayton shook his head. He wanted to say something else, but nothing came to him. Climbing into the train car, he looked around, but Prescott was already gone. The damp, fetid darkness stank of spilled blood, and when he raised his hands to the light, he saw they were glistening red.

Somehow, he found a gap between the door and the crimped wall and shoved his good shoulder in, braced his legs and pushed. The metal yielded an inch or two, enough for him to push through and crawl out into the heat and blinding glare, into the screaming of the tiltjets. He groped his way forward, hands outstretched, into a vortex of dust and sand churned up by the downblast.

A disembodied, metallic voice boomed overhead, ordering him to stop and lie down on the ground. Cracked, scorched earth spread all around the track bed, a vast, unbroken expanse of open space, going on and on until it met the sky. He struggled to draw breath through a rapidly narrowing throat. The train car lay on its side, half on and half off the rails, its front end charred and crumpled like an empty can, bodies and wreckage spilled everywhere. He caught his foot on a corpse leaking dark red into the thirsty ground, recognized the long, rawboned frame. O'Rourke's body was broken, his arms and most of his face torn to shreds. His head was turned at an unnatural angle, one dead eye staring up at the steel carrion-bird circling above.

The metallic voice repeated its command.

Further down the line, armored figures carrying shock-sticks and plasteel riot shields were advancing in formation. Sunlight flashed off their black-visored helmets. Behind them came the green biohazard suits, bagging the dead for removal and finishing off the wounded. A soldier in a torn uniform crawled out of a derailed car and ran toward them, making wide, clumsy slashes with the trench knife in his hand, his voice rising in an inhuman screech. Two batons brought him down in a flash of sparks, left him retching and convulsing in the dirt.

Someone called out his name, shouting over the boom of the rotors. A hand waved from behind one of the cars. He made his way over, fighting the urge to give up thought and run blindly forward, toward the dark bulk of the wall. To run until they caught him or cut him down.

Prescott was kneeling in the shadow of the broken train car, bloodied and cradling O'Rourke's rifle. When he moved aside to make room for Clayton, he used his arms to drag his right leg and grunted in pain. "The charge went off when those idiots rushed O'Rourke," he said, pushing a strand of wet hair out of his eyes. "We flipped over and the whole goddamn train folded like an accordion. I jumped off and almost broke my neck. O'Rourke never had a chance." He attempted a smile, but it turned into a hard grimace. "I don't think we'll make it through that wall after all. Looks like this is the end of the line."

Clayton chanced a look back. The survivors were coming out of the derailed cars, hands above their heads. Some were dragging or carrying wounded and unconscious comrades. The figures in black armor were rounding them up in groups and disarming them. Bolt-guns hissed and clacked as the green suits dispatched those too injured to get up. Others were hauling the body bags into two transports some distance away, half-hidden by a fog of rotor dust. A cluster of black dots hung in the sky, a second formation flying low on approach.

One of the armored Scavs was pointing his baton at the car behind which the two men were hiding. Prescott propped the rifle against his shoulder and sighted down the barrel.

"What do we do now?" Clayton asked, glancing down at his bayonet.

"Time to give the audience something to remember," Prescott said, and fired. The pointing figure dropped its baton and fell, blood spurting from his throat. The rest broke and ran for cover. The hovering gunship began to turn, bringing its railguns to bear on the train car. A second shot pinged off the cockpit glass and the nose of the gunship dipped, then swung from side to side, the pilot wrestling with the controls. Clayton felt a blaze of savage joy. Against the flying machines the rifle was useless, but the pilots were frightened; they had never faced fire before, couldn't know how many of the soldiers were armed.

"Move, move." Prescott dragged himself under the car, crawling as fast as his broken leg allowed. Clayton followed, one eye on the gunship which had righted itself, guns pivoting. He tumbled down the track bed, pain bellowing in his hurt shoulder. The front of the train car disintegrated in the screaming scrape of the railguns and the shriek of tearing metal, the wreckage rocking with the impact of thousands of titanium flechettes. A cloud of smoke and dirt rolled over the tracks, obscuring the middle of the train.

Coughing and spitting, he crawled on all fours over the ground. Prescott lay flat on the tracks under the back of the car, seeking his next target. The rifle sounded again, and a black figure went down, but its cerametal armor held and it got up and scrambled to safety. "We take a shot, then pull out," Prescott said over his shoulder, already on the move. "Work our way to the back of the train. They won't shoot because they might hit their own."

No sooner had he said that than another gunship took off, whipping up a maelstrom of grit and sand. Twin railgun blasts tore through the overturned car, raising great gouts of dirt and metal fragments. Shielding their eyes against the scouring wind from the rotors, they felt their way toward the rear of the train, barely able to see their own hands.

"This way," came Prescott's voice from the blur. Clayton hunched down between two cars, held onto the connecting platform like a drowning man to a piece of driftwood. From somewhere not far off to his left rose the din of destruction as the gunships strafed the train, taking it apart.

On the other side of the train, in an indeterminate distance, red lights strobed and flashed. Green shadows moved through the dust-storm, vanished toward the lights.

"Clayton." Prescott had pulled himself up, using his rifle as a crutch, breathing heavily. He leaned on Clayton's shoulder and shouted into his ear over the noise of the engines. "You have to go. One of us can still get out. You'll have a few moments before the dust settles. Make them count."

Clayton started to protest, but Prescott grabbed him by the collar and nodded at the lights. "The lawyer I told you about lives in East Central. Down by the slums. Name of Hymes. Joseph Hymes. Tell him I sent you." He uttered a bitter laugh. "Tell him you need one of my skins and my key. You need a different set of eyes to see the key. Remember that."

"Go where?" Clayton asked, but the hand on his collar dropped to his chest and shoved, a quick foot tripped him up and he went tumbling head over heels down the gravel of the bed.

The fall robbed him of all sense of direction. Railguns fired from somewhere above him, a thin, grating sound. Dazed and disoriented, he got to his feet and ran into the haze. Away from the wreckage, toward the blinking lights, nothing in the world but his feet and his lungs, the body's brute need to survive.

Out of the dust-storm a shape appeared, clad from head to foot in a green protective suit and dragging a body bag backwards. It raised a goggled head and dropped its quarry, one hand moving to the bolt-gun at its belt.

Momentum on his side, he dove and tackled the figure, pinned it to the ground. His fingers found the lower edge of the protective mask and his bayonet stabbed beneath. Once, twice. The writhing body under him shuddered and went still.

Working quickly, knowing that to stop and think about the task would mean failure and death, he knelt and stripped the body of the mask and the biohazard suit, removed the undergarments. Other figures moved past him, vague outlines in the thinning cloud. He wiped off the bayonet and pulled the moist, bloody suit over his uniform. The mask stank of rubber and spoiled meat and another man's sweat. He tore the body bag off the naked corpse inside, worked it over the dead Scavenger and closed the zipper.

The muscles in his back sang with the weight of the bag. Ahead in the swirl loomed the hulk of the transport, the red light strobing above its great open mouth. He concentrated on the rhythm of his strides, on the intake and exhalation of breath. No time to think about what he was doing. No time to think at all. Every moment, each new shard of time, existed on its own, separate from the others. Heaving the body bag through the door of the transport, he waited for an alarm to sound, for his ruse to be discovered. But nothing happened.

To the right of the door was a large refrigerated chamber, scores of bags stacked against its ice-crusted walls. A man in a green suit moved around the chamber, lugging the incoming bags across the slick metal grate floor. His mask was off, and his wet head steamed in the cold. Dozens of carcasses hung from hooks that slid along rails beneath the ceiling, raw and red and glistening with ice. Bodies cleaved open and pried apart, frost filming the open eyes, gathering on the lashes. Clayton dropped his bag over the threshold, like he'd seen the others do, and followed the line of green suits further into the belly of the transport.

The seat he strapped himself in bore dark brown stains. He thought he felt eyes on him and forced his breath to slow. Looking up, he realized that no one was paying him any attention. Most of the men had removed their protective masks and were staring blankly into space, faces pale and exhausted, eyes sunken and lifeless. Their heads were shorn, and their bones jutted under their skin like knives. They could just as easily have been the soldiers from his platoon after a battle, waiting for the whistle to blow, the guns to start pounding again.

Engines whined louder and the aircraft rose with a ponderous lurch. Dashboard indicators tracked across the dark glass of the cockpit. Beneath the transport windows the barren plain came into view, the shining track winding across it, the train like a snake cut in two, spilling scrap-metal innards from its smoking middle. Two gunships were banking away from the gutted shells of the cars. Tiny dots milled across the cracked ground. Beyond the black strip of the wall, in the brilliant, quivering distance, the ocean shone like an enormous mirror.

The formation angled east, toward the sparkling expanse. Clayton caught a flash of massive concrete barbettes, the sun flaring off rows of antenna arrays. Then he was over the wall, racing into the orange afternoon light.

Seven

He had closed his eyes for what seemed like a minute, but when he opened them again the aircraft was already over the water, flying above the levees and canals of the South Atlantic dam system. Barren crags nestled between immense concrete bulwarks, the last remains of what had once been a resplendent, vibrant coastline, its white sands and coral cays long vanished under the undulating, encroaching sea. Far to the north lay the southernmost tip of the megasprawl, a long gray smudge on the horizon.

Around the cabin men were sleeping, unperturbed by the turbulence or the racket of the powerful engines. Unbuckling his straps, he got out of his seat and removed his protective mask. A few heads turned in his direction, eyes rolling open, but without curiosity. Clutching at the seats, he picked his way across the rolling, thumping deck, toward the cold storage area.

The main door of the transport was closed, and the emergency lever refused to move. He searched the zippered pockets of his suit for an ident card or a key, came up with nothing. Further up the aisle was the cockpit, the pilot hunched over the controls, bringing up and dismissing tactical displays. He ducked out of sight and crept back down the aisle, looking for a way out. Sooner or later the transport would land, and that would be the end of it.

His eyes went to the closed door of cold storage and he thought of the frozen carcasses dangling from hooks in the ceiling. Better to jump to his death than to let that happen to him. He had come too far to go that way.

At the back of the cabin was a small hatch set into the deck. Kneeling behind the bulkhead, he removed the bulky biohazard suit and tucked the bolt-gun into his uniform belt. He bent over the hatch and turned the handle.

Wind blasted in through the opening, bringing in heat. On the underside of the transport a red light began to blink. Far below, the ground skimmed by, cracked earth furrowed by old canals whose rundown sides had crumbled into the stagnant water. Beyond them lay the desert, scorched a sickly yellow. He remembered reading about the hydroponic farms, the grand solution proposed by the transnationals to end food shortages and the dependence on food from the orbitals. Artificial lakes sprawled through the network of canals, the towering cylinders of farming tanks sprouting from their shores like metal toadstools. Long abandoned, or at least he thought so. Rust bloomed along the roofs of the cylinders, and islands of bilious green sludge floated around the tangled outflow pipes.

He dangled his feet over the drop, feeling queasy. Dull, murky water opened beneath him, rippling in the wind from the rotors. There was no guessing the depth. His hands gripped the rim of the hatch. He could not bring himself to jump.

Sensing a presence, he glanced up. The pilot was standing in the middle of the cabin, staring with his mouth open, fumbling with his service pistol. The rocky shoreline was approaching fast. Clayton pushed off and let the wind carry him back and down.

He hit the surface like a rock, the impact jarring through his soles, rattling his teeth. Water, warm and brackish, invaded his nose and mouth. His feet could not find bottom and the depth took him by surprise. Silt billowed up from beneath, smothered him with blackness. He flailed and sank, the fetid water taking him in and under, drawing its blanket over him. Thrashing and struggling, he freed himself and kicked up to the surface.

He spluttered and trod water, lungs screaming, trying to get his breath back. Across the orange sky, the aircraft thundered on. The pilot had seen him; they would be coming for him. A removal team could already be on the way. He had to hide.

Peeling, rusty tanks circled the lake like cliff faces, casting long shadows over the water. Nodes of blackened and burst pipes sprouted from the concrete foundations like roots. With stiff, tentative strokes, he struck out for a pair of stone pilings sticking out of the water like rotten teeth, the remnants of a collapsed dock, overgrown with reeds.

Soon his feet touched the muddy bottom and he pulled himself onto a half-sunken concrete slab. A quick inventory turned up both the bayonet and the bolt-gun. The gun's gas cartridge was damp but didn't look damaged. The bandage covering his ear had come off in the fall and when he tried to move his injured shoulder the pain was so intense that bright spots appeared before his eyes. His insides were cramped and sour with hunger, his tongue thick with thirst. He hadn't eaten since the previous night, and even then, he'd not been able to stomach more than a pair of soy wafers. But he was alive, and that was all that mattered now.

He climbed out on the bank and walked around the base of the tank. Out of the shadow the heat was unbearable, the parched ground almost white in the late afternoon glare. One hand shielding his eyes, he gazed out into the distance, saw only dust haze and shimmering air and the great vault of sky. The desolation went on beyond the reach of his eyes. No one around for miles. No food and no water either.

He thought longingly about last night's meat ration and his stomach clenched. Even knowing what he knew, he would have eaten it now, every last scrap of it. Hating himself but unable to stop, he went back to the bank and stared at the dirty, sludge-choked surface of the lake. Nothing could live in it, or in the salt desert that stretched past its shores. He had escaped the killing zone only to die a long, slow death of hunger or thirst. Alone on the necrotic border of a sick, dying world.

Taking off his waterlogged boots, he moved back into shade and waded in the shallows. Pieces of junk and broken, black-slimed concrete jutted from the mud like the bones of some great foundered beast. He stripped naked and laid his boots and clothes to dry on the warm slab, then walked into the lake until the level reached his shoulders. The water reeked of brine and rot, but it offered relief from the heat. Exhaustion swept over him. He swam along the bank, nestled under a cluster of corroded pipes, and slept.

Somewhere on the lake a motor chugged, the sound traveling across the water to his ears. He roused, shivering,

and crept out under the pipes. The shadows of the hydroponic tanks had grown longer; a hot, foul breeze rippled the
still surface. Out by the far bank he made out a small scow,
silhouettes moving inside it.

Crossing over to the slab, he covered his face in mud
and took the bayonet in his teeth. He slithered into the
shallows and waited, as silent and still as death.

The noise got louder, and the boat appeared around
a bend. Two men sat inside, one in the bow and the other
handling the outboard, an old combustion engine rigged
with a solar power recombiner. Close to the pilings, the one
in the stern killed the engine and allowed the scow to touch
the concrete slab. The man in the bow, the shorter of the
two, looped a mooring line over one of the stumps. Both
men were naked to the waist and barefooted, their skin
burned a deep brown by the sun, hung from their emaciated frames like borrowed clothes. But neither one seemed to
be armed. They climbed out on the slab and started turning
over the pieces of uniform, lingering over the boots.

Clenching the bayonet in his teeth, Clayton swam to
the stern and lifted himself over the edge. The sun was behind him now; even looking directly at him, the men would
only see a dark blob against a burning background. But
they didn't turn around, sifting through his clothes like a
pair of apes faced with some unsolvable enigma. At the bottom of the boat lay a pile of greasy rags, a large steel jug,
two oars and an ancient, rusty bolt-action rifle. Behind the
engine was mounted a crude device consisting of a metal
cage and a row of blunt circular blades, used to collect long
strands of the floating green scum. He tossed his bayonet
on the pile of rags and heaved himself into the boat.

The men heard the commotion and turned, still holding
the clothes. He racked a round into the breech and pointed
the rifle at them. The taller of the men glanced down at the
bolt-gun but made no move.

Steadying the weapon with one hand, Clayton picked
up the steel jug, opened the top and sniffed. He tipped it
back and drank as slowly as he could. The water smelled
stale and carried a faint mineral taste. A painful spasm
gripped his stomach, but he kept his gorge down. When
the jug was empty, he set it down and raised his eyes to
the men.

"Do you have anything to eat?"

They looked at him with dull, uncomprehending eyes. Perhaps they were imbeciles, or perhaps they spoke another language. "Food," he said, opening his mouth to indicate hunger. He felt ridiculous, naked and mud-smeared in the middle of a wasteland, taking water from a pair of idiots at gunpoint. "Eat."

The shorter man laid down the boots with a sigh of regret. "In the back," he said, "under the rags."

Clayton probed the pile with the rifle barrel, pulled out a foot-long brick of something dark green and hard. He tested the chunk with his nail. It was as solid as a rock and smelled like a mudflat at low tide. "What is this?"

"Food," said the shorter man. His voice was smooth, educated. "That's all you want to know. You break off pieces from the block and soak them in water until they're soft enough to chew."

Clayton cast a guilty look at the empty jug. "That was the last of the water."

"Well," the taller one said patiently, as if speaking to an irascible child, "I guess we all go hungry, then."

Clayton scowled to hide his embarrassment and motioned the men off the ruined dock. They climbed down into knee-deep water and regarded him warily, but without great fear. Holding the gun, he stepped out on the slab and pulled his clothes on. If they recognized the uniform, they gave no sign. "Where do you come from?"

The two men exchanged glances. "A place on the other side of the lake," the taller one said. "We don't bother anyone, mister. We're not tribals. Let us go our way. You can keep the gun and the food, if you want."

"Are there more of you out there?"

Again there was hesitation. "I don't want to hurt or rob anyone," Clayton said. "I'm on my way to the city and I want to trade for food and water."

This brought forth twin expressions of incredulous surprise. "The city is more than a hundred miles from here," said the shorter man. "You'll never make it that far on foot. But if you want to trade, you can come with us. We can always do with another pair of boots."

"It's not safe," the other man said, glaring at the speaker.

63

"We'll let Cal decide what's safe." The shorter man held out his hands. "But we're not taking you over without the gun."

Clayton handed him the rifle, but not before removing the clip and the round from the breech. He knew the men had noticed the ease with which he handled the gun, realized he was giving himself away, and didn't care.

"You'll get them back when we're across the lake," he said, holding up the ammunition.

The shorter man nodded and got in the boat. His companion followed and bent over the outboard, yanking the cord so it sputtered to life. Clayton sat in the bow and watched them, one hand on the bolt-gun in his pocket. Again and again, his mind played over his choices and found them wanting. The tribals on the city fringe were cannibals. Pallid and malnourished, the men in the boat didn't look the part, but he couldn't trust them. No one would live in this desert unless they had good reason to. Cannibals or not, they might still kill him and loot his corpse. Out here, human life couldn't count for much.

Either way, he didn't like his chances. He didn't like them at all.

Eight

They tied the boat to a dock and led him up the sloping shore, past a pair of derelict tanks, their twisted outflow pipes overgrown with slimy fronds. Green paint flecked
off dented metal, the remains of a wind-abraded company
logo. Behind the huge cylinders stood an irregular circle
of low, rust-roofed outbuildings. The cement yard between
them was littered with industrial flotsam—piles of brick,
chunks of trucks and construction machines, dented steel
sinks and rusted plumbing fixtures. A large firepit full of
charred ashes took up the center, crates and metal drums
arranged around it. From the largest of the outbuildings
came the steady hum of a diesel generator and the grinding,
ratcheting noise of segmented wheels on a track.

Faces appeared in the open doorways and windows,
watching the arrivals. A tall, rangy old man came out of
the generator building, wiping his hands on a greasy rag.
He was thin but sinewy, his short silver hair and beard
streaked with yellow ivory. Following him were four younger denizens, dressed in ragged trousers and long, stained
aprons and carrying what looked like spears fashioned out
of sharpened rebar and heavy masking tape. A fifth aproned
man trundled an empty wheelbarrow behind them. They
halted a good distance away from Clayton and the duo from
the boat and waited.

"We found him on the other side of the lake," said Clayton's shorter companion, apologetic. "He wants to trade."

The old man approached slowly, as if Clayton were a
dangerous dog that had slipped its leash. He took in Clayton's uniform, the bayonet and bolt-gun hanging from the
belt. His eyes, already half-hidden in their nests of wrin-
kles, slit further.

"You boys go on and get the stuff from the boat," he
said, addressing his entourage. They glared at Clayton but

obeyed. The old man tucked the rag in his back pocket but didn't offer his hand. "My name's Cal," he finally said. He was sizing the newcomer up, trying to decide what to do next.

Clayton found the old man's wariness reassuring. Cal didn't look like a killer. Besides, if they were going to kill him, they would have done so already. He introduced himself and apologized for the trouble. "I'll trade you for provisions," he said, holding out the bayonet and the bolt-gun.

"Don't look like you've got much to trade with, fella." The old man jerked his head toward a group of stick figures standing in the far corner of the yard. Men and women in torn, filthy clothes, armed with nail-studded clubs, iron spikes and knives. Sunken visages and distended bellies, bodies poorly nourished on basic rations of crude algae-derived carbohydrates and aminos. There was no mercy in their gaunt, sun-leathered faces, only sullen resentment. "We have more weapons here than we have people."

With some reluctance, Clayton stepped out of his boots. "These are good boots. Last you awhile. They're all I have."

"Where you headed to?"

"The city."

"That's a long way to go barefoot," Cal said. He didn't smile, but the tight set of his shoulders relaxed. As if having made up his mind, he turned around and walked toward the open door of the building. "Come on in. It's cooler inside, and the food isn't much, but there's enough to spare."

Clayton followed him into the building. The interior was a single high-ceilinged room with bare walls and a stained concrete floor. On one side of the structure was a large, rumbling generator, its exhaust pipe running out through a hole in the siding. The rest of it was filled by a bulky contraption of wheels and belts and rollers which terminated in a cutting press, rust-specked blades spinning slowly in the heat. Reams of dripping, congealing green fronds hung from overhead drying screens. Sweating workers, stripped down to shorts with rags tied around their heads, dragged wire-tined rakes through piles of algae on the floor and smeared the soggy fibers across the screens. Water slopped around their feet, pooling near the drains. Blocks of dark green matter were stacked to one side like bricks. The damp, stifling air stank of brine and decaying seaweed mingled with diesel exhaust fumes.

The old man flipped a switch and the generator belched, rattled and died. From a shelf near the entrance, he removed a lidded metal bowl and a spoon and handed them over. Clayton sat down on an overturned crate and lifted the lid off the bowl. Inside was a thick green soup, half congealed, clumps of vegetable matter rising from it like pale islands. It smelled faintly of fish concentrate. Gingerly he dipped and brought the spoon to his mouth. It was the best meal he'd ever tasted. He ate quickly, ravenous, washing the fibrous clots down with water from a tin cup the old man had poured for him.

Cal sat across from him and waited for him to finish. Clayton wiped his mouth with his sleeve and looked around the room. "What is this place?"

"The Ocean Vista Hydroponic Farming Cooperative," the old man said. "Or what's left of it. In its time, it was considered the largest corporate land reclamation project in the world. Owned and operated by Monarch Emergency Management Group, which you've probably heard of."

Clayton nodded. "They took over the crisis areas after the government collapse. Drafted the deregulation accords."

"Monarch initially planned to build a luxury community on the coast, with the Cooperative providing its food supply. Completely self-sustainable, the first of its kind. When the dams failed and the sea decided to move ten miles inland, they scrapped the arcology idea and tried to convince investors that the farming project was still viable." He gave Clayton a small, ironic smile. "The lifeline of the south, the ads called it. Claimed it could feed two hundred million. After the fourth or fifth flooding disaster, the investors packed up, Monarch cut their losses, and everyone left town."

"I've heard about it," Clayton said. "Didn't think there was anyone out here."

"There wasn't. Not for a long time." Cal took a sip from his cup and sloshed it around in his mouth before swallowing. His look was contemplative, distant. "Back in the day, before the collapse, I worked for Monarch. Chief geneticist for the Cooperative's food program. We were developing high-yield crop strains with different macronutrient ratios—krill, algae, edible varieties of kelp. After the project folded, I moved back to the city. My career never recovered. A few years ago I found myself in dire financial straits, so to speak. Moving to the slums was out of the question, as was enlistment. I was too old. Then I thought about this place." His eyes warmed. "Monarch had sold off the machinery and flooded the tanks, but there was plenty of junk to be salvaged. When I came out here, I saw that the water was green. Some of the crop strains had spread out through the tank pipes and invaded the lake. It was a sign. With some effort, I could carve out a living from the remains of the farm. But I knew I'd never make it on my own. So I looked around. Turned out there were others in the same boat."

"How many others?" Clayton had a vision of the old man as a religious prophet, leading an army of the dispossessed into the desert. Out in the yard he had counted two dozen, maybe thirty, most of them men, all of them sickly and starved.

Muscles worked in Cal's leathery face. "Seventy-two," he said, his voice hoarse. "The first few months took a toll. The work on the cycler and the desalination plant lasted longer than expected. The algae turned out to be well adapted for survival but missing key nutrients." Almost absently, he picked up one of the dark green blocks and turned it in his hands. "It was a hungry time, and still is, for the most part. Even with our present numbers, many are suffering from deficiency diseases. But those first months were hell. Backbreaking labor in the heat. The sick and the weak dying a terrible, lingering death of thirst. Bodies rotting under tarps. If we stopped long enough to bury them, we'd never get the machines running in time to save the rest of us."

He swallowed around a lump, but his eyes were dry. "There were children among us. None of them lived through it. I lost faith. It had all been for nothing, the delusion of a crazy old man. I'd brought the others to this, brought them here to die. But eventually we found a way out of the darkness, a second chance. The start of a new life. Such as it is. Better than what we left behind."

Freedom of choice. The words lodged in Clayton's head, stripped of meaning through endless repetition. That was what they'd left behind. Buying things was a choice, as long as you could afford them, and credit was a choice. Those who owned you owned your choices and let you choose between them. Once you lost those choices, you could choose between killing yourself or killing others on primetime television. Having children was a choice, and when they got sick there was the choice of ruining yourself trying to save them or putting them down like dogs. Freedom of choice, free will, provided you did what you were told.

Cal and Cal's people had chosen, and he could guess the same was expected of him. But what choice he would make, where it would lead, he didn't know. "Are there other groups like yours? On the other lakes?"

"Not that we know of," Cal said. "But it's possible. We just never thought to go look for them. Nor do we intend to. We're doing just fine on our own."

Clayton thought about what he'd seen outside. "You're not as cut off as you're making it out," he said. "Machines break down. Oil runs out."

Cal mulled this over for a moment. "There's a man who calls himself the Deacon," he said. "He's the only outsider we've seen, apart from you. Got an old truck, the kind you have to drive yourself. He travels around picking up junk—scrap metal, tools, machine parts. Trades with us and with the tribals up in the slums." Noticing something in Clayton's expression, he frowned. "You don't want to bargain with the Deacon, fella. Something about him isn't right. When he's not trying to pull a fast one on you, he's preaching the end of the world. Oceans rising, cities falling, atonement in flood and fire. Earth baptized in blood. Some here buy into that, hold him to be some sort of clairvoyant."

"But not you."

"I think we've already been through hell," the old man said. "That whatever lies ahead can only be better. I have to believe it, or none of what happened makes sense." His face hardened. "Here's the deal. I don't know how you got out of where you were, or why you're headed back to the city. What I know is that you'll die out there, in the desert. Either the heat will get you, or the thirst. Even if you make it as far as the slums, the tribals will flay you alive and put your head on a stick."

"Doesn't sound like much of a choice."

"You could stay with us instead," Cal said. "We're through the worst of it. I've been experimenting with the crop, selectively breeding varieties to improve their nutrient profile. Some types can be gene-tailored for use as biofuel. This community continues to exist, and in time it will begin to grow. People like structure. We'll need someone like you, a soldier. Someone who can help us maintain order. Fight for us when the time comes."

"I'm not a soldier," Clayton said. "I only enlisted eight months ago." But even as he spoke, he wondered if that were true. Once there had been a man with the same name as his, a husband, a father; a man with ambition and a career, with plans and dreams. A man on track for a mid-level executive position, a safe, simple life, preferential housing on the corporate compound. Away from the tiny, stuffy one-family unit, the sirens and flashing lights at night, the stench and silent desperation of Canalside. A man who thought he could shut out the insanity of the city, keep his loved ones safe from harm. That man was long dead, and Clayton couldn't decide who had replaced him.

"If you say so. Still, I'd like you to think about it." Cal clapped his hands on his knees and got up. Outside, a red, heavy sun hung low over a purple dusk sky. The area around the firepit was filling with people carrying metal bowls and cups. "Stay the night with us. If you still feel the same way in the morning, we'll give you all the water we can spare and see you on your way. But for your sake and ours, I hope you'll change your mind."

Nine

The truck whined and groaned across the torn concrete and came to a stop at the edge of the yard. A single slitted headlight cut through the gloom, the other a gaping hole. A battered pickup with a sagging suspension, it sat askew four bald tires, canting visibly to the right. Its front fender was gone, and the passenger door was held shut with wire. From the pickup bed rose a huge pile of junk, bound with rope and ripped tarp.

There was a commotion around the firepit, and several men and women got up from their seats. The others did not seem alarmed or reach for their weapons. From his place by the fire, Clayton watched the smaller group approach the truck. Some of those who had remained seated were staring at the vehicle with blank, shiny eyes.

Earlier on that evening, Clayton had listened to them discuss Cal's plans to fertilize one of the other lakes and seed it with tailored strains of algal crop, to jury-rig a second generator for the desalination plant. In their previous lives, the colonists had been skilled workers, engineers, technicians. Cal had chosen his people well; it was one of the reasons they had survived. But hardship and isolation were slowly stripping away the last vestiges of civilization, eroding rational thought. Now their body language suggested curiosity and a fearful deference, like savages gathering around a religious symbol. Instinct and superstition were asserting themselves in this dark open waste, far from the battlements and towers of the city.

The truck door opened, and the driver got out. He was a big, fat man with a round, jowly face, his head clean shaven and pink from the sun, his bulk shrouded in a loose suit of dirty white linen. Stepping into the narrow beam of the single headlight, he turned to the approaching figures and opened his arms in greeting. For a man of his size, he moved with surprising lightness and grace. One of the women said something Clayton didn't catch, and the driver threw his head back, the bellow of his laughter drifting over to the fire.

Cal stood outside the circle of firelight, his face invisible in the darkness. The big man walked over to him, hand outstretched. They shook.

"We weren't expecting you, Deacon. Not for another week."

"Change of plans." The big man turned toward the fire and smiled. It was an engaging, self-deprecating smile, the smile of a man taking you into his confidence. Yet the eyes above it remained cold. He accepted the proffered cup of water with a small bow, drank it at a draught. "There's rumors of a fuel shortage in Southeast. Tribal gangs have blown up two or three major serviceways and are attacking all inbound tankers from the refineries. Standard Energy and PetroMobil are deploying heavy ordnance into the area. Getting ready to lay waste. I figured I'd get out of the city and wait it out."

"How long do you think it will take?" asked a sharp-featured man standing to his right. The Deacon shrugged and returned the empty cup.

"Not long. Two days, three at most. They'll pound the whole slum to rubble in twenty-four hours, spray the ruins with poison gas. I've seen corpmercs at work before." He ran a hand across his shiny scalp. "They'll jack up the fuel prices, though, especially with the cold snap coming. Thousands will die in the streets, come winter. But that's only the beginning of it." His eyes swept the gathering with calculating slyness. "The wheels have been set into motion. We are seeing the first signs."

"What signs?" said a woman with gray-streaked hair, her lips parted. Cal crossed his arms over his narrow chest but said nothing.

"This is a holy war," the Deacon replied, his voice shifting gears, becoming deeper and portentous. "It's a great clash of faiths we're witnessing. The savage creeds of the tribals teach of blood sacrifice. They believe that cutting the veins of the tanker and spilling its oil, its blood, will bring divine favor. The transnationals worship their own false gods. Anything that eats into the profit margin is blasphemy of the highest order." In the firelight, his slab-like face took on a dreamy, vacant mien. "They're both wrong. The last times are upon us. To the north lies the great harlot, clad in a raiment of avarice and lies. Herald of the fall of the empires of man. At her mouth, a river of blood, leading into an ocean. Sin cries out for expiation. There will be much sorrow and pain before the tears are wiped away from our eyes—before the truth is revealed to us in flood and flame."

A low whisper began to build around the fire. This sort of hellfire-and-brimstone talk was hardly news to Clayton. Harbingers of the impending apocalypse filled the airwaves and the already crowded streets, delivering sermons and handing out leaflets. Deserted warehouses were converted into temples, bars and back alleys turned into pulpits. New faiths proliferated, old ones rose refreshed: Magians and Methodists, Epiphanists and Evangelists, True and Reformed Catholics, Sunnis and Sufis, Karaites and Reconstructionists, Buddhists and Pentecostals, Little Brethren and Neopagans, Sowers and Baptists, all offering their brand of salvation. Doomsday cults and fundamentalist splinter sects sprang up everywhere, taking root and gaining followers as the food and water allotments grew smaller, as precious farmland disappeared under the spreading concrete or turned into poisoned, dusty desert. There was no use denying the influence that the Deacon's huge, fire-lit figure and the solemn bass in which his message was delivered held over the gathering. Clayton wondered if Cal knew he was losing control of his people and what the old man meant to do about it.

The Deacon must have noticed Cal's silent disapproval, because he caught himself. "Enough of that. I have something to show you."

He went back to the truck and pulled out a folding table, which he set near the firepit. With a flourish, like a magician doing a trick, he tossed a tattered, stained length of cloth over it and began to lay out his wares; a frayed timing belt, a pair of shapeless shoes with new rubber soles, a few greasy brass fittings and valves, a gauge with a broken needle. With a wink toward the women, he added two faded hand-dyed dresses to the pile. The group pressed around the table, conferring in an excited murmur. Their dirty faces were grave and thoughtful, as if they were discussing a matter of life and death—which, Clayton supposed, was exactly what it was for them. Even Cal had come into the circle, gesticulating with both hands, his earlier animosity forgotten. For his part, the Deacon seemed to have abandoned the role of doomsayer; he preened and charmed and haggled, his eyes dancing in the firelight. Not once did they turn in Clayton's direction, but still he had a sensation of intense scrutiny.

Finally a price was offered and accepted, the group taking the belt and the valves, the Deacon receiving a tall stack of food blocks and filling two jerrycans with water. *Barter,* Clayton thought. Hominids standing around a fire, exchanging food for a pelt, fresh meat for a spear-point or a flint arrow. He lifted his eyes and found the Deacon staring at him, the pink, bulbous face like a jovial rubber mask, another set of features lurking underneath.

They made room for the big man by the fire and passed him a bowl and spoon. At first the conversation was stilted, the group unnerved by the presence of two strangers. Unfazed, the Deacon told jokes and improbable stories, his booming, gregarious voice rising over the crackle of the fire. It was a warm night, but the low flames did not put off much heat; sitting in the circle made Clayton feel like he was part of the community. Another throwback to pre-civilized times, the tribe gathering around the light to listen to the storyteller, the fiery ring keeping the night at bay. Maybe this was inevitable; maybe civilization had to perish for humanity to find meaning in its struggles. Maybe none of it made a bit of difference and the sweeping waste, the nothingness, was all there was to it.

Movement brought him out of his reverie. The Deacon was standing over the fire, holding up a book bound in scuffed, black leather, the lettering erased from the cover, the pages dog-eared and yellow. The amiable face was gone; in its place was a wild mask, gleaming with sweat, lit from below by the orange tongues of flame. Spittle flew from his mouth as he described buildings and towers ablaze, the seas washing over the handiwork of man, the flea-pits of sin and gluttony and lust washed clean by dark waters. The eternal throne surrounded by beasts, the breaking of the seven seals, catastrophes ravaging the earth. He spoke of years of toil and tribulation, of submission to the terrible mercy of the Lord, of the world being set to burn in order to be renewed. His words became increasingly incoherent, moving toward some awful climax but never attaining it, whipping the colonists into a higher and higher frenzy.

Most of the audience had left, but the remaining few listened in utter fascination. The sermon, Clayton observed, was a mishmash of apocalyptic teachings taken from the mainstream religions and graphic images of devastation which he suspected came out of old books and films. Lips moving soundlessly, eyes alight with black glee, the congregation devoured every word. Clayton felt dizzy and sick, the tasteless, meager meal he'd eaten earlier threatening to come up. He'd never been a religious man and he found the ease with which Cal's group had split into camps deeply troubling. The big man had power, and the longer his listeners spent in the desert, the more that power would grow.

Abruptly, the Deacon fell silent and set the black book down. As if a switch had been thrown, the group by the fire began to break up and vanish into the night. Clayton tried to make up his mind about approaching the preacher, almost turned around. When he looked back the Deacon was smiling.

"A military man." His bright, cunning eyes bored into Clayton's. His smile grew wider, baring strong yellow teeth. "What brings you out this way?"

"They tell me you're going up to the city." Clayton nodded at the truck, ignoring the question. He wasn't going to be intimidated by this self-made revival preacher. "I want to come with you. I can trade for passage."

The Deacon seemed to mull this over, fingers locked over his expansive gut, his great head cocked to the side. Clayton had an unpleasant feeling that the man had anticipated his words from the outset, that he was being toyed with. "I've already got everything I need," he said at last. "But I have a job for you if you want it. You may have heard that there's a bit of trouble brewing in the Southeast. My usual sources have dried up. It's hard to find new ones, and some of them tend to be rough customers. Savages, for the most part, and they can't be trusted. They're just as likely to rip out your guts and strangle you with them as they are to trade with you. If things go badly, I could use someone who knows how to handle a knife and a gun, who isn't squeamish about getting his hands dirty. Do that and we're square."

"What happens after that?" The idea of killing for hire bothered Clayton, which was ironic considering where he'd come from and what he was planning to do when he got where he was going. But that was different. If he took a life again, it would be on his own terms.

"We part ways and I forget I ever saw you," the Deacon said with a smirk. "I don't know who you are or where you're going, and I don't want to know. Life's easier that way."

Clayton considered his options. The old man's warning came back to him, telling him not to bargain with the Deacon. A bad feeling was spreading up from the pit of his stomach, but there was no help for it. The big man's hand engulfed his as they shook. "How long will it take us to get there?"

"A day and a half, two days tops." The Deacon's nonchalance seemed feigned. "It's slow going, traveling through the desert. No roads out here, and we'll have to go further west to circle around the fighting. We'll leave at dawn, find some shade by midday and continue in the evening. Stay out of the worst of the heat. If the engine boils over, we'll be stranded in the middle of nowhere and die of thirst. Are you armed?" He took Clayton's bayonet and ran his finger along the blade, handed it back. "It'll do the job. Have you killed many men?"

"I've killed enough."

"Then you know the feeling. You never get quite accustomed to it, but it gets easier over time. After a while, it becomes part of you." The big man stared into the fire, lost in some inner calculation. "Get some rest, sleep if you can. I'll wake you."

Clayton left the fire and walked to the nearest building. A pile of canvas and netting was pushed against one wall. He stretched out on it, inhaling the musty smell. Before the darkness took him, the last thing he saw was the Deacon squatting by the fire, inside the island of light, a huge and shapeless idol wreathed in a nimbus of flame.

Ten

It was still dark when they set off, the truck struggling over bumpy ground, rocking like a small boat in high seas. The bleak, barren contours of the desert slipped in and out of view as the narrow headlight beam sliced into the night. Above, the stars shone hard and bright, unwinking, the thin crescent of the moon washing the rolling wasteland a watery silver. To the east, the massive bulwarks of the dam system formed a dark line against the lightening sky.

Two or three times during the night, Clayton had woken up, confused by the darkness and unfamiliar surroundings, sweating and clutching his bayonet. Lights played in the sky and the chop of rotor blades filled his ears. The meat transports were coming for him, opening, their frozen breath steaming in the night. At last he could not sleep at all and tossed on the canvas until the Deacon came to get him. Now he sat back in the cracked vinyl seat, exhausted but awake, jolting over the ruts.

The Deacon kept both hands on the wheel and squinted through the dusty windshield. Pistons wheezing, the truck moved at a walking pace, protesting like an exhausted animal. Even at this hour, the cab was hot and stank of old sweat and worse. Junk and debris filled every available space. Dozens of trinkets—amulets, bone carvings, shards of shiny stone and gaudy glass beads—bobbed from the ceiling on lengths of string. Inset into the dashboard was a battered radio console, trailing frayed wires. The glovebox underneath it held the black book and a heavy revolver. "In case we run into trouble," the Deacon had said, showing him the gun. There were three rounds in the cylinder and the barrel was dirty. What if it didn't fire when he needed it to? Clayton hoped he wouldn't have to find out.

He drifted in and out of uncomfortable half-sleep and when he opened his eyes the sun was up, blazing through the windshield and the missing windows. Sweat ran from his hairline into his eyes, down the back of his neck. The shadows of the ridges and rocks fell across the barrens, but in an hour or so they would be gone. He leaned out of the window and looked back. Far behind, sunlight flashed off the metal tanks of the abandoned farms.

The Deacon was eating a soy wafer, straight out of the wrapper, unheated. His jaws moved in a slow circular motion. He had stripped down to a gray, stained undershirt and a pair of yellowing shorts. His great bulk was pale and the sun-darkened skin of his face and neck and hands looked incongruous against the whiteness, like some odd disguise he hadn't bothered to remove. Without a word, he held out the packet. Clayton's mouth flooded with saliva. He bolted the remaining two wafers down and licked the crumbs from his fingers.

"All this used to be swampland," the Deacon said with no preamble. One thick finger traced the unbroken salt desert around them, blinding white in the sun. "Hard to believe, but it was. Swamp and trees everywhere. When my granddaddy was a boy, people used to come here on vacation. Then the sea came in, and the droughts. Nothing grows here, and nothing has for a long time." He pointed to the east, to the thin dark line of dams. "Before the deregulation, the government built tidal barriers along the coast. I heard there's a whole big city out there, half buried under sand and half sunk in the sea. Six million people lived there once. A Gomorrah of corruption and fornication, of drug addicts dying in the streets, of men selling their wives and daughters for credit. Gone, just like that. Such is the price of conceit. Man can rail against God's design, but he can't hinder it."

"I've never seen anything like this." Clayton rubbed his stiff neck. A headache throbbed at the back of his skull. "They don't talk about it on the Newscans."

"A land of salt without inhabitant." The big man nodded slowly. "The deceitful and the immoral turn a blind eye to it. They want us to forget what they did. But it won't be long now. The blight is spreading into the city. I've seen it happen over the years. When I started trading out here, the city line was six or seven miles from where the slums began. Today it's more than twenty miles back. The city is retreating, the desert moving north. People are leaving the southern Districts. Abandoning their homes."

"Why is that?"

"It's the way they live in the city," the Deacon said. "The blasphemous perversion of the gifts He bestowed upon us. Farming consortiums ravage what's left of God's land for the sake of increased production. Soil erosion clogs up streams and rivers. Drinking water must be filtered or pumped from farther away. The southern parts get hit the hardest, but in the end, none will be spared." The Deacon reached between his knees to retrieve a metal flask. He pulled the stopper with his teeth and took a long drink. "It's the beginning of a chain reaction. Profits fall, so corporations pull out. More and more people leave. The ones who can afford to move out, that is. Where do they go? Away from the desert, deeper into the city, where the housing projects are already crowded beyond capacity. More starving rats, and the box keeps getting smaller." He grimaced and snorted and drank again. "It's happened before, out west. Conurbations buried under dust and drought and smoke. Abandoned streets sinking into the sand. We knew what was happening and all we did was talk wastewater management and reclamation, carbon credits and pollution infractions. The invisible hand of the market at work." He closed his eyes and smiled. "It has all been foretold. *He will make Nineveh a desolation, parched like the wilderness.*"

"Is that what you think? That this is God's work?"

"Everything is His work," the Deacon said in a conversational tone, a man reflecting on the weather. "How can you doubt it? His mark is on every stone, every grain of dirt. The god of fear, of darkness, of blood and retribution. A blind, pitiless god, howling in the center of an insane universe. The only god mankind has ever known. Look around us." Tears rolled down his jowls, bracketed his smiling mouth. His eyes were muddy and bloodshot. Clayton could see madness capering inside them; madness and something else, a conscious desire to do harm. "This is the temple we have built for Him. The climate, the befoulment, the poisons we keep pouring into the ground and air and water. We knew what we were doing, and we did it anyway. Even now, on the brink of destruction, we refuse to overcome our greed, to renounce our selfish desires. It's deliberate waste, a kind of ritual desecration."

He took another pull from the flask. "Man has always been fascinated by the abyss. Show him a high ledge, and his first thought is to get up there, his second to jump. But the suffering and violence are sacred, necessary. God sees that the world is corrupt, for the flesh has corrupted its ways upon the earth. After all this destruction will come a glorious rebirth."

They both lapsed into silence. Clayton watched the desolate landscape pass by and tried to imagine lush greenery sprouting from the rocks, blue water and white beaches in place of the monolithic dams. It didn't work. He had never seen a forest outside of corporate propaganda messages and old movies on television. Vivid pictures and sounds, evoking concepts that no longer had any meaning. The world he had lived all his life in was one of steel and concrete, and all that existed beyond its borders was farmland, acres upon acres of biotech crop tended by complicated machinery. Some of the men in his platoon told of war zones set in jungles, where the trees grew tall and thick and their branches shut out the sun. Some even claimed to have fought there, but he didn't credit such stories. Among the enlisted, few lived long enough to serve out their contracts with the network, and of those who did, fewer still signed up for a second tour.

He thought about what the Deacon had said, the cycle of apocalypse and rebirth, God sending down a terrible vengeance on His wayward creation. That didn't sound right either. Even if there was a God, this world was one thing He had nothing to do with.

A few hours later the Deacon swung the truck into the scant shade of a rockpile. "We'll take a break here," he said, tapping a gauge on the dashboard and watching the movement of the needle. Wisps of steam curled up from under the hood. Clayton unwound the wire holding the door together and stepped out. The heat struck him like a blow. The metal chassis ticked as it cooled. Beyond the rocks, the flats shimmered like the bottom of a cauldron.

The Deacon wrapped a rag around his hand and lifted the hood, thrusting his head into the steam. He emerged flushed and grease-stained and gave Clayton the thumbs-up. "Looks like we still have a ride. Give me a hand with those tarps in the back."

They tied one end of the tarp to a piece of cast-iron beam and weighed the other end with flat stones, rigging a makeshift canopy. The Deacon folded over a second tarp, laid it under the canopy and lowered himself onto it with a groan. Clayton did the same. Sitting cross-legged in the shade, they prepared their meal, scraping thin slices off the green blocks into tepid canteen water, mashing the mixture with the butts of their knives until it softened. Clayton didn't feel like eating, but he swallowed the bland gruel and washed it down with more water. Dehydration could set in quickly. He had seen it take its toll on the long, deadly march from the beach—collapsed men left behind in the arid dust.

Noontime sun leached shadow from the ridges and furrowed earth, washed out all color from the sky. The heat bore down upon them, smothering, unforgiving. On the other tarp, the Deacon lay on his back and snored, blackened hands folded over his huge, flabby chest. Half-delirious with the heat, Clayton covered his eyes with his arm to shut out the light.

The desert rippling in the glare. Dirt walls closing on a rectangle of blue sky. The Deacon moving in the flickering firelight, hawking his wares. The vast face sheened with sweat, the eyes like burning coals.

Clayton grunted and turned, skimming the border between sleep and wakefulness. His mind was telling him something, the cascade of images unraveling like film.

Dull, thudding voices sounded from the far end of a long hallway. The bloodred darkness behind his eyelids pulsed like the inside of a heart.

The Deacon was shaking him awake. He sat up, groggy and aching. The shadows were long, and the sun was a red line in the west. They packed up their belongings and got back in the truck. The engine coughed, spluttered, then caught, the tires kicking up dust.

They drove on under the darkening indigo dome of the sky. The terrain was changing, rocky badlands and dust basins giving way to low rolling hills. Dirt tracks traversed the broken ground, merged with the tumbled remains of old, ruined roads. Beyond the coastline to the east, distant streaks of fire rose into the heavens like ascending meteors. Transport shuttles and agrolanders blasting off from Canaveral City, hauling equipment and material to the orbital colonies, bringing down food to a starving world.

Try to go off world, Salvesen had said on the death-train. What did he mean? The only off world Clayton knew about were the Gyges penal colonies, huge ring-shaped habitats in high Earth orbit. A complex of farms and industrial research laboratories, the colonies grew food for the United Nations famine relief program and assembled space probes in microgee. He scanned the night sky until he found them, the brightest constellation among the stars. There was no way of getting there. It didn't bear thinking about. Salvesen's words had been nothing but the babbling of a dying man.

Far ahead, flashes of explosions lit up the dusk. "Bombing runs." The Deacon followed the flares with his hand. "That's where the serviceway tunnels are. We should play it safe and go around them. Too many lurking tribals and corpmercs with itchy trigger fingers. There are many other ways to get into the slums."

Clayton started to reply, but a harsh metallic squawk from the radio unit cut him off. Both men jerked back from it. The cab filled with the crackle of radio voices. Clayton didn't make out the words, but they sounded like orders.

Quick as a striking snake, the Deacon leaned over and turned it off. "I keep it on for the security drones," he said with a dismissive shrug, but for a moment his calm, collected mask had slipped and suspicion—or fear—had shown through. "Sometimes you can pick up their signal if they're flying nearby. Gives you a few seconds to try and hide."

"Drones?" Clayton could feel the slanted gaze on his face, studying his reactions. "How far do they range?"

"About a mile or so from the edge of the slum. But sometimes they go haywire, or lose their bearings, or I don't know what, and stray into the desert. Vicious little things. No recon missions out here—they're programmed to destroy anything that moves." The Deacon saw Clayton's anxious look and laughed. "Don't worry. When the corporates send their troops and armor into the slums, they usually shut down all the drone towers within signal range. Reduces the risk of friendly fire. Besides, we'll drive with the lights off. They won't see us."

He dug for the metal flask and tossed it into Clayton's lap. "Here, try this. A tribal I trade with brews it from fruit concentrate. It'll take the edge off some."

The sharp stink of alcohol made Clayton's eyes water. He took a cautious sip. Liquid fire caromed down his gullet, exploded in his belly and rocketed up to his brain, trailing hot fumes. He coughed, snorted, took another, longer drink. It went down more smoothly. He stretched the next one into a gulp.

"Easy there." The Deacon chuckled. "You don't want to overdo it. Tastes awful, and you can go blind from a bad batch, but it does the trick."

"You never told me what you want me to do," Clayton said. The liquor was a tight ball of fire in his empty gut and his thoughts were thick and sluggish. "When we get wherever it is we're going."

"Nothing to tell," the Deacon said. "You take the gun and hide in the back of the truck. I'll drive to the meeting place and make the trade. If there's trouble, you'll take care of it. Simple as that."

"They know you're coming?"

"They are expecting me."

"You had any trouble before?"

"Once or twice." The big man hitched up his undershirt. Long, uneven streaks of purple scar tissue crisscrossed the pale mass of his flank, trailed from his waist up to his armpits. "But not for a long time. I know better now."

"You seem awful sure of yourself."

"The tribals are bloodthirsty savages," the Deacon said. "But they're a superstitious bunch. To them, I'm an evil spirit, a beast from the pit, feared and reviled." He set a few of the hanging ornaments into swaying motion with his finger. "A demon who disappears into the desert for weeks and returns with unimaginable treasures. Their chieftains like to show off to each other, especially when it comes to shiny baubles. Most of them do their best to appease me, which suits me just fine. But I don't want to push my luck."

"They're worse than animals," Clayton said with contempt. "They deserve to be wiped off the face of the earth."

"They are the light in the darkness," the Deacon replied. "God's own scourge. The blessed fire that purifies the land. Who among us is without sin, above judgement? We all have a role to play in the great transformation."

"I don't know about that," Clayton said. "Whatever this transformation is, I want no part of it."

"That's not yours to decide. Neither of us is in control of the fates remitted to us. Providence put you on my path, or me on yours. We have been shown the way, and we must not stray from it." The Deacon's voice took on a distant note. "The old faiths, they spoke about hell, a place of everlasting torment and punishment in the afterlife. But that hell was no more than a metaphor, a parable. The real hell is the absence of God. The real hell is on this earth. Around us. Damnation is a state of mind, a state of existence. Only through blood and torment shall we be redeemed."

Before their eyes, the last of the orange sunset faded from the sky. The night was upon them. The faraway crump of the explosions reached their ears. Clayton leaned back and counted the flashes. God's terrible miracle, the cleansing fire upon the fallen world.

His head was still muddled with drink. Something was bothering him, and he wasn't sure what. He didn't fully understand the Deacon's apocalyptic gibberish, the riddles and parables in which the man spoke, but there was meaning in them, a sinister echo, that struck strange chords at the back of his mind. He resented the notion that it was getting to him, that this nightmare figure, this grotesque prophet of death and damnation, was trying to impart some sort of lesson, to poison him with deranged visions.

The moon was halfway up when the Deacon turned off the lights and shut down the engine. The truck coasted to a stop on the crest of a rise. Below was a flat, moonlit plain, huge dark structures tumbled across it like a child's building blocks, a silent, empty heap of concrete ruins. No lights burned in their walls. These were the slums of the megacity, the petrified bones of a dead civilization.

The big man got out of the truck and surveyed the land through a pair of powerful thermal binoculars. Nothing stirred, but he watched for a long time, sweeping the glasses from one end of the plan to the other.

"Down there," he said, passing the binoculars to Clayton and pointing down. Clayton followed the finger. Enhanced-feedback optic circuits turned the night to day. The line of buildings leapt into magnification. Between two massive accommodation blocks, rising in tower upon dark tower-like ziggurats, nestled the spire of a ruined church. "We'll meet them in the churchyard. After that you're free to go your own way."

Clayton studied the dark streets, searching for escape routes. Nothing but narrow nooks and alleys, broken sidewalks piled with garbage and debris. Behind the church was a collapsed Loop entrance, a circular hole leading into blackness. "Looks like a good place to get ambushed and killed."

"They'll keep their word." The Deacon came around the truck and leaned through the missing window. He rummaged through the glovebox, the door creaking under his weight. "There's a flashlight somewhere in the back. Under the tarps. Bring it here and I'll show you something."

Clayton pulled back the tarp and climbed into the truck. Scrap iron and pieces of machinery formed the bulk of the pile, but smaller bits had sifted to the bottom. He shuffled through the junk with his hands. Rusted tools, old clothes, odds and ends of gear. A stack of brick-sized parcels behind a pair of old tires. He bent over and unwrapped one of the parcels. Hard and smooth to the touch, a faint smell of salt and seaweed. Next to them, three full cans of water.

The instant he saw the cans he knew what it was, knew what had been bothering him since the night before. Pieces of the puzzle fell into place. The Deacon showing up at the lakeside settlement unexpected. Trading for food and water he didn't need. The crackle of voices from the radio. The big man must have known that the network was looking for an escaped soldier, that they would be willing to pay to have him delivered.

Frozen with alarm, he didn't hear the footsteps until they were almost on top of him. Even then, he dropped to one knee and tried to turn round, one hand going up to protect his head, the other moving to the bayonet.

He almost made it. A pale and enormous shadow filled his vision, as big as the world and everything in it. The butt

of the revolver descended. White light exploded behind his
eyes. Then darkness, the night sky falling away, shrinking
down the far end of a spyglass.

Eleven

When he came to, all was darkness. He lay on his face, breathing in dust and gasoline fumes, the rough floor rocking beneath him. Pain thudded in the side of his head and he could feel blood cooling on his temple and cheek. The sound of an engine revving up, falling off, revving up again; he was in the back of the pickup truck.

His hands were behind his back, his wrists and ankles bound with plastic ties, cutting off the circulation to his extremities. He reached behind, ran his hands over the surface of the cast-iron beam. When he tried to wriggle free, the motion rustled the tarps over his head. Something heavy clanged behind him and rolled around.

"You can't get out." The Deacon's voice came from the front, over the noise of the engine. "I shouldn't have hit you that hard," he said, sounding almost apologetic. "But I didn't think I'd get another chance. I knew you'd figure it out eventually. Damn radio gave me away."

Clayton braced against the beam and tried to push himself upright. Pain hammered in his head. The bonds cut deeper into his wrists. Another tie secured his bonds to the beam, with no give at all. He was trussed up so tight he could barely breathe.

"There's a contract out on you. The network is offering a reward. Enough to live off for a while, even with the gas shortage." The engine labored up and down the ridges, tires scraping across dirt. "Like I said, it was fate. Had to be. God provides for those who do His work."

Clayton's brain worked restlessly as his muscles strained against the ties. He tried to estimate where he was, how much time he had left. Before they stopped, the explosions had been growing closer, the delay between flash and report shortening. They had to be heading east, closer to the fighting. At times, the truck picked up speed over sections of paved road, only to slow down and crawl across rough, pitted terrain. Every bounce sent a stab of pain through his injured shoulder.

The voice droned on, muffled by the noise of the engine. Clayton caught some of it—the sun shining on the path of righteousness, the wages of sin, blood washing the stain away. "You're His chosen instrument, my friend. A bearer of destruction. A creature of terrible purpose. Where the tribal heathens are a brush fire, you're a killing blade, a spiller of blood. The light that burns in you must be allowed to grow brighter." Laughter, dry and cracked. "But a man's got to eat, so this is the end of the line for you. The Lord's killing light may just have to wait."

Loose objects scraped across the truck bed. He fumbled around in the blackness, as far as his bonds would allow, trying to find one of the tools he'd seen earlier, or a piece of metal with a sharp edge. Something rolled to a stop against his thigh. Holding his breath, he moved it up his body, closer to his hands, with agonized concentration. A plastic cylinder under his fingers, smooth with a ridged rubber grip, like the handle of a screwdriver. He felt a small thread of hope. But there was no blade. Careful not to drop it, he felt along its sides, found a button.

A burst of light illumined his surroundings, the junk piled above him, the tarps like a dusty, tattered sky. A flashlight. He switched it off and listened. The truck kept moving, the Deacon jabbering away. Leaning forward, he flexed his legs and stomach muscles, pushing down with all his might. The mass of iron strapped to his back moved a little. He bit his lip and strained, blood humming in the sides of his neck, just under his jaw. With a loud crash, the beam came free of the clutter and fell on top of him.

"What's going on back there?" No worry in the Deacon's tone, only curiosity. "Hope you're not planning to do anything foolish now. Fall off the truck and you'll break your neck."

Clayton got his knees under the weight and pushed. The beam toppled sideways, wrenching his shoulder, drawing a scream through clenched teeth. He was on his back now, staring at the black sky through a rent in the canvas. Dark shapes of gutted machinery limned by moonlight.

There was no way out, not with the iron weighing him down like a ball and chain.

Was it his imagination, or were the explosions getting nearer?

Suddenly the Deacon stamped on the brake. The pick-up skidded to a halt, sending the loose junk in the back tumbling. Clayton was thrown against the back of the cab, jerked painfully against his restraints. For a terrible moment, he thought that the flashlight was gone. Then his hands found the plastic and tightened around it in a death grip.

The engine turned off. Clayton waited for voices, for approaching footsteps, but none came. There was no sound at all. Even the Deacon had gone silent and still.

A whirring noise cut through the night, rotor blades scything the still air. Between the tarps he saw a triangular shape dart overhead, a darker shadow against the stars. The Deacon had been wrong about the armed drones. One of them was up there, a shark gliding under the surface, stalking prey.

An irresistible urgency took hold of him now, and yet he held onto the piece of plastic with both sweat-slicked hands, waiting for the sound to get closer. He worked his arms around to give himself more room, pointed the flashlight as straight up as he could and clicked the button. On and off, on and off, revealing their position to the circling predator.

The noise from the sky rose to a high-pitched hum. The sleek, deadly shadow swept down on the truck, resolved into sharp angles and matte surfaces, guns locking on target. He could almost hear the delicate circuitry of the drone's brain humming, cold and ruthless, laser targeting rings closing on the truck, stored schematics pinpointing the engine, the wheel-axle system, the location of the operator. He heaved onto his side, ignoring the pain, dragging the heavy girder over him. Tried to make himself as small as possible, to burrow into the clutter like an animal.

A scream from the front as the Deacon gunned the truck to life, a futile attempt to escape the inevitable.

Fire from the sky cut the vehicle in half, precise as a surgeon's knife. Metal groaned. The chassis rocked under the impact of titanium needle-rounds. The truck bolted forward, shattered engine trailing smoke and steam. Hard, hot light streaked from above and the front right wheel vanished in an explosion of dirt and rock. The pickup tilted forward, teetered, then rolled onto its roof, spilling its cargo across the darkened plain.

Guns poised, the drone hovered over the destruction, sailing on the warm currents from the desert floor. Its ducted fans raised small eddies of grit around the wreckage. Intricate systems swept the night, searching for signs of life.

No movement below. Minimal probability of survivors.

Out on the plain, a pinprick of light blinked in the cratered void, drawing the drone's sensors like a moth to a flame. Telemetry was beamed to signal towers that studded the border of the slum, reams of data parsed in microseconds, identifying its new target. The drone's inertial navigation gear calculated distance and direction, payload clicking home into the firing chamber.

Sensing heat and blood, the predator angled its wings and veered off over the dead city, its shadow dancing along the empty streets.

Twelve

He waited for the drone to return, but it never did.

At dawn he crawled out of the wreckage like a monstrous hermit crab, the girder dragging in the dirt. His body felt as if it had been through a meat grinder in one of the bioprotein factories. It took him hours to get out of the plastic ties, sawing them against the sharp edge of the tailgate. When he was done his wrists and hands were cut and bleeding and sweat coursed down his face and neck. His eyes and mouth were full of sand.

The bayonet was missing, and so was the bolt-gun. He rifled through the debris until he found them, took the gas cartridge out of the gun and shook it to dislodge the dirt. Then he stripped out of the uniform and put on some clothes from the back of the truck. The shirt was too large, and trousers only came down to his ankles, but the cloth was good. He tucked the weapons and the flashlight into his belt and used a section of canvas to make a sling, into which he placed two food blocks, a change of clothes and a few of the tools.

As he balled up his uniform shirt, he felt something crinkle in the pocket, reached inside. A faded photograph, water-stained and peeling at the edges, showing a smiling baby with a fringe of dark hair. At first, he couldn't remember how it had gotten there. Then it came to him. Prescott must have put it there.

He didn't have to turn the photo over and see the name penned in large, clumsy letters to know who the child was. Something made him fold it over and put it back in his pocket and he wasn't sure what.

He found the Deacon in the cab, crushed behind the wheel, head-first in a puddle of blood and broken windshield glass. One arm was trapped under his bulk, the other bent backwards at an odd angle. Somehow the huge man was alive, his breath rattling in and out of his chest like gravel in his ribcage. Blood painted the inside of the cab, still dark red but congealing quickly.

Clayton got on his knees and leaned in to open the glovebox. The cab reeked of death, the sharp, stinging stench of gasoline rising beneath. A dark circle spread under the rear of the truck, seeped into the cracked ground. He took the revolver, a pack of matches and a water canteen and slipped them into his improvised pack. When he looked up, the Deacon's eyes were open and staring.

"The flame of His vengeance." The voice was choked, struggling through blood. A spasm went through the vast body, and a balloon of blood burst on the Deacon's smiling lips. His teeth were bloody shards. "God has shaped your path. I should have known not to interfere. It was a vain thing to do. The signs were clear, but pride is the curse of will."

Clayton stood, uncapped the canteen and drank. A wave of blackness came over him and he leaned on the overturned truck until it passed. Shadows were retreating across the scoured land, the first faint streaks of sunlight bringing another scorching day. Ghosts of roads peered through the stony yellow dirt.

Under the truck, the Deacon laughed, a harsh, rasping sound. "Do it," he said. "You can use the knife. Save the bullets for when you need them."

Low hills, flatlands and ridges. Nothing out there but dirt and twisted, scraggly shrubs. Across the desert, the city wavered and shifted in the heat shimmer, its towers and walkways now distinct, now merging into a gray blur. Dead quiet. No sound of gunfire. A pall of smoke hung over last night's battlefield, where the serviceways began.

They knew he was here. They were waiting for him, letting him come closer. They were everywhere, or nowhere, perhaps watching him even now, his image playing on a huge studio screen in front of a frenzied audience. It was useless to run. There was no real escape.

He walked around to the back of the truck and soaked the uniform shirt in spilled gasoline. He stuffed the rag into the fuel tank and took the matches out of his pocket.

"Every moment in life is a crossroads." The voice was rising, with panic or ecstasy. "Every choice a turn. Coming and going, life and death, don't matter. Both are marked by terrible suffering."

Clayton lit the bottom of the rag and stepped away. Yellow tongues caught the wet cloth, licked hungrily upward. The overturned truck did not explode but bloomed into flame with a low whoosh. High, thin cries came from it, snatches of prayer, laughter. Then nothing, save the crackling of the fire.

He moved further back and watched it burn, sending up a pillar of black, oily smoke and ash. If there were any drones within range, the fire would attract their attention. Out on the burning boulders he would be all but invisible to their heat-seeking sensors. But the sky remained empty.

He flung the pack over his shoulder and set off across the desert, following the line of a half-buried highway. Ten miles to the city, maybe a dozen. One foot in front of the other. The dry wind covering his boot prints with dust.

The blaze fell away behind him until it was no more than a trail of gray on the horizon, and then not even that.

Thirteen

At midday he left the packed dirt that had once been a road and descended into a dry ravine that cut the land like a great jagged wound. Pipes jutted from the yellow earthen walls, each opening large enough for a man to crawl into. Grave markers of a dead industry, stripped and gutted by labor gangs, vanishing slowly under the dust.

Inside the pipes the air was cool and damp and when he shone the flashlight, he could not see the end. He ate some of the concentrate and took a few measured sips from the canteen. It took considerable effort to stop himself from drinking more. Then he stretched out in the welcome dark, folded the pack under his head and slept.

When he was rested, he took the spare shirt out of the pack and wrapped it around his head. The heat had abated some and when he got back to the sunken highway, he could make out the shanties and tenements of the slum, vacant shells from which squatters had fled or been rounded up and executed. Reddish dusk fell across a landscape darkened with soot and dry oil spills, abandoned auto freighters stripped of windows and tracks, mired to the hubs in dust, rusted oil tankers from which every piece of salvageable metal had been removed.

Heat burned the back of his neck, his exposed skin. There was no saliva in his mouth, and his legs seemed to be moving of their own volition. Instead of getting closer, the structures were receding. The last of the water in his canteen did no more than wet his parched lips.

Visions danced in the shimmering inferno, distorted shapes and patterns ebbing and flowing like a tide upon the dust and rock like the nightmare residue of a Synthazine fugue. Ghostly voices called out to him from the white glare. Behind the line of shanties and crude shacks, miles and miles away, windowless, monolithic housing projects soared into the cloudless sky. Perpetual dusk ruled between them.

There was no one in sight as he passed the first of the shanties, but he knew he wasn't alone. Up close, the demolition was evident, old tribal-infested tenements leveled in air raids, more recent structures growing on their bones; lean-tos placed against foundations and standing walls, shacks built of corrugated sheet metal and plastic. No sign of habitation save for primitive murals scrawled or painted on every available brick. Layers upon layers of them, crude but unsettling, at once childlike and totemic. What they lacked in skill and detail they more than made up for in powerful suggestiveness. A band of hunters with spears surrounding their prey, stylized but distinctly human. Monstrosities breathing fire from the heavens. Figures dancing and leaping and coupling around a central symbol, made to resemble a skull. He found no water in the empty shelters, only a few pieces of broken pottery and in one of them an ash-pit full of charred, gnawed bones.

He walked on through the silent settlement, guided by the high towers of the accommodation blocks. If the Deacon had been right, the streets closer to the District would be empty, the megastructures abandoned, converted into what the conglomerates euphemistically referred to as a cordoned zone. A no-man's-land separating the slums and the megasprawl, strung with electrified fencing, patrolled by militias of various stripes and drones programmed to kill. He would have to wait for night before venturing in.

Sometime later he came to a derelict tube station. The entrance had once been boarded up, but both boards and gates were now gone, recycled into squalid shelters. Unlike the structures to either side, its walls were pristine, unmarred by tribal drawings. He didn't know what this meant, but the dust at the entrance had been recently disturbed. Perhaps there was water in there. He entered with the revolver cocked in his hand. Three bullets. That was all he had.

Inside the vast, cavernous space, the smell of old engine oil mingled with the cloying, meaty taint of corruption. Holes in the high ceiling let in dusty beams of daylight. The escalators and moveways had been torn out, and a great black pit yawned in the middle of the station. Here too the

walls were untouched, shadows moving over them like water, erasing depth and proportion. In places the floor and
ceiling were scorched black, as if great fires had burned
here, spaced an even distance apart.

In the dim light, a squat and heavy shape stood on the
edge of the pit. He moved closer, exhaustion and thirst forgotten, a chill at his back in spite of the ferocious heat. It
was a car of the old type, its insides and wheels removed, its
undercarriage resting on cinderblocks. White bone shone in
the gloom of the station. He reached his hand and touched
it.

Skulls, hundreds of them, maybe a thousand, arranged
in neat rows inside the chassis. All had been picked clean
and bleached by the sun. Long necklaces of small bones
and teeth were draped across the empty windows. Bowls
and jugs were arranged around it in a semicircle. An offering to appease the machines, a gruesome altar to the new
gods of this stark, hellish realm.

He shone his flashlight into the pit, quickly turned it
off. It was an eighty-foot drop from the upper level from the
platforms. Blocks of stone and twig-like bones wrapped in
scraps of cloth littered the bottom. Offerings, or suicides, or
both. The ripe smell was stronger here, overpowering.

Suddenly the place seemed darker, more threatening.
It felt like a trap. He took a step back from the edge and
scanned the empty station. Nothing. On the other side of
the pit, a defunct escalator well, its stair treads long gone,
led down into the chasm. Broad dark sweeps stained the
top of the well, turned into trickles as they ran lower. He
thought of blood spraying from a slit throat, bodies tumbling into the darkness. Nausea closed his gullet. Behind
the escalator well, a pyramid of smashed television sets, a
shrunken head placed inside each one, grinned with yellow,
desiccated lips.

He reeled back against the wall. Something was waiting for him in the hole, something hungry and beyond understanding. The thought was irrational, but too strong
to deny. He could hear its labored breathing, the noises it
made as it moved through the rubble and the corpses. He
wanted to pull his eyes away from the pooling darkness,
but he was powerless to stir.

A runnel of dust and pebbles struck his cheek. It took him a moment to grasp the significance of this. Then survival instinct flared up, driving the terrible lassitude out of his body. He wheeled around, raising the revolver. On a ledge above his head, a shadowy figure crouched. Muscles pulled taut, poised to pounce like a cat. Moving without a sound. A dark gargoyle, naked but for a loincloth, his skin blackened with coal-dust or soot to blend in with the shadows, eyes white and wild. Silver flashing from the knife in its hand.

They moved at the same time, Clayton aiming and pulling the trigger, the man springing down with a cry, curved blade arcing toward his target's neck.

The gun boomed and the back of the tribal's head exploded in a fine red mist. The body hit the ground at Clayton's feet, jerked a few times and went still.

Shadows raced across the open entrance, shouts and howls coming in from outside. They must have been following him all along, waiting to catch him unawares. He'd been trapped by his own stupid confidence, and not for the first time, either. Two rounds left in the revolver. He swung round and fired at a man who rushed in through the doorway, swinging a wicked-looking machete. The bullet went wide and struck the wall. Stone chips flew. Before he could adjust his aim, the tribal scurried back into the open.

Clayton knelt behind the altar of skulls, thinking frantically. Now they knew he was armed, but they would try again. Come in through the high windows and the door at the same time, or from some other entrance, and that would be the end. He felt the weight of the gun in his hand. Whatever happened, they wouldn't take him alive. Or dead, if it came to that. He would jump into the pit, where they could not follow. Use the last round on himself if the drop didn't kill him. He had not fled the carrion machines only to have the tribals feast on his corpse.

A tense wait ensued. He could hear them scuttling beyond the entrance, murmuring to each other. "Come out, brother," a voice called to him. Two faces darkened the opening, as if taunting him. Heads shaved, etched with ritual scars and tattoos. Bodies swathed in dirty robes, hands clutching staves and knives and hatchets. He hoped they didn't have guns. More of them huddled in the background. He couldn't get out. They had him surrounded.

Or did they? Before the enlistment, he'd taken the Loop every day to the office. Now he remembered the signs over the moving belts, the scrolling tickers directing the moving human masses. There were service tunnels down on the platform level, used by maintenance crews and repair automatons. His skin crawled. Down in the lightless pit, surrounded by corpses. It was his only chance. That, or his shrunken head joining the ghastly display, grinning into the silent, staring dark.

He raised the revolver and fired, forcing the boldest ones back into cover. Before the echo of the shot had died out, he was up and running, heading for the blood-streaked escalator well.

It wasn't much of a head start and his legs were not used to running. Feet pounded behind him. Hoots and cries erupted, rang off the station walls. The flush and heat of the hunt. Already they were gaining on him, closing the distance. A second group was circling the pit from the other side, trying to cut him off. His vision narrowed to a tunnel. Something sailed past his head and clattered on the cracked tile floor. He ran on.

At the edge of the sacrificial ground, his pursuers slowed down, and their hesitation bought him a few precious seconds. He hurtled over the side of the escalator and pitched down the concrete slide. The station spun about him. The rough surface tore at his hands and knees. He threw his arms out for purchase and felt something give in his bad shoulder. He screamed and slammed to a jarring halt, almost biting his tongue in half.

The domed ceiling blinked in and out. He shook his head and clawed himself up, bending his knees to maintain his balance. A huge chunk of stone had stopped him halfway down. His arm was ablaze with pain. Dark silhouettes squatted at the top of the well, looking down at him. He bent over instinctively, then realized that the dim light didn't reach this far. They couldn't see him unless they decided to follow.

Feeling his way along the side, he inched down the steep incline. He had spilled his pack but didn't dare use the flashlight. Pitch black engulfed his surroundings, his body, his hands. A space without depth or dimension. Sections of the well had collapsed and his progress was slow. When he turned to look up, the mouth of the hole had receded to a small pale circle, the heads of his pursuers gathered around the perimeter.

After a while, his feet found level ground. He turned the flashlight on, shielding the lens with the palm of his hand. The trickle of light revealed fallen stones and twisted, desiccated husks. He was on the platform, alone with the dead.

Rustling in the dark. He knew that it wasn't real, that he couldn't hear it, but he imagined he heard it—and in a way, that was worse. His mind conjured images of moldering faces turning toward him, fleshless fingers rooting through the rubble. Bones shifting inside parchment skin, crawling across the pit floor to wrap him in their embrace.

Panic reached inside his chest like a giant's hand, squeezing the air out of his lungs. He could hear himself gasping. His brain refused to form coherent thoughts. The blackness of the pit invaded his head.

He lurched and lost his balance, went sprawling. The flashlight dropped from his hand and clicked on the platform. The light fluttered. His heart stopped. If the flashlight went out, he would never find his way out of the pit. Just he and the corpses and the moving, breathing dark. The beam stayed on. He felt himself go limp with relief. Picking the light up, he swept it around to get his bearings. Most of the bodies lay at the foot of the escalator well, where they had tumbled from above. Their skulls had been caved in and their throats had been cut. Tatters of long robes wound around the bones. Rival tribesmen, or intruders like himself. Mummified children wrapped in faded cloth. All color drained from both the remains and their burial cerements.

The platform seemed to go on forever, further than his light could reach. Beyond the pile of rocks and bones were banks of empty elevator shafts. Concrete struts and supports loomed overhead, curved deeper underground. Core rods stuck out of bare walls. Fine dust covered the ground. No turnstiles, no tickers, not so much as a cable in sight. Once the station had closed down, the labor gangs and machines had picked it clean of everything that could be reused. The transportation cartel faced a chronic shortage of materials, and new stations had to be constructed to fulfil the demands of the ever-expanding population. The city fed on itself, built on itself; a sleepless and ravenous beast, grinding its own bones to dust.

He almost missed the caved-in doorway opening off the central concourse. For an agonizing moment, he stood in front of it, trying to decide. It might lead to salvation or it might lead nowhere. His light was fading, the batteries running out.

Beyond the doorway was a passage, and at the end of it, a ramp leading upward. He shone the beam inside. Series of lines and notches covered the walls, instructions for the repair automatons to navigate by. His nostrils flared. The passage smelled of damp stone. He ran his dry tongue over his cracked lips. His thirst was a monumental craving. He tapped the flashlight against his palm and went in, running the beam along the walls.

It didn't take him long to find it—a glistening wet trail in the stone, trickling from a broken pipe near the ceiling. Kneeling, he removed the shirt wrapped around his head and used it to soak up the moisture. The wait was excruciating. After a few seconds, he wrung the cloth out over the mouth of the canteen, careful not to spill a drop. The result was half an inch of water, barely enough to cover the bottom. He repeated the process until the canteen was half full of cloudy liquid. The simple, repetitive movement calmed him. Sipping slowly, he leaned back against the wall and stared up the ramp.

The flashlight flickered. He tapped it again, but the bulb didn't brighten. It didn't matter. He sat in the shrinking circle of light and thought about the life he had left behind. For the first time ever, he was alone and drifting, unmoored.

He had never been a political man or held strong opinions. Ideals and causes were for other people, professional do-gooders, grumbling deadbeats and borderline asocials. Those who longed for a return of the old ways, for market regulation, for government bureaucrats to take them by the hand and tell them what to do. The lazy and the vicious living off the sweat of the diligent citizen-consumer. Disdain for all forms of activism had been fed to him from the cradle. His parents, staunch members of the middle class, had worked themselves ragged to ensure he received a college education, a ticket to the upper end of their credit bracket. Neither of them had lived long enough to see their grandson born. His father had died in a factory accident, the consequence of a faulty assembly line. Emphysema had taken his mother a year or so later, decades of pollution exposure finally taking their toll. Yet through it all he had kept his faith in the system, in the freedom to choose. Even with the Newscans telling him what to eat, what to wear, what to want. Even with the consortiums and conglomerates running sales algorithms to determine what he could afford, his consumption index creeping lower and lower every year.

The family life he and Linda had built together was a fragile shell over a roaring black hole. A respectable existence, a corporate job with solid prospects of advancement, maybe a second child permit down the line. Yet the signs were there, even then. Somewhere along the way his ambition had atrophied. He had begun to hesitate over the smallest decisions, terrified by the endless chain of consequences each action led to, by the threat of redundancy and being cast out into the low-credit zones. It was like walking blindfolded across a narrow precipice over a bottomless gorge, holding the hands of those you loved the most. Knowing that a single misstep could send you all plummeting below. Josh's birth had helped solidify the ground under his feet. Then things had changed. His son had died, and the carefully crafted illusion he'd weaved around himself and his family had burned away in the harsh light of that terrible, burning truth.

What did he believe now? There was nothing left to fight for. Josh was gone. Linda wanted nothing to do with him. He didn't even know where she lived. Their old friends and acquaintances would turn him in without a second thought. But those rational considerations were becoming secondary. His mind was turning inward, finding someone strange and unfamiliar inhabiting the space inside his skull. Perhaps that someone had always been there, pulling his strings from the primordial depths, forever unseen and unreachable. Perhaps every man had one, hidden beneath the surface he saw in the mirror. This inner self had its own, older imperatives.

The light went out. He reached into his pocket and took out the matches. Struck one of them against the box and held it in front of his eyes. Watching it, he wondered what else would burn before he was done. Anything and everything.

Fourteen

Warm rain cascaded onto Clayton's upturned face. Neon lights flared red behind his closed eyelids, a shimmering fretwork of corporate logos draped across the concrete and glass.

He stood in the middle of the moveway, buffeted by passing bodies, drinking in the smells and the noises of the crowd. The curses and shoves. The drum and sizzle of rain on hot stone. The vibration of the tunnels and transportation tubes miles beneath his feet. The tide picked him up and bore him away like a piece of flotsam, jammed him against the hard cement railing. He laughed and opened his eyes, filling them with the sight of the city.

Vast planes and straight, unforgiving lines carved his visual field into rectangular slivers. Unbroken miles of dirty ferroconcrete spread to the limit of vision, lashed by sheets of driving rain. There was a subtle, severe beauty to the megacity, hidden in the crowds and the squalor and garish lights; inhuman architecture that awed with its scale, a haughty rejection of measure and proportion, of all that could please the eye. A brutal aesthetic laid out with unsparing, mathematical precision.

A torrent of faces pushed through the downpour, eddied around food stalls and neon-lit cafes. Wet nylon and plastic reflected the stark light of signs and tickers and immense LCD screens. Computer-generated vistas of nonexistent forests and beaches glistened in the rain, overlaid with the intricate calligraphy of trademark logos and advertisements. Great incandescent faces, pixel-polished beyond perfection, leaned over the pavement, accompanied by a ceaseless stream of ad broadcasts.

Touch the future today with TransCore.

A leap forward with Titan Hydroponics.

Standard Energy; delivering smart power solutions.

Buy PetroMobil, buy Glasser-Kamada, buy Vidal Morris.
Think bigger. Never settle for less. Make the most of the
moment.

Subliminal messages were coded into the signs and
advertisements, the rate of pulse calculated to the most
infinitesimal firing of light, stimulating deep-buried response centers. He tried to ignore them, walked past a food
vault—a concrete-walled, fortress-like structure surrounded by concertina wire, studded with gun towers. A patch of
leaden sky hung over the canyon, as dead as the stone and
glass of its walls.

People were everywhere; on the arching risers, on the
crowded sidewalks, rumbling through underpasses. They
swarmed up and down narrow aisles in the bright windows
of shops and supermarkets. Without conscious input, his
body reverted to familiar movement patterns, pushing and
being pushed, weaving through the crowd, the head angled forward, the shoulders hunched and rolling from side
to side. He didn't know exactly where he was—he'd lived
in Canalside and never ventured further south than Trac-
tion Mile and the old Industrial Belt—but he thought if he
kept moving north he would eventually cross into one of
the Spokes, peripheral settlements that grew around the
main transportation lines connecting the Free Enterprise
Districts. From there he could find his way to East Central.
On the Loop, the trip there would take no more than an
hour, but he had no identification and no credit. That was
his biggest problem, bigger than the exhaustion and the
gnawing hunger. People without credit didn't exist outside
of the slums. The streets of the megacity opened and swallowed them without a trace.

After the tunnel he had crawled into the dead streets
of the slum and made his way toward the lights of the cordoned zone, watchful of the guards, of silent footfalls in
the night. Either he had not been spotted, or someone had
decided he wasn't worth the risk. Taking it slow, timing his
movement to the low whir of the drones, he had used the
empty buildings to sneak past two corporate militia checkpoints. Utility cartels lacked the manpower and resources
to monitor the entire length of the ever-shifting border, and
security was lax. For the past seven days he'd been making

slow progress north through increasingly crowded streets, sleeping in alleys and doorways, scrounging in refuse for food. Out in the desert he had stuck out, but here he was invisible, a nonentity, one of the thousands of freeloaders roaming the crawlspaces of the city.

Bodies milled and rumbled, nudged him like an implacable tide, faces constantly changing in the rain, blending into one another; some indifferent, some hostile, all drained and glazed by the dancing glow of neon and liquid crystal. All his life he had loathed the crowd, the blind multitude surging across the cramped pavement, threatening to engulf him and snuff him out, to render him invisible. He had lain awake nights, afraid of going to sleep, feeling the walls of his tiny apartment close in on him, the breath of a hundred million lungs hissing in his ears. But now the anonymity suited him. After some thought, he had tossed his weapons into a garbage chute to avoid being picked up by a hidden weapons detector or security screen. As long as he kept away from ident scanners, he would stay invisible.

Even if they were still looking for him, finding a needle in the proverbial haystack would be child's play in comparison. The national police force, gutted by the Freedom from Intrusion Act three decades before, was running on a skeleton staff and dealt only with capital crime. Corporate security teams had their own investigators and databases, but there was no central registry and little to no sharing of information; industrial espionage and asset extraction posed a far greater danger to transnationals than a criminal on the street. Perhaps the networks could pool their resources and operatives to coordinate a manhunt, but he doubted it. They had a show to run, troop movements to coordinate, scripts to be written and rewritten. The machine had to be kept in smooth, seamless motion. No time to look for a single slipped cog, especially one that could not have survived the desert. He was safe, at least for a while. Long enough to find Prescott's lawyer and see if there was any truth to the story.

The smell of frying oil and krill patties wafted from an open door, flooding his mouth with saliva. Fantasies of food invaded his mind. Warm, crusty bread spread thick with spicy lentil paste. Soft strings of cheese substitute. Ice-cold soymilk, sweet and flavored, tiny beads of condensation clinging to the glass. How long had it been since he'd eaten anything other than rations and concentrate? He saw a group of laughing youths clustered around a food stall, tucking into greasy paper. Caught the security guard watching him with open disgust, hand on shock-stick, and hurried away.

His torn shoulder pulsed with pain, red-hot tendrils reaching all the way between his shoulder blades. He had felt something give in there during his tumble down the escalator well, and now the arm below was almost unusable, a solid mass of pain from wrist to neck. Every jostle was agony, every breath hurt. He needed medical help, but he couldn't afford the clinics, not even a self-help dispensary. Besides, all they would do was pump him full of painkillers and send him on his way. It wasn't worth the risk of being caught on a security camera feed.

But he was free. Out here he could blend into the dregs of humanity, the bums and homeless and dope pushers who crowded dark passages and Loop station entrances, offering chemical escape from the bleak drudgery of the day, from the claustrophobic confines of swarming, pressing flesh. Synthazine wasn't always available—Glasser-Kamada ran a network of plainclothes trademark enforcers around the city, armed and licensed to kill—but other, generic drugs could be found on every corner: off-brand neurotransmitters and alertness enhancers for the office drone on his way to another grueling twelve-hour shift, megamphetamines for the dedicated partygoer, antipsychotics and tranks for everyone else. It was how the world worked. Psychosis and depression built up like steam under pressure. Some sought an outlet in drugs and mindless consumerism, others gave in to more atavistic tendencies—violence, vandalism, riots, murder.

He descended a dripping, graffiti-scrawled underpass and followed the flow into a maze of old walls and sunken passages that spread below the busy sidewalks. Every ward of the megasprawl was crisscrossed with underground thoroughfares, layer upon layer of them, running at different depths. The many sloughed skins of the city held defunct subway tunnels and maintenance shafts, entire neighborhoods leveled to make way for more efficient housing units, or simply built over. It was a buried necropolis, hidden both from the teeming hive of shoppers and commuters above and the traffic serviceways and tube tunnels deep below, an eternally twilit domain of the wicked and the hopeless, of Synthazine freaks and stewbums, of dull-eyed drug burnouts skulking in the dark. Here black market organ-harvesting clinics nestled next door to doomsday-cult temples, illicit shelters shared walls with soup kitchens for the poor. Police and corporate militias sometimes raided the undercity, but nothing could deter the denizens from coming back. They had nowhere else to go.

He elbowed his way through a cluster of peddlers holding up bags of derms and syrettes and hypodermic injectors, nursing his shoulder and trying not to show how bad it hurt, not to expose himself as a target. The underground concourse wasn't as crowded as he expected it to be, but that was fine... fewer eyes, no security cameras. He scanned the people around him quickly, avoiding eye contact.

He hadn't gone far before he found what he was looking for; a wizened old bum sitting slumped against the wall of an alley, surrounded by a mess of dirty newspapers, an empty liquor bottle between his knees. The bum's nose was broken and swollen, but there was no crusted blood on his face and a clean bandage, stained yellow with iodine, adorned his wattled, hollow neck. He directed Clayton to an unmarked door around the corner. Clayton watched the door for a while, then went and knocked. From inside came the low, muffled hum of a generator, and a crack in the boards that covered the empty windows let out a thin stream of light.

On the fourth knock, a bolt slammed, a lock clicked, and the door inched open. Narrow, bloodshot eyes flicked left and right over an unruly growth of beard. "What do you want?"

"I need help." With his good hand, Clayton pulled down his shirt collar and pointed at the bruise.

"What's that got to do with me?" The round, scruffy face twisted in a scowl. Behind it a bare bulb spilled muted yellow light. The sharp odor of disinfectant wafted from the interior.

"The old man on the corner." Clayton saw the door started to close, lunged forward. "He said—"

"Get lost, asshole," said the man on the other side, his eyes dark and hard. An automatic charge-pistol appeared in the doorway. The hand holding it was delicate but strong, incongruous with the rest of the man's appearance. A surgeon's hand. "Don't make me ask you again."

Behind the man, Clayton saw a second shadow pass. A patch of light coming through the boarded-up window was blocked from the other side. Someone was watching the street. "Please. I have nowhere else to go."

"Not my problem." For a second the hard mask slipped. He could see the man struggle with himself, trying to decide. Then the door swung open and the man stepped aside. Before he could change his mind, Clayton climbed the steps and went in.

The door closed behind him. He was in a small, bare room, ducts running overhead, torn fittings protruding from the walls. To his right, a second door led into the building. "Strip," the man said wearily, waving the gun. He was big and flabby, his hair and beard shot through with gray. He kept the charge-pistol on Clayton, but without conviction.

Clayton removed his rags and boots and stood naked against the wall. The door on his right opened and a short, bald man in a white lab coat emerged, pulling on a pair of surgical gloves. He passed a handheld device over the pile of clothes, checked the readout and nodded.

"He's clean."

Wrinkling his nose at the smell, the man with the gun picked the clothes up and carried them into the next room. Moments later, Clayton heard the hollow clank of metal and the whoosh of an incinerator.

"Just a precaution," the bald man said, ushering him through the door. He spoke with quiet authority, his eyes wandering to the door and back. "You don't look like a stoolie, but one can never tell. Two weeks ago, a team of goons from Allied Therapeutics busted a welfare clinic in Park Circle. The crew who ran it are all gone now. We have to be very careful about who we let in."

Clayton gazed around himself. The room had a workshop look to it, cryo-freezers stacked atop metal filing cabinets, carts of dusty medical equipment parked in the center. Bags of real and artificial blood and plasma hung behind the glass door of a soda dispenser. Bright surgical lights shone down on a pair of examination tables and a bed surrounded by IV drips. A biomonitor panel duct-taped to the side of a wheeled life-support unit.

Crude as it was, the setup had to have cost a fortune. If it were discovered, its owners would be in a world of trouble. The police turned a blind eye to welfare clinics and soup kitchens, but the transnationals were another story. Newscans and corporate propaganda programs thundered against groups of well-organized asocials, who distorted consumption indices and encouraged freeloading and social decay under the guise of charity. Known offenders ran the risk of losing everything. Private property and individual rights were allegedly sacred, but a corporation could refuse to sell to asocials, rendering their credit useless, or blackball them and make it impossible for them to get work. Laws could be superseded by contracts; everything could be arbitered, negotiated. To sin against the corporations was to be summarily executed while remaining alive. Like the poor, asocials could either enlist, or sign up for one of the labor gangs in the cordoned zones.

Or bleed to death on the floor of a stinking train car, Clayton thought, *their hands full of their own slick guts, like Salvesen.*

Yet the flophouses and missions remained open, despite the danger. Some were established by religious organizations—even the Virtus Foundation, the all-powerful conglomerate think tank, was reluctant to go after those—but most were run and funded clandestinely by private groups. He flushed with hot shame, remembering an argument he'd once had with Linda. They had both been half drunk. It had ended with him ranting about freeloaders and lazy deviants and how they ought to bring back the death penalty for bleeding hearts and whiny do-gooders and everyone else who refused to understand how things worked in the real world. Now these two men were putting their lives on the line to help him.

"Here." The bald one led Clayton to one of the tables and told him to sit. Gentle fingers probed the edges of the bruise. "It's not broken, only dislocated. The bone is out of its socket, but I can put it back in." He clasped Clayton's injured arm by the wrist and placed his other hand on the lump in the shoulder. "It's going to hurt like hell, but only for a moment. Can you stand a bit of pain?"

Clayton nodded and held his arm out straight. The bald man gripped it firmly. "Give me a hand here," he said to the bearded man, who moved in between them and enfolded Clayton in a bearhug. "Here we go," the shorter man said, braced himself and pulled.

Something cracked inside him, and agony exploded in his shoulder. The room grayed out for a few moments. When it came back into focus, he was slumped in the bearded man's arms. The other man handed him a paper cup with two pills and a steaming mug. The coffee substitute burned his mouth, but he drank it down greedily.

"Eat these." The bald man gave him a packet of fortified crackers. "In your condition, those pills will knock you out, and you can't stay here. It's not safe."

Clayton sat up and moved his arm around. It was still sore and stiff, but sensation was returning. He wolfed the crackers down and tried to stand. The room wavered unsteadily before his eyes, seemed to darken.

"He's in no shape to walk," a voice said above him.

"He better get in shape," another replied.

A piece of soap was thrust into his hands, followed by a towel and a change of clothes. The two men led him to a portable shower stall and started up the water pump. Dirty water sluiced around his ankles and disappeared down the drain. The allotment was no more than three-quarters of a gallon, but the water was warm, almost hot. It felt like heaven, and it helped clear his head.

He scrubbed and shaved under the tap, then dried off and stood in front of a full-length mirror to dress. His scrawny, emaciated body greeted him, a revenant from a nightmare of starvation. The flat bones of his skull pushing through tightly stretched skin, his sunken chest over jutting ribs, his distended stomach supported by a pair of bony legs. The clothes the men gave him were well-worn but clean—a faded shirt and baggy pants, a pair of scuffed but comfortable shoes. He muttered his thanks and started toward the door.

"Hold on." The bearded one took him by the elbow and placed something in his hand. "I found this in your things. Your kid?"

Clayton looked at the crumpled photo in his palm and nodded. It was easier than trying to explain. The man's face quivered with a mix of emotions: pain, anger and fury struggled under the skin, surfaced as a thin smile that had nothing to do with mirth. "I know what it's like," he said, clipping each word with great reluctance. "I had a kid, once. A daughter."

"He's got to go," the other man said in a warning tone, looking away. "Now."

The bearded man took a blue plastic Loop pass out of his pocket. "You have six hours. Then I have to report it stolen. Got that?"

"Thank you," Clayton said again, but he was already on the front stoop and the door was closing fast. He made it as far as the corner before the passage around him went through a slow spin and the hard pavement rose up to meet him. Somebody laughed drunkenly, and an empty can bounced off the wall behind him. Cautious feet stole across the concrete, circled around him and drew away.

After a while, he found his feet and climbed up into the light of the streets. Two blocks ahead, the white cupola of a Loop station swallowed and disgorged streams of people. His hand closed around the plastic pass to make sure it was still there.

He fought his way onto a mobile sidewalk and fell in behind a group of rowdy, well-fed men in business suits. A plump, middle-aged woman eyed with him open distaste. Hunching his shoulders, he turned away and stared over the railing until she moved along.

His head wouldn't clear. Everywhere he looked, he saw patterns in the movement of the crowd, too quickly gone for his brain to get a fix on. Had he been recognized? A procession of bland and handsome faces stared down at him from the huge screens, smiling, preening in designer casuals and glamorous evening wear, strolling cool and collected through fashionable shopping sections. People seemed to push closer to him, hemming him in, cutting off all possibility of escape. There were eyes everywhere, faces everywhere. He forced himself not to run, to take deep breaths.

At the turnstiles, a bored, grizzled station guard was ogling a trio of scantily-clad girls walking down an escalator, craning his neck to peer under their short skirts. Clayton inched forward behind the group of overweight businessmen and pushed his pass through the slot. The light above the stile turned green. The metal arms parted, and he slipped through.

Fifteen

He came out of the roaring darkness into the enormous, brilliant space of East Central Station, all stained glass and stately brass domes and mosaic-decorated walkways. The ivory marble floors were slick and wet, but when he stepped outside the sky was clear, the sun setting behind the glittering towers of downtown.

Two station guards in full riot gear were standing by the nearest exit. He lowered his head and moved past them without looking up. The guards took no notice of him, their eyes fixed at someone or something behind him, faces hard with anticipated violence. He hadn't gone ten steps before he heard a cry and the sounds of a short, savage scuffle, followed by the crackle of shock-sticks. While the gawkers crowded around, he wiped the Loop pass on his shirt to remove fingerprints and dropped it into a recycler. The computer screen in the battered info kiosk outside the station was broken, but he thumbed through the yellow pages and found a listing for a Joseph Hymes, attorney-at-law. The address given was in South Mall, on the other side of the concrete-covered river.

He walked fast, the polished stonework and sun-streaked windows falling behind him, his gut still in free fall from the ride. With every mile the accommodation blocks grew farther apart, seedier, dirtier. For all its architectural excesses, East Central was a declining industrial area that stretched through several FEDs but belonged to none, most of the industry in question having migrated to the peripheral Districts, leaving behind a contaminated water supply and an astronomical air pollution count. A dirty orange haze muted the sun and his borrowed clothes stuck to him with sweat.

Everywhere he looked he saw the same sight: a blighted expanse of abandoned construction sites, barren lots, chain-link fences around factory yards heaped with trash. Crumbling factory walls rose in an untidy jumble over girdered roofs and glassless, iron-latticed windows. Stooped crones picked through the landfills while scarecrow men sat on the stoops of slum shacks and passed bottles around. Dirty children clambered and chased each other through condemned buildings, raced around the dumps. The reach of the Department of Demographics and the eugenics boards did not extend to the poorest neighborhoods; disease and starvation served as their own population control.

Yet for all the obvious dangers he was safer here than he had been before. There was no cordoned zone in East Central, no corporate security checkpoints or ident screens. Even the government police didn't take chances in these squalid blocks, where the policy was containment, not law enforcement. Evidently there were others, like Prescott's lawyer, who preferred the anonymity of the slums. He spotted a few scrap collectors amid the ruins, followed them down to the salvage yards and the remains of the business park.

Joseph Hymes' firm was in an old steel mill repurposed into offices. The lawyer himself was fat and balding, a prominent potbelly straining the confines of his cheap brown suit. His office—a small, dim room dominated by a cluttered desk and a tiny reception nook thick with dust—smelled of carryout food, cigarettes and stale booze. A creaking paddle fan on the ceiling stirred the torpid air without cooling it. At the mention of Prescott's name, he got up, locked the door and fired up his ancient-looking computer.

Seeing that Clayton was about to speak, he held up an admonishing finger. "Before you say anything, I'm required to inform you that all communication between my client and myself is privileged. You, on the other hand, are not my client. Privilege is not operative in your case. So don't tell me anything you don't want others to know." He opened a drawer, shook two antacid tablets onto his palm and dry-swallowed with a grimace. "The less you tell me, the better. The police are bound by the law, but corporate thugs often choose to pursue, shall we say, alternative methods of questioning. Is that clear?"

Clayton managed a nod.

"Does anyone know you're here?"

"No," Clayton said. "At least, I don't think so."

"How many of you made it out?"

"I'm the only one."

"I see." The lawyer slumped back in his chair, looking deflated. "I want you to repeat what my client said to you, in his exact words. Can you remember?"

Clayton spoke slowly, trying to recall the brief exchange. "He told me to tell you I need one of his skins."

"Did he say which one?"

"He just said skins. Also something about a key."

Hymes drummed his fingers on the desk and stared through his visitor, as if thinking it through. His hands went to the keyboard and tapped. A blue text box came up on the monitor screen. He pressed a combination of keys, then reached under his desk and produced a small fingerprint pad. Sweeping a pile of papers onto the floor, he placed the pad in front of Clayton.

"Press your right thumb to the plate."

Clayton did as he was told, then the index finger. The lawyer jacked a cable into a portable retinal scanner and told him to look inside. When Clayton raised his head from the scanner, his picture was on the screen and Hymes was clicking away, filling out a set of forms.

"I'll rout your biodata through the local police servers and into the national consumer database. It will be good to go in the morning."

"Good to go?"

"Your new identity." The lawyer hit enter with a flourish. Clayton leaned over the desk and stared at the screen. The face on the ident form was his own, but different—the jawline stronger, the hair longer and fuller, the brow and cheekbones more prominent. The features were recognizable, but only because he knew they were there. As a disguise, it was effective enough to fool facial recognition algorithms. Under the image was the name DECKER, CONRAD. "What do you think?"

"It doesn't really look like me."

"That can be taken care of. Plastic surgery would be risky, but there are other options. More anonymous ones. Collagen injections, syntheskin, temporary implants."

"Implants?"

"Whatever you want." The lawyer scrolled down the form. "You're a wealthy man, Mr. Decker. You can afford it."

Clayton read the credit rating field, then read it again, waiting for it to sink in. It had to be a mistake. Hymes' sober, impassive expression gave way to a small smile.

"This is—"

"This is the new you. A better you. Conrad Decker, a national of the Antillean Union, employed by the Emergency Relief Agency in Hispaniola. Here on business." Hymes shook out a cigarette from a crumpled pack and lit up, without offering one to his visitor. "Here in the Districts to negotiate a big purchase of dam turbines from Associated Engineering for a recovery program in the Leeward Islands. You travel a lot. Upper-crust family, playboy lifestyle, cushy government job. It helps plug the holes in your consumer history and the high credit rating."

"Who came up with the story?"

"Like I said, that's privileged information." The bland look was back on the lawyer's face. "Let me give you a piece of advice, Mr. Decker. I don't know what you're up to, and I don't want to know. But whatever it is, make sure it's done quickly. This ident is a patch job. Good enough to pass casual scrutiny, but the cracks are easy to spot if you look closely. You're harder to trace because you're a foreign national, but it's just a matter of time. The Census Bureau in the Antilles has no record of a Conrad Decker, and the paper trail leads nowhere. With me so far?"

"Yes."

"Good." Hymes steepled his hands. "Everything you do leaves behind traces, fragments of personal information. The longer you use the identity, the bigger your data footprint. Patterns will emerge. The system picks up patterns. When they add up, you'll be tracked down and arrested. They'll find out about your connection to my client, and when they do, they'll come after me. Do you understand?"

"Yes," Clayton said. It took his confused mind a moment to grasp the import of the lawyer's words. Prescott was dead. He was in this alone. "I understand."

"Good." Hymes fed a blank plastic card into a thermal printer. When it came out, he pushed it across the desk. "Wait until tomorrow before you use it. There hasn't been anything on the Newscans, but you can bet they're looking

116

for you. Go downtown. It's too dangerous for you to stay here."

Clayton held the card in both hands. It was still warm. Conrad Decker stared back at him from the laminated plastic. He felt a wave of dreamlike unreality wash over him. "How long will it be safe to use this?"

"A month. Maybe six weeks, if you stay low." The lawyer exhaled a plume of smoke toward the ceiling and lit a fresh cigarette from the smoldering stub of the first. "But I have a feeling that staying low isn't what you're here for."

Clayton said nothing. Hymes leaned across the desk. "Of course, there are alternatives. You could use the credit to disappear forever. No one would be the wiser. No one could stop you. Conrad Decker's accounts with the Union Bank of Antilles are real and intact. They still use legal tender there, and don't ask many questions. Or you could convert your windfall into digital bearer certificates, or cryptocurrency. Something anonymous that can't be traced to you. Move somewhere beyond the ambit of extradition treaties and transnational warrants. Someplace where they still have a government that's not appointed and run by corporations. You can still walk away from this and start over. I'm very much in favor of this option. It would make both our lives much easier."

The thought had crossed Clayton's mind before. There was nothing to hold him in the city but bad memories and a vague conversation he'd had with a man who was now dead. The dream of bloody revenge seemed impossibly distant now. He had never thought it through. But where was he to go? On the long nights after enlistment, he had explored a hidden place inside himself, a place both terrible and beautiful, and in doing so had let something out, a black, poisonous fog that might otherwise have swelled and swelled until he burst. That poison was inside him now, curdling, burning in his blood. He would carry it with him wherever he went.

There's something in you that goes beyond the madness of this place.

He turned the ident card over in his fingers. Conrad Decker grinned up at him, a face familiar but strange, like a thing glimpsed in a twisted mirror. Self-assured and confident, set in hard lines. The face of a man who knew what had to be done. He felt he was locked on course, moving toward some inevitable conclusion. "I have to get a few things," he heard himself say. "Can I use your computer?"

"No." Hymes folded over a sheet of paper and jotted down instructions. "But there's an Epiphanist Public Library on the other side of the river. They'll let you use one of theirs for free. No ident required. Whatever you buy, use a post office box for delivery. It'll make you harder to track down." He tapped his cigarette ash into a cheap ceramic tray and gazed at the burning ember wistfully. "A place for every man, and every man in his place. In our society, that's how things work. If you're rich enough—and you are—your status allows you to get away with anything." Hymes settled back. "My advice is to forget this conversation and our meeting. Forget everything, including who you used to be. Become Conrad Decker. That's the best way to keep from standing out. From being noticed."

"I'll keep that in mind."

The lawyer nodded, clearly unconvinced. Turning in his chair, he pressed a button under his desk to reveal a safe-deposit box. He punched in a combination and the box clicked open. Inside were bundles of paper and stacks of blank ident cards. Hymes took out a small oblong of solid black metal and tossed it to Clayton. The piece was smooth and unmarked, about the size of a box of matches.

"What is this?"

"The key you asked for," the lawyer said. "You can only use it once, so when you do, make sure your mind is made up and you're not going to change it. Goodbye, Mr. Decker." He rose and held out his hand. His palms were slick with sweat. Clayton shook his hand and walked out into the long, dimly lit hallway. The lock clicked behind him.

He stood there for a while, staring ahead and seeing nothing. A crescent smile appeared in the darkness. Frank Clayton didn't want to think about where he was going and what lay before him, but Conrad Decker was beginning to know.

Sixteen

The man who stepped out of the chartered FanWing Gazelle and onto the rooftop pad of the Lafayette Regency Hotel in the heart of the Federal District bore no resemblance to the dirty, half-starved creature who had walked into Joseph Hymes' office a week and a half ago.

The rumble of the cooling duct-fan turbines fazed him not at all, nor did the sweltering heat that rolled across the shimmering tarmac. He was wearing a well-tailored microweave suit and his hair was cut in a fashionable but casual style. Mirrored wraparound sunglasses protected his eyes from the noonday blaze. A small leather valise swung from his right hand. He wore hand-tooled shoes of Old World leather. At the edge of the landing pad, the photovoltaic skin of the FanWing shone dully in the blinding burn of the sun.

To the harried hotel clerk, steaming on the hot asphalt in a high-collared, starched uniform, the arrival looked impossibly cool and collected. *Must be nice to be rich,* the clerk thought with envy, bowing slightly and trying to blink sweat out of his stinging eyes.

"Pleasure to have you with us, Mr. Decker," the clerk said. The man in the immaculate suit regarded him with a bland, meaningless smile—the kind of smile reserved for well-trained underlings and service people who knew when to bend the knee. The clerk's own servile expression felt frozen on his face. That morning he had used up the last of his weekly water allotment and there were still two days to go. The new day manager took a dim view of employees who neglected their personal hygiene.

"Glad to be here." The flat smile remained. The guest looked around himself as he passed his ident card over the portable reader's electric eye. "Looks like it'll turn out to be a nice day."

"Indeed, sir." Not for the first time, the clerk wondered what it would be like to grab one of these rich assholes by the collar and pitch him over the safety barrier at the end of the roof. *See if it still looks like a nice day then.*

On second thought, perhaps it wouldn't do to start with this particular rich asshole. There was something peculiar about him, something off. Something that made the clerk nervous. Apart from the expensive clothes and haircut, he didn't look like the typical fat, florid corporate lobbyist or sales executive who stayed at the Regency; thin, but fashionably so, his shoulders set in a rigid line, free hand clenching and unclenching at his side. The corollary, no doubt, of some new designer drug making the rounds in the circles of the wealthy and powerful.

"Right this way, if you please." He glanced behind the guest to make arrangements for the luggage, but the landing strip was empty. The rich asshole apparently traveled light.

For no reason he could identify, the clerk suddenly felt cold. The sweat on the back of his neck was clammy. He turned around. The guest's face was inches from his own. The curved surface of the mirrored sunglasses threw back his distorted reflection. The smile below the glasses didn't look bland anymore. It didn't look like a smile at all. It gave the clerk a bad feeling. The guest nodded once. The clerk looked down at his hand, still holding the magnetic key card.

"Please see that I'm not disturbed," said the man in the expensive suit, plucking the card from the clerk's damp fingers. "I have some business to attend to in the District. I'll be leaving tomorrow."

"Certainly, sir. My apologies, sir." There was a piece missing from one of the guest's earlobes. The clerk found himself wishing he were somewhere else, anywhere but here. He mumbled something about enjoying the stay, but the man was already stepping into the elevator and didn't bother with a reply. The metal doors closed, and the car dropped down the transparent fiberglass shaft.

Sweating and shivering, the clerk stood on the tarmac for a long time, then went inside. He told the day manager he wasn't feeling well and asked for the rest of the day off. The manager, usually not a man to be lightly swayed, didn't require much convincing. From the look of him, the clerk was coming down with something nasty, and the Lafayette Regency had a reputation to think of.

The room was enormous—at least four hundred square feet, the size of an average living unit for a family of three. Clayton pulled the door closed and allowed himself to relax. His fingernails left bloody crescents in his palms. An iron spike of pain was lodged behind his forehead and his heart was beating fast. The ident card had worked. No alarm was raised, no plainclothes security agents had jumped him from the shadows. Hymes had done a thorough job: Frank Clayton no longer existed. For all the world he was Conrad Decker, a digital ghost, a specter conjured from consumer directories and credit reports.

The sheets on the big double bed were fresh and scented, the towels on the marble shelf in the bathroom white and neatly folded. A massive television screen on the wall opposite the bed displayed a welcome sign and a list of the hotel's amenities. The room was pleasantly cool after the heat of the roof. Air scrubbers and water purifiers hummed inside the walls and under the polished-wood floor. He walked over to the broad windows and gazed outside. The glass was polarized, with inbuilt microfilters to simulate dawn, sunlight, dusk or night. He reached out and touched the smooth surface, sensing a trickle of the day's heat through it.

Eighteen floors below lay the nation's administrative center—the presidential residence with its wide stretch of green lawn, stately neoclassical buildings of marble and limestone spreading from it in concentric circles, hemmed in by the towering sprawl of residential neighborhoods in the west and the south. To the north and west, the titanic conurbations broke into a checkerboard of industrial parks and processing plants, following the spoke-and-hub layout of the city.

Half of the District was government, the other half owned by lobbyists and corporate advisors, the government share diminishing from year to year as it tried to prune itself down to a size its shrinking budget could support.

121

Standing at the window was like standing on the prow of a ship sailing into a dark bank of cloud.

Coming here had been a mistake, a fool's errand. Clayton knew that he was wasting time when speed was of the essence, but he had been unable to help himself.

Moving away from the window, he went over to the minibar and poured himself a drink. Straight Scotch, the real kind. Even with the air conditioning on full blast, his silk shirt felt glued to his back. He took his jacket and shirt off and tossed them into the closet. Motion-sensor lights flicked on and off.

The drink was almost gone, so he made another. It came to him that he'd forgotten to ask the hotel clerk for water tokens. Maybe he could call the front desk and have some sent up. Conrad Decker could do whatever he wanted, bend the world to his will. When credit spoke, everyone listened.

Inside the dark television screen, his face offered a sick, hollow grin. His second drink was disappearing fast. The bathroom was all porcelain and white tile, single-use toiletries in sterilized wrappers lined up next to the towels. He put the glass down on the sink and struggled out of the rest of his clothes. There was no water meter under the shower nozzle. He stepped in and turned on the tap. Icy water blasted him from above and he gasped and almost slipped. He'd never seen a shower without a meter or a timer. Brass spouts set in the tile dispensed soap and scented oils. When the water got warmer, he turned the faucet all the way to hot and closed his eyes under the drumming spray.

Much later, he stepped out of the bathroom in a billow of shower steam and ordered a meal from room service. By the time the discreet knock came, he was already halfway into his third drink and the room had taken on a pleasant, mellow glow. He waited until he was sure the waiter had left, then opened the door and wheeled in the table. Steak, fried potatoes, green salad and a small insulated dish of ice cream. Half a bottle of red wine. He regarded the food reverentially, the Scotch he'd drunk burning a hole in his empty belly.

The salad was fresh and tossed with a light dressing, soil-grown, with none of the briny aftertaste of seaweed he'd become used to. He chewed slowly, took a cautious bite of the steak. Rich, savory juices flooded his mouth. Real meat, almost three ounces of it. Tender muscle and fat instead of centrifuge-grown soy fiber. The dessert was creamy and sweet, the wine dark and heady. He ate it all, savoring each mouthful, and managed to keep it down when his stomach rebelled.

Another drink to chase down the food, then another. Sharp angles softened into a pleasant blur. The welcome sign and the menu icons from the screen floated in the middle distance. He unplugged the television from the wall socket and lay down on the bed. The mattress was too soft, and he couldn't arrange his arms and legs right. His thoughts went around and around, got lost in the thick fog of liquor and veered in odd directions.

Some part of him wanted to hurt himself, to scourge himself with the memories over and over, but he couldn't. All of it—the life he'd once lived, Josh and Linda, the war zone—felt like it had happened to someone else. He tried to remember his son's face and got only a hazy outline, the vague impression of a smile. Already the fragments were coming apart under his fingers like mist. There was wetness on his cheeks, but he was hollow and empty, dead inside.

He had no right to be alive. None at all. But that made no difference. Right and wrong never entered the equation.

He fell asleep with the glass half full, and it tumbled out of his hands and off the bed, gurgling out on the deep carpeting. In his dream the screen turned into the mouth of a tunnel through which he dragged himself, broken and bleeding, aware of something closing in on him, its shape not yet revealed. The Deacon was waiting for him in the darkness; naked and immense, smiling, cradling Josh in his huge arms. Suffocating his son, snapping the delicate neck like a twig. His pale, doughy flesh moved under the skin like crawling insects. Josh's head lolled to the side, eyes open and staring under blue eyelids, filled with the black of nothing. When Clayton tried to cry out, yellow dirt spilled from his mouth, his throat.

Seventeen

The light woke him, and the screaming of shells. Small-arms fire rattled close, followed by explosions. He sat up and didn't know where he was. An iron, grinding clank resounded in his head. The long barrel of a trunk pushed out of a stand of tropical trees, the treads churning mud, heading straight at him. Lost and terrified, he rolled aside and tumbled off the bed, landing on his hands and knees.

Outside it was morning, the first arc of sun rising over the high-rises in the east. Through the light-sensitive glass, he could see a rectangle of green jungle in the concrete side of a building across the street. The tank closed in, growing bigger and bigger until it filled the entire screen. Fire bloomed from the muzzle and credits for the Kill Zone began to roll, followed by clips of the island fortress rising vast and unassailable from the sea. Hidden speakers in the headboard of his bed blasted marching music over the sounds of warfare.

The gunfire faded away, replaced by bland, canned music. The twenty-foot holovid on the rooftop across from him flickered, and the rumbling tank was replaced by a stock market report. Clayton got up and turned the speakers off with clumsy fingers, fumbled a yellow lozenge out of a small plastic dispenser and dry-swallowed it. A gritty, chemical taste at the back of his mouth was followed by a warm glow spreading down his spine, working loose the bunched muscles between his shoulder blades, all the way to his ankles. The smooth caress of the drug soothed his ragged nerves. Ice oozed across the back of his skull, throwing the edges of the room into sharp contrast. He turned the trank dispenser in his hands. There would be consequences later; minute increments of memory shivering out of focus, paranoid fixations. He had to start tapering off.

Breakfast arrived while he showered—eggs and toast, hot, bitter coffee. He shoveled the food down without tasting it. The image of the tank lurked at the back of his mind like a bad omen. He pushed the tray table away, laid his valise on the bed and undid the clasps.

Inside was a pair of plain slacks and two shirts, some underwear and a toothbrush. He dumped the contents on the bed and felt along the bottom of the valise until he found an indentation under the lining. The bottom gave with a click, revealing a hidden compartment with a small metal box inside. Next to the box was the metal piece Hymes had given to him. He took the kit into the bathroom, opened it and laid out the components on the marble shelf. After inspecting his face in the mirror, he used Skintox dermals and a fine-needle injector to alter the shape of his chin and brow.

Piece by piece, Conrad Decker disappeared, and a different face took shape, an unsettling amalgamation of old and new features. A face that meant nothing to anyone. He had to be careful; frequent treatments could cause painful inflammation of the skin and underlying tissue, even scarring. Already there was a stiffness in the muscles of his left cheek and his eyelids were puffy, twin dull aches flaring in his sockets. He ran his fingers along the line of his jaw, watching the stranger appear in the mirror, studying the result. Raw, but it would have to do. He dressed, put on the wraparound sunglasses, hid the paraphernalia in the false bottom of his valise and went out.

Some deep instinct told him to avoid the nearby Loop station and mobile sidewalks. Within minutes his light linen shirt clung to his shoulders and back in the hothouse damp. He joined the stream of morning commuters gushing out from turnstiles and escalators and followed the street signs toward the Triangle, a labyrinth of arches and tall, colonnaded porticos. A long, gently rising promenade cut through the middle of the Triangle, with the huge marble dome of the Capitol at its peak.

Keeping an eye out for scanners, Clayton passed through a shadowy arcade and emerged into a broad, stone-flagged quadrangle. A solitary, bored security guard shuffled around the perimeter, head down, hands in his pockets. Screened by a row of pillars, Clayton made his way along one side of the quadrangle, checking the inscriptions above the vaulted archways.

The Department of Demographics was on the far side of the plaza, a wide stone staircase winding up between two marble columns. Inside it was cool and dark like a museum. He took the sunglasses off and put them in his pocket. Two more guards sat at the entrance, a wiry red-haired woman and a heavy man who looked to be in his sixties. He steeled himself and walked past, ready to run. The woman stared right through him, fingers weaving commands, tapping virtual keys, images and video reports coursing across the insides of her glasses. Her companion yawned and flipped through a paperback. Neither guard paid him any mind.

The long, echoing corridors were all but deserted. Cardboard boxes, sagging with age and the weight of yellowed paper, lined the walls. Most of the doors were closed, the glass panes dark and dirty, the numbers on them out of sequence. He went deeper into the building, his heartbeat hurrying along, his throat tight with anxiety. *Caught,* a voice shrilled inside his head. *You want to get caught. You don't have the guts to go through with it.*

A door on his left opened suddenly and he flinched and turned his face away from the man who rushed out, cradling an armful of ledgers. Further along the passage was a half-open door, a light burning on the other side. Feeling like a man in a dream, Clayton read the faded letters on the glass, walked in and closed the door behind him.

The man behind the desk didn't look up at the intruder. He was leafing through a sheaf of stapled forms, making notes with a red pen. Sensing a presence, he made a quick, terse gesture with his head.

"I said later," he said, without lifting his eyes from his work. "Paperwork isn't going to fill itself out. Come back at nine or ten."

He was a tall man, thin but with broad shoulders, his curly black hair cropped close to the skull and sprayed with gray at the sides. When Clayton didn't move, he glanced up irritably. "Didn't you hear me?"

Behind small wire-frame glasses, his eyes first narrowed, then bulged in their sockets. His mouth hung open. The red pen dropped and rolled across the report.

"Oh my God," said the man. The words came out as an exhalation. His dark face seemed to pale, and he gripped the edge of his desk like he was afraid it would float away. He gaped at Clayton for an interminable moment, his brain arranging and rearranging the individual pieces of his visitor's face, trying to fit them into a familiar pattern.

"Hello, Charlie," Clayton said, suddenly at a loss on how to proceed. It had been a mistake to come here, but there was no turning back.

"Frank." The man behind the desk licked his lips and ran both hands through his hair. He looked like he had just been punched hard in the gut. "Frank, what are you doing here? I thought... I heard you'd enlisted."

"I did." Clayton pulled out a chair and sat down. The reality of the situation settled down on his shoulders like a tremendous weight. By coming here, he had put Charlie in danger. Charlie, who was the best friend he'd ever had. Maybe his only real friend. Charlie, who had a wife and a young daughter to think of. "But I decided to get out." *It was a cut-throat business,* he thought of saying, and bit his lip against an uprush of black hilarity.

"My God," Charlie repeated. From the pocket of his neat, carefully pressed suit, he produced a white handkerchief and mopped his forehead. "You look good," he finally managed. His eyes went from Clayton to the door, then to the opposite corner of the small, dusty office.

"So do you. Lost a bit of that paunch you were carrying around last time I saw you."

Charlie's face hardened. "Diabetes," he said. "My insurance company tried to stiff me. Said it wasn't covered by my medical plan. It was rough for a while. Bootleg insulin costs a bundle, and you can't exactly get it on credit. You got to trade." A small pause preceded the last word. "But I'm good. Getting treatment now. I turned the tables on the bastards. Nobody wants to get on the bad side of a Demos employee, even if he is only a lowly statistician. One of the few perks of a government job."

"That's good to hear. Mary and the kid?"

"Doing great," Charlie said. A touch of pride warmed his voice. "Abby got into a pre-med program with Allied Therapeutics. They pay for her college and guarantee an indentured traineeship afterwards."

127

He remembered and caught himself short, looked at his hands, embarrassed.

"She's a smart kid," Clayton said. A stab of grief, sharp and unexpected, twisted his heart. He turned his face aside before it could show. "Listen, Charlie, I don't have much time. I have to find Linda. Can you look up her address for me?"

He half-expected Charlie to refuse outright, but the other man only looked doubtful. "That kind of search takes time, Frank. It's above my clearance level. I can't just type her name into a database and hit enter. I'd have to rout the request through back channels and wait. You're not thinking of seeing her, are you?"

"I don't know. I haven't really had a chance to think this through. How long?"

"Could be an hour. Could be two days." Charlie removed his glasses and rubbed his eyes. "This Freedom from Intrusion bullshit has tied our hands. One-third of the Department is on furlough, and there's another round of budget cuts around the corner. You saw it yourself—you waltzed right up to my office without so much as an ident scan. But let's see what we can do." He put the glasses back on and turned to the screen, his fingers moving over the keyboard. "Bingo," he said, after a pause. "I think I can find her."

"What about the clearance?"

"My boss is out today. He gives me his password so I can access his files. He's not supposed to do that—technically it's a felony—but God forbid he should do his own work. I'll put in a request through his account and mark it high priority."

"I owe you one," Clayton said. "More than one. I never thanked you for what you did for us after—" He couldn't finish. "I was in a bad way back then, and I stayed that way for a long time. You gave me a second chance, and I threw it away. I gave up. It was all my fault."

"It wasn't anybody's fault," Charlie said in a distant voice. "Can't keep blaming yourself, man. Sometimes things happen just because they happen. That's all there is to it." The screen before him turned black and strings of ciphers started to scroll across it. "Got it. I'll run a consumer index check, cross-reference it with her targeted-ad profile. Shouldn't take more than a few minutes."

Clayton sat back in the chair and gazed out the window. He had first met Charlie in elementary school, on the wrong side of Canalside, and they had been friends ever since. Even after Charlie had gotten the job with the Department of Demographics and moved his family to the Federal District, they had remained in touch, seeing each other a few times a year. Charlie's work as a Demos statistician often took him back to the old neighborhood; they would get drunk in one of their old watering holes, swap old stories and bitch about new accommodation blocks being put up and food shortages and how the low-credit poor were ruining everything because they just couldn't stop breeding. Those had been good times, and when the bad times had come, Charlie had come through for him. Just like he was coming through now.

He should have felt relieved, but he couldn't relax. His pulse was racing, and his mind was working fast, some sixth sense kicking in, trying to get him to listen. He shifted in his seat and glanced over Charlie's shoulder. The computer was still running its search program, filaments of data weaving across the background: food allotments, credit ranks, purchasing habits, child permits, vital statistics. Everything that made a consumer-citizen what he was.

The last thought brought with it an unpleasant chill. He tried to push it away, but it kept stealing back, roiling up the muddy bottom of his brain. He got up and stood at the window. The flagstone plaza was empty, a gap between tall white columns and arches that seemed to prop up the sky. Charlie was hunched over the keyboard, the screen reflected in his glasses.

You got to trade.

Charlie, who had a wife with expensive tastes and a daughter with big dreams.

Charlie, a government paper-pusher, destined to stay behind this same desk and computer, looking out this same window, until he grew sick or too old to work and got tossed on the scrap heap.

It wasn't something you talked about in polite company, or even consciously acknowledged, but it was always there: an unspoken undertone to all that was being said aloud. For the old, sick and unprofitable, the options were few: a slow death as the organ-harvesting outfits claimed them piecemeal, or a quick one in the quiet, dim chamber of a euthanasia clinic, erased from existence to the funereal dirge of synthesizer music.

Unless an offer came their way, one too good to pass up. To prove their worth to the conglomerates.

They pay for her college and guarantee an internship.

It was rough for a while. But I'm getting treatment now.

Was Charlie trying to tell him something, give him a signal? The man's face was inches from the screen, but he wasn't looking at the changing numbers. His eyes were fixed on the far corner of the room. On a mirror mounted there, high up on the wall.

Clayton's pulse quickened. If the office were under surveillance, a micro-camera hidden behind the glass could cover the entire space. He glanced out into the courtyard. The lone guard had been joined by two more, shock-sticks swinging at their sides. They hovered near the Department entrance, ordering the office-workers back into the buildings and looking nervous. The yard was emptying fast.

From the other side of the quad, a second group of guards was approaching. These did not look nervous. They wore bulky riot suits and helmets and carried caseless submachine guns.

It wouldn't have been hard, the thought came to him through the sudden haze of adrenaline. *They knew exactly where I would go, and they made sure they got there before me. All they had to do was wait.*

Everyone was capable of betrayal because everyone had a weak spot. Charlie's was easy to find.

"Are they watching us, Charlie?"

His friend's face remained fixed. "Yes," he said in a cold, dead voice, still not looking up. There was no apology in it. "They have the whole area covered."

Clayton pushed him out of the way and tried the computer. The numbers on the screen continued their crawl, unresponsive. He brought his fist down on the keyboard hard enough to hurt. Keys scattered like broken teeth.

"It's locked out of the system," Charlie said out of the corner of his mouth. "All drives have been wiped." He folded his glasses and placed them on the desk. When he spoke

next, his voice was no more than a whisper, his lips barely moved. "Linda moved out. She's staying with her dad.
They're watching his place too."

Clayton looked around for a weapon, picked up a pa-
perweight from the desk—a miniature of the Demos building
encased in a half-sphere of heavy fiberglass—and smashed
the mirror to pieces. He could hear commotion outside, the
thud of booted heels. "How do I get out of here?"

"There's a serviceway escalator up by the Archives
building, if you can make it that far." Charlie looked old
and beaten. His shoulders sagged. "Let it end here, Frank.
You won't outrun them. There's nowhere to run."

"I know," Clayton said, and struck his friend across
the side of the head. Charlie slumped down in his chair. A
trickle of blood ran down his cheek, soaking his shirt collar,
but he was still breathing. Clayton dropped the bloody pa-
perweight into the waste basket and raced out of the office.

The two security guards from the entrance were rounding the corner of the hallway, the woman in front, the big
man huffing and red-faced behind her. Both held shock-
sticks. At the sight of Clayton, they stopped in confusion.
The man fumbled with a can of teargas at his belt. It fell
from his hand and rolled back down the corridor. The woman jerked at the noise and spun around, baton raised to
strike. Clayton took advantage of the confusion, ran in the
opposite direction, past the closed doors.

Shouts as they came after him, doors opening and
slamming, voices raised in alarm. The guards were slow,
but they had the angle on him, and more were joining the
chase, trying to cut him off. He saw an exit sign at the end
of a corridor, the door beneath it swinging open, and sprint-
ed for it.

The guard coming out of the stairwell could do no more
than throw his arms up in front of his face. Using the full
momentum of his body, Clayton drove his shoulder into the
man's midsection and slammed him into the wall, eliciting
a grunt of pain and surprise. His baton clattered to the
floor. Clayton doubled him up with a kick and darted down
the steps.

The staircase plunged as steeply as a ladder. He careened down flight after flight, gulping air into his lungs,

the muscles in his thighs burning. Echoes of footfalls and voices came at him from all sides.

The stairs ended on a narrow ground-level landing, one door leading outside, the other locked solid, the ident scanner above the lock glowing red. He burst through the exit, saw the bulky uniforms crowding the north corner of the plaza. Riot police, he realized, huge and slow in insulated plasteel armor, their heads encased in soundproof helmets. One of the policemen saw the door open and shouldered his caseless submachine, but the figure next to him pushed his gun down, signaled with his hand. The formation parted, and a riot cop stepped forward, pointing his weapon at Clayton. It looked like a rifle, but, instead of a barrel, it terminated in a wide, snub-nosed muzzle.

In an instant, Clayton knew what it was. The Scav teams used concussion guns when a situation threatened to get out of hand. As the cop squeezed the trigger, Clayton threw himself back onto the landing and rolled, clasping his hands over his ears.

The swinging door took the brunt of the blast, shuddering in its frame. A sound that wasn't a sound thrummed through Clayton, sending waves of nausea out from the middle of his guts. He strained to sit up, but all the muscles had gone out of his stomach and back. His legs made feeble jerking motions.

Boots appeared on the steps above him. A security guard, sweaty and winded, looked down at him over the staircase railing. Capacitors buzzed as he thumbed the safety off his shock-stick. Poised to strike, he took a step down onto the landing, right as the second blast ripped through the door.

A great invisible fist of subsonic discharge and compressed air hit the guard like a freight train, knocking him back against the stairs. His skull bounced off the concrete and he lay on the ground convulsing.

A monstrous buzzing filled Clayton's head. He tried to get up, but his balance was shot, and his feet tangled, sending him sprawling next to the unconscious guard. Strings of bile trailed from his mouth. He could hear others running down the stairs, the ones outside approaching the bent exit door. They were coming in. Any second now.

He used the railing to drag his recalcitrant body to its feet. The floor and the ceiling twirled in a mad kaleidoscope. Picking up the guard's ident and baton, he shambled to the locked door and placed the card on the scanner. When the light turned green, he slipped through the door. Behind it was a set of metal stairs going down to a long underground passage. As soon as the door whooshed closed, he turned the baton to full charge and smashed in the electric lock on his side of the wall. The weapon bucked in his grasp, rolled on the floor, useless. Smoke and sparks belched out of the carbonate-fiber casing, and the scanner went black. It would not hold them long, but he hoped it would slow them down.

His head had cleared a little and strength was coming back into his legs. Wincing, he hobbled down the steps. The passage curved into the distance, its walls marked with signs and lines and brightly colored symbols. Thick ferro-concrete shielding and blast doors were everywhere, the legacy of the riot years before the deregulation. According to the map, the tunnel ran the length of the Triangle, connecting the various government offices through a profusion of branching pathways. The more the better; the cops and the guards could not seal off every exit, at least not this fast.

He studied the map briefly, then set off in the direction of the Archives. A deep tremor reverberated through the ground, followed by another. Overhead, lights crackled and flickered. He started to run.

He was almost there when another shudder went through the lights and a section of the corridor ahead fell away into a black hole.

They were shutting the power off, trying to blind him. Even as he realized it, the overheads went off, burying him in instant darkness. The power to the doors would go next. He would be locked in.

Both his hands went out to the wall, but it was no longer there. The open space around him felt enormous and threatening. He chanced a step into the void. Something cold and damp touched the tips of his reaching fingers. The solidity reassured him a little but did not quell the rising tide of panic. He shuffled along the wall, one hand on the cold stone, the other groping forward.

Was he moving closer to the exit, or away from it? His breath whistled through his teeth. His mind threatened to slip its moorings. He was back in the sacrificial pit on the edge of the desert, dying of thirst and starvation, listening to the rustle of desiccated corpses, to the howls of the tribals above. He had never left. The solid surface of the wall ended in emptiness. A whimper escaped his throat, loud in the silence. He held his breath, waiting for the rustling to come nearer, for bony fingers to close around his wrist and drag him into the expectant dark.

Instead, his hand encountered the cool metal of a railing. Breathing fast, he found the steps and willed his numb body to move.

Above and ahead, a dim reddish glow began. He realized he could see the outline of stairs. The glow emanated from an ident scanner. The cops had killed the power, but the automatic doors ran on their own generators and had to be switched off one by one; the underground tunnels had to remain operational in case of an emergency or crisis.

At the touch of the guard's card, a section of the wall slid open and he walked into another stairwell, squinting in the sudden brightness. There were noises here, doors opening and slamming, but they seemed distant. He climbed up to a landing window and peeked through.

The plaza outside was crawling with guards. No other way but into the building. Deeper into the trap. He ran up to the next landing, opened the door and went inside.

He was in the great central hall of the Archives, a silent space filled with shadows. Floor-to-ceiling bookshelves, loaded down with volumes of all sizes, creaked like masts at sea. The smell of decaying paper and rotted bindings permeated the musty, stale air. Pale, terrified faces blinked at him from dusty cubicles and crates full of books, over tables buried under avalanches of old paper.

Clayton headed for the exit on the other side of the hall, stopped when he saw the door open and ducked behind a bookshelf. Four guards walked in and started ushering the archivists out of the hall. A short, bespectacled man paused to speak to them, gesturing wildly and pointing in Clayton's direction. The guards clicked on their shock-sticks and one of them spoke into his palmer. Clayton tried to backtrack, found his way blocked by a second group of guards coming in from the tunnel-side door. They had him surrounded.

He fled through the narrow lanes between the shelves, knowing it was useless. Behind him, he could hear them gaining, the ancient wooden floor sighing under their heavy boots. Shouting back and forth to each other, leaving him no room for escape. Yet he felt no fear, only a strange sort of elation. His concentration narrowed down to a fine point— find a weapon, take as many of them as he could down with him before they killed him.

He turned a corner and crashed into a library cart, sending it rolling across the floor. An archivist was pressed up against the bookshelf. He was tall and gangly, with straw-colored hair and a pasty complexion, and looked all of sixteen. He cradled an armful of paper he'd just picked up off the cart against his chest and stared at Clayton in mute horror.

I'm the boogeyman, Clayton thought wildly, and felt his mind slip and catch again. The cart came to a stop against a bundle of old newspapers. The squeak of its wheels snapped him back to reality. He bent over and tore open the bundle, twisted several pages into a spill. Ink and grit stained his hands. On the top page was a grainy black-and-white picture of a missile-carrying ship. Headlines warned of blockades and nuclear hellfire in black bold print. History stacked on shelf upon shelf, dozens of feet high. Distant and meaningless, if this was what it had led to.

Looking over his shoulder, he crumpled the newsprint into a small pile and reached for a second bundle. The boots were closing in. They knew they had him. He worked quickly, piling the paper up from a broad base to a tapering summit, then patted his pockets. Through all this, the archivist's eyes, wide and wet, never left him.

"You got a smoke?"

The whey-faced youth nodded, unable to speak. Clayton found the pack in his shirt pocket. Inside it was a cheap plastic lighter. He snicked it on and held the flame to the spill until it took hold. Once he was sure the flaming spill would not go out, he used it to light the pile and watched the fire eat eagerly into the curling paper.

Thick smoke built up, drifted. Flames curled up the tall bookshelves, crawled along the aisles, spread wider. Heat rushed at him, building quickly, pouring down his throat. The hairs in his nose and on the backs of his hands were crisping. His eyes watering, his lungs raw with smoke, he picked up handfuls of burning newsprint and stuffed them into gaps in the shelves.

Boxes of dry paper went up like kindling. The blaze feathered up to scorch and blacken the ceiling. Old wood crackled and spat. A rising wave of panicked screams drove him forward, in the direction of the exit door. Figures were fleeing through the curtains of smoke, coughing and weaving like drunks.

Somewhere, an alarm began to bray. Water gushed from overhead sprinklers but could not control the devouring conflagration. Clayton pushed past a guard who was staggering blindly and pinwheeling his arms, trying to beat at the flames climbing up his uniform. The guard's face was distorted, his eyes huge and unbelieving. Others were making for the exits without looking back. Using the smoke as cover, Clayton followed.

There was a stampede on the stairs. The building was a death trap with only one fire escape. People were screaming in the smoke and confusion, trampling each other in the mad rush to get out of the suffocating stairwell. A woman tumbled past Clayton and lay on the landing below, unmoving. He punched and clawed at the wall of flesh, swallowing back the taste of panic. Without warning, the barrier gave way and he reeled out into the open.

Guards and riot police wandered around the sunlit plaza like a routed army, watching dark clouds of smoke pour out of the Archives building. Government workers swarmed down the Triangle's central thoroughfare and more were joining in from all sides. Up ahead, at the end of the promenade, a pair of troop carriers were landing on the capitol steps. On their sides was emblazoned the red-and-black emblem of Tristar-Paramount Studios.

Clayton tried to break and run, but the crush of bodies carried him forward. Black-armored troops streamed out of the carriers and marched in formation. An unbroken line of plasteel shields had already formed at the bottom of the steps; teargas canisters hissed into the frantic multitude. Mechanical voices squawked from mounted amplifiers, ordering the crowd to disperse.

Pandemonium broke out, those nearest to the canisters collapsing on the ground or retching, others pushing to escape. An amplified voice crackled over the street and was promptly swallowed in the uproar. The front ranks of the crowd crashed into the wall of shields and started to crumble and retreat, trampled by those behind them.

He pulled his shirt over his face and forced his way against the tide. The elevator box was mere feet away, the peeling metal door almost close enough to touch. The acrid haze filled his eyes and nose with tears. Elbows and shoulders jammed him against the filthy glass of the box window, dug into his ribcage. Clinging to the doorframe, he worked one hand free and slapped the guard's card on the call sensor.

The line of shields was advancing. The pressure of bodies slackened. Remnants of the crowd swept past him, bruised and bloody. A booming, static-filled voice exhorted them to submit to ident scans in an orderly fashion.

The elevator arrived and the doors opened. The inside of the car was dark, and the control screen displayed an emergency shutdown message. Clayton went in and slid the ident through the reader slot. The light came on. He touched the button for the serviceway level, and the door rolled shut. Seconds before the elevator started down, a visored face peered in through the narrow window, gesturing wildly. He had been spotted.

The car sank rapidly, tunnels and platforms sliding past the window like layers in a cake. He slumped against the rear wall of the elevator, heart leaping in his chest. Flat concrete planes came up at him in a vertiginous swoop, shaped into enclosures and ramps and moveways. Armed men in the blue-gray uniforms of the East-West Urban Transit Corporation were waiting for him on the elevated bus concourse. He had time to register the surprise on their faces as the car rushed past them without stopping.

The earth swallowed him up. Constellations of signal lights blinked in the black gulf below. Cables groaned as the elevator began to decelerate.

He was descending from the roof of a vast cavern, a tunnel high enough to accommodate a tower block. Ribbons of twenty-lane serviceways ran into the darkness, each crawling with automated traffic. The car came to a halt at the serviceway embankment. Dust and oil fumes gusted in through the open door. Covering his mouth and nose, Clayton stepped out onto the concrete strip and gazed down through the chain link security fence.

The serviceway was a mass of shifting shadows, directed by light signals, operated by sensors and feedback circuits. Oil tankers trudged by in long, evenly spaced columns. Freighters the size of small islands rolled past, their colossal wheels stirring up clouds of dirt, their blunt prows studded with sensors and lights. Elevated buses straddled the lanes, rumbling overhead like moving bridges. Headlight beams slashed at the eternal night.

The roar of sound was enormous, a hurricane in his ears. Even from where he stood, the slipstream whipped his hair, snatched at his breath. Blue strobes pulsed behind the slow-moving behemoths, splashed up the tunnel walls. He didn't have much time. Grabbing the top of the fence, he swung over and dropped onto the maintenance walkway running the length of the tunnel.

Metal grates sent a thrumming vibration up through his feet. Oily, noxious air filled his burning lungs. Endless lines of haulage vehicles thundered beneath him, pistons thumping, gears whining and grinding. The blue lights grew brighter, throwing the serviceway into sharp relief. When he glanced back, he could see the bullet-shaped police cruisers weaving between the trundling giants, closing in fast.

Around the tunnel, signal constellations whirled, and traffic slowed to a crawl. Down below, flashing yellow lights and orange construction signs girdled a section of the road. Repair machines clanked and pounded. A labor gang in grimy yellow overalls and filter masks was hard at work between them, breaking up the paved surface and clearing away rubble. The crew boss and two blue-gray guards were standing by the construction barrier, watching the approaching cruisers. Manned vehicles were a rare sight on the underground roads, and the recent spate of tribal attacks had everyone on edge.

Clayton climbed over the side of the walkway and pushed off, landing in the dirt with a thump. The laborers scattered in alarm. The three men at the barrier had their backs to him. He picked up a length of pipe and swung it at the back of the nearest guard's head. The man went down like a sack of grain, his eyes showing white. Neither of the other two took any notice. Clayton raised the pipe and brought it down on the other guard's forearm, feeling its weight smash deep into the bone.

The man screamed in pain and surprise and sank to the ground. His arm lay in his lap, useless. The crew boss turned white and raised his arms. He looked over at the strobing lights, then at the bloody pipe in Clayton's hand.

"I won't tell," he said, voice muffled by the filter mask. Above it, his eyes pleaded. "Just don't kill me. Please. I don't want to die."

The cruisers were close now. Clayton shifted his grip on the pipe and swept his eyes across the site. There had to be a way out. Behind the ranks of whirring construction machines, a shaft traveled up the tunnel wall, vanishing into the ceiling shadows. Inside it, suspended on thick steel cables, was a double-deck cage. He started toward it, then pulled back.

Standing in a line, blocking his path to the cage, were the laborers, picks and sledges hanging at their sides. In his mind, Clayton was suddenly back in the desert, entering the lakeside settlement, surrounded by hard, pitiless faces. If they held their ground, it would be all over.

One of the men took a few steps forward and removed his filter mask. He was old and bent from heavy labor, his knuckles swollen with arthritis, bowstring tendons standing out in his neck. His left eye was filmed over with cataract and it was impossible to tell the color of his skin; tunnel dust had turned it an ash-gray. The good eye stared over Clayton's shoulder, at the two men leaning on the construction barrier. The old man took a pair of gloves off his belt and pulled them over his gnarled hands. On his toothless lips was a strange smile. He extended one gloved hand, palm upraised.

Clayton held out the pipe. Without raising his eyes, the old man took it and moved forward. The labor gang moved with him, parting around Clayton like water around a rock.

Out by the barrier, the crew boss screamed.

The line of yellow suits closed to fill the gap. There was a solid clunk of metal on bone, then a series of wet, crunching sounds. Clayton kept walking toward the cage and didn't look back.

Around him, the machinery ran on and on, tracking along preprogrammed routes, grinding forever in the subterranean dark.

Eighteen

He thought they would be waiting for him at the hotel, but no one tried to stop him when he walked into the brightly lit, airconditioned lobby. The concierge held the door open for him and greeted him by name. The well-groomed receptionist flashed her dazzling professional smile without noticing him. His disheveled appearance was accepted without so much as a raised eyebrow. At the Lafayette Regency, discretion was a given. The bars and clubs and underground dens of the Federal District catered to a variety of illicit tastes; when well-heeled patrons decided to seek out snuff parties or neurohack cubes or rough trade, it was hotel policy to smile and look the other way.

The elevator rose smoothly, a soft ding indicating each floor. A strange man with a raw, dirt-streaked face was trapped in its mirrors with Clayton. The closed-circuit camera in the top corner stared at him unblinking. Hidden facial recognition scanners caught him and a beaming hologram welcomed Conrad Decker back, rattled off the stock market headlines for the day.

He slammed the room door shut, dimmed the windows and headed straight for the minibar. The lights came on and the television blared to life. His hands shook so badly that the liquor sloshed around the glass. His face burned, every nerve under his skin on fire. It wasn't safe to stay here. The risk was unacceptable. Time to get out of the Federal District. He'd had his purchases forwarded to a post office box in the old neighborhood. They knew where he was going, but he was sure he could give them the slip. Canalside was his home turf. They were in for a surprise.

He sipped his Scotch and grinned. The screen had filled up with elegant curves of white beaches, lazy waves caressing the sand. Laughing couples strolled down broad, white avenues lined with lush trees and baroque filigree facades.

WHEREVER YOU MAY DREAM, appeared at the bottom of
the screen, fading into the sky-blue logo of TransCore and
the slogan THE NUMBER ONE CHOICE IN SYNESTHETIC
VACATIONS. He tossed off the last of his drink and went
into the bathroom to clean up.

When he emerged, the corporate propaganda broadcast was over and the Newscan had come on. He went to
unplug the television set, changed his mind and flopped
on the bed. The presenter, a severely pretty blonde in a
dark blue pants suit, was announcing a merger between
two waste management megacartels. The camera cut to an
oak-paneled conference room and two elderly men signing
a document in a large leather-bound folio. A ticker in one
corner of the screen displayed the fluctuating share price of
the newly formed company.

He waved through to the next news item. Flooding in
the coastal parts of the District, muddy water washing down
hillsides, swirling around blocks of vertical farms. Motioned
again. Columns of old trucks and even older farm machinery stopped at a border crossing on the edge of a vast dust-
bowl. Starving dark-skinned children covered in flies, thin,
dirty men and women staring down phalanxes of armored
infantrymen with faces like granite. Clayton scrolled further. Riots up north, below the border, farm workers protesting the introduction of a new strain of genetically mod-
ified, high-yield wheat. Automated harvesters burned on
an access track in the middle of a rippling golden sea of
grain. An indignant corporate spin doctor was explaining
that a five percent reduction in workforce was necessary
to stabilize the market and ensure continuous supply, that
the riots were the work of asocial radicals illegally trying to
unionize the labor force. The CEO of Titan Hydroponics had
signed a food assistance loan to Katanga Free State, shaking hands with a heavyset man in sunglasses and a parade
uniform covered in decorations.

Another wave of the hand. He sat up.

The screen showed smoke rising from the Archives
building, police and security guards helping fleeing government workers to safety. The camera was angled in such a
way that the stampeding crowd in the Triangle was never

in full view and the swarming Tristar-Paramount troops remained completely invisible.

FIRE AT ARCHIVES BUILDING read the headline beneath the location shot. SEVERAL INJURED.

The report indicated that the fire was caused by faulty wiring and segued into a commercial for the Omni Insurance Group. That was it. No mention of a manhunt or an escaped fugitive or troop carriers landing on the capitol steps. The coverup must have been massive and very expensive.

Thinking about it made him smile.

He got up to get another drink, but the bottle paused over the glass. The screen had cut to a stark panorama of Canaveral City, great circular platforms and silos thrust out over the sea, blast walls of pitted steel reflecting banks of Atlantic cloud. Domes and launch gantries cast long shadows across the water. Cylindrical agrolanders, singed and dented by repeated atmospheric entries, bobbed inside floating docks like dead whales. Grimacing, Clayton poured, took a long gulp and turned up the volume.

The presenter was talking about the upcoming four-day summit between the President, the Secretary-General of the United Nations and the Colonial Governor of Gyges over the famine crisis in the southern hemisphere. Also attending would be the Chairman of the East Asian Cooperative Zone and a slew of minor heads of state. He sat back down on the bed and drank some more, fueling the comforting blossom of heat in his stomach.

A rooftop shot of the conference hall showed a great structure of slanting columns and glass wall panels panned over to the speaker's podium and islands of tables beneath a row of furled flags. Suddenly he was aware he was breathing hard. The picture reminded him of something unpleasant, something hovering on the periphery of his consciousness. Another swig blotted it out. He held the bottle up to the light, turning it from side to side, watching the oily amber liquid sparkle.

Canaveral City faded away, gave way to an ad for Glasser-Kamada's new hormonal rejuvenation line. DISCOVER A NEW VITALITY, the ad proclaimed. Behind the letters, a handsome father swept a curly-haired little girl up into his arms, while an adoring mother looked on, smiling. All three radiated health and contentment, eyes sparkling, cheeks glowing.

He brought the bottle to his lips, swallowed as much as he could keep down and hurled it at the television. It hit dead center and shattered with a loud crash, without so much as scratching the smooth, reinforced surface. Glass and liquor trailed down the screen in long strings of rainbow-colored diamonds. Through them, a smiling weatherman was pointing out a high-pressure front settling in, burning away the clouds, bringing good weather.

Nineteen

Canalside in summer, the heat like an iron dome over the sky, the dust and clamor of construction swirling around forests of smokestacks. Sullen crowds roaming the dirty streets, lining up in front of food vaults. Men and women huddling under the broken marquees of shuttered arcades, inside concrete arches and piss-stained entryways. Hawkers touted wares piled on foldout tables: clothes mended and new, used household appliances, fried food studded with fat, lazy flies. Where credit and consumption indices had failed, bartering stepped in to fill the gap.

Eyes followed him. Eyes that he remembered well, sullen or glazed over with any number of pharmaceutical combinations, escape from the abject drudgery that lay on this side of opiate dreams. Primitive cunning and a kind of vacuous hunger sheened their faces. Food was in short supply, but a burgeoning drug market was there to take its place, generously subsidized from a public utility fund that all transnationals contributed to. The familiar stench of the place, sweat and sewage and industrial waste thickening and brewing in the stifling air, filmed Clayton's skin like dirty oil, welcoming him back into the fold.

It was the smell of home.

As Conrad Decker, he had rented a berth in a capsule hotel on the other side of the canal and had the post office forward his purchases there. At first, he'd planned to stop there and collect his deliveries, but he changed his mind. The feeling of being watched was back, and it was stronger now. Behind polarized glasses, his eyes studied the passing faces, searched the crowd.

If the network agents knew where he was, they would take him right here and now. They knew he was alive, and they were looking for him; the quick, brutal raid on the Triangle had shattered any illusions he might have held on that count. He had slipped through the net, at least for now. Yet the feeling stayed with him as he made his way toward the pedestrian bridge, crossing sidewalks and doubling back to throw off pursuit.

In his absence, the neighborhood had changed, and not for the better. Factor pricing and changing regulations as the FEDs competed for investment had driven high-tech industries away, making room for steelworks and mills, for chimneys belching dirt at the heavens. Islands of worker tenements sprouted around the industrial complex, covering the remains of malls and office blocks like an infestation. The computer chip plant he had once worked for had closed shop and moved to another ward, its bones stripped back to steel and ferroconcrete, the road eroded by the tracks of armored vehicles.

His eyes sought the tall, neon-lit Standard Energy tower at the end of the central square, but it was gone, replaced by a demolition site. It had been a landmark of the neighborhood, its harsh geometries rising over the Canalside roofscape for over twenty years. He remembered sneaking up to the roof with a girl, sixteen and single-minded, their fumbling haste and the warm feel of her skin. Remembered sitting up there through the deep of night, every sense alive and awake, watching the rosy glow of dawn spill across the drab mosaic of accommodation blocks, their summits come alive with holovids and advertisements. That made him think first of Linda, and then of Josh. He pushed the memory away and kept walking, careful to keep away from their old block and the memories that lurked there, waiting to snag him.

Close to the canal, the crowd thickened and slowed to a crawl. Factory whistles sounded over the din of machinery like temple bells summoning the faithful to service. He followed the rush onto the shadowed walkways of the bridge. Beneath the great iron spans and girders, sunlight scattered thousands of sparkling colors across the river's oil-scummed surface. You could smell the ocean from the bridge sometimes, if the wind was right, but today it just stank of trash and diesel. Fiery gas plumes rose skyward from the factories, cast long reflections across the black water.

When he and Linda were first married, they would come down to the concrete bank of the canal and watch the bleary sun bleed into the vivid oranges and pinks of petrochemical sunset. They would hold each other and try to imagine what lay beyond the dirty block units and train tracks of Canalside. Thinking there had to be more to life than this, there just had to be.

A bitter smile crossed Clayton's face. Together they had dreamed of running away to the end of the world, but made it no further than across the canal. Now he was coming full circle, right back to where he'd started.

They were waiting for him outside the tenement block entrance, two plainclothesmen sitting on the wide steps, smoking and pretending to pass a bottle back and forth. He spotted two more lounging at the far end of the block. Big men, thick through the chest and shoulders, looking out of place among the underfed denizens of Canalside. The stooped and begrimed factory workers coming off night shift instinctively kept out of their way. Either they were careless, or this was a ruse to lure him to one of the rear entrances, where there would be fewer witnesses.

Part of the crowd, anonymous, he walked past the entrance, ready to run. Close enough to be spotted, but the plainclothesmen stayed where they were. The man they were looking for was not the one whose face he was wearing now. Even without the syntheskin and facial injections, it would have been hard to tell him apart from the dozens of gray, tired faces in the street.

He got to the end of the block and turned the corner. More big, stony-faced men loitered around, trying to look inconspicuous. They had all the doors covered. He kept on walking. On the next block over, he made sure none of the plainclothesmen were in sight and ducked into the building entryway.

Inside, it smelled of piss and refuse and neglect. Slogans, names and obscene drawings covered the walls above rows of vandalized mailboxes. The elevators were out of service and the stairwell lights were gone. A skinny old man in a gray, frayed T-shirt and shorts, his wasted legs bent at an odd angle, scowled from a folding chair by the elevators and made incomprehensible noises. His placid, watery eyes

147

bore the look of drooling imbecility. Plastic garbage bags lay heaped around his chair, many torn open and spilling their contents across the floor. Clayton stepped over the refuse and started up the stairs, feeling his way along the bannister.

By the time he reached the top of the building, he was gasping and covered with sweat. The hallway was empty. Loud music, laughter and shouts blared behind peeling doors. Somewhere a woman screamed. The roof was accessed through a set of metal stairs and a horizontal door. As he'd expected, the lock was broken, the handle removed.

He pushed the door open a slit and looked through. Under the low, hazy sky, empty rooftops blended into one another, dotted with ventilation shafts and the squat pillboxes of elevator rooms. Peeled billboards, covered in graffiti and bird droppings, sat on skeletons of struts and triangulated framework. One of them showed a group of young soldiers, faces blackened with powder, raising a flag on a barren mountaintop. The flag bore the red-and-black symbol of Tristar-Paramount. A low wall ran around the edge of the precipice. On the far side, a narrow span of welded-together pipes and metal tubing, stayed by cables to a broken antenna tower, extended across the gap, high above street level.

In Canalside, the flat expanse of rooftops formed a well-established travel route with its own distinctive kind of traffic, from heated young lovers to thieves and traders in illicit goods. Makeshift bridges, made of rusty scaffolding and the remains of neon signs, held together by cables and tangled wiring, spanned the emptiness between the roofs. Those who knew where to find the crossings, or which roofs were close enough to jump between, could travel for miles without touching the dangerous streets.

But his pursuers would know that and expect him to come that way. He went out and crossed in a crouch, watching the opposite roof for movement. There was none. Instead of relief, he felt a gnawing anxiety. Things were going too smoothly. He leaned over the parapet and a wave of dizziness washed over him at the sight of the sheer drop opening up beneath.

Could he make it? When he had been a boy, the gap between two rooftops had been no bigger than a drugstore aisle. He and his friends would dare each other to walk it upright, keeping low to fight the wind, arms out for balance. Now it seemed as wide as one of the underground serviceways, wider than the canal itself.

He rubbed his eyes and stood there, looking at the roof of Linda's old block. Every corner, every hidden nook of it he knew like his own hand. The sense of having come full circle was stronger than ever. Time repeating itself, tightening around him like a noose against which he was helpless.

He hoisted himself up the wall and straddled the top, trying not to look down. The other end of the makeshift bridge leaned on the opposite parapet, tied down with ropes. Metal hummed and creaked in the hot wind. Blackened welding marks showed through the rust. Holding onto the wall, he set one foot on the bridge, then the other.

The span was two feet wide, but it felt like a tightrope. He lowered himself on his knees and hands, letting the bridge take his full weight, wrapping his legs around it. The metal groaned and shivered, but the welds were strong.

Hot steel singed his hands as he groped his way forward, across the dizzying emptiness of air. Thirty stories below, the threadlike street spun in his vision. Squeezing his eyes shut, he worked his way forward, hand over hand, until he felt rough wall under his fingertips. He rolled over the edge of the parapet and lay on the sunbaked concrete, chest heaving, waiting for feeling to come back to his limbs.

The door leading to the roof was unlocked, the hallway beyond it empty and dark. Discarded needles and broken glass crunched under his feet. Silence ruled the topmost floor. At this time of day, most of the residents of the block would be at work, or on the streets. Those who stayed behind were even farther away, bodies inert inside their cubicle apartments, their central nervous systems riding brilliant pharmaceutical clouds, yielding to the searing chemical imperative written in their blood. Or glued to their cable sets, drowning in the tidal wave of ad overload and hyperreality shows; the sustaining pipeline poised to deliver the next fix, the only thing worth living for.

He took the stairs down to Linda's floor, moving as quietly as he could. There was no guard posted in the corridor. It had to be a trap. He came to the familiar door and stood with his hand raised, feeling physically sick, ready to turn around and leave, go anywhere.

Instead, he knocked.

Footsteps on bare floor. The eyehole clicked open. *This is it,* he thought. If the network heavies were inside, waiting for him, he wouldn't run. He had just about reached the point where he no longer cared.

The moments stretched. Heavy bolts shot back, and the door opened. Linda was standing in the semidarkness of the single room on the other side—the same Linda he'd last seen a year and a half ago, but paler and thinner, her face drawn, arms crossed on her slender bosom. Her hair was longer than he remembered and streaked with white. She was looking at him, but her look said nothing. Behind her, lights blinked, sterile machines clicked and hummed.

"Can I come in?"

Her eyes scrutinized him, warily, prying away his disguise. Then recognition set in, a sudden flare that she did her best to tamp down. Still she said nothing. The lack of reaction was more chilling than the tears and recriminations he had prepared himself for. He was at once desperate for her to speak, and terrified of what she might say. She moved aside to let him in, closed the door behind him.

The single room was stuffy and hot and smelled of disinfectant. Muted daylight came in through the shatterproof polymers of the windows, caked with ages of grime and dust. Linda's cot, neatly made, sat next to a nightstand made of faux-wood-grain fiberboard. A rickety ventilation unit clattered in one corner of the ceiling. Underneath it was a tiny kitchen alcove with greasy walls and a retractable fridge-pantry unit.

The remaining space was taken up by the double bed and the life-support equipment, hospital surplus bought from black-market dealers, some of it still bearing property stickers and defunct meter gauges. Valves and pumps clacked and wheezed around the shriveled, crooked body in the center of the bed; tubes and dermatrodes wormed under the covers, connected to bodily orifices and shunts embedded in slack yellow skin. A wizened hand, like a monkey's paw, curled protectively over the leads of a Glasser-Kamada transdermal unit. Crinkled, red-rimmed eyes above the oxygen mask regarded Clayton with bright, cold hate.

Linda edged past him and sat down on the cot, under the ventilation unit. She took a pack of cigarettes from the nightstand, lit one and watched the smoke trickle up into the ducts. When she looked up, her eyes were shiny and hard. "Why are you here, Frank? What do you want?"

He didn't know how to answer her, couldn't explain it to himself. "I came to see you," he said. The words sounded feeble and inane in his own ears. Why *was* he here? It felt unreal, like something he'd dreamed.

"You came to see me." For a split second, her face worked with emotion—grief or fury, he couldn't tell. Then the bland mask slammed back shut like an iron gate. She took a deep drag on her cigarette and stared past him, at the snaking line on the vitals monitor. "I know where you were, Frank. Where you went. You don't get to leave that place before your contract is up. Or until you're—what's the word? Reclaimed. No one gets to leave." She looked at him with open resentment. "I know all about it. They sent me the paperwork to countersign. Something to do with us still being married, I suppose. The network shill told me it would benefit both of us, protect the studio from liability and give me the rights to the royalties."

"I wanted you to have that."

"I didn't want anything to do with it. But I didn't have a choice, either. Our credit was sunk. If I refused, I would lose the apartment." She let the smoke out in a dry, rueful sigh. "Then Daddy got sick, and I lost the place anyway. The health conglomerates foreclosed on it. Now you're here. You've broken the contract, and I'll be on the hook if they sue."

"What happened to him?"

"His lung disease got worse. Then he had a stroke." She waved the cigarette at the life-support machines. "He needs all this junk to stay alive, but I can't keep up with the bills. Not without the royalties propping up my credit. The collection agency is coming next week to repossess it." With a bright, hateful smile, she indicated a pile of unopened mail on the dresser. "Estimates from the harvesting clinics. I don't think there's much for them to salvage, but you never can tell."

"I didn't know," Clayton said. He felt sick with guilt and self-loathing. The past merged seamlessly into the present;

he saw the two of them in another room, by another hospital bed, watching another life ebb under the hum of machines. Linda had already lost her child and she was about to lose the last person she cared about. He had failed then and he was failing her now. Failed his son, the memory of him and the life they'd all built together. He had loved Linda more than anything, but Josh had been what carried him through this awful world. "But I can take care of it. I have credit."

"I don't want your credit," she said with sudden fury, her inscrutable front swept away. He caught sight of the hatred in her eyes and was astounded by its depth and intensity. Her shoulders were tensed, her jaw clenched. "I don't want anything from you. Or from anybody. We tried to take what they gave us, and this is how it turned out."

"It doesn't have to be that way."

"What were you thinking, coming here? That we could act like nothing happened, pick up where we left off? That we could—" She clapped a hand over her mouth, as if horrified by what she was about to say. "Is that what this is about?"

"No." But that was a lie. The unspoken hung suspended between them. Seeing her this way, the naked misery and pain in her face, tore at his heart. "Linda, no. It doesn't have to be that way. I'll explain everything, but not here. We'll go away from here. We can leave right now."

Even before the words were out of his mouth, he realized he had miscalculated, made a mistake. Her face closed up once more, turned to stone. He felt the world drop away from under him. It was all wrong, all of it; nothing good was ever going to come out of him being here. The past they'd shared, so close in a temporal sense, was utterly irrecoverable. It was a terrifying thing to recognize—the hidden gulf separating them from each other, from the people they had once been. Anything he said would only make it worse.

"I don't want to leave." She spoke without anger, her voice flat and toneless. The cigarette had burned down almost to her fingers. She ground it out in a tray on the nightstand. "All I want is to never see you again."

"I'm sorry," he said. "About what happened after Josh died. I wish I could change it, but I can't. I fell apart, expected you to be the one to carry us through. I had no right. You deserved better than that."

"Josh didn't die," she said, very clearly, enunciating each word. "We killed him. We killed our son. A fresh start, that was the plan. A clean break. But there is no such thing, is there? Everything comes 'round in the end."

There was nothing left to say. A surge of hopelessness overwhelmed him. He turned to leave, paused with his hand on the doorknob.

Someone spoke his name. Linda's father was staring at him from the bed, propped on one elbow. The plastic oxygen mask was off the old man's white-stubbled face, the tube hooked over the respirator's meter gauge. Scrawny shoulders in faded, stained pajamas trembled with the effort of drawing breath into the rattling lungs.

"If there's a hell, I hope you burn in it, you sonofabitch."

The voice was weak, no more than a rasping croak. Linda got up, turned the old man over gently and settled the mask back into place. Clayton didn't wait to hear the hiss of the respirator. He turned the knob and let himself out.

Twenty

Out on the bridge, heading back across the canal, he popped another trank into his mouth and crunched it with his teeth. Tremors were spreading from the center of him, chemical-starved nerves screaming, the cold, muddy swell of paranoia. Crowds melded behind him, around him, a curved wall of bodies, faces driven and hungry-looking. His cheeks were wet, although he hadn't felt the tears start. He leaned over the railing and stared at the oil-scummed swirl of water below, hand clenched around the trank dispenser. Better to end it here and now. One foot over the side, then the other. Then the drop in the water and oblivion. Anything was better than this pathetic display of self-pity. Anything at all.

He let the half-raised dispenser drop back into his pocket. Something rattled against it. A smooth black metal oblong, curved as if to fit the inside of his palm. He looked at it dully, struggling to remember what it was. Prescott's key, the pass to the Aventus arcology. The answer to that final question he didn't want to ask himself.

On closer look, the shape wasn't as smooth as he'd taken it to be. One side was indented, fine lines raised in the metallike fingerprint ridges. A tiny crescent-shaped groove at the back, just wide enough to slip a thumbnail into. He almost did but thought again and put it away.

The trank turned circles around the inside of his skull; he flashed on the Deacon in the middle of the street, surrounded by flames, smiling and shaking his great bald head. He couldn't feel much now, and part of him sensed that this was bad, that he wasn't as frightened as he should be. That the border between the things in his head and the things around him was fraying, and soon wouldn't be there at all.

Reality snapped back, hard and sharp. He was in the foyer of the capsule hotel, a large, hollow hall whose ceiling rose away into darkness, broken at intervals by the neon lights that marked the floors. Tiers of fiberglass cubes, bracketed by battered steel panels, reflected the pulsing glow. A receptionist clad in black skinweave and leather looked up at him from behind the virtual pages of a celebrity magazine and pushed a chipped token through a slot in an iron-barred window. The cube was already paid for; the ident reader blinked green and spat out a thin plastic strip with a number printed on it in black.

He took the creaking elevator to the fourth floor. The cubes were stacked one atop the other, fifteen to a row, corrugated gangways and staircases weaving between them. Epoxied fiberglass and identical hatches, the number stenciled above an oval porthole window looking into darkness. An open space between the tiers of cubes served as a kind of lounge; there were chairs here, a scuffed vinyl sofa and an old television set playing the latest Newscan on silent. More footage from the water war in Central Asia; dust blowing across fields of slag, bearded figures in mismatched uniforms firing anti-tank guns at a barren hillside. The chiaroscuro of burning oilfields under a night sky, peasants scavenging the wreckage. Cutaway to a gunship belonging to a coast guard subcontractor opening fire on a slow-moving garbage scow, tearing up a makeshift camp of tents and shanties, refugees scampering overboard. On the sofa sat a man in a light climafiber duster, smoking and staring at the screen of a tablet computer. Apart from him, the lounge was empty.

He went up the stairs and fed the plastic strip into the lock of his cube. Fluorescents came on behind the frosted glass of the porthole. The packages he'd ordered were inside, laid out on the green memory foam, along with the valise that held his clothes and facelift kit. He counted the boxes to make sure they were all there, locked the hatch and started back down. Staying the night was out of the question. He had paid for a room in a hotel in Pennsport, a gated commercial-residential complex west of Canalside, next to the Associated Engineering arcology. If he showed up there with his purchases in tow, he'd draw unwanted

attention to himself. There were no laws restricting or reg-
ulating possession of their contents, but many transnationals, wary of anti-corporate terrorism, enacted their own
measures. He'd come back for the goods tomorrow.

The sensation hit him before he'd made it two flights
down, the awareness that someone was right behind him,
watching him. Trank paranoia, cold and fast, nerves on fire,
adrenaline surging behind the false calm of the drug.

Cold and sweating, Clayton stumbled into the empty
lounge.

On the screen, graphics indicated falling industrial
output in Free Enterprise Districts Two and Eight, two hundred thousand jobs on the line in the northeastern Spokes.
A spin doctor from the Trade and Finance Committee was
gesturing the projections away, her smile fixed, her skin
gray and sick under the layers of studio makeup.

"Excuse me." The man he'd seen earlier was at his elbow, hand extended. He seemed to have materialized out
of thin air. Pale eyes in a fine-boned face, a shock of light
brown hair. A nondescript face, forgettable and ageless,
anywhere between thirty and fifty. An athlete's arms and
shoulders on a lean, spare frame. "I'm looking for someone.
A guest of this hotel. Perhaps you can help me."

"I haven't seen anyone," Clayton said. He wanted to
move away, but the overhead lights held him still. In a single fluid step, the man closed the distance between them,
blocking the way to the elevator.

"This is the right place," he said, holding the tablet out
for Clayton to see. The screen lit with a map of Canalside,
the location of the capsule hotel a red, pulsing dot. "I think
that the man I'm looking for is here. It's very important that
I find him as soon as possible. Before something untoward
happens."

"I don't know what you're talking about." Fear, raw and
pure, distilled to a single crystal-sharp point. He scanned
the hallway behind the man with the tablet. No one there,
but he felt surrounded, without knowing how or why.

"Take a closer look." Swipe of the finger and the map
faded away. An image grew steadily on the screen, expanding from a pinpoint of black. The angles and planes of a
face, long and saturnine, topped by a mop of dark hair,

156

against the backdrop of a network recruitment poster. Next to the Tristar-Paramount logo, a name hung suspended in red capitals. Clayton's breath caught in his throat.

His old face. His old name.

"Let me tell you something about this man." Not so much as a flicker in the stranger's eyes. One was brighter than the other, Clayton noticed, the pupil tracking a fraction of a second slower. High-grade visual inlays analyzing the dilation of his irises, the rate of his breathing, the pulse in his neck artery, infrared emanations from his skin. "He's desperate and confused. He's starting to make mistakes. That makes him a liability, to himself and others. A dangerous liability."

Clayton eyed the distance between them. The man read his expression. His other hand came out from under the duster, holding a short-barreled pistol. "Sabot rounds," he said, as if apologizing. "Messy, but effective, especially at this distance. Please don't try anything foolish." The uncanny speed and smoothness of his movements suggested some sort of neural enhancement.

Realization sank in like a knife, chilled Clayton's blood. The man was a fabricant, a made-to-specs cloned assassin, riddled through with wetware. Corporate property. Somehow the studio had found him, just when he'd started to think he'd given them the slip. In Canalside, of all places.

"Who are you?"

"Sit down." The fabricant motioned with the gun. Clayton slid to the end of the sofa. Moving like oiled smoke, the stranger snapped the tablet shut, tucked it into his coat and folded himself into a chair opposite. "My name is Ethan Quain."

"I'll take a guess. You're the studio's hit man. Or a contract enforcement thug."

"I'm the new head of security for Tristar-Paramount." Quain's augmented gaze was the coldest thing Clayton had ever seen, probing and intelligent, ruthless. "Your contract breach doesn't concern me, Clayton. Or do you go by Decker now? I'm here on my own. I came to offer you a deal. A settlement, if you prefer."

"Why would I believe that?"

"Because you're still alive," Quain said. "Because you don't have a choice. You'll understand that once we're finished talking. You'll come to see the situation from my point of view. Do you know how long it took me to track you down?"

"No."

"Seventy-three seconds." It was a plain statement of fact, without a trace of triumph. "Through the credit exchange. A crawler program picked you out when you paid for the room, a few days ago. Lit up the system like a Christmas tree—a foreign official staying the night in Canalside. Didn't mean much on its own. But the same foreign official was picked up by an ad screen in the Federal District right before the fire. The same foreign official bought firearms. A quantity of CorpSec-grade, customized firearms, deliverable to the same Canalside address. All I had to do was sit tight and wait for you to show up." The assassin touched his ear in the same spot where Clayton's was missing a piece, pointed at the flesh-colored prosthetic covering the scar. "Also that. Good enough to trick a facial scanner, but I can always tell."

"How many of you?"

"I came alone."

"Right," Clayton said. "To make me an offer."

"You think you have everything under control." Quain stretched his legs and slipped the gun into a shoulder holster. "You don't. This isn't going to go away. You owe the networks fourteen months of your life, but now it's gone beyond that. It's not about the contract anymore. The execs are out for your blood." Something like curiosity crept into the corporate agent's voice. "They're afraid. Of what you represent. Of what Douglas Prescott taught you, or thought he did. You've become an unknown."

"Not to you."

"Not to me. But for the elites, you're the ultimate fear. Loss of security. Collapse of the established order. Terrorists breaching the corporate sanctum. Prescott was an insider. He saw the chink in their armor. The fortress they have built around themselves, the same rules that keep them untouchable, protected Prescott as well. You could become the virus in the system, disguised as one of their own, breaching their defenses. Insidious and invisible, lethal. These aren't people who take chances. Some other corpmerc will track you, like I tracked you. Or you'll make another mistake."

A hard grin found Clayton's face. "I got away once."

"That was a debacle." Quain pulled out a silver cigarette case and offered one to Clayton, lit up with a thin square of engraved metal. For a moment only inches separated them, but Clayton knew that the gun was still within the man's reach, that if he tried to make a move, he'd be dead before he left his seat. "Tristar-Paramount pulled a lot of strings to bring it off. Government police don't get involved in contractual disputes, and the private ones tend to be protective of their turf. Any security operation in the Federal District must be cleared weeks in advance." He smiled and wagged a finger. "You caused quite a commotion. The fallout was unbelievable. Heads rolled, including that of my predecessor. But it was a fluke, a bad call. It won't happen again."

"You're sure of that."

"Yes. I'm in charge of the operation now. There's a contract out on you, redeemable in stock options. Removal with extreme prejudice. Even if you get lucky once or twice, which is unlikely, they'll just send someone else. Or you'll be taken alive and shipped to one of their containment facilities. You don't want that to happen. There's no coming back from what they will do to you there."

Clayton shifted on the vinyl seat. He could feel his exhaustion as a living thing, a physical presence in the room with them. "They."

"What?"

"You keep saying they. Like you're not one of them."

A pause. "Tristar-Paramount pays my salary, but I represent a different interest."

"Who?"

"I'm not at liberty to say." Cold eyes watched him closely through a stream of smoke. "Some time ago I was approached with an offer. At the time, I was a senior field operative, assigned to follow Prescott Junior and make sure the situation didn't get out of hand. Pay off the right people, threaten everyone else. What the other party wanted was detailed information about his movements. Places, names, dates. Standard industrial espionage. A rival network seeking to use Tristar-Paramount's problem heir for blackmail. Or so I thought."

"So you sold out and became a mole."

"It's a cutthroat business," Quain said, unoffended. "In every sense of the word. You don't need me to tell you that."

"What did they want with Prescott?"

"Everyone is looking for an edge. The corporates are like sharks, always looking for a weakness they can exploit to devour the competition. For the studio, Douglas Prescott was that weakness. Groomed from birth to be a leader of industry. All for nothing. Asocial behavior from an early age, rejection of authority, disdain for hierarchy. Our birth clinics claim to have engineered such traits out of the arcology gene pool, but it still happens. When it does, the children are taken to behavioral adjustment centers, or to undergo psychosurgical treatment. Sometimes they don't come back. Cancer must be cut out before it's had a chance to spread. But the top echelons, they play by their own rules. A controlling interest in the studio makes up for a multitude of sins. Everyone knew about Fulton Prescott's son, yet somehow it never came up in screening."

The lighter in his long fingers caught the fluorescent overheads and glittered. "Had it been anyone other than the heir to the Tristar-Paramount empire, he would have been *disappeared,* or turned into a vegetable. The Board thought he could be treated or argued into reason."

"But you knew better."

"After they told me to back off," Quain said, ignoring the barb, "I decided to work my own investigation. That's how I found out about the lawyer in East Central and the fake identities. About the cyber criminals who helped him tunnel into the corporate servers and set up infiltration points. I was paid very well to keep my new employers abreast of the situation. Then Prescott Junior signed up for the show and my services were no longer required. Until you came along. This other party is intrigued by Conrad Decker. Which brings us back to the offer."

"Why me?"

"Haven't you guessed already?" Hidden amusement played around Quain's mouth and eyes. "They want Decker to do what he does best. They want him to kill."

Clayton said nothing.

"You didn't have a problem with it in the war zone," Quain said.

"It's not the same," Clayton said slowly. His mouth was dry, and the words clogged in his throat. *Someone who knows how to handle a knife and a gun,* the Deacon spoke up in his head. *Who isn't squeamish about getting his hands dirty.*

He saw the man in gray uniform wheeling Josh into the white building. His son's eyes, haunted and beyond hope of rescue, resigned to the sacrifice.

"It's the same, no matter what side of the wall you're on. The violence is inside you. Like it or not, Tristar-Paramount made you, Clayton. They did things to your brain. Chemical conditioning, disorientation techniques. The same tried and tested method the government used in the military before the deregulation. Anyone can be turned into a killer. All it takes is the right mix of conditioning and circumstances. That was how armies operated. Recruit a psychotic and turn him into a soldier. Drugs silence the voices in his head. Soldier kills for drugs. Over time, violence becomes a coping mechanism. Without it, you start to come unraveled."

"I'll take my chances."

"You're not paying attention," Quain said. "Fulton Prescott wants you dead, whatever it takes. It's personal for him. He refuses to believe the psych reports on his boy and he's blaming you for everything. For brainwashing him, getting him killed. He's quite irrational about it."

"So you're offering a trade. Someone else's life for mine."

"The studio used you as an expendable asset, just another body to throw in front of the cameras. My employers recognize your potential is far higher." Quain finished his cigarette and laced his fingers over one knee. "You took to the conditioning better than most others. Every enlisted man is converted into numbers and fed into a computer. Did you know? They call it survival modeling. Thousands of preprogrammed statistical profiles. The networks use it to work out the odds, make sure they don't run out of cannon fodder. Maximize the return per corpse."

A slow, almost appreciative nod of the head. "You were a face in the crowd, unremarkable. No prior combat training, no athletic background. Desk jockey from Canalside. Married, but separated. One child, deceased, euthanasia by consent. History of depression, blacklisted for alcoholism, loss of credit and status. There are thousands like you in the slums, maybe millions. They die in the gutter, or as debt slaves, or under an autosurgeon in some back-alley organ trafficking outfit. The models gave you eleven days in the zone, with a delta of thirty-seven hours. You survived almost seven months, at the end of which you escaped the zone. Beat all expectations."

"Lucky me," Clayton said. The muscles of his face seemed to have set, stiff and unyielding, exposing his teeth. Quain was right. He had not escaped. The killing zone spread on both sides of the wall. It went on forever, and no matter how far you ran you always came back to where you'd started. They had been ahead of him at every step of the way. Perhaps even the rage driving him was a conditioned response, the pain he felt at the memory of Josh a chemical phantom burned into his mind. Even that belonged to them. Even that he couldn't claim for his own.

"It wasn't luck. You're the survivor type. No statistical model, no behavioral program, no matter how sophisticated, can pick out survivor types for certain. Who breaks down under pressure and who thrives. Not until they're out on the killing field. That's what makes the show such a success."

"There must be others who are better at this sort of thing. Contract killers, corporate assassins."

"True, but they are real, and Conrad Decker is a ghost. No credit transfers, no paper trail, no fake accounts to set up." Quain studied Clayton's face. "Whether you succeed or fail, there's nothing to trace back to the source. You don't know who's behind the hit, or what it means. If you get caught, you're just a delusional psychotic with an ax to grind against the system. No connection to us. Tristar-Paramount will be too busy covering themselves to try to figure out the how and why. Bleeding hearts in the media will point the finger at the post-traumatic stress disorder and dehumanization in the zone, demand the networks take the war shows off air. A few days later it will all be forgotten."

"What if I say no?"

"I'll turn you in. Tell the network that one of Prescott's identities has gone active. In twenty minutes, they'll be all over Canalside."

"You're not going to bring me in yourself? Claim the big payout?"

"Tempting," Quain said. "But it would raise too many questions. I took too many risks, broke protocols. My new employers prefer to keep a low profile. They may decide I'm no longer an asset. That I know too much." The pale eyes caught Clayton's gaze, held it. "There's nothing for you to think about. Prescott's dream of vengeance is dead. Without him, you do not stand a chance of getting in. Aventus Spire is the best guarded corporate arcology on the eastern seaboard. If you try to go through with it, you'll die for nothing. An awful waste."

"Is that the only reason?"

"No." The same secret amusement lit up the agent's eyes again. "I'm also interested in seeing how this will all play out. There's something about you I can't put my finger on. But I feel that we have more in common than either of us can imagine, you and I. Like that stunt you pulled in the Federal District. Burned down half the Archives to get out of a trap. Killed a labor gang boss to get out of the tunnels. Survivor reflexes explain some of it, but not all. Nothing explains *you.*"

Instinctively, the fabricant's hand moved an inch closer to his shoulder holster. "One part of me wants to destroy you like one would a rabid weasel. That would be the rational thing to do. Another part wants to let you into the henhouse and watch what happens." Quain shook his head, as if amazed. "Perhaps there's a beast inside us all. Someone unknown, pulling the strings. Sooner or later we all have to face that someone. Confront what's inside."

Through the fog of rage and despair, a single thought pulsed in Clayton's mind. Quain had the upper hand but didn't know about Prescott's key. "I still haven't heard the offer," he said, trying to keep his voice even.

"Certainly," Quain replied. "We kill Conrad Decker and you get to keep his credit. All of it. You'd have to leave the country after the deed is done, of course. Start again. Go to Honshu Conurb and check yourself into a gene recoding clinic. Get a new face while you're at it. Then head over to the Parana Economic Area or the Great Lakes Republic, launder your newfound wealth. Wipe out all traces of both Decker and Clayton. Wealth and longevity, the opportunity to begin anew. No doubt you've thought about this already." He moved his head from side to side. "There are other things we could do. Psychosurgery could erase your memories. Take away the pain. But I have the feeling that none of that matters to you. The pain is what defines you. Without it you'd be dead already."

"That doesn't sound like much of an offer."

"There's your ex-wife to think about."

Clayton started up, his fists tightening. Quain held up his hands. "We don't intend to harm her. But you could help her. A better job, a higher credit rating. She could keep her father alive or give him the best hospice care available. Move on. Her child permit is still active, you know." He regarded Clayton calmly, let his words sink in before delivering the final blow. "She could have the life you were never able to give her. It's not too late for that."

Helpless anger rose inside Clayton, a cold fury at himself, at this engineered killer, at the invisible bars surrounding him. He struggled to tamp it down. "If I do this for you," he said, forcing the words through closed teeth, "she can never find out."

"You have my word on that," the agent said. "Do we have a deal?"

"Just one other thing." Clayton leaned forward on his knees. "Who do I have to kill?"

Twenty-One

Mirrored blast walls threw brilliant shards of morning sun across the ferry terminal. Spires and gilded domes formed a tangled grid of light, the vast shapes of the launch platforms edged in red beacons. As the automated ship approached, dark ramparts rose out of the sea, waves spuming and frothing at their base. With a grind and a shudder, the engines reversed, and the ferry drifted between the 'lander docks, aiming for its berth.

Through the misted windows of the first-class salon, Clayton watched the floating agrolanders, each the size of a skyscraper laid on its side, their metal shielding scoured and scarred, being towed to the launch gantries. There was nothing beyond the 'lander docks, save the vastness of the Atlantic. He left his drink unfinished, picked up his bag and went down to the exit ramp.

It was the second day of the famine relief summit, and security in Canaveral City was tight. Armed drones and heavy gunships circled above the harbor; soldiers in full assault armor prowled the glass-fronted terminal building, rifles at the ready, corralling the disembarking crowds into lines for the customs and immigration checks. The launch center was an independent territory, administered by the United Nations through international agreement. There were few chairs at the negotiating table, but no limit had been set on the number of observers from the participating nations. Dignitaries were arriving in force, each trailing an entourage of aides and bodyguards, swelling the already crowded ranks of Canaveral City's engineers, workers and bureaucrats. The harbor swarmed with people.

A bleary-eyed, overworked immigration officer took no more than a passing glance at Conrad Decker's summit observer pass. His bag came through unopened. He followed the signs through customs and into the arrivals hall, mov-

ing in cadence with the crowd, avoiding the patrolling soldiers.

Outside the terminal gates, connecting walkways
weaved between the dark, forbidding shapes of silos and
platforms. Orbital shuttles sat cradled in skeletal gantries,
geared for liftoff, noses pointed at the heavens. Visitors
clustered under the blast walls and behind fences, posing,
taking pictures or perusing commemorative holos. On the
far side of the platform, a pillar of fire roared into the sky as
a booster took off for the orbitals. The wind carried the salt
tang of the ocean under heavy layers of oil and kerosene.

Clayton walked down to the concrete promontory,
bought a bag of fried soybeans from a food stall and sat on
a bench looking down at the foaming waves, the simmering
horizon. Bright blue over ink-black waters, clouds building in the distance like a phantom fleet. He took the photograph from his valise and smoothed it out on his knee.
Tried to close his eyes and see Josh, but time had blurred
the image in his head, worn it to blankness.

He let the photo slip through his fingers. The wind
picked it up and it turned a lazy somersault over the railing
and was gone.

The hotel room, booked at an exorbitant price, over-
looked the conference hall, its entrance festooned with
flags. His packages were stacked in one corner, delivered
in a sealed diplomatic shipping crate to skirt customs. That
sort of thing took serious clout and insiders in more places
than he could begin to imagine. Whoever Quain's employers were, they would pull out all the stops to get what they
wanted. He blacked out the windows, piled the foam boxes
on the bed and started unpacking.

Assembling the Bushmaster-Bofors graphite rifle took
him the best part of an hour. His palms sweated over the
unfamiliar parts, the firing cell refused to slot into place
behind the electrochemical propellant charge. The rifle had
an automatic setting but was primarily designed for snip-
ing. Ultralight frame, smart targeting imager to guide the
ceramic bullets. Taken apart and folded, it fit inside a briefcase or under a long coat and didn't show up on a weapons
scan. He had bought the rifle for the assault on Aventus,
back when his plan—if it could be called a plan—had been

to move fast and shoot from cover or a distance, avoiding a direct firefight with the corpmercs until the last instant. Kill as many as he could before they gunned him down. Escape had never factored into the equation before. He took the rifle apart, then restarted the process, timing himself, forcing his fingers to work faster. There wasn't much time left for practice.

The charge pistol was easier to handle, a heavy eleven-millimeter Tokarev KBP with a recoil brake, almost identical to the old firing-pin weapons he'd used in the war zone. Explosive-tipped rounds guaranteed to stop a man in his tracks from one hundred and twenty feet away. At close range, in a confined space, it could take off a limb or spread a target's insides over a wide radius. It was a nasty weapon, a last resort.

Both weapons came with full warranty. The seller had thrown in two clips for free and included a coupon for ten percent off next order. He tucked the pistol under the pillow and opened the remaining packages.

The caster rig consisted of a simple headset with a transparent eyescreen and a wireless feed to a long-range transmitter worn on the belt. Microcams were mounted in the set for full three-sixty view. He had seen camera operators wear similar rigs in the war zone and knew how to work them. Calibrating the uplink module would take time and effort, but he wasn't sure he would end up using it after all.

The medikit, a combat-grade Allied Therapeutics model, held a hypodermic injector, a small can of coagulant spray and another of antiseptic, a pair of syntheskin derms, two units of blood and a set of liquid ampules. Blue for endomorphin peptides, if he got hit, red for amphetamines, to keep him going. The last package contained several vials of Synthazine and a month's supply of tranks. Contraband currency he could use in the streets, worth far more than Conrad Decker's credit.

He swept the empty boxes to the floor, folded the rifle into his valise. Locked the remaining items into the room safe and lay down on the bed to think.

Quain had narrowed it down to two options; take down the target when he stepped up to the podium to address the audience, or somewhere along his way to the conference hall, which he accessed through an underground security tunnel. The first option made the killing part easier. Several locations in the high gallery offered a clean line of sight to the stage, an easy shot for even a mediocre marksman. But shooting from the gallery made it difficult to get out of the building before security locked it down, and there was no margin for error. If he wanted to escape, he would only have one shot, maybe two, to get the job done.

The second option was messier and less reliable. It necessitated taking out the target's personal security detail, which meant a gunfight in the close space of the tunnel. But the tunnel afforded several escape routes into a network of old service shafts beneath the launch platforms. He didn't have long to decide. The target would deliver the closing remarks on the day after tomorrow.

Getting in would not be a problem. He had a valid observer pass identifying him as Conrad Decker, a diplomat with the Antillean Trade Mission, and a UN maintenance keycard with another name for access to the security tunnel. It was the getting-out part that would pose difficulty, if it could be done at all. Somehow, he didn't think saving him had factored into Quain's calculations.

He flipped through the loose pages in the folder the security agent had given him. Maps and floor plans from satellite imagery and building blueprints. Routes, security rosters and timetables, the rotation of the target's bodyguards in minute detail. Quain's mysterious employers must have been planning this for some time. An operation this big took a lot of support, involved dozens of key players in high positions to make sure there were no leaks.

Large glossy photographs pulled from Newscans and corporate websites showed the target from a variety of angles. Ramesh Rustin, the twelfth Colonial Governor of Gyges, one of the first generation of human beings born and raised Topside, in the orbital colonies. In one of the photos he was disembarking from a landing shuttle, looking up at the sky above Canaveral City, his expression indecipherable. A sojourner in an alien, hostile land. The Governor's torso and limbs were strapped into a powered exoskeleton to counter the crushing gravitational grip of a world that didn't recognize him as its own. Filter mask and oxygen hoses provided air to lungs unaccustomed to Earthside's toxic brew of pollutants. In another photo, he gazed at the camera with a smile: a thin face, elongated eyes like jags of black glass, delicate bones and organs shaped by life in perpetual free-fall. He and others like him were the next step in mankind's evolutionary line, a testament to the skill of Topside genetic engineers determined to carry the human germ into the dead infinity of space.

There had been rumors of strange experiments up in the colonies, some doubtlessly exaggerated, some ground-breaking—new crop strains, developments in spaceflight mass driver technology. Rustin had declined to comment on them, repeating instead for the United Nations' official line: the orbitals existed for the benefit of mankind, a life-line ferrying food to Earth's starving billions. Now someone wanted him dead. Clayton studied the floor plans, thinking through possible approach and escape routes. His brain ached from trying to take it all in.

At some point he must have dozed off, because when he opened his eyes he was face down on the bed and the contents of the folder lay scattered across the floor. He rubbed a hand over his face and sat up. The digital clock on the wall screen showed early afternoon. He couldn't remember much of the dream, but Salvesen had been in it, blood pouring from his mouth and the gash in his belly, finger pointed up at an unwinking black sky.

Try to get off world. Look for the orbitals.

Getting up, he rooted through his pockets for the trank dispenser. It was empty. He tossed it into the trash basket, dug into the pocket again and took out Prescott's key.

The smooth metal parted as he slid his thumbnail into the groove on its side, separating into two pieces. One of them looked like a datawafer. The other one was hollow in the middle and when he held it up to the light, he saw a tiny button inside. He waited for his hands to steady, then used a bent paperclip to press the button. On the outer surface, a red LED blinked once and went out. He pressed the button again and the same thing happened.

Queasy anxiety filled him, the feeling he had done something that couldn't be taken back. Metal glinted, cold in his palm. He sat on the bed, trying to think.

You need a different set of eyes to see the key.

The memory of Prescott's parting words brought back the bland, generic face of the cloned killer in the neon flare of Canalside, his faded blue eyes threaded with top-notch wetware. Perhaps the message was coded, scrambled to keep it from being revealed by accident.

He couldn't make the connection right away, but it would come to him. Pulling on his clothes, he snapped the pieces back together, slipped the key into his pocket and turned the wall screen on.

Twenty-Two

Dinner was greasy soy steaks washed down with luke-warm beer in a cafe at the top of the waterfront wall. The only other patrons were two oil-rig toughs glued to the television above the bar and an old drunk slumped in a corner booth. Clayton sat facing the windows and watched the night rise out of the sea, the stars come out like the lights of a limitless city scene far away. He smoked the last of his cigarettes and studied his own face in the glass, or the face that had become his own.

The waterfront was stirring to life when he walked out. Diplomats rubbed elbows with workers in overalls, flight engineers crowding the gaudily lit bars and clubs alongside somber-suited bodyguards and UN soldiers in dress blues. Holograms shifted and swarmed above the entrances, blurring into each other, a snarl of brilliant angles and flowering phosphene forms. Modulated music from the bars pumped subsonic rhythm through his solar plexus, shivered the concrete walkway beneath his soles.

Three blocks from the cafe he found the entertainment complex, a huge empty warehouse broken up into booths. Machinery hummed under a conduit-laced ceiling. Bright counters cast holographic corporate logos into the half-light of the main hall. Behind the TransCore desk, a shaved-headed girl in a tight polycarbon suit gazed up at him with a vacant, automatic smile. Simulated landscapes and phantasmal skylines undulated on the walls of the booth, melded into one another, spelling out WHEREVER YOU MAY DREAM in hi-res sky blue.

"I want a single cube," he said, handing over his ident card. "Full immersion. Half an hour."

The girl nodded and passed the card across the scanner. Long blue fingernails tapped keys, returned the plastic strip over the counter. Her smile widened as the credit rank popped up, lustrous eyes under microblade eyebrows. "Certainly, sir. Have you decided on a destination?"

He scrolled through the synesthetic vacation options on the display and chose one at random. "Excellent choice," the girl said, handing him a folded bathrobe and towel. A number appeared on the screen and a door slid open behind her.

Soft lights in a long corridor, the faint smell of soap and antiseptic. No sound came out from the numbered doors. Muted red lights shone from the empty cubes, hidden motion sensors picking up his presence, holographic flesh slinking down from overhead demonstration screens, stretching, twisting, moaning.

He undressed and scrubbed himself in a white-tiled shower stall, stepped out into the bathrobe, his clothes folded over his arm. Further down the hall he found his cubicle and pressed his ident against the black glass of the reader.

Magnetic locks clicked open. The cubicle was barely wide enough for him to stretch his arms out wide, lit by adhesive fluorescent strips, walls and floor padded to render it soundproof. Music piped in from overhead speakers, bland and almost inaudible. The black polymer coffin of the isolation tank took up most of the room. As soon as the door closed behind him, the tank's instrument panels lit up and a dial started counting down from thirty minutes. The top of the tank slid open and a nest of dermatrodes emerged from the left armrest.

He took off the bathrobe and lowered himself into the tank, his right fist closed around Prescott's datawafer. The back of the coffin was molded to fit the contours of the body and the inside was filled with a ten percent magnesium sulfide solution. The tank was designed to hold the inert body suspended in warm, directionless darkness, placing it into a state of deep relaxation while synthetic memories and sensations were fed into the brain. Touch, smell, sight, taste and sound were streamed directly into the cortex and etched deep, more vivid and longer-lasting than any real experience. He had never used one before, but a coworker had once told him that the synesthetic unit removed all sense of time; thirty minutes in the tank could stretch into weeks in this altered headspace.

When he sat down, the liquid rose to his chest, unpleasantly warm, wrapping itself around his bare skin with repulsive intimacy. The headgear descended from the ceiling, a huge sensor-studded helmet trailing a thick fiberoptic cable. On his right, a compartment opened to reveal a pink derm of MDMA analog. Animated instructions popped up on the console screen, showing him the arrangement of the gear, the application of the drug.

He reached behind the helmet and unplugged the mainframe cable. The console blared red. He pulled the disconnected headgear on and lowered the eyepiece. Under the surface, his left hand found the synesthetic switch and flicked it on.

Cold, wet dermatrodes at his temples.

Multiple sensations at once; the taste of metal and ashes in his mouth, a disorienting sense of intrusion, cruel fingers plucking at his optic nerves.

Shimmering layers of color exploded on the rim of his consciousness. The walls and ceiling folded into themselves, disappeared down the black hole at the back of his head. Automated warnings flashed across his field of vision.

Clayton thrashed helplessly, clawing for purchase, finding only spinning void. Cut off from the mainframe feed, the gear's sensory input overlapped with his own, garbled visuals trickling like rain on a window. The room bled in through the hypnagogic shapes like broken film. Competing realities tugged at his sanity as he careened toward the precipitous edge of neural burnout.

Somewhere at the end of the universe, his right fist opened, pushed the button.

It was working. Blue streaks rose in his vision, a street grid with the coordinates traced in green, superimposed over the dark room and the angles of the tank. The program, a simple loop of encrypted code, had been designed to stream directly into Prescott's optical implants, and meshed imperfectly with his jury-rigged solution; the lines blurred together and some of the symbols were scrambled. Location crosshairs closed around an address, and a telephone link came up. He tried to focus on it, but the pixels dissolved, drained like dirty water down a sink. Darkness spread out from the center of the grid, and in the darkness a half-formed face.

173

White worms burrowed in his eyes, squirmed in his brain. He tore at his face and his fingers scrabbled on the plastic of the eyepiece. Throwing the headgear off, he leaned over the armrest and retched.

Green and purple afterimages burned on his retinas.

Fear sheened him in slick, slimy sweat. In a brief flash of vision, he had seen his body on a mortuary table, the automated processing unit poised above him like a polished steel spider. Meat knives glistening in cold light, descending. Cutting into the waning warmth of him in a thick spray of blood. Dark redness inched down the runnels. There had been no escape, no Conrad Decker, only the wreckage of the train and the war zone wall. It was all a dream, the death-fantasy of a fading consciousness.

Angry beeping from the console brought him back. He rolled over the side of the tank and lay on the floor, the liquid puddling around him. A synthetic voice informed him that connection to the mainframe had been interrupted. Perspective shifted; the planes of the room changed places. He was upright, the rough padding of the wall under his hands and cheek. Grabbing his clothes from their hook, pulling them on, he stumbled out into the corridor.

The passage melted into a blur. From an open door, a fat man with a towel knotted around his ample waist stared at him. Hologram bodies flickered in the darkness behind the man, naked and shining.

Then the meat grinder was back, its blades slashing down. The fat man vanished, and the Deacon took his place, laughing without a sound, the ruins of his teeth wet with blood. Carnage glistened red inside the cubicle, bodies contorted at odd angles.

Reality snapped back like someone had thrown a switch. He rubbed his cheeks. The world felt thin, like ice. The address and the telephone number burned in his mind with unnatural clarity.

Subliminals. The bastard had fed him subliminals through the key unit's encrypted broadcast, a trail of breadcrumbs to follow to the bottom of the mystery. Even in death, Prescott had kept an ace up his sleeve.

The girl at the counter started to say something but stopped when she saw his face. He walked past, into the night. Outside, the visions lingered, and he had to work to shake them off, to piece the real world together.

Beyond the edge of the water, the warm night split with a crash of thunder. One of the agrolander boosters roared into the blackness. Fire unstitched itself from the waves, threading through the concussed sky, rattling the windows.

He shut his eyes, but the fiery trail remained, sketched across the backs of his eyelids, spinning away.

Back at the hotel, he sat over the telephone for a long time, then dialed the number. On the fourth ring, a voice answered. "Hello?" A man's voice, flat and weary. On the screen, the phone link showed IDENT WITHHELD. "Hello?"

Clayton hung up.

Twenty-Three

He came out of a nightmare of blood and pursuit and into the darkened hotel room. The sheets were damp with sweat, and his stomach was in knots. In a corner of the wall screen, a small window displayed live updates from the famine relief summit. He checked the agenda. The Colonial Governor's address was scheduled for the end of the afternoon session, broadcast across all the major networks. That gave him almost eight hours.

Gathering the plans and photos, he dumped them in the bathroom sink and ran the faucet until the paper dissolved. He packed his things, dressed and walked across the square to the conference hall, flashing his observer pass through the checkpoints. His dark microweave suit, light coat and valise made him indistinguishable from the droves of reporters and politicos milling through the gates.

At the entrance, he removed his mirrored glasses for the camera, scanned his pass and shoved his coat and valise through a weapon scanner. He steeled himself, but the device remained silent. The UN trooper manning the scanner nodded him through. "Have a good day, sir," he said to Clayton. Clayton thought he caught a knowing look in the trooper's eye, but the press of new arrivals carried him forward before he could be sure.

It was nine thirty-four when he entered the crowded lobby. He crossed the marble-paneled vestibule and climbed the staircase to the upper galleries. The morning coffee break was underway, and most of the top rows were empty. He walked behind the seats and let himself into an empty maintenance room at the end of the gallery.

The door opened at the touch of his keycard. An iron ladder bolted to the wall led to a narrow catwalk that ran under the roof. He went up slowly, carrying the valise in one hand, hugging the ladder in the crook of his arm.

The catwalk terminated in a wide ledge, heaped with broken equipment and coils of dusty cable. Several stories below, delegates mingled and strolled across the conference floor. He sat and opened the valise, took out the stock and firing mechanism of the graphite rifle. From hidden compartments sewn into his overcoat he removed the scope, the magazine and the broken-down barrel. He assembled the rifle, mounted the scope and sighted down to the speaker's podium.

Elevation, distance and range focus scrolled down in the scope's optic feedback screen. He swept it across the floor, swung it up to the row of projection and lighting booths above the other wing of the gallery. Nothing yet. Far below, the commotion settled, the observers filing back into their seats. He lowered the rifle, leaned back and waited, his eyes on the dark windows of the booths.

Hours trickled by. The hall echoed with voices and applause, the faces of the speakers changing on the conference screen. Spotlights burned, multiplied in the booth windows.

Movement caught his eye. A shadow twisted behind the dusty glass of a booth and the pane slid aside, a rifle barrel protruding over the sill. A backup shooter, zeroing his weapon.

Either they doubted his ability to get the job done or suspected that he wouldn't be able to go through with it. Perhaps they didn't believe in leaving loose ends and the bullet was intended for him. It didn't seem likely; the angle was wrong, and the cramped space left little room for the shooter to maneuver. That left the podium as the most likely target.

He raised the scope to his eye. The figure was a darker smear against the gloom of the booth. From his perch, all Clayton could see were the barrel and a hand in a black glove. He glanced at the clock behind the platform. Murmurs among the delegations as the afternoon session drew to a close.

On the lighted podium, the Secretary-General announced the final speaker. Approval rose from the floor as the bulky form slowly made its way across the platform, spotlights glistering on the duralloy and carbon of its exoskeleton. The face of Governor Rustin, magnified to fill the

screen, loomed over the heads of the audience. He had removed his oxygen mask in the filtered atmosphere of the
hall and was smiling at the auditorium. Through the scope,
Clayton counted the security detail at the edge of the platform. They would not be close enough to intervene.

He found the target in the scope, took a deep breath
and held it. Light pressure on the trigger, mind empty of everything but the aim. Green lights lit the vision field as the
nanocircuits in the ceramic bullets came online.

The Governor's voice boomed out of the speakers.

On the other end of the gallery, the rifle barrel moved
imperceptibly.

Feedback optics locked on the target, dialed adjust-
ments into the scope field. Clayton waited for them to line
up, then squeezed the trigger. Once, twice, three times, exhaled breath merging with the sigh of the firing mechanism.

All three rounds exploded through glass and flesh. The
figure jerked and fell back into the booth, dropping the rifle.
One by one, the tracers in Clayton's scope turned red, con-
firming that the smart rounds had found their mark.

Shouts of shock and confusion rang out as bloody
shards showered the spectators on the gallery. The shots
had gone unheard beneath the noise in the hall, and people
were craning their necks to see where the glass had come
from. There was no movement behind the shattered window. He wrapped the rifle in his coat, tossed it behind a coil
of cable and started across the catwalk.

By the time he came out of the maintenance room,
commotion had spread through the gallery. Security agents
were pushing through the spectators, climbing toward the
projection booths. Down on the conference floor, the Governor had stopped speaking and was gazing up, eyes half
shut against the glare of spotlights. Heads were turning toward the noise. Security staff in dark suits swarmed the
platform, waving their arms and shielding the delegates.
Fractured frames flashed on the conference screen as television cameras roamed the auditorium.

Up on the gallery, anxious spectators gathered in the
aisles. Clayton moved unnoticed through the crowd, an-
gling toward the stairway. He had to get out of the building
before they sealed the exits. The layout of the conference

center revolved in his mind. Down below he could hear soldiers rushing up the stairs, orders being relayed.

Three flights later, he felt a roar of fear and shock reverberate through the walls. The security detail must have found the shooter. He shouldered his way to an emergency exit, opened it with his maintenance keycard and stepped in.

He took the curving stairs several at a time, listening for sounds of pursuit. Deeper and deeper into the building, he headed for the basement, navigating from memory. Every second he spent here, every mistake, could be his last.

At the bottom of the stairs was a row of metal doors, padlocked and chained. Clayton went to the second door on the right and rattled the handle, as he'd been instructed to. The padlock was cut, and the chain slithered to the floor. He squeezed into the narrow opening, ducking his head under a rusty pipe and brushing cobwebs aside.

The passage led to the back of the conference center. He stripped off his suit, rolled it up with the sunglasses and stuffed it in the space between the pipe and the wall. Underneath he wore the blue-gray coveralls and shirt of the UN maintenance crew.

Out on the checkpoints, two armored cruisers were pulling up to the riot-control barriers. Walking fast, but careful to avoid attention, he crossed the square and turned into an alley that ran past the hotel's staff entrance and kitchen door.

The pistol and the small durafiber backpack were where he'd left them the night before, taped to the wall behind one of the huge trash compactors. Inside the bag were the caster rig, the medikit and the drugs. He pulled down his coveralls, slung the backpack on and zipped them back up. The pack barely made a bulge. His handmade shoes went into the compactor, rubber-soled slippers on his feet. He glanced around to make sure no one was watching, tucked the pistol into his front pocket and started back toward the conference center.

Time was running out.

Sunset poured through the glass and steel archways of the United Nations residential complex, pollution smearing the sky in glorious shades of burnt-orange and carmine.

News of the dead assassin had spread, and the foyer and corridors were full of stone-faced security personnel, their eyes moving behind dark glasses, reading incoming messages. Diplomats and members of delegations were being herded back to their quarters, looking lost and frightened.

He emerged from the underground tunnel and used his keycard to get into an elevator. As the ground floor fell away, he saw the Colonial Governor enter the foyer from the same direction. He had only minutes left to act. As soon as the glass doors dinged open, he headed for the suite, his false credentials held chest high, his other hand on the pistol.

"You can't come in here." The guard was half up from his seat, but his eyes were looking past Clayton, toward the commotion in the lobby. His earpiece crackled and his eyes squinted, trying to make sense of the information crawling across his lenses. Something hard dug into his ribs. He looked down, saw the blunt curve of the Tokarev in the maintenance worker's hand.

"Open the door," Clayton said, removing the guard's gun and palmer. "No sudden movements and no noise. Nod once if you understand." Uncertainty flashed in the man's eyes, but his head went up and down. Clayton steered him around the weapon scanner and to the door. The guard passed his ident across the lock. They went through.

Inside the suite was a second guard, a young woman with closely cropped hair. Clayton pressed the gun into the side of the man's neck. "Stay where you are." She raised her arms and took a step back. He shoved the male guard forward, covering them both with the pistol.

"You're not getting out of here alive," the man said. The woman said nothing, her face unreadable. Clayton's eyes moved from one guard to the other. If there was a second backup shooter, it had to be one of them. Only one way to be sure.

"Quain sold us out," he said, watching both faces for reaction. "Our cover's blown. We have to get out of here."

The man stared at him in utter incomprehension. Fear in the eyes of the female guard. No more than a flash, but it was enough.

"What are you—"

Before the guard could finish the sentence, Clayton moved in and slammed the butt of his heavy pistol into the man's temple. The guard's knees buckled, and he went down bonelessly.

With desperate speed, the woman went for her holster. Clayton shot her four times, point-blank into center of mass, tungsten rounds expanding, roaring through bone and organ and muscle, punching into the masonry behind her. She staggered back and slid down the wall, leaving bright smears of red blood, eyes wide and uncomprehending.

He squatted and placed his hand on the man's neck. Heavy, irregular breathing, but the pulse was strong. Stepping over the prone form, he checked the female guard's pockets. Nothing in there save for her ident card. He removed her earpiece and blood-soaked glasses.

Behind him, the double doors to the suite opened with an electric sigh. Pistol aimed, he retreated into the darkness of the bathroom.

Harried voices from the entryway. Slow, awkward footsteps sounded across the wooden floor, the whir of tiny servomotors.

Ramesh Rustin appeared in the doorway and took another heavy step before his brain caught up with his eyes and the bodies on the floor. For a moment he was paralyzed, the gray joints and struts of his exoskeleton frozen mid-motion. Then a finger went up to summon the security agents outside the suite. Clayton came out of the shadows, silent in his rubber soles, the heavy-caliber pistol pointed at the Governor's midsection.

"Bang," he said. "You're dead."

Twenty-Four

They faced each other in silence. Clayton motioned with the gun. Carefully, the Governor removed his headset and placed it on the coffee table. Strange eyes followed Clayton as he picked up the device. Inside them, initial fear was being replaced by curiosity.

"You're the one from the conference center," the Governor said after a while. "The one they're looking for. The second shooter."

"No." Clayton lowered his weapon. "I'm the first shooter. The guy on the gallery was supposed to be my backup. Finish you off if I missed." He nodded at the dead woman. "That right there is what's left of the third shooter."

"But they're both dead, and I'm not." The Governor's gaze slipped to the pistol. He spoke slowly, trying to put it all together. "I suppose there's a reason for that."

"I haven't decided yet," Clayton said. "Your being alive presents a whole host of problems. But if I kill you, they win, and I can't let that happen. I'm not going to play their game." He put the gun away and walked over to the balcony door. "Besides, something tells me you won't last long, no matter what I do."

"Meaning what?"

"Meaning that whoever wants you dead is well connected. They knew your every move here. Floor plans, security rotations, protocols. They infiltrated your UN security detail. They're big, bigger even than the transnationals, and they don't seem like the sort of people who know how to quit."

"Where does that leave you?"

Out above the harbor, surveillance aircraft flocked like seagulls, wheeled over the broken water. Clayton watched one of them bank toward the residential complex, a slow, elegant hundred-and-eighty-degree turn, close enough for him to catch a flash of late sun off its underside plating. By now the facial recognition software would have gone through the security footage from the conference hall. Conrad Decker's face would be streaming onto the soldier's palmers, into the visual displays of the security personnel, the memory banks of the aerial drones and sentry bots. Hastily erected checkpoints in the streets would be choking off his escape routes. The trap was closing tighter.

The situation didn't seem real somehow; he found himself observing it from a distance, like something that was happening to a vaguely familiar stranger. He knew he should be more afraid than he was but couldn't convince himself that it mattered.

"Damned if I know," he said. "But I'm open to suggestions."

"You could turn yourself in." Moving over to the bed, the Governor unstrapped himself from the metal frame and lowered himself to a seated position. The lines of his face tightened with effort. "I can vouch for you. The city administrators will protect you in exchange for information."

Clayton looked pointedly at the corpse, blood pooling around its feet. "You'll forgive me if I don't find that entirely persuasive."

"What else are you going to do?"

"I don't know," Clayton said truthfully. "I don't know how it came to this. One thing led to another, and all I did was roll along with the momentum." He stepped away from the glass door and inspected a small bloodstain on the side of his shoe. "Maybe I thought there was something coming out of it, some kind of bigger pattern. Something that would make sense of it all. But I no longer think that."

"Locked in," the Governor said with a smile. He was a tall, stately man, with thick black hair sprinkled white above his ears. Next to him, at the foot of the bed, the empty exoskeleton stooped like a grotesque metal insect. "I feel the same way. You were maneuvered. They left you no choice."

"You knew about this? That someone was coming to kill you?"

"Our intelligence suggested that they might try." The Governor's eyes skidded away. "We decided to take precautions. Some months ago, two of our deep-cover field operatives entered the Tristar-Paramount war zone. Word was

out that the son of one of the studio heads had enlisted and
that he could be persuaded to trade information about the
Aventus arcology. The plan was to break him out and bring
him to Canaveral City, then extract him Topside."

Salvesen. O'Rourke. Clayton's mind spun gearless for a
moment. "You tried to deal directly with Prescott."

"He was kept in the dark. Our men wanted to find out
more about the information he had, decide if it was worth
the risk. Then you came along, and Salvesen must have
decided to bring you with them. There was an extraction
team waiting on the other side of the wall, in the desert. It
didn't work out that way. You were the only one to make it
out, but we lost track of you in the desert. The other side
got to you first."

"Who are they? This other side?"

"The Virtus Foundation," Ramesh Rustin said. "Offi-
cially, it's a think tank funded by a handful of transnationals, conducting free market policy research. Behind the
scenes, they trade in influence, control entire economies.
They finance warlords and guerrillas in small nations. Then
let their investors swoop in and cash in on the killing. A sort
of shadow government, determined to preserve the domi-
nance of the transnationals."

"What does this have to do with you?"

Dark eyes studied Clayton with grave consideration.
"How much do you know about Topside? Other than what
you've seen on the Newscans?"

"They're prisons in space. Free labor for science experiments and orbital farms."

"That's not entirely true." The Governor shook his
head. "The Gyges stations started out as shared research
facilities for multiple national space programs. The first
wave of Topsiders were scientists and engineers, working
on plans for a manned expedition to Mars. They developed
specialized agricultural and life support modules, designed
environmental habitats and great colony ships to be assembled in zero gravity. Already there were signs of trouble
down here—crop failures and famines, revolts and resource
wars in the Eastern and Southern Hemispheres. Governments losing ground to the corporations. Everyone was
scrambling for a solution. One of the working biogen modules was turned into the first torus-farm, and disaster relief

agencies lobbied for a policy change. The space program was abandoned, all funding diverted into crop research and development. Convicts made up the initial labor force, sent up to relieve the overcrowding of prisons. When the governments collapsed and people started killing each other in the streets, the United Nations took over and created an autonomous zone, a home base for their food aid campaign."

A vague childhood memory came to Clayton; hulking cargo lifts squatting on their landing gear, relief packages stamped with the four-ring logo of the Colonies. The blackened bodies of dead rioters and soldiers rotting in the street. Feeling his father's rough, callused hand on the back of his neck as they walked over to the relief trucks. Telling Clayton not to look, his usually booming voice small and tight with fear and shame. Warm, mealy gruel served out of a self-heating pouch.

"By the time the corporations stepped in and divided up the world," the Governor said, "the orbitals were the world's fourth largest breadbasket. But we had become something more. Over the years, thousands had fled to the colony, leaving behind the strife and hunger and brutality for a chance to start over. People who believed in the vision of a human settlement among the stars, free from the trappings of nationalism and corporate greed." He leaned forward, grimacing. "We didn't have the resources to do it on our own. Not at first. We needed raw materials to build the greenhouses and solar mirrors, to power the generators. Everything had to be manufactured, even the air we breathed. Now the balance of power has shifted. We're on the brink of a breakthrough. Mass driver technology, capable of moving asteroids, or sending colony ships around the sun. A viable space program would make us fully independent from Earthside. The Virtus Foundation can't allow that."

"Why not?"

"Millions down here look up to the colony for sustenance. Without the agrolanders, there would be chaos and bloodshed again, cities burning. To the transnationals, we are a threat, a sword hanging over their revenue projections and shareholder interests. But they need us, and they know it. We're a necessary evil, a distasteful compromise which must be made to keep things the way they are. It's different with the Virtus Foundation. They want to obtain a controlling interest in our space program."

"That's a hell of a risk for them. Big investment with no short-term payoff to count on."

"Profit means nothing to them. In the world they inhabit, the only currency is power. Control over the individual lives that make up the corporate organism. Credit is no more than an accounting tool. They are ideologues who want to turn corporate propaganda into truth, to be vindicated by history. To show that all this," Rustin turned to the window and spread his arms, "this dying world, this devastation and suffering, was ultimately worth it. That their ideology is the only way forward, a new faith for a new wave of humanity. They want to be the first to the stars, to build a new empire in the image of the old, but with open, ever-expanding frontiers. Unlimited raw materials and energy, profit and wealth beyond their wildest dreams. A clean slate on which to build their model society. Their vision of the future is a great human diaspora spanning the Solar System, chained to the machine and the assembly line, toiling for the benefit of the elite."

"They tried to buy you out?"

"They made me an offer. I turned it down." The Governor's headset bleeped, but he made no move toward it. "I believe humanity can start anew. That we can build a better world elsewhere, free from hate and fear. A place where no man owns another. That we can break the cycle of greed and exploitation. I have to believe that."

"So now they want you out of the picture." Something vibrated in Clayton's pocket. He took out the dead assassin's earpiece and turned it in his fingers, wondering if Quain was on the other end of the line. "You knew what they were going to do," he said, "and you still came here."

"The Foundation thinks in terms of social hierarchy and power structures. Like you said, building an orbital station from scratch ties up immense amounts of capital. The orbitals are already up and running, just waiting for investors to move in. The Foundation expects my death to cause upheaval, to sow fear and confusion. It's been part of the corporate playbook since the Collapse. Create or exploit chaos to stake your claim. Once I'm out of the way, they'll be looking to cut a deal with whoever replaces me."

"Or with your bosses here at the UN."

"The UN has no real authority Topside," the Governor said. "We started out as an autonomous zone, but we're much more than that now. It's an arrangement of convenience. Only a handful of governments recognize the United Nations mandate, and most of those do no more than pay lip service to it. There aren't that many nations or governments left, not in the old sense of the word. But they all still toe the line of international treaties. Without the agrolanders coming down, without famine relief, there'd be open riots in the streets, market disruption, loss of profit. Without the Colonies, the UN is a toothless tiger. The leverage they have will be gone."

"Sounds to me like you off-worlders know a thing or two about power structures yourself."

"It's not like that." The Governor's voice remained even, but Clayton could tell that his barb had found its mark. "Topside doesn't work that way. Everything is shared, from the labor to the food to the decision-making. The governorship is no more than a ceremonial function, a public face for the colony. Killing me won't change any of that. Someone else will take my place."

"There's always someone looking to cut a deal."

"Not in the colony," the Governor said. "We know the cost of greed. We see it every day. The earth is changing before our eyes. Deserts spreading, storms ravaging the coasts, cities abandoned to ruin. Poverty and misery and disease, the gated enclaves of the privileged surrounded by slums. Industry-funded slaughter abroad, profiteers getting fat off the corpses. Razor wire and walls to keep out the hungry and the desperate. Up there in space, nobody owns anyone else."

Sudden anger raced through Clayton—at this man and others like him, looking down on the damned in silent judgment. "That's right," he said, feeling his lips skin back from his teeth. "Not like us. You're so much better than that."

The Governor's face clouded. "I can help you. There's no—"

"I don't want your help." Movement outside the glass door. The drone he had seen before was making a second pass. Had they found him already? He took out the Tokarev and tracked the drone in its sights until it disappeared round the edge of the balcony. Unmarked, lights blinking, with something that looked like a fat, blunt-nosed missile slung under its belly.

The security guards hadn't seen him come into the suite or they'd be in here already. But they would know soon enough. Patrols would be searching for him, street by street, the electronic eyes in the sky scanning the grid from above.

The earpiece in his hand went off again. He clipped it on and settled the receiver under his ear. Ramesh Rustin frowned, but Clayton motioned him quiet.

"Decker." The words cut through the static of the dead line. "Don't hang up."

Clayton raised the gun, looked around the suite. No cameras in sight, but he felt exposed. He edged away from the balcony and grayed out the polarized window.

"Put the girl's glasses on." A rasping, unnatural tone, sifting in through layers of voice pattern filters. "Hurry up. You're wasting time."

Wiping the congealed blood from the lenses, he slipped the dataglasses on. A mosaic of text boxes and video feeds slid across the lines of the room. The icon in the corner of the viewscreen blinked with an incoming message. He swiped his hand left and it unfolded itself, a layout of the residential complex and the streets around it with a route traced in red.

A way out.

"Follow the route if you want to live," the voice said, and clicked off.

He took out the earpiece and ground it under his heel. The red line on the map trailed from the complex all the way down to the industrial docks in the harbor. Pulsing dots marked the UN checkpoints and security teams. Tucking the pistol into the waistband of his pants, he slid the balcony door open and scanned the sky, but the unmarked drone was out of sight.

He didn't expect to make it out alive, so he let his thoughts go where they would. To Linda in the cramped apartment, watching an old man die slowly, holding onto each minute. To Ethan Quain's eyes as he spoke her name, nothing inside them at all, nothing human. To Cal and his followers in the desert, their abiding hope to raise Eden out of scorched, lifeless stone. He had made his choice and he was at peace with it, but there was still a chance something good could come from it.

"I know what you want," he said, without turning to look at the Governor. "So I'll trade you. Fair trade for a chance to get back at the bastards who tried to kill you. But it's going to cost you."

There was a long pause before the reply came. "I'm listening."

"All right, then." Clayton studied the movement of dots in the viewscreen. "Here's what we'll do..."

Twenty-Five

The drones were on him in seconds, homing in, dark shapes against the reddening dusk. He swung out over the balcony railing, lowered himself down and hung by his fingers. Fully extended, he still had four or five feet to the balcony below. One slip or a few inches to the side, and it would be an eight-story fall to the street.

Noise from the suite—doors slamming, running feet. He swung his body once and let go, hit the floor with a jarring impact. Like the viewscreen had shown, the room on the other side of the balcony door was empty. He took out the pistol and fired twice. The glass webbed with cracks and shattered inward. Clearing the shards from the frame with his shoes, he leapt inside and was out in the hallway before his pursuers could regroup.

Turn right. Down. Through the door. Run.

In his lenses, bright dots converged, video feeds alternated on virtual screens. Steering clear of them, he took the service stairs down to the ground floor and went through an emergency exit, onto the crowded sidewalk. Around the checkpoints, then down to the harbor. It was his only hope. He walked fast, head down, avoiding eye contact.

Two blocks later the surveillance craft picked him out of the crowd, a hunched figure floating on a video feed, shot from above. He tucked his chin to his chest and broke into a jog. Passersby were looking now. Ahead the street was narrowing, rifles and barriers funneling the pedestrians into a checkpoint. He tried to dart into a side alley, saw a pulsing dot light up as armed soldiers barred the other end. Above the street, electronic eyes locked on him, held him in their gaze.

In the viewscreen, his face—Conrad Decker's face— was frozen in a snarl of fear and defiance.

He looked up to see the unmarked drone drop behind the formation, bearing down fast.

Then the lenses turned black and the streetlights went out and the drones were falling into the crowd, shattering against the sides of the buildings, metal and plastic raining down.

The world shaded to black.

He took the useless dataglasses off and kept moving, pushing through the panic. At the checkpoint, the soldiers jerked and shook their heads, clawing their earpieces out. Burnt-out palmers lay at their feet. One of the soldiers was tapping his ident scanner against the heel of his hand, cursing at the dead screen. The unmarked drone had emitted an electromagnetic blast of some sort, like a charge-bomb, blowing up a black crater in the data nexus.

The pulse had shorted out the lights as far as he could see, and the streets swam in shadows. He skirted the checkpoint and walked downhill to the warehouse blocks, climbed over the retaining wall. The harbor opened out below, narrow channels of dark water between great rusty hulls, loading cranes and booms and heavy machinery unmoving and silent. Unseen birds cawed past the edge of the sea.

It was dark here, the only light coming from the fading sky. He passed through an open electric gate and into the old container port, a maze of corrugated-steel shipping cubes stamped with the logos of extinct transnationals. A group of dock workers shouted something at him from the roof of the main building, but he walked on. At the end of the terminal, he ducked under a chain and went out on the stained concrete pier and dropped the interface glasses into the water.

The boat was where the message had said it would be, bobbing on the dirty water, its ethanol outboard idling. A man in an oilskin jacket was sitting in the stern, watching him approach. His face was heavily tattooed, and his shoulders bulged under the jacket.

Clayton moved a few paces forward and halted, unsure what to do. The man grinned, a sly flash of steel teeth.

"That's close enough," said a woman's voice behind Clayton. Before he could turn around, a shadow darted from the cover of a shipping cube and the barrel of a pistol pressed into the back of his neck. "Take your gun out with your left hand. Thumb and forefinger only. Toss it into the boat and move one step forward."

He did as he was told. The woman walked around and stood in front of him, holding an old-fashioned cartridge revolver. Slim and angular in faded militia fatigues, black hair cropped short, she had a cold, hard expression on her face. She looked young, barely out of her teens. The man in the boat picked the Tokarev up and weighed it in his hand with a low, appreciative whistle.

"CorpSec grade," he said, pointing the gun and making shooting noises. "Heavy duty stuff. You pick this up at a garage sale, brother?"

"Where's Prescott?" the girl asked.

"He's dead," Clayton said, and saw the impact of his words. Her eyes narrowed and her mouth moved, but only for a fraction of a second. "Killed trying to escape. I'm the only one who got out."

"Do you still have the key?"

"Yes." Clayton thought fast. He couldn't let the boat leave without him on board. "But I'm not giving it up. You have to take me with you."

"This wasn't part of the plan, Liss," the tattooed man said, looking up at the girl. "We should get rid of him. He's a corporate plant. Gotta be."

"We could kill you," the girl said. The revolver barrel moved up. "Save ourselves the trouble."

"You could." Clayton took a step closer to the edge of the pier, held his clenched fist above the oily water. "But if I fall in, you don't get what you came for. It's your call."

Liss studied Clayton, the lines of her face tense and stern. "Just who the hell are you?"

"Decker," he said. Slowly, he took out his ident and held it out to her. "My name is Conrad Decker. Doug Prescott sent me. I got this from a lawyer in East Central."

"You're lying. He would never have given away the name, or the key."

"He wanted me to have them." Clayton cocked his head in the direction of the port gates. "Believe me or don't, but you better make up your mind fast."

The girl snatched the card away and inspected it closely. He watched the struggle on her face, read the fear beneath the hardness. The two of them didn't seem like killers, but there was a desperate intensity about them, a hunted look in their eyes. It wasn't him they were afraid of, and that made them all the more dangerous.

"Is he who he says he is?" The man's anxious eyes moved from Clayton to the girl. Despite his intimidating bulk and appearance, there was no doubt who was in charge. "We can take him over to the Mothership, see if his story checks out. If it doesn't, we'll throw him overboard."

Liss glanced at Clayton, her mouth set in a grim line. Weighing the odds. "Get in," she said, and leapt into the boat.

Clayton climbed in clumsily. The tattooed man revved the outboard and the vessel nosed between the silent hulks, through the floating oil stains and debris. Over their heads, metal walls closed, then parted.

Terrified of the open, he gripped the sides of the boat. They were heading past the ships, toward the breakwater, where the waves hissed and boiled, and dark water reached up to swallow the sky.

The tattooed man saw his fear, threw his head back and laughed. "Welcome to *Freezone,*" he said with a wink as he opened the throttle. The boat thundered past the broken walls, out to the sea.

Twenty-Six

Within minutes, the sun slipped over the edge of the horizon in a final blaze of pink and scarlet. Night dropped over the heaving sea like a black velvet curtain. Battered by wind and spray, Clayton clung to the gunwale as the boat veered between mountainous breakers, rearing and plunging like a frightened animal. Behind him, Canaveral City was a thin bright line, vanishing fast. Ahead, a point of light tossed up and down in the roaring, surging darkness.

It was toward this point they were heading, the big man wrestling with the tiller, his tattooed face like stone, the girl huddled in the prow, drenched and unmoving. The light grew and became the outline of a ship, rolling heavily on the swell. Even from a distance, its sheer size and odd shape took Clayton's breath away.

The boat came into the range of the behemoth's floodlights and the tattooed man turned the engine off. They drifted beneath massive iron protrusions crusted with barnacles and tufts of seaweed. Up close, the ship looked like a mountain rising out of the sea. The girl took out a flashlight and signaled to someone up on the deck. In response came a shout from above and she swung onto a metal ladder. The tattooed man pulled the boat into a haul cradle and helped Clayton out.

"*Mothership Freezone*," he said as they climbed the slippery ladder. "Class Three ultralarge, capacity seven hundred thousand deadweight tons." He sounded proud. "They don't make them like this anymore. Used to be part of the Vladivostok Commercial Enclave merchant marine until the oligarchs decided to put an end to that particular endeavor. We bought her for scrap and got her running again, all the way down to her hot little heart."

"Her heart?"

"Nuclear reactor," came the reply. "Keeps the lights on, the engines running, and the hardware juiced up." The tattooed man reached out and thumped the corroded metal plating with a laugh. "This here's the world's last free republic, sailing through international waters. No laws, no corporate treaties. Around three hundred of us here, all in the business of facilitating information flow. You get what I'm saying?"

They emerged on the windswept deck near the middle. The ship was easily half a mile long, segmented into four enormous cargo holds, the floodlit bridge towering at the stern. A forest of prefab cubes and satellite dishes sprouted from the deck and the cargo hold roofing like mushrooms on a log. Some of the prefabs were adorned with brightly colored murals, others with peeling political slogans and stenciled symbols, wires and insulation showing through worn durafoam siding. A group of armed men stood off to the side, smoking and swapping jokes.

Liss was waiting for them, leaning against a hatch door. "Let's make one thing clear," she said to Clayton, handing him his pistol. "You're here because Prescott trusted you, but that doesn't mean I do."

"Then why'd you get me out?"

She didn't reply but yanked the door open to reveal a steep metal staircase leading belowdecks. "Take him down to the hold," she said to the tattooed man. "He's not going anywhere but keep an eye on him. We've come too far to blow it now."

They descended into the suffocating heat of the great ship's belly, iron walls creaking under the assault of the sea, engines pounding and rumbling. Miles of bioluminescent strips lit the way. The vast space below had been sectioned off by colorful plastic partitions and hanging tarps into a gypsy camp of smaller compartments. Thick braids of bundled fiberoptic cables crept up the walls and ceiling, trailed across the floor of the camp like exotic plants strung with red and green LED eyes.

Between the partitions, Clayton could see people sleeping on cots, eating canned rations, staring at rows of computer screens. Feral-looking children raced and played on the gangways. The tattooed man, whom the others called Sage, led him through the camp, keeping up a steady flow of chatter. *Mothership Freezone* was a nexus of data crime, home to hackers and grifters. Like the pirates of old, they ran illicit data havens, pirate servers and warez exchanges, using decommissioned weather platforms and communications relays to spread into corporate and government networks like a cancer.

"Everyone here's a free agent," the tattooed man said, pushing aside a canvas curtain emblazoned with a red nuclear hazard sign and Cyrillic letters. "Some are lone wolves, some work in crews, like me and Liss. We run a strictly cryptcoin business, no questions asked. *Mothership* takes a cut of the profits for maintenance and food."

"No one's tried to shut you down?"

"The governments have no real authority to come after us, and the UN has no jurisdiction outside territorial waters," Sage replied, sinking into a foam couch beneath a rack of monitors gridded with lines of code. "The corporates don't bother because a lot of them have interests here. We do their dirty work, they maintain full deniability. Minor stuff, for the most part. Hack the competition and steal a covert bid, sneak a virus past their ice to mess with production. Bring their share price down a few points. We're no threat to them." Steel teeth glistened in the glare of the monitors. "At least, we weren't until you showed up."

"How'd you meet Doug Prescott?" Clayton asked.

"Long story." The man's eyes darted reflexively to the curtain over the entrance. Then he relaxed slightly. "Every six months or so *Freezone* docks in an independent port for supplies. Tangier-Kebdana or LADOL, Svalbard in summer. So the four of us are in a seedy bar in Apapa, and this guy is buying us drinks, waving his plastic around like it's going out of style. Talking about a business proposal, big figures. We figure him for a rich arcology kid, out slumming. Except he knows a whole lot about what we do, he's setting up a run on the biggest corporate enclave this side of the Atlantic and he's got the credit to back it all up."

"You figured you'd give it a shot."

"We should have known better, but at this point we're drunk off our asses and high on adrenaline, plus a few choice designer drugs. Also, he has a way with words. When he speaks, people listen." His eyes shone in the dimness. "Just think about it. There isn't a single soul in *Freezone* who hasn't dreamed of sticking it to the man, and here's this insider, one of the elites, telling us he's got it all worked out. Fake names and backgrounds, fake accounts, access to corporate data vaults. With him on our side, Aventus Spire would be wide open for the taking."

Clayton nodded. "Is that how you found me? Through Decker's ident?"

"Yeah." Sage pulled up a file on one of the monitors. "The call you made from Canaveral City went to an encrypted router. We saw it and ran a search for Prescott's known aliases in the area. Every transaction you make using Conrad Decker's plastic tags you for the grid crawlers. We traced you to the hotel, lost you, picked up the short-range signal from the key. We figured it was either Prescott, or a trap. I didn't want to risk it, but Liss couldn't walk away."

"She didn't seem too happy to see me."

"She'll be fine," the other said, with a shrug. "This is hard on her, man. Her and Prescott, they had a thing going, you know? Really got her hopes up when she saw Decker's name."

"You said there were four of you," Clayton said. "What happened to the others?"

"Dead," Liss said from the entrance. She flung her sodden jacket onto the back of the couch and walked over to the programming console in the corner, leaving a trail of droplets in her wake. "Rider went out on recon and never came back. I was with Hiro when he was shot in Port Nyali. Barely made it out myself. Killer knew exactly where to find us, knew our every move. He let me get away. It was a warning."

"What did the killer look like?"

"He was a synth, one of those cloned custom jobs. Pale eyes, moves like a cat. Wired to the gills." She called up a virtual keyboard and busied herself typing. "Any of this sound familiar to you?"

Clayton weighed his response. There was no need to bring up the Virtus Foundation or Ramesh Rustin, at least not yet. "The man who killed your friends is with the studio. Tristar-Paramount."

"How did he find out about us?" Sage asked.

"He figured out what Prescott was doing. Where he was going, who he was meeting. All about the fake identities.

He'd had you followed, knew you were trying to get into Aventus' computer system."

The girl turned and fixed him with a cold stare. "You seem to know an awful lot about him."

"I know enough."

"Yet you're still alive." She folded her arms and seemed to ponder for a moment. "Why are you doing this? What's in it for you?"

Clayton gave them an abbreviated version of his escape from the war zone and transformation into Conrad Decker, leaving out his encounter with Quain and the business in Canaveral City. The girl leaned against the translucent blue cube of the console and listened, her face impossible to read. The tattooed man watched him from the couch, massive and unmoving like a statue.

"The studio's onto us," he said when Clayton had finished. "They know about Prescott. It's all over. We have to flush the files."

"You do that," Clayton said, "and your friends will have died for nothing." He reached into his pocket and took out the datawafer, held it out to the girl. "If you won't help me, I'll go in alone. Prescott sacrificed himself for the key to be delivered to you. I don't know what's on it, but you know how to find out. You can finish what you started."

"Forget it." Sage looked up at Liss for support, but she wouldn't meet his eyes. "Prescott was crazy. He made us crazy for a while. We thought he was in it for the money, but it was blood he was after. Wanted to raise up an army and burn Aventus to the ground. This isn't a game. We're way out of our league, and we've already been warned twice. We don't mess with the corporates, not on this scale. That's why we're still walking around."

Annoyed by the lack of response, he got up and paced the enclosure. "Poke Tristar-Paramount again, and they'll zero us out. They can blow *Freezone* right out of the water. Everyone on board, we'll have their blood on our hands."

The girl ignored him, her eyes fixed on Clayton. "Maybe we can," she said. "The question is how you got our number. Prescott had it encrypted. Coded into subliminals. You couldn't have cracked the sequence, and you don't have the implants to view it."

"I used the headgear filter from a synesthetic immersion cube," Clayton said. "Unplugged the feed and ran the projection from the other part of the key. A map came up in the visual, along with an address and number."

Sage stared, his mouth open. "Mainline into the occipital lobe? You could have burned out, man. Fried your brain like a circuit breaker."

"I read an article about it one time. About neurohack addicts breaking into TransCore centers, vandalizing the synesthetic tanks to get high. The headgear apparently runs off a similar program as top-notch wetware. I didn't understand most of it, but if a junkie could figure out how to work it, so could I."

"Close enough." Sage whistled through his steel teeth. "Neurohack works off augmented vision, just a really primitive version of the program. If you do it right, a five-second ad subliminally played on repeat becomes a hallucinatory trip of a lifetime. If you don't do it right, you never wake up from it. Augments target specific nerve clusters in the brain, converts any type of patterned signal into synthetic vision. Same deal with wetware, except you gotta shrink it about a million times."

"Prescott put you up to that?" Liss asked. The hard look was gone from her face, replaced by frank surprise.

"He told me where to look."

The girl took the smooth metal oblong and closed her hand around it. "Then let's look." She turned back to the blue programming console, slotted the drive into place and punched in.

Traceries of data filled the monitors like frost on a windowpane. The console hummed and ticked to itself. Liss and the tattooed man leaned forward, faces rapt, glowing lines of logic reflected in their eyes. Neither of them spoke a word.

To Clayton, none of it made any sense at all. He sat back on the couch and watched the code descend across the screens, endless rows of text unspooling behind the cursor. When it reached the bottom, the girl got to her feet and pointed to the top left monitor. The first lines of code were flickering, changing.

"It's rewriting itself," she said, awe plain in her voice. "Evolving interface wrapped around a viral payload. The rootkit burrows through the wall and mutates before the security system can pick it up. Leaves no tracks." She traced a finger across the flickering crystal lattices. "Beautiful."

The tattooed man reached over and yanked the metal drive out of the console. The screens turned black. "It couldn't have been Prescott," he said, licking dry lips. Under the tattoos, his dark face was ashen. "He's not a programmer."

"It wasn't." For the first time, Clayton saw the girl smile. Tears shone in the corners of her eyes, sparkled in the light from the screen. "I wrote it. All he did was tinker with the code, tailor the core program to Aventus' icewall."

"What does this thing do?" Clayton asked.

"It's a virus," Liss said. "An intrusion program. Made to cut into Aventus' power grid and shut it down. Burrows into the core servers and sends fake signals to the system that manages the electric load in the arcology. Causes a massive power surge that burns out the main grid and all the backup systems." She mimicked an explosion with her hands. "Total blackout. It would blow the gates wide open, disable Aventus' security systems."

"Was this part of your plan?"

"No, it fucking wasn't," Sage said angrily. "We were doing this for the credit. Find a back door into the studio's DataVault, steal a few bank codes and become filthy rich. Retire to Parana, or somewhere temperate like Novomsk, and drink ourselves to death. Not this. This is different." He wheeled on Liss and waved the datawafer in her face. "You went behind our backs with this shit. You're just as crazy as Prescott was. You want to go in, be my guest. But this isn't what I signed up for."

"Nobody made you do anything," the girl said, staring him down. "You took your chances, and I took mine. No guarantees, no promises of even breaks."

"Why would I go for this? What's in it for me?"

"You'll get your payoff." Clayton placed his ident card on top of the programming console. "Help me get into Aventus, and Conrad Decker's credit is yours."

The tattooed man paused and regarded him sullenly. "All of it?"

"All of it. Bank chips, cryptcoin, digital certificates. Whatever you want, transferred to an account of your choice."

Sage rubbed his jaw. "Crazy," he said under his breath, but he picked up the card and stared at it, transfixed.

"There's a catch," Liss said. "Studio security patched up all of our intrusion points, and we don't have an inside man any longer. Which means we'll have to get around their ice."

"Can't be done." The big man shook his head. "Nothing gets through arcology ice. The code just can't be written. Hiro tried an end run and got burned, and he was the best we had."

"So we're stuck."

"Depends." Sage hesitated, as if unsure whether to go on. He turned the ident card in his thick fingers. "There might be another way."

A look passed between them that Clayton couldn't read. Liss broke it first. "It's too risky," she said, shaking her head.

"What other way?" Clayton asked.

"Get in there and plant it yourself." Sage held up the datawafer. "Find a terminal, jack in and download the virus into the core. Ice is designed to deal with threats from outside. Prescott must have planned to use this as a last resort."

"Impossible," Liss said. "The ground level is a fortress. Walls three feet thick. Automatic gates with sentry robots. The only way in is through the gates in the defensive perimeter, clearing five or six security checks. Unless your DNA or biometrics are loaded in the system, you can't take a step without setting off alarms. Cameras and weapon scanners everywhere. Software screening to pick up malware on the way in and proprietary data on the way out. Corporate security on the other side—and that's before you even walk into the residential areas."

Clayton gave Sage an inquiring look.

"Prescott had some kind of backup plan," the tattooed man said. "In case the run didn't work out. Had to do with this Aventus studio exec, a real nasty piece of work. Likes to go slumming in Liberty. You ever been to Liberty, man?"

"Heard about it."

Sage chuckled. "Liss here, she was born and raised on the *Mothership*. I grew up behind the fence, right in the middle of the Ellis Relief Zone. That's what they called Liberty back then. Migrants in makeshift camps around the old baseball stadium, refugees on ships in the harbor, the military in between. No food, no water, barely room to breathe. I was a little kid when the dam broke and the sea came in. Government tried to keep things going for a while, but after they pulled out the gangs took over everything." He clicked his tongue. "Ugly old place, Liberty. The gangs make their own laws. Get you whatever you want for the right price, no questions asked. Our friend the studio exec, he's got a deal going with one of them."

"What kind of deal?" Clayton had difficulty forming the words. Grayness closed in, his vision tunneling to the middle of the nearest screen. The flat surface was warping, sweeping into curves and depressions. Something was taking shape in the shadows of his mind, close but incomprehensible.

Synesthetic shock tingled down his spine. He blinked and shook his head, tried to fix reality into place.

"Little boys, little girls," Sage said with a grimace. "Doesn't make a difference, long as they're young. There's an underground club he goes to. Private membership, invitation only. Tight security, but he brings his own hired muscle. The circles he moves in, the only person he can really trust is himself." He frowned and peered at Clayton. "You all right, man? You don't look too good."

"I'm fine," Clayton said, looking away from the monitor. Blood everywhere, streaked across the partition walls in bright arterial splashes, dripping from the green canvas curtain, the red letters sloughing off like dead skin. His shoes smearing it into bloody prints. Two faces like raw wounds stared at him. "Who runs the club?"

"Former corporate mercenary by the name of Papa Tchang. Old school military sociopath, from back when we still had government armies. Used to work for Aegis Tactical but split off and went freelance. He did a lot of dirty work for TransCore back in the thirties, in the Biotech Wars. Led a death squad in Greater Zaire, torched down Asian wetware labs and raided their compounds. Kept a collection of shrunken heads, or so the legend goes. After it all blew over, the UN wanted to try him for war crimes, but TransCore tangled them in red tape. Papa Tchang got a quiet payoff and moved to Liberty, where he could continue to put his talents to good use. He runs one of the biggest operations there. Snuff flicks, drugs, puppet racks, real whores. You name it."

"How's this supposed to help us?"

"Prescott never said." Sage shot a sideways glance at the girl. "There were things he kept from us. From all of us. If we'd known the whole story, we wouldn't have gone for it, no matter what it paid. Anyway, the studio exec's name is—"

"Eastlake." The name floated to the top of Clayton's thoughts, strange on his tongue, a false memory spinning up from unknown darkness. The missing piece, the face rising up through the grid of blue lines, frozen in a cruel leer. "His name is Eastlake. He's in the club every other week. Owns a custom-made Aerospatiale, Aventus biometric registration. Travels with his pilot and two bodyguards, all armed."

They watched him, too stunned to speak. "How do you know that?" the girl said. For a split second, she looked very young and afraid.

"Because he told me." Clayton's legs slipped out beneath him and he sat down on the couch. "Prescott told me. It was in his key. The address I saw was in Liberty." Everything came together in a flash of recognition. "That's where I'll find Eastlake."

Twenty-Seven

The ruined dam was a long, uneven curve of cracked concrete and buried levees, moored between crumbling earthworks, pounded by the sea. A network of pontoons and floating docks and derelict ship hulls lay nestled within it, lashed together with polycarbon ropes, painted red and green by blazing neon. Ghostly hologram faces and shapes leaned over the dirty polythene and aluminum of Liberty, advertising brothels, gambling dens, black market organ labs, illicit plastic surgeries and gene therapy services. To the west, over the locks and redoubts of the inner seawall, burned the white lights of Aventus and the glass towers that surrounded the arcology.

Sage pulled the boat in next to a half-sunken scavenged barge and climbed out onto the dock. Clayton and Liss followed, silent but watchful. Black water, scrimmed with oil and garbage, gurgled under the pontoons.

Unlike the rest of the city, Liberty ran faster at dark. Any appetite could be sated here. Light and music spilled from a strip of waterfront bars, durafoam walls alive with moving images and reflected shadows. Neon and halogens bled the brightness out of colors, turned the twilight into bleak, eternal day. High above them, lurid projections twined and overlapped, blended into a featureless white sky.

"You think you can just walk in, man?" The tattooed man glanced around as Clayton steered them into a rat-warren of narrow alleys, navigating from subliminal memory. "Swipe your rich-man card at the door and Papa Tchang's boys let you in? You'll get us all killed."

"Everything can be bought." Clayton's hand went into his jacket, came up holding a small vial of pale amber crystals. "The free market always finds a way. You just have to find the right currency."

Sage cursed and his eyes darted around nervously. Liss laughed in disbelief. Pharmaceutical-grade Synthazine fetched several times its factory price in the streets, where barter was the sole form of exchange and addiction ran rampant.

The waterfront had vanished behind rows of prefab shanties; the makeshift streets opened around them in a roar of sound and bustle. They passed massage dens and loud bars, hookers beckoning from open store windows, a neurohack parlor fronted by a whirlwind of hologram body parts twisted in ecstasy. Brothels and arcades strung along like gaudy beads of light. Crowded streets swarmed with greed and lust, awash in neon and synthetic pheromones. Hard faces and predator eyes, biolume gang tattoos glowing on exposed skin.

The reassuring weight of the Tokarev pressed against the small of Clayton's back, nestled below the caster rig harness. Earlier on he'd asked Sage to program the rig's relay module to an old satnav registered to the Orbital Colonial Authority. Now the device was on board *Freezone,* two dozen miles off the coast of Liberty, well within broadcast range and awaiting activation.

One street over, the hull of a grounded freighter reared up from the huddled styrene prefabs. Surveillance cameras leaned over a door of heavy beaten steel. Security stood out front:, two shaven-headed hulks in black jackets, their sides bulging with concealed firepower. Clayton tapped Sage on the arm. "Here."

The three of them moved behind a street vendor's food stall. Clayton took out the pistol and handed it to Liss. The girl balked for a moment. "Take it," Clayton said, pushing the gun into her hands. Implanted visions stirred in his head, gnawed at him from within. "They won't let me in if I'm armed."

"One of us should come with you," Liss said. The tattooed man didn't say anything, but his glum expression spoke volumes.

"I have to do this alone. Find Eastlake's ride and meet me at the back entrance. I won't be long."

The bouncers spotted him as soon as he walked out from behind the stall and shifted their stances, immediately alert, their faces seamed with old scars, muscle knotted under leathery skin. Professional killers—former corporate militia, barcodes tattooed into the sides of their necks, luminous in the light above the door. A low throb of music pounded from within, heavy bass lines like competing heartbeats. One of the men stepped forward to block Clayton's way. Half of his face was covered by a smooth syntheskin graft, the eye on that side a cheap prosthetic. Its red lens zoomed in and out, changing focus. "Private club. Invitation only."

"I have an invitation," Clayton said, his lips stretching into a broad, jittery grin. He fumbled in his pocket. A quick exchange of looks and the other bouncer moved behind him. Strong hands grasped him by the back of his collar, shoved him against the wall of the arcade. He felt them pat him down, trace the straps and buckles of the caster through his clothes. "Sonofabitch's wired," said the second bouncer. "Some kind of bodycam rig."

"Get the hell out of here, friend," said the one with the face graft. "Before you get hurt."

"Don't want any trouble." Still grinning, Clayton opened his hand, held it palm up. Light flashed off the glass vial. The bouncer's eyes went very wide and he took a step back. "Just going in to see the show and do some recording for my own personal use. That's all. Or I can take my business elsewhere."

The man with the graft waved his companion away and took a step forward, his bulk shielding Clayton from the security camera. With a practiced gesture, he plucked the Synthazine vial from Clayton's hand and made it disappear into his pocket. Powered hinges hummed and the door scraped open. A hideous smile opened across a slit of broken teeth, stopping at the livid edge of the scar. "Enjoy the show," the other bouncer said, nodding him in.

Blue and pink neon danced across the gutted walls of the arcade. Moans and shrieks of pain, real and synthetic, mixed with the thumping of amplified speakers. Highlights darted through the tinted gloom, reflected on drinks and jewelry and metal-studded leather. The walls and floor reacted to the music, colors oscillating to the beat, each note a hypnotic swirl of reds and purples and blues. Pale, sexless bodies clad in sleek polycarbon and taut leather and chains writhed in the pulsing light, reached out for him as he pushed toward the bar and ordered a drink.

Apart from him, the bar area was empty. Smoke curled above a long, narrow stage around which a silent audience gathered, watching a trio of biosurgery freaks engage in some sort of elaborate performance, projection gear replicating their movements on the rear wall of the club. Gleaming metal on flesh, surgical implants fused to withered, stunted limbs. Two screens flanking the stage flashed speeded-up footage of splice surgery, set to a relentless electronic beat; wires inserted into an exposed spinal cord, a neural interface lowered into the bloody hole at the back of a skull. Faces moved and changed in the sudden flares of lighters, in the weak glow of wearable cameras and palmers recording the performance.

Behind the bar, a red-lit corridor lined with doors led deeper into the peeling shell of the building. Two CorpSec thugs in expensive suits sat at a table near the entrance, looking uncomfortable. Clayton took a long pull of his scotch and waited for the bartender to make his way over.

"I need some information," he said, leaning across the counter. "Something you could help me out with."

"Can't help you." The bartender swabbed the stained plastic with a dishtowel, without looking at Clayton. He was a tall, hulking man, the remains of his hair gathered into a lank, greasy ponytail. Clayton took out another vial of Synthazine crystals and tapped it on the counter. The bartender frowned, shook his head. "That's not the way things work around here. You want something, you go see the man upstairs."

"I was told certain arrangements can be made, if you ask the right person. Someone I can do business with."

"Don't know anything about it," the bartender said. For the briefest of moments, his eyes betrayed him and skittered toward the darkness at the back of the bar. Clayton followed his gaze. Behind the dusty bottle racks, a lone light shone above a curtained doorway. Glowering, the bartender refilled Clayton's glass. Numbers and letters glowed under the skin of his right forearm, a registration tattoo from the Polar Circle interment colonies. "Drink your drink and shut up, if you know what's good for you."

Clayton raised his hands defensively, gestured at the row of bottles. "Tell you what. I changed my mind. I'll have one of those instead." When the bartender turned his back on him, he reached over the counter and jabbed the injector into the side of the man's neck.

The bartender grunted and jerked away, his hand going up to the wound. Then the double dose of endomorphin hit his bloodstream like a jolt of lightning and his eyes rolled into the back of his head. Clayton went behind the bar and caught the big man as he sagged, laid him down on the floor. Crouching by the counter, he looked around. All eyes were on the stage and the wall behind it; the holoprojection was changing, prostheses and scarred stumps melding together into a shapeless horror of claws and tentacles and eyes that stared in mute agony, or rapture. He searched under the counter for a weapon, found nothing.

Behind the curtain was a doorway into a bare concrete room stacked with barrels and cases. To the left was a scuffed metal door. A voice was humming on the other side, the key too high, unnatural. The handle turned in his hand and he went in.

A haze of heavy perfume and old sweat hung in the air. Mirrored desks lined one side of the room, their few remaining bulbs shining on a clutter of discarded jars and brushes, dusty wigs on blocks. Stacks of empty boxes were scattered in the corners. Tattered costumes lay draped over chipped racks. Old posters covered the damp-stained walls, their colors faded, yellowing edges curling under the tacks.

A slim figure wearing a light blue chiffon robe, bald and bejeweled and heavily made up, reclined in a worn armchair next to one of the dressing tables, holding a rouge puff and an eyeliner pencil. Standing in front of the chair was a small girl dressed in a miniature corset and skirt, her pinched face caked with makeup, her dark hair elaborately coiffed. At the back of the room, a boy of seven or eight, pale and thin and naked to the waist, sat on a stained chintz sofa. The figure in the armchair ceased its humming and raised eyes ringed in black kohl at Clayton. One hand darted under the dressing table.

"You're not supposed to come in here." The voice was rough, masculine, threatening. The girl looked up at him,

208

licked her thickly painted lips in a dreadful, mechanical parody of lust.

"Take it easy," Clayton said, trying on a glassy-eyed leer. He held up the Synthazine vial. "Eastlake sent me. He's interested in some fresh action, and he's willing to pay extra for it."

Beneath the powder and rouge, the smooth face drew tight with suspicion. "I wasn't told about this," the show-master said, his gaze following the yellow crystals. "Such short notice too. I'll do what I can, but I can't promise any-thing."

Clayton tossed the vial into his lap. The showmaster tut-tutted and shooed the girl away. Long, manicured fin-gers picked the vial up and removed the stopper. "You'll have to settle with the club separately, of course." He closed his eyes theatrically and passed the vial under his nose. "Thirty percent over the usual rate."

"Don't worry," Clayton said, crossing to the dressing table and picking up a tall cut-crystal atomizer. The show-master's powdered bald head was bent over the vial in his lap, old costume jewelry sparkling in the lights. "I intend to settle fully before I leave."

He swung the heavy bottle down like a sledgehammer, felt the solid crunch of impact with the other man's skull. The showmaster made a strangled grunt and slumped to the floor. Blood poured from a cut above his temple, stained the lapels of his robe. His mouth worked, trying to form words. Clayton bent down and picked up the vial, forced it between the man's clenched teeth. Dark-ringed eyes flared wide in horror. He knelt on the showmaster's chest and drove his elbow under the trembling chin, grinding the jaw shut, crushing the glass.

A muffled howl, pain mixed with horrified disbelief, bubbled through the blood and saliva. Painted nails dug into his shoulders, raked his cheeks, sought his eyes. Using his full weight, he pinioned the flailing arms and clamped both hands over the writhing figure's nose and mouth. The showmaster's eyes bulged and began to glaze over. His throat moved in convulsive shudders. Clayton released him and stood. The other man tried to roll onto his side, clawing at his closing throat, his swollen face turning blue. A terri-ble whistling rasp came from his heaving chest.

Reaching under the dressing table, Clayton brought out the showmaster's weapon—a microfilament whip with an engraved metal handle. Small and innocuous, each of its five graphene-coated strands tipped with small steel bearings. One clockwise turn of the handle and current would flow through the whip, molding the graphene lattice into a razor-sharp edge a few molecules thick. Switched off, the whip was a fetishist's toy, capable of inflicting pain without serious injury. At full power, the strands would slice through skin and strip flesh from bone. He pressed a button and the microfilaments reeled into the handle, which he dropped into his pocket.

From the sofa, the two children watched the scene with still, flat eyes. The showmaster lay face down in a puddle of bloody froth, his back jerking, broken nails scratching a spasmodic pattern into the dirty carpet. Clayton walked over to the sofa and held out his hand. The girl took it and climbed down, pulling the boy after her.

Together they walked out into the fractured light of the projectors, the two children in front of Clayton, his hands on their bony shoulders, steering them toward the corridor. The two CorpSec men looked up from the drinks they were nursing and the closer one slid a hand inside his suit. The other one nodded to Clayton without meeting his eyes and waved him through.

On the far screen, an autosurgeon peeled the bloody membrane off a neatly exposed skull, threaded delicate wires through quivering brain tissue. Beneath the ridge of sawn-off bone, the Deacon's face twitched and leered, and blood poured from its eyes. Hallucinations or a reaction to the subliminals; Clayton couldn't tell. He let the children lead him into the red-tinted darkness of the passage.

Steel doors lined the blotchy walls, paint flaking off them like leprous skin. An exit sign glowed red at the far end of the corridor. A dozen paces in, the boy stopped in front of a door and looked up. Clayton squatted down so that his face was level with the children's. He held out the last vial of Synthazine. "Get out of here," he said, pressing the vial into the girl's palm. "Take this and get some food. Don't come back here. Ever."

Two small faces regarded him with a peculiar look, remote and not quite human. Finally, the girl tucked the vial into her corset and led the boy away. Clayton watched them walk toward the exit, then went to the door and knocked gently.

Bedsprings creaked and the door cracked inward a few inches. Beyond it was a small room, its floor covered in tile and its walls bare concrete, a single bulb shedding weak light on a nightstand, a sink and a stained mattress. A man stood in the middle of the room, wearing only a pair of well-cut silk trousers. Trim and finely muscled, his handsome, chiseled features set in a half-smile.

His eyes wandered past Clayton and the smile faltered, became something else. He turned and lunged for the nightstand, toward the glowing screen of his palmer.

Clayton flicked his wrist; the man hissed in pain and shrank back, his hand pressed to his side. Five angry red welts rose from the pale skin of his stomach. Clayton pointed the whip at the mattress and the man sat, his eyes wild, his face flushed and working. He didn't look so handsome anymore.

They faced each other across the room. Eastlake glanced from the palmer to the whip in Clayton's hand, shrugged and tried to smile.

"You don't have to do this," he said. "Whatever you're being paid now, the studio can double. More, if you give them the names of whoever sent you."

The tiled floor, Clayton saw, sloped to a drain in the center of the room. He watched the hole as if hypnotized. The metal ring around it was speckled rusty brown. He saw blood sluice down into the blackness, his thoughts sluicing away with it.

Encouraged by the silence, Eastlake said, "They've been after me for some time. You're not the first. Can't get to my level without making a few enemies." He chuckled and rubbed his nose. A strange light had come into his eyes. His grin was stronger now, but fear was pushing through it, like dirt under ice. The negotiator, the power broker, looking for an opening, a way back to familiar ground. "You could just walk away. I can make it worth your while."

Clayton gazed down at the man's face. The high sweep of brow and cheekbone, the firm lines of the jaw. Genome taken apart and rebuilt to specifications, scoured of hereditary flaws. He wondered what else had been taken out alongside the flaws, something hidden in the infinite twists of genetic code, some essential element of humanity—what was left behind the perfect front of skin and tissue and bone.

In his hands, the whip clicked and hummed to life. Eastlake's tightly held composure dissolved. The look in his eyes was one Clayton knew well from the war zone. "Get on your knees," he said. "Over there. Turn around."

"Don't." Eastlake knelt over the drain, his face pleading. He could see what was coming, yet he still couldn't believe in his own death. "Look at me. Please."

"Turn around." Clayton raised the whip. When the man obeyed, he wrapped his fingers around one of the steel tips and snapped the microfilament wire taut, careful not to touch its thrumming surface. He stepped closer to the kneeling figure. The head was hunched between the heaving shoulders, either with fear or in the anticipation of a blow or both.

"I have to do it," he said, leaning closer to Eastlake's ear. "There are threads in our lives, connecting everything. Sometimes they get tangled. Or they come loose. Then you must make the world make sense again. Piece by piece, one thread at a time."

"What?" Eastlake said and Clayton rammed his knee between the rounded shoulder blades, slipped the thrumming wire over the man's head and pulled back on the ends.

Muscle and gristle parted. Blood poured out of the gash in a red rush, ran down the runnels in the sloping floor. Warm spray on his face. Eastlake flailed and kicked, gurgling, drowning in his own blood. They thrashed in it like lovers in a monstrous embrace, feet slipping and sliding across the tiles. Clayton felt the wire snag as it bit into bone; he pulled back harder.

The dying man jerked once and was still. Hands twitching as the last warmth of life drained away, the gleam of white from severed digits where they'd thrust under the slicing wire. Clayton got up, breathing hard and wiping blood from his eyes. The strand was broken in two. He flung the dripping piece into the corner and looked around. Bright red splashes covered the walls and the bed, inched down the closed door, thick and already congealing.

Red all around him. Red behind his eyes.

He stood at the door and listened, but he could hear nothing. Moving over to the body, he spat to clear his nose and mouth and bent to his work.

Twenty-Eight

They were waiting for him in an alley behind the club, crouched behind an overflowing trash compactor.

He stepped out of the slatted neon shadows and caught movement out of the corner of his eye, turned to face the blunt muzzle of the Tokarev. Sage squatted behind her, a long piece of iron pipe gripped in his massive fists. Clayton raised his free hand. "You took your time," Liss said, lowering the pistol.

He reached and took his gun from the girl. Their hands brushed and she jerked hers away, turning away from him in disgust. Clayton looked down. He'd cleaned up as best he could and thrown Eastlake's suit jacket over his ruined shirt, but there were dark brown streaks on his hands and his hair felt stiff with caked gore. In his haste, he had sliced through his thumb and bound it with a strip of bedsheet. Not all the blood was his and the bundle in his left hand made a wet sound as it swung.

"Did you find the jet?" he asked. Sage was staring at the bundle, red stains soaking through the dingy gray of the pillowcase. His mouth curved down and he looked sick.

Liss averted her eyes. "There's an old barge down there." She pointed down the street, toward the remnants of the dam wall. "Half buried in the sand and turned into a private airfield. Razor wire around the deck, four executive jets sitting on the tarmac. One of them is Eastlake's."

"You sure about that?"

"I didn't exactly hang around to ask," the girl said, glowering. "But there's a Sterling Aerospatiale parked at the very end, Tristar-Paramount logo on it as big as a door. I'd say it's likely."

"They got guards down there?"

She shook her head. "No cameras, no security. Easier not to leave a trail. Prescott used to fly around in one of

those things. The pilots are armed, and the doors have biometric locks. You can't get in without a face scan."

"Even if you could, no one's going to try to jack a corporate jet," Sage said. "Not in Liberty. The gang bosses take
care of their exec customers. Look at them the wrong way
and you'll get killed."

Clayton checked the gun's firing cell and counted the
rounds. "This is as far as you go," he said. "I'll call you when
I'm on my way to Aventus. If you don't hear from me in an
hour or so, destroy the relay." He tapped the eyepiece of his
caster rig. "I don't want them to track the signal back to the
ship."

He saw the fear in their eyes, surfacing like a rock at
low tide. Fear of what they read in his face, in the rust-col-
ored stains on his clothes. Somewhere inside him the old
rage called, the dark joy high and strong, a beast that would
not be denied. Whispers at the back of his thoughts, and
beneath them, rising as if to drown them out, the roar of
tiltjet turbines. Scavenger teams homed in for the kill. He
packed the rest of his gear, nodded and left the two *Freezoners* standing in the alley. They were gone when he came
out on the main thoroughfare, swallowed by the light and
the noise. He kept walking.

Closer to the massive ruin of the old seawall the streets
fell back, the neon frontages and shimmering holodisplays
winked out and vanished abruptly. Iron walkways clung to
the walls of empty warehouses, led down into the dark bowl
of the harbor. Remains of an ancient civilization left to decay, waiting for something new to emerge from them. Over
the dam, the first wan traces of dawn leaked into the sky,
the ocean a heaving blackness beneath.

The barge Liss had described was a bright square of
light, stripped of engines and plating and drawn up on a
slip. Cables and pipes sprouted from the ship's cavity like
entrails, dripping in the dark. He climbed up to it under the
cover of darkness and hid behind a crooked pylon, watching the deck and interior for movement. There wasn't any.
A long, wide ramp led to the top of the barge. He put a full
clip into the pistol and went up.

At the top was a chain link fence with a gate and beyond it, a makeshift landing pad, four tiltjets parked next

to a maintenance shack. Powerful floodlights washed all shadows from the tarmac. He crept along the fence to East-lake's jet and waited. Minutes passed and nothing moved. The cockpit was dark, and he couldn't tell who was inside. He rose slowly and bounced a pebble off the glass. No lights came on and the cabin door remained closed. He tossed the bundle over the fence, grasped the top and hauled himself up.

The pilot heard the door slide open and scrambled himself up, snatching off his glasses. Streaming during work hours went against company regulations, but the boss wasn't due for another hour at least and he always called ahead. He cleared his throat and fumbled for an apology.

The lone figure stood at the back of the cabin, its face hidden by the shadows. The pilot squinted and frowned, blinked to clear his sight. Something about the shape seemed wrong. He had time to register the soaked bundle of rags in one of the upholstered seats, red seeping into the expensive leather.

"What the hell—?"

In two long strides, Clayton closed the distance and whipped the pilot with heavy pistol. Bone and cartilage crunched. The pilot cried out and threw up his hands to his gushing nose. Clayton grabbed him by the hair and slammed his head against the dashboard, shoved him onto the floor. The pilot whimpered and tried to roll into a ball, all resistance gone out of him.

Clayton searched the man's pockets, removed a palmer and a flechette pistol. He sank into a deep leather chair and propped his feet up on the low teakwood table.

"Get up," he said. The pilot spat blood and clambered up into his seat, tilting his head back and holding his nose. His terrified eyes moved from the dirty, bloodstained apparition to the cabin door. Clayton caught him looking and waved the gun. "Start the engines. We're all ready to go."

"Go where?" The pilot tried to make sense of it but couldn't. "Who are you? How did you get in here?"

"I'm a friend of Mr. Eastlake's." Clayton lay back against the headrest and closed his eyes, felt the soft edges of exhaustion close in. The steep edge of a long fall into nothingness. He had not slept in days. "Your boss was delayed. There were some urgent, last-minute details for him to attend to. But none of that is your business. What you need to consider is how to get us home in the shortest possible time. We have an appointment to keep, and we don't want to be late."

"Appointment?" It was a dream, the pilot decided, had to be a dream. He had fallen asleep earlier and become trapped inside it, some nightmare place where his worst fears came up through the veil of sleep to torment him. The maniac with the gun, he realized, was wearing Mr. East-lake's dinner jacket, but it was dirty, the cuffs and lapels stained brown. His gaze fell to the bloody footprints and the bundle of rags by the table and his mind shrank back in revulsion.

The intruder nodded. All animation had fallen away from his face, turning it into a death-mask, drawn and dirty, lit from within by a glaring and inhuman light. He didn't open his eyes, but his free hand went up. The hand was wrapped in a torn strip of cloth, stained with red. A finger black with dried blood pointed inland. Above the dark, silent walls of the seawall, above the vast agglomerations of housing projects, where Aventus blazed like a second moon.

"They're expecting us," the man said, smiling.

Twenty-Nine

They thundered off the barge moments before dawn and swung away into the lowering pearl-gray sky, circled out over the ocean. Below them, the lights of Liberty glided along the dark water, holograms shifting and flickering in the morning mist. When Clayton opened his eyes, the Deacon was sitting in the seat across from him, a placid expression on his great, smooth face. At the front of the jet, the pilot hunched over the navigation readouts, hands moving over the instrument panels. A floating screen glowed with numbers and colorful tags, expanded across the dashboard.

"Aventus air traffic control," the pilot said, swiping at the alphanumerics, trying to sound composed. "They painted us on their scan. If we don't reply, or if we deviate from one of the approved flight trajectories, they'll want to know what we're doing here."

"Hold off on that." Clayton got up and looked out the starboard window. Over the rim of the seawall, past the massive locks holding back the weight of the ocean, slums clustered around the dikes and canals. Further inland, beyond the squalor of the cordoned zones, the rising sun drew the grim, massive lines of the accommodation blocks out of the darkness. Holovids and company logos shimmered above their summits like mirages in heat. He searched the web of light for twin flares of vivid green, the crossed grain sheaves of Titan Hydroponics. He tapped the gun against the thick glass to get the pilot's attention. "Get us closer to the food vaults. Something's going on down there."

"Did you hear what I said?" The pilot looked up at him, incredulous. "Air traffic control has blanket authority to blow us out of the sky. We either request approach clearance or we get the hell out of Aventus airspace."

"You've got more pressing concerns right now," Clayton said, pushing the gun hard into the man's temple. Over the sea, through the shiver of holograms, Aventus loomed, a pyramid of gleaming steel, white stone and smoky glass, covered in red navigation beacons. High walls and razor wire around it, level upon level of ferroconcrete bunkers studded with smart-weapon perimeter defense systems. Floodgates glinted on the banks of the river, silent sentinels over the black water. "How much time do we have?"

"Depends." The pilot's face was gray. Rivulets of sweat rolled down his forehead, continued down his cheeks. "When we fail to respond, they'll make a threat assessment. Establish level of response. Thirty seconds, maybe forty-five." His voice was dreamy with horror and his hands twitched on the controls. The screen glowed again, more urgently now. "Another sixty for the system to notify short-listed vendors and for the bids to come in. Within the next minute or two, the contract will be signed and the drones on their way." He stared ahead through the cockpit glass. Blue radiance from the instrument panels leapt across his face; bright orange patterns projected across his retinas. "I don't want to die," he said, as if to convince himself.

"Then do as I say." Clayton tapped the dashboard. "Give it two minutes. Stay away from their airspace. They know this is Eastlake's jet. They won't shoot us down. Not immediately, at least." He felt the floor shift beneath him, the noise of the powerful engines changing pitch, rotors cycling higher. The cityscape tilted; the sea raced past; concrete ravines and mazes slewed below. Between the housing blocks, the streets were already thick with people. He pressed his face to the glass of the window. From afar, a voiceless roar reached him, rising and falling over the thunder of the turbines.

"What's that—?"

Proximity alerts blared and the tiltjet lurched sideways, almost throwing him off balance. Dark shapes plunged from the sky, burst through the rooftop holograms in a scatter of broken light. He caught a flash of sun on metal, bright corporate logos on black fuselage, railgun barrels slung under sensor-tipped noses. Four gunships falling out of the red sun, bearing down on them fast.

Clayton's fingers dug into the soft leather of the seat. Nothing to do but watch the approach of his own death.

Next to him the pilot gibbered and sobbed, head bent as if to fend off the coming impact, the lethal hail of rail guns.

The gunships screamed past them and swept around the corner of an accommodation block two streets ahead, low and fast, dust and refuse storming in their downblast.

"Not us," the pilot said and uttered a shrill laugh. His eyes were wet. "They're not coming for us." The tiltjet swiveled on its vertical axis, climbed over the rooftops and headed for the dark slash of the river. Between the steep walls of the blocks, Clayton saw armored cars and soldiers outside the food vaults, barricades going up in nearby streets, gunships hovering overhead. Pressing up against the barriers was a crowd of tens of thousands, more and more bodies trickling in from the side streets, like floodwater bursting through a dam.

"What's happening down there?"

"Deadbeats," the pilot said. Contempt had edged out the fear from his voice. He listened to the chatter in his headset, frowning. "One of the pirate 'casts been spreading rumors of a crop failure in the hydroponics. The vaults will run out of food in a couple of days, so everyone's coming out to grab what they can. Security is closing off the streets, diverting all air traffic away from the area." He wiped his face and leaned over a display. "There's going to be a riot."

Clayton had listened to the *Freezoners* lay out their plan, but the nonchalant ease with which they had set things into motion was nonetheless astounding. It had begun with a snippet of misinformation, carefully prepared and inserted through independent channels and online feeds. A new strain of blight fungus, a genetically engineered pathogen, attacking stocks of hydroponic grain; images of closed gates and biohazard signs, footage of green-suited, masked workers with flamethrowers torching down vertical farms. The grain sheaves of Titan Hydroponics engulfed in flames.

Within an hour, the story had been picked up by four corporate propaganda channels owned by Titan's smaller, more vicious competitors, who had run it as breaking news. Anger and fear had swept the housing projects like an epidemic, and by the time Titan Hydroponics had put togeth-

220

er a press release, no one believed their denials. Clayton imagined he could hear cries below, the railguns opening fire. Red sunrise heralded violence and blood, a carnage in the streets. Feeling sick, he turned away from the window.

"Take us in."

The pilot swallowed hard. "They'll know by now that something's gone wrong," he said. "Mr. Eastlake's body-guards will have called them. They'll never let us get close."

Clayton aimed the pistol, set the recoil brake and fired. The headrest of a seat in the back of the jet disappeared in an explosion of upholstery and polymer foam. A rough hole the size of a fist smoked in the bulkhead behind it, spilling torn insulation. Warning lights went off around the cabin and the air filters whirred louder, compensating for the in-flow of tainted air.

The pilot winced and hauled on the controls, spoke into his headset. The tiltjet banked over the black water of the river, curving toward the glass and light of Aventus.

The panel chimed twice and Liss' face appeared, tired but alive. "It's all over the feeds," she said, pointing at something offscreen. "Both vaults have been looted. Titan's sending in armored units, trying to push the mob across the river. Aventus just declared an emergency. How far are you?"

"Not far," Clayton said, donning the headgear and palming the caster rig on. Soft, translucent amber and green view panes slid over his view, overlaid by a shifting grid of composition guidelines. Digits flickered between them, tracking contrast and exposure and distance. "Are we online?"

"We have satellite uplink. Sage is working on the News-can channels. Want to try it out?"

Dizzy, he set the cameras to auto and dismissed the viewfinder aids. The video panel in front of him blinked and the girl's face was replaced by the interior of the tiltjet, com-peting camera angles melding in vertiginous false focus, like falling forward.

He got up, took a step to the side. The headgear lens swept in a tracking shot of the cabin. The microlenses on his shoulders and chest zoomed and adjusted, sifting solid forms from a clutter of virtual screens. He blinked a few times and the rig followed the tiny dilations of his pupil, its main processor smoothing the input from the lenses into a continuous feed. "Are you getting this?"

"Loud and clear." The panel cut to the inside of *Freezone,* a rack of monitors displaying his camera feed, then panned to Sage, bent over a programming console, giving him a thumbs-up sign. "We're seeing everything you can see, plus a few degrees to either side. We're going live as soon as you touch down. Scramble the feed, bounce it off the satnav and play it over the corporate broadcasts. Just in time for the morning Newscans."

"What about the crowd outside?"

"We'll beam directly to the ad holos. You can see those from as far away as Liberty. Hack into the news servers too, flood the online columns. It'll take the studios a few minutes to shut us down, but that's all we need to get the crowd moving."

Liss came back on screen, winked at him. "Pretty big audience out there, looking through your eyes. Hope you don't choke."

"So do I."

She held his eyes for a moment. "There'll be a boat waiting for you at the mouth of the river, down by the barrier gates. It's your only way out, but you got to be quick. You have to get out before they lock everything down. Corporate thugs are already cordoning off the area. Stay inside for too long and you won't be coming out at all."

"I'll be there," Clayton said. The girl nodded, that wry smile surfacing again. She knew better. "I have to go now."

"Decker?"

"Yeah?"

"What's your real name?"

He broke the connection and the panel blanked, dissolved into a spray of pixels. His weariness was long gone now, replaced by singing nerves and sharp, heightened sensations. Emotions and reason retreated to some deeper place inside him; adrenaline gave the world an edge of sharp clarity.

Below the nose of the jet, sun gathered on angular glass canyons, the arcology expanding to engulf the horizon. In the streets around it the mob swelled and eddied, moving toward the shining steel gates.

"This is the world they have made for themselves," the Deacon said in his ear. With a sweep of his hand, he took in the surging mass of bodies, the sprawling rooftops. His arms were red to the elbows. "The world they never expected to turn against them. You are the messenger of God's wrath, the herald of a new and terrible dawn. The bringer of a great levelling. Not a single choice brought you here that wasn't your own."

"I don't want to be a messenger," Clayton said. "I don't care about choices. All I want is to see this whole rotten thing blown open. That, and to see people pay."

The pilot turned and frowned at him, pointed at his headset. "That was Control," he said. "Last warning. They'll shoot us down if we don't respond."

As if to confirm his words, a squadron of drones rose from behind the glimmering towers, approaching on an intercept course. The pilot put the tiltjet into a holding pattern, the drones gliding into formation behind them, locking on target.

"Raise them," he said to the pilot. He picked up the bundle and held it up to the dashboard camera. When the red transmission light winked on, he reached inside and tore the bloody pillowcase away.

Static from the speakers. Somewhere far away the pilot was screaming, the anguished howl of an animal insane with terror.

Clayton held his grisly trophy aloft and faced the camera.

"Tell them my name is Conrad Decker. Tell them I want to speak to Quain." The pilot blubbered into his microphone, face shiny with tears and snot. "There's an old serviceway running along the coast. A section of it passes right under the seawall. There's nothing between the tunnels and the ocean but a few feet of stone. We've rigged it with blasting charges. If they fire on this jet, I'll give the order to blow the locks. Flood the arcology from the inside out." He paused to let the man repeat his message, thought about what he'd say next. "Tell them that there's a bomb on the jet. Twenty pounds of plastic explosive. Tell them that their boss knows we're coming."

No response. Either they hadn't heard the transmission, or they were about to call his bluff. He turned the severed head in his hands. Eastlake's face bore a grimace of faint surprise, blood clotted around the neck like a string of red-black pearls. It looked almost alive, the expensive haircut unruffled, as if he were about to deliver the closing remarks at a board meeting. But something had gone out of it; some subtle transition had taken hold, hollowing it out from inside. He wondered what it would feel like, letting himself slip away, consciousness dwindling to a tiny bright point. There, and then gone.

The pilot was slumped over the controls, his shoulders hitching. A dark stain spread from the front of his trousers down his leg. The autonav kicked in and the aircraft veered over the riverbank, close enough for Clayton to make out layers through the polarized glass; bright office spaces laid out around a green core of vertical farms, living quarters and manicured gardens linked by paths and walkways.

He thought about the lives that went on inside, oblivious to the suffering on the other side of the walls, the poisoned air and the baleful heat. There would be more like Prescott among them, in steel-and-glass enclaves all over the city; tiny cells floating inside the corporate behemoth, metastasizing in silence. Ready to grasp the wrath boiling in the streets and mold it to their purposes.

Perhaps all it took was a signal to wake them up. Before their excursion to Liberty, the Freezoners had released Prescott's intrusion program through a network of unlicensed servers, giving it away as freeware. All it would take was another freelance group, desperate or daring enough to try breaking in. Sooner or later someone would try. Many might die, but some would strike true. He pictured the program spinning out, growing; a viral disease, shapeless and unstoppable, infecting corporate defenses, ravaging counter-intrusion systems. Lights winking out one by one, the foul breath of the streets invading the oases of privilege and plenty.

In the glass he saw the Deacon smile, felt his own smile come out in response; the lightest of touches on his head, as if bestowing a blessing.

"Mr. Decker." Quain's voice poured in from the speakers, smooth and featureless. "This is most unexpected.

Anyone else would have vanished without a trace by now. But I suppose you just couldn't help yourself."

"I have a little unfinished business to attend to. Get me a landing pad and I'll tell you all about it."

"I'm afraid I can't do that." Background noise faded, cut off sharply. "You said that you wanted to speak to me. So speak. We're on a secure line. No one can intrude."

"I think you know what I'm going to say. That's why we're having this conversation in private."

"Let me guess. The bomb in the tunnel." A dry laugh. "That was a good try. Very logical, guaranteed to get attention. But it's not true. That serviceway was filled in years ago. Besides, we tracked every purchase you made. There was no way you could get your hands on high explosives on the street."

"Maybe. But let's see if I can hold your attention anyway." Clayton watched the shadow of the tiltjet skimming in the arcology glass, the small, lethal shapes of the missile drones following it in lockstep. "I've taken a few precautions. Blow up this jet and a message goes out to Tristar-Paramount, routed through every pirate satellite over the Atlantic. Something to do with their new head of security and the recent events in Canaveral City. It won't take them long to check things out. Find out whose payroll you're on."

"Another bluff," Quain said. But Clayton could hear a pause, a momentary loss of poise. He felt a small jolt of triumph, knowing he had been right. Just for a heartbeat, he had the cloned killer backed up. "Even if it isn't, no one will believe you."

"Then do it. Pull the trigger." Clayton snickered. "If you thought you could get away with it, we wouldn't be having this conversation. But I don't think you do."

A moment of silence stretched out. "It would seem that I have underestimated you, Decker. But I'm not the only one. That's what you do, isn't it? Defy the odds. Bluff on a bad hand and never fold."

"You dealt me in. I never asked for any of this. Now you're not holding all the cards anymore, and I'm planning to stay in the game until the end."

"Then we're at an impasse." Quain sounded almost regretful. "It wasn't supposed to happen like this. I had one last card to play. We had a contract, you and I, and contracts come with liquidated damages clauses. After you disappeared, I went back to Canalside to collect my collateral. But she was already gone, along with her father."

The words hollowed Clayton's belly. He had to grope for their meaning. Linda. The bastard was talking about Linda. This creature, this thing that existed only to kill, had come for Linda, but she'd gotten away. Ramesh Rustin had kept his bargain. His men had reached her before the studio thugs. She was safe, or as safe as she could be. He had to believe that.

His relief didn't last long. Sick hatred coiled and turned inside him, curdled his blood. He pushed back against it. This was no time to lose control. "I guess you can't think of everything."

"I guess not. So where do we go from here?"

"You still don't get it." Clayton let out a mirthless laugh. "There's no deal on the table here, no angle left for you to play. You're burnt, Quain. You tried to bend the rules, but they weren't the kind that can be bent. I don't know much about the Foundation, but I'll guess they're not big on second chances. Not after your fuckup with the Governor. As for the studio, you're nothing but property to them." He tried to infuse his voice with all the hatred he felt. "Not even human. A piece of faulty biotech to be scrapped and sent down a recycler chute. You know that better than anyone."

"This isn't going to do you any good, Decker." Quain's voice was cold, but there was anger underneath, pulsing like a heart. "You'll be dead the minute you step off that jet. All these cheap heroics will have come to nothing. There's only one way this can end."

"Then let's end it." Clayton leaned forward, grinning into the black screen. "I'm coming to kill you, Quain. I want you to know that. I want it to be the only thing you think about in what little time you have left. I'm here to make sure you get your dues. You and everyone else in there. I'm here to blow you all to hell."

"There's no bomb on that jet." Quain seemed to have regained some of his composure. "Only a sad, deranged man, looking for someone to put him out of his misery. Let it be so. Perhaps I owe you that much." On the dashboard, a display lit up and a glowing schematic unpeeled from its center. "Landing pad eighteen," the voice said. The line went dead.

Clayton glanced out the cabin window, saw the missile drones veer off, sweep behind the expanding glass skyline. "We're cleared to land," the pilot said, taking the controls. There was no reading his expression.

With a low, mechanical whine, the autonav switched off. The tiltjet's engines settled into a steady pitch, swiveled into landing mode. In the cockpit glass, the swooping, tangled geometries of Aventus rose like crystal walls, studded with red navigation strobes. The river and the crowded streets fell away.

Close up, the dimensions of the arcology wreaked havoc on Clayton's sense of scale and proportion. Curves and planes of steel-girded glass closed around the jet like a trap, swallowing the sky. It was like descending into a hole filled with bright light, a field of stars on the wrong side of heaven.

Visions of carnage and destruction spun before Clayton's eyes. Cracks spidering the smooth angles of glass, flames rising in the reflective panes; bodies plummeting from the shining towers. A voice whispered in his head, scratchy and distorted, speaking in a language that his conscious mind could not comprehend. But some other part of him, a hidden part, got the message. His hand wrapped around the gun.

"What happens if something goes wrong midflight?" he asked the pilot. "If you have to make an emergency landing on water?"

The pilot looked up at him, eyes red and unfocused with shock. "There's a distress beacon," he said, his voice old and strained. "The autonav protocol—"

"No." Clayton blinked, trying to make sense of the muddled subliminals, a meaning that floated just out of reach. The aircraft was nosing down toward a row of scarred ferroconcrete circles, vertical thrusters howling with strain. He watched a tiltjet take off from one of the pads, soar into the receding sky as if sucked up. "Underwater. If you're sinking. How do you open the doors?"

"Blow them out." The pilot raised a switch guard to the left of his seat. A red toggle appeared, blinking. "This arms the emergency bolts. Got to turn the engines off first. When you're ready," he pointed to a handgrip set into the base of the dashboard, "you pull the lever and the doors come off."

Below the tiltjet, the red-and-black logo of the landing pad grew. Figures clustered around the massive security doors that led into the arcology. Clayton searched for Quain but saw only polished black helmets and cerametal armor plates, the dull shine of machine pistols. Visors raised against the downblast of the engines, guns pointed, ready to fire. He could almost see the frantic messages streaking across the inside of the photochromic glass, sorting and compiling tactical feeds, calculating ranges and rates and angles.

With a shuddering clang, the aircraft unfolded its landing gear and settled in the center of the pad. The roar of the turbines dwindled to a murmur. Clayton watched the corpmercs. They were spaced along the wall, but they held back, hesitant to come closer: word of the bomb must have gone around. One armored figure, lean but powerfully built, was motioning as if giving orders.

Quain.

The armored guards shuffled closer to the jet, bodies low, uncertain. Sunlight spilled down the sides of the towers, turning the windows into burning mirrors. Even with the visors down, even though the filtered dataglass, the glare would make it hard for them to see.

Forty feet from the jet to the gate. Maybe fifty.

"What now?" the pilot said.

"Move." Clayton pointed with his gun. "Get in the back and stay there."

The pilot got up and started toward the rear of the cabin. As soon as his back was turned, Clayton stepped in and caught the man under the ear with the pistol barrel. The pilot went down with a grunt and didn't move.

Clayton sat down in the pilot's seat and thumbed the arming switch. An error message appeared on the main control screen. Outside, the ring of corpmercs had tightened a few steps. He pulled on the headset and flipped up the toggles on the comm panel.

"Stay where you are," he said, hearing his voice crackle around the jet, "or we all go to hell. There's a bomb on this jet. One of you comes forward and I pull the trigger.

They'll be scraping you off the windows, all the way to the top floor."

The line wavered and broke. Some of the corpmercs retreated all the way to the wall, heads swinging left to right, searching for cover. Quain urged them forward, impatient now. The fabricant had bet everything on this gambit. There would be questions to answer later, but he could deal with that. Silencing the only person who could challenge his version of events was what mattered now. It was his last chance.

Clayton fumbled with the engine controls, trying to find the throttle. The drumming of the ducted fans slowed, idled to a stop. Readouts winked out and the dashboard went black.

He tried the switch again. Red signs lit up above the doors; soft illumination traced an evacuation route across the cabin floor. His fingers curled around the handgrip. He tried to memorize Quain's location, the relative positions of the security personnel.

Forty feet. A few seconds of confusion. It would have to be enough.

Time slowed to a crawl. A cold, bleak calm had settled over him, part fatigue, part acceptance of whatever was to come. If this was the pivotal point his life had led to, there was no resonance to it, no great and secret revelation to be had at the end.

"Action," he said to himself, and pulled the lever.

The doors blew off with a sharp crack. Crumpled metal clattered across the tarmac. Corpmercs dove and rolled for cover. Some froze in place and turned their heads, as if trying to fend away the anticipated blast.

Clayton was already on the move, running through the smoke, pistol in one hand, the severed head under the other. Using the aircraft as cover, he dropped to the ground and ran for the entrance.

Heat rolled over him in a wave, rose from the burning concrete. A corpmerc in front of the jet, bulky in cerametal armor, had recovered from his surprise and was raising his weapon to fire. Clayton shot him and the man toppled backward, a gaping hole in his chest. Without aiming, he squeezed a short burst in Quain's direction, but the cloned killer was gone.

He kept running.

Several of the corpmercs had recovered from their surprise and were shooting at him, bullets ripping past his head. Something tugged at his side, followed by a sting of pain. He reached the heavy doors just as one of the corpmercs lifted his head from behind an electrical junction, swinging his machine pistol to bear. The Tokarev kicked faintly against its recoil brake and half of the corpmerc's helmet disappeared, blood and bone splattering the wall behind him.

More fire rained on the entrance. There was nowhere to hide. He felt a blow in his left thigh, nerves going numb. Thick warmth seeped into his trousers. He shot back blindly and raised the severed head to the plate of the facial recognition scanner, doing his best to hold it steady.

Lines began to form in the black glass, sketching the outline of Eastlake's face. Inches from his head, the wall exploded, leaving behind a crater the size of a fist. He glanced behind. Quain was walking across the tarmac, his sabot gun held in front of him, straight into the line of fire, heedless of the screaming, ricocheting bullets.

Slowly, too slowly, he saw his hand raise the pistol. Then green light exploded at the fringe of his vision and he was falling backward, into a field of cool, quiet white.

Thirty

Brightness like ground glass in his eyes... Featureless tunnels in every direction...

His hand trailed broken lines of dark red along the sterile walls. Spaces opened into each other, light and dark alternating toward infinity.

He fell and got up again, the floor sticky with his blood. Pain surged within him like a wave, sudden and excruciating, filling the hole left behind by ebbing adrenaline. There was commotion behind his back, but no one came. He loped on past virtual floorplans and interactive screens, silent imperatives, unimpeded by memory or thought, guiding him through unfamiliar space.

Bursts of static crackled across his sight.

In one of the screens he saw himself limping down a long corridor, tracking red footprints across the polished floor.

In another, his blood-slick hand raised a gun and fired, a visor split and the face behind it exploded into shreds of meat and gristle.

He went away for a moment and when he came back, he was on the floor of a dark, cramped place that smelled of motor oil, machinery thudding on the other side of the wall. His shirt and trousers were stiff where the blood had begun to dry. He peeled the clothes away and inspected his wounds. The hole in his side was small and puckered, bleeding slowly. The one in his leg was bigger, the skin around it bruised, but the bullet had gone clean through.

Reaching under his jacket, he snapped open the medikit and swabbed both wounds with antiseptic. Sprayed the disinfected flesh with coagulant, waited a few beats and sprayed again. There was a burning, itching sensation as the wounds began to clot. He slapped syntheskin patches over them and tore the plastic wrapper off the blue ampules. His arms were numb, fingers struggling to fit the ampule into its slot. He dialed the injector down to half-dose and stabbed it into his thigh, right next to the wound.

Instantly the pain retreated, shrank to a pinprick at the edge of his awareness. His breathing slowed, teeth stopped chattering. He ejected the half-spent ampule and loaded a red one, pushed the injector against his skin one more time.

The amphetamine hit his nervous system like a bolt of lightning. His pulse hammered at the base of his throat, his weariness gone in an instant. Already the bleeding had stopped: the syntheskin plugs were designed for battlefield use, could hold ripped guts together long enough for medics to arrive.

He looked around and saw metal cabinets filled with spare parts, the dismantled frame of a repair robot in one corner... a pair of stained overalls hanging off an articulated arm. He followed the trail of his blood to a ladder that descended from a ceiling hatch. To his right was a door secured with an electronic lock. Behind the repair robot was another door through which a wedge of thin light shone on the dirty floor.

He limped to the unlocked door and pushed it open. Beyond it was a narrow ledge and a tunnel with stark white walls, bisected by a monorail track. Nothing to hear but the faint buzz of electric lights. He followed the ledge to where it widened into a marble-lined platform. As soon as his foot made contact with the platform, a virtual screen pixelated into existence and a pleasant feminine voice requested him to select his destination. He chose the last stop on the line and was given an estimated arrival time of two minutes. The screen menu gave way to an ad for a gene recoding clinic, offering a ten percent discount to customers with a corporate residential permit.

He stared at the glass wall on the other side of the tracks and counted silently. When he got to one hundred and fifteen, a silver car shaped like a sphere pulled up to the platform without a sound. The doors opened and he got on.

Inside the car were two occupants, a man and a woman. Their eyes flicked rapidly behind interface glasses, staring in Clayton's direction, but seeing only feeds. Fingers moved with practiced deftness across trackpads, twitched over invisible keyboards.

Clayton leaned on the closed door and the car set off with a barely perceptible tug of acceleration. The woman noticed him first and sat up very straight and removed her glasses. Her eyes were large and blue, vivid with shock and disbelief. The man sensed a change in the car and did the same. It took him a moment to comprehend the situation and decide how to react. There was a dazed half-smile on his face, as if he were anticipating some sort of joke.

Clayton pointed at his eyes, then at the floor. He didn't trust himself to speak. He glanced down at the empty seat next to the door and decided against it. He didn't think he'd be able to get up again.

Slowly, the woman placed her glasses and palmer on the floor. Her shock had worn off, replaced by a cool look of contempt and hatred. The man followed her example mechanically. Realization was finally coming through to him and his tanned, handsome face sagged like all the bones in it had been removed. He wore a flashy dark blue suit with a gold Tristar-Paramount pin on his lapel but marked with the insignia of a junior executive. A foot soldier who had worked his way up the rungs, his bland, inexpressive good looks bought off the shelf from a plastic surgery clinic.

The woman, on the other hand, was top brass, board level or premier-grade, dressed in a carefully tailored but sensible jacket and skirt. Her pin held the symbol of Yasuda Kumiai Mutual, an insurance conglomerate. No need for her to flaunt her status and wealth. The flawless, ageless skin of her face and body had never been touched by a surgeon's knife; she was a product of the corporate creche, her perfection coded right down at the cellular level, permanently written into her genes. She would be the one to watch out for.

Both had been surprised by Clayton's appearance, and the monorail was still running, which meant that no alarm had been raised. Clayton picked up the woman's glasses and scanned through the chatter on the public channels. Nothing. Maybe Quain still thought he could resolve the situation before it escalated.

"Are you going to kill us?"

He took the glasses off and looked at the man. Amphetamine turned slow circles inside his skull. The car slid noiselessly along the track. The window framed a false distant vista of snow-capped mountains. He reached over and turned off the projection, closed his eyes in sudden vertigo as the view of the outside slid into place. The walls and the rail had changed direction and the car was gliding down a vertical shaft. He tried to focus his gaze on the tops of his shoes. The woman was watching him intently, her lip curled in a disgusted sneer.

He suddenly saw himself through her eyes—a filthy, wild-eyed freeloader, flakes of dried blood under his fingernails, stinking of slaughter and sweat and exhaustion—and the black poison spilled over, heightened by the stimulant. In that moment, he wanted nothing more than to kill them both, to pull the trigger and turn those perfect bodies inside expensive clothes to bloody ruin. Bodies untouched by rickets or scurvy, impervious to cancer and genetic ailments.

Bodies that would never succumb to disease, never see the inside of a euthanasia clinic.

"Maybe," he said, risking a look through the window. "Maybe not. How far does this car go?"

"I don't know how you got here," the woman said, ignoring the question. Her tone was clipped, precise. "But you can't get out. Both of us are expected somewhere. If we don't show up, security will track us down and come for us. You'll never have a chance."

"Main lobby of the west wing," the man said. The woman shot him an angry glance, but he paid no attention. Eyes fixed on the heavy pistol, he shrank back against his seat and gripped his knees with manicured hands. "That's where we're going. The side facing the river. Please. We'll do whatever you say."

"I need to find a computer terminal," Clayton said. "One that's connected to the central servers."

The man thought for a moment. "There's a surveillance room two levels up from the lobby." He spoke fast, as if the words were crowding his throat. "Under the rail station. West wing security is subbed out to Langley Consulting. All their video feeds are backed up on the mainframe. I used to supervise the studio's Ops and Facilities Department. I know."

"Don't tell him anything," said the woman. "If he hurts us, security—"

"Forget about security, you stupid bitch!" The man's face had gone from white to brick-red. Cords stood out in his neck. "How do you think he got inside in the first place? Someone in security must be on the take. This is a planned hit, has to be. There's a mole, a leak. Someone's trying to get rid of you, or me, or both."

What Eastlake had said in the basement of the club suddenly made more sense to Clayton. *Whatever you're being paid now, the studio can double.* Paranoia and suspicion seemed to be the order of the day in the arcology, an instinctive fear of betrayal from within, of being stabbed in the back by hungrier, more ruthless peers and subordinates. Voting blocs shifted, power and control changed hands; competition and volatility kept the killer instincts sharp.

There was a way to use this fear to his advantage, but he was having trouble thinking straight. The dead-meat chill of the endomorphin filled his head, fought with the feverish release of amphetamines.

Somewhere far away, a man and a woman were screaming at each other, the shrill, unintelligible noise a white-hot agony searing his brain. He wanted to speak out, to silence them, but words wouldn't form.

Bright light exploded in the window, glared from a boundless expanse of mirrors. The sky hung aslant. The monorail had shot out of the tunnel and was speeding across the outer edge of Aventus, hurtling between glassed-in walking bridges and steel buttresses. Other cars snapped by, enhancing the sense of speed. There were dozens of them, silver beads careering up and down monorail strands in flagrant defiance of gravity, passing one another with clockwork precision. His gorge heaved, squeezing his throat. Blinded, he moved away from the window on undone legs, swayed and caught his balance.

A faint rustle of clothing was enough for his drug-sharpened senses to alert him.

The woman was already out of her seat, scrambling for her palmer. He tried to grab her, but she twisted away, pulled him off balance. His feet shot out from under him and he went down hard, dropping the gun.

The woman was on him in an instant, hitting him with her small fists, trying to claw his face. She was stronger, in better condition, but rage and amphetamine gave him the edge. Wedging his palm under her chin, he pushed her head back, gaining enough leverage to shove her off him. The woman tumbled back and struck her head against the metal wall of the car, the noise like a muffled gong.

Clayton scrambled for his gun and froze. The man was standing over the weapon, an uncertain look in his eyes. They faced off for a long second, tension pulled taut. Then the man's nerve broke and the moment was gone. He sat back down and stared at the floor.

Clayton crawled over to the Tokarev, picked it up and righted himself shakily. "Don't try that again," he said. On the other side of the car, the woman was sobbing, more out of frustration than pain.

The car shot into another white tunnel and started to slow down. Holding the two executives at gunpoint, he herded them to the front of the car.

"Take off your clothes," he said to the man. Trembling, the executive did as he was told, hands fumbling with the buttons of his shirt. Clayton made them stand back to back and used the belt to tie their hands together. The executive was heavier in the shoulders and arms, but his jacket fit reasonably well over Clayton's own clothes, hiding the blood.

"I'm going to let you go." They looked at him as if they didn't understand. "I'm here for someone else, and I don't do freebies. I won't kill you unless you leave me no other choice. Get out and stay out of sight. Wait an hour before calling for help. Do as I say, and you won't get hurt."

Going for the weaker link, he pushed the pistol barrel against the man's cheek. "If you try anything else, you'll be very sorry. You were right about the security. We have insiders all over this place. Wherever you go, whatever you do, I'll know. You understand all that?"

The man nodded slowly. The woman didn't bother answering. Clayton picked up one of the palmers and requested a stop.

When the monorail rolled up to another empty platform, he marched the man and the woman out the door. They shuffled along awkwardly, interactive screens flaring into existence around them, stricken faces bathed blue in the light. He smashed both palmers under his heel and swept the debris onto the monorail track with the edge of his foot. The door closed with a soft chime and the car accelerated away, descending down a long tube of brilliant white.

Thirty-One

The vast, sleek lobby of the arcology's west wing faced out over the river, concrete barriers and automated antipersonnel defenses running down to the water's edge. It was built to admit as much natural light as possible, marble and chrome and frosted glass softened by blooming cascades of hydroponic greenery. Corporate logos twenty feet tall, wrought in burnished brass and copper, took place of honor in the center, surrounded by virtual screens and brand-name holos. Glass-bottomed walkways rose up to the galleries and open terraces, crisscrossed the great dome ceiling, connecting the residential areas and the business districts. The subtle scents of flowers and cool moisture mingled in the purified air.

A small crowd had formed near the entrance, faces pressed against the filtered-glass walls, watching out for the rioters. Others clustered in small groups throughout the lobby, staring at the interactive screens. No one seemed to notice him at all. Beneath the canned music and the chatter of ads, an unnatural stillness clung to the lobby, as if everyone were listening.

He pushed through to the front and gazed out past the guards, past the automated gun emplacements. The huge fortified gate at the entrance was closed, the doors sealed tight. A line of armored militiamen stood on the plaza between the gate and the defense barriers, carrying shields and bulky riot guns. The sun was just coming over the arcology, chasing away the shadows.

For a second, he didn't know what he was looking at. Then he saw it. A throng so great it blackened the streets beyond the barriers, spread over the bridges and floodgates. Rioters, forced across the river by Titan's armed response units. Yet the surge had lost its impetus; the same eerie calm reigned on both sides of the arcology glass. From where he was standing, he couldn't see faces, but the people in the streets seemed to be intent on something above them, necks craned upward.

His look followed theirs to the rooftop of a housing block overlooking the arcology's outer perimeter. The deluge of floating ads had faded into the background, making room for a corporate propaganda message. But instead of a Newscan, the thirty-foot holovid was showing shaky live footage, the feed going in and out of focus, camera jerking from side to side.

A view of the west gate of the Aventus Spire, shot from the inside, people crowding around it, looking out. The pale blur of a reflected face smeared on glass.

One by one, the rooftop holovids around the plaza winked out, replaced by the feed from his caster rig.

It took a moment for the crowd inside the arcology to realize what they were seeing. Someone was inside with them, an intruder, a pair of hostile eyes prowling among them. A man glanced around as if dazed, watched his own profile appear above the streets, scaled up to gigantic dimensions. Confusion rippled outward, heads turning away from the spectacle outside, bodies jostling against each other. Someone laughed, but it sounded shrill and forced.

Clayton moved away from the glass wall and started toward the nearest monorail platform, trying not to attract attention. At first look, his headgear was indistinguishable from a pair of interface glasses, but it wouldn't take long for someone to spot the difference. Or a sensor would pick up his face and set off a silent alarm, sending Quain's men his way. He had to get away from the busy areas, closer to the studio.

There were fewer people on the platform and the car was nowhere in sight. He keyed in his destination and thrust his hands in his pockets, desperate not to show his anxiety.

On the opposite side of the track, a holovid showed an aerial view of the perimeter defenses and the accommodation blocks around Aventus. It wasn't just the west wing now. For miles ahead in every direction, the streets were choked with people. No telling how many.

Faces like his own. Watching.

The holovid zoomed in on the nearest of the rooftops, aligning its feed with the point of view of Clayton's camera, the platform receding in an infinite tunnel of mirrors.

A man was staring at him over lowered dataglasses, glancing back at the holovid, a frown wrinkling the smooth, handsome face.

Clayton held the man's gaze, his hand creeping back toward the gun. The man shook his head at the screen, smiled and moved his shoulders in a what-can-you-do gesture. Then he clicked down his glasses and went back to flipping through the newsfeeds. A zippered leather briefcase was clutched under his arm, the zipper half open.

Platform lights blinked and two silver cars emerged from the tunnel. They came to a stop at the far end of the station and let out a handful of disembarking passengers. The lights inside went out and the doors remained open. A rumble of complaint went up from the waiting passengers. The frozen virtual screen told Clayton that the line was temporarily out of service.

He looked out over the lobby. A detachment of black-clad security guards was making its way through the crowd, led by a figure in a tan duster. There was no mistaking the easy, fluid gait.

Around him the platform was emptying. He fell in behind a line of passengers heading for the escalators, scanning the area for an exit. More armored forms on the upper level galleries, a cordon forming in front of the bank of glass-walled elevators. Several of the guards in Quain's entourage were holding handheld biometric scanners and one of them carried a large, box-shaped device wired to a portable high-density power unit on his back. They were moving from group to group, scanning faces and asking questions.

Quain seemed not to notice the bystanders around him. Every few moments he would stop and stare hard at his palmer, then raise his head and issue instructions to his men. He was streaming the signal from the holovids, using the camera angle to home in on the source of the feed.

The line to the escalator had stopped moving. The steps were choked with people, abuzz with angry protests. Looking up, Clayton saw a pair of security personnel standing on the top landing. He stepped out of the line and tracked back to the middle of the lobby. A huge brass sculpture shaped like the logo of Tristar-Paramount stood facing the entrance. Pretending to check an information screen, he paused behind the tall pedestal and considered his chances. No way up to the galleries, no way out into the street. There were uniforms everywhere he looked.

He felt the gun under his jacket and measured Quain's progress. The guards were heading directly toward him.

He was cornered, but there was no fear in him, only a vague sense of regret. It was the same feeling he'd felt in Canaveral City, looking out over the edge of the ocean. Something that was part hate and part raw pain but altogether impossible to describe. One final choice to be made. Take down as many as he could before they shot him to death. Make sure Quain was the first to die.

Then an idea occurred to him. He removed his headgear and placed it on top of the pedestal, making sure that the tiny camera was pointed at the gate, continuing to film. Head down, he walked out into the open, hand on the gun under his jacket, eyes on the black uniforms. The circle was tightening, moving closer, the guards rounding up the residents and sorting them into groups. Exasperated murmurs spread through the waiting crowd. Ident readers flashed and the guard with the metal box moved from group to group, sweeping the device back and forth.

A dozen feet behind, Quain had stopped mid-stride and was signing to someone out of sight, his free hand on a bulge in his coat pocket.

Clayton moved along the edge of the gathering until he spotted the passenger with the zippered briefcase. The guards were still a distance away, working their way down the lobby, converging on the Tristar-Paramount sculpture. He lowered his shoulder and shoved the man from behind.

The passenger reeled forward, grabbing at arms and shoulders, trying to steady himself. His briefcase dropped to the floor. Clayton stooped over and picked it up. When the man whirled around, flushed with anger, Clayton was handing him the briefcase, apologizing profusely. Ignoring the shouts of protest, he elbowed his way deeper into the crowd.

Frowning, the man straightened his jacket and clutched his briefcase tighter. He bounced on his heels and checked his palmer, looking annoyed by the delay. A few feet away, the box-shaped device tracked from left to right, halted, reversed direction.

Hidden by the press of bodies, Clayton saw the man shift his briefcase from hand to hand, do a double take and set it on the floor. His irritable expression was replaced by a look of utter puzzlement. He reached down into the briefcase and came up holding the Tokarev eleven-millimeter, the big, ugly weapon incongruous against his expensive suit. He stared at it, uncomprehending.

Almost at the same time, the scanner box flashed red and emitted a high-pitched, warbling hum. The nearest security guard reacted without hesitation; blue sparks crackled as he rammed his shock-stick into his target's solar plexus. Black uniforms piled over the man with the briefcase as he went down.

Bedlam broke out around the struggling bodies, people running for the exits, trampling each other. Quain was pinned back by the surge, waving his credentials and his gun, his voice lost in the screams and shouts that ensued. Guards were coming into the lobby from the galleries, holding shock-sticks but reluctant to use them on the residents.

Clayton flowed with the crowd up a motionless escalator. The steps seemed to go up for an eternity. The pain was something he was distantly aware of, a bright white-hot crack running along the floor of his mind, buried under soft fathoms of endomorphin. His lungs worked like an engine tearing itself apart. Step by step, he urged himself to go on.

Two levels up, the brightly lit galleries were emptying, the residents heading for the exits, flocking into crowded elevators. The holovids had been switched off and the information screens played a meaningless loop of advertising messages.

Clayton paused at the landing to catch his breath, patted his pockets for the injector and came up empty. No amphetamines and no gun and the arcology was going into lockdown. He couldn't see any guards, but he knew they had to be close by. The crowded escalators would not hold them for long.

Trying not to limp, he set off across the mosaic floor. The gallery ended in a short flight of stone steps leading to the monorail platform. Flanking the steps were two small, neatly trimmed lawns, skirted by flowerbeds and decorative bushes. Hologram screens cast a projection onto the surrounding walls, turning the lawns into a clearing in the middle of a deep, dark forest. A white gravel path wound across the grass and into the virtual trees. He walked through the projection and found a security door stamped AUTHORIZED ACCESS ONLY. Beneath the sign was a Langley Consulting corporate logo. He touched the fingertip lock, leaving a bloody smear on the plate. Nothing happened. He leaned on the door and tried again.

"Langley Consulting," a male voice said from somewhere above the door. "How can I help you today?"

"I'm with the studio." He shifted a step away from the door and braced a hand on his forehead, hiding his face. One last desperate effort. "We have an emergency situation in the lobby. Possible shots fired. I need to take a look at your surveillance footage."

"I can't do that, Mr. Pearson." The name meant nothing to Clayton. Then he remembered the pin on his lapel, the frightened face of the executive in the car. It made sense; the studio would keep their executives tagged. "I'm sure you're familiar with our contract clauses. What you're asking us to do would constitute an infraction of security and compliance protocols. If you could please submit—"

"Listen to me," Clayton said, with as much arrogance as he could muster. "We don't have time for this. There's an armed asocial in the building. He has a bomb. Our security team is trying to handle the emergency before it escalates further. I'm here on direct orders from Ethan Quain."

"Sir, our contract—"

"We have reason to believe that the terrorist got in through the west wing lobby. Right under the nose of Langley Consulting. If that bomb goes off, you can wipe your ass with your contract clauses. I'll make sure you're held responsible. Personally responsible. You'll be lucky to get a beat in the slums. Am I making myself clear?"

There was silence as the man behind the door weighed his orders against the authority vested in the Tristar-Paramount lapel pin. If he decided to check Pearson's credentials, or to call Quain, it would all be over.

The door whirred and began to slide into the wall.

Three men sat in the surveillance room, surrounded by tiers of closed-circuit flatscreens and computer monitors. The one closest to the door tried to scramble to his feet, but Clayton was ready, his hand-to-hand combat training taking over. He punched the guard in the throat and the man collapsed back into his chair, gasping for breath.

In a single motion, Clayton pulled the taser out of the holster on the man's belt, flipped the dial to full charge and fired at the second guard, whose weapon was already halfway out. The darts slammed into the target's chest. Forty thousand volts surged through the trailing wires and the man went down twitching. The remaining guard raised his arms over his head.

Clayton crouched over the tasered guard and unclipped a pair of plastic zip ties from the man's belt. He used the ties to bind the third guard's hands and feet behind his chair. Spinning the chair round, he held the taser close to the man's face, the blue arc of electricity playing between the darts.

"Which one of these terminals connects to the mainframe?"

No response. Clayton aimed the taser at the guard's crotch and the man jerked against his restraints. "All of them," he said hoarsely.

Clayton glanced around. The flatscreens showed images relayed from cameras in the west wing's communal areas or poised on top of the accommodation blocks outside of the arcology's defensive perimeter. Empty galleries and seething streets. The broadcast from the headgear camera was still playing on the holovids. He removed the datawafer from his pocket and plugged it into the nearest computer terminal, keyed in a handful of basic commands Sage had made him memorize.

A small black window opened up on the screen, a cascade of script scrolling from top to bottom. Green and blue schematics unfolded in the background, bright dots of terminals and servers linked by long, fine lines of communication protocols. He accessed a menu of security files and tapped download. Swirling text clumped together, converged into a tightly coiled vanishing point: a black poison nova spiraling through the lattices of data, leaving destruction in its wake.

He stood and blinked purple flashes from his eyes. The guard in the chair had relaxed slightly. Clayton could almost read the man's thoughts; this was a corporate skirmish, an asset-stripping raid. A crisis for the company's security division to handle. It had nothing to do with him. If he kept his mouth shut, he might come through this alive.

Clayton searched behind the desks until he found the weapons locker. The guard gave him the code to disarm the lock. Three nine-millimeter charge pistols, each with a spare clip, looked new and unused.

He cast another look at the flatscreens. The floor had been cleared of residents. A team of armored troops had reached the top of one of the escalators and was moving into position. Another group was coming out of a parked monorail car on the platform above him. The elevator bank was unguarded, but he suspected that was a trap to lure him in.

He scanned for Quain but didn't see him. The team on the platform was holding position. They had to know he was in the surveillance room, directly under their feet. He stripped off his jacket and caster rig and gagged the guard in the chair. Other screens showed the second team making quick progress down the gallery, checking the side corridors, leaving nothing to chance.

If he wanted out, he'd have to run a gauntlet of gunfire.

He sat silent for a long moment, then picked up the taser and walked up behind the man in the chair.

Thirty-Two

The sound of the door below opening cut through the tactical chatter. One by one, the members of the rapid response team leaned out from their points of cover and raised their weapons. Four laser sights swept over the edge of the platform, laying down a luminous red grid. The three corpmercs looked over to the Commander, who consulted the tracking software in her visor overlay and shook her head. Their target was stationary.

They waited, breath held, fingers poised on triggers.

Plastic wheels crunched hollow on gravel. The chair rolled into view, came to a stop at the edge of the lawn. A body was slumped over in it, hands tied behind the backrest. Dark blood stained the front of the uniform, dripped from a gash in the forehead. The Commander couldn't see the man's face, but the uniform belonged to contractor security. There was a pistol tucked into the front of his trousers, a nine-millimeter service weapon, unfired.

The terrorist was taunting them.

She pulled up a Bioscan in one corner of the tactical menu, followed the symbols crowding the sidebar. The man in the chair was alive, but not by much. By the looks of it, he'd lost a lot of blood and his breathing was so shallow that his chest barely moved under the sodden uniform shirt.

The Commander blinked sweat out of her eyes. The backup team was on the way. There would be no more than a few seconds to make a decision. Take the target down, or play it safe and wait, which meant splitting the performance bonus. Headquarters had advised caution. The studio's security division had never dealt with an intrusion before.

She worked her tongue around her dry mouth and signaled to the point man to check it out. It was a search-and-destroy operation. No finesse required, just a lot of firepower. Nothing the four of them couldn't handle.

The corpmerc set his charge rifle to full auto and advanced down the steps, keeping his sightlines clear. Smart sights picked up the signal from his suit, friend-or-foe tags eliminating the chance of friendly fire. In the overlays of the other three, the point man's figure was a black stain on the targeting grid. He reached the chair and stood over the bloodied form, turned around and relayed his visuals to the others. The holographic forest had vanished and the walls around the steps were bare. The door to the surveillance room was closed. He kept his rifle on it as the rest of the team made their way down, graceful and silent as wraiths.

Tactical software whispered information, estimating the target's location, calculating lines of fire. Two team members took up position on either side of the doorway, the commander in the middle, the point man covering the rear. The Commander took first pressure on the trigger and nodded the go-ahead. The corpmerc on the right short-circuited the electronic lock.

Gridlines leapt up and shrink-wrapped around the tracking beacon. Electrochemical firing mechanisms engaged, poured a lethal fusillade into the open space ahead. Slugs thudded into bodies and walls, ripped through chairs and desks. Screens burst into flames and shards of plastic. Overhead lights exploded, showering glass and yellow sparks.

The Commander raised her arm and gave the order to cease fire. Nothing moved in the surveillance room. Nothing could be alive. Yellow and green graphics appeared at the bottom of her vision, the Bioscan indicating three bodies in the wreckage, high probability of massive trauma. Stuttering lights made it hard to tell, but she thought she could see the shredded remains of a suit jacket on one of the corpses.

She called up the comm menu, blinked to clear her vision. Something was wrong. In her visor, tactical constellations were winking out, nodes of garbled graphics streaking across like comets. Static hissed in her earpiece, climbed up to a painful, deafening whine. All along the gallery, lights were going out, information screens falling apart in pixels and smears of corrupted data.

One of the corpmercs by the door had lowered his rifle and raised his visor and was taking off his right glove. His face wore a puzzled expression. The other one was shouldering his weapon, mouth wide in a shout she couldn't hear.

She swung around just in time to see the bloodstained man rise up from the chair, aiming a pistol at her. Her mind froze as she brought her own rifle to bear, squeezing the unresponsive trigger, knowing it was already too late.

Through half-closed eyes, Clayton focused on the massive figure approaching him, a nightmare of matte black armor and weapons, its only human part a narrow strip of face between the gorget and the visor. The corpmerc gave him a cursory scan and turned his attention to the surveillance room door. He hadn't bothered to check the plastic ties. Slowly, almost imperceptibly, Clayton shifted his wrists.

Heavy steps on the stairs. Three other corpmercs fanned out around the door. He heard a faint electric crackle, followed by a deluge of automatic fire. Slipping off the ties, he took the pistol out of his waistband. The nearest corpmerc had his back turned and was tapping his earpiece. Two more to either side of the door, shaking their helmeted heads as if trying to dislodge something. A smaller shape, a woman, was standing on the threshold of the devastated room, uncertainty in her stance.

Prescott's virus ate through their tactical software, scrambling information into nonsense.

It was the only chance he would get.

He came up from the chair, both hands on the pistol, aiming at the gap between the neck guard and helmet. Shot through the throat, the corpmerc made a choking noise and dropped his weapon. Clayton caught the man as he sagged and held him up as a shield, staggered back under the unexpected weight.

The woman and the man on her right were fast, moving in tandem, trained combat reflexes taking over, rifles coming up. But the weapons wouldn't fire, their friend-or-foe system tagging the dead corpmerc as one of their own. Clayton aimed the pistol low and pulled the trigger, the burst shattering the woman's ankle. She went down with a cry and a curse, tried to return fire, her teeth bared in rage as the trigger jammed again. He put two more rounds into her torso, and she twisted in pain. The man shouted some-thing and wedged the rifle between his knees, frantically clawing at the weapon's targeting sights.

The fourth corpmerc, the one to the left of the door, had his visor up and a dazed, shocked look on his face. Clayton snapped off a couple of bursts and the face disap-peared in a cloud of red mist, the body thrown back against the wall. His comrade tore his targeting sights off and shot back without aiming, rifle chattering on full auto.

Impacts shook the body in Clayton's arms. He emptied his pistol into the remaining corpmerc's chest and hit the floor, the body coming down on top of him.

Pain rolled in, a slow, smoldering fire. His ribs burned with every breath. He got up and reloaded the pistol, went over to the doorway. A thin red thread flowed from the corner of the corpmerc's mouth. The armor had stopped most of the pistol slugs, but the sternum underneath was broken, or at least bruised. The corpmerc heaved for air, flashed a bloody grin and reached for his rifle.

A single gunshot echoed up the empty gallery, loud in the sudden silence.

Clayton stood over the female corpmerc and picked up her weapon. Green eyes stared defiantly from under the cracked visor. He aimed between them and tried to fire. The trigger felt like it was set in stone and a red dot winked on the tactical menu. He slung the rifle over his shoulder and tottered up the stairs to the platform.

Thirty-Three

The sun poured through the glass walls, shone on the great red-and-black sigil above the entrance to Tristar-Paramount. He limped out of the monorail car and through the open door, listening for the security guards. They couldn't be far behind. All they had to do was follow the telltale red trail behind him. His wounds had reopened in the melee by the surveillance room and his head swam with the blood loss.

From below came a noise like a rush of wind, sweeping through the marble lobby, traveling up the tunnels. He supposed the mob had stormed the gates and battlements, past unresponsive gun turrets pointed up at the sky, and was inside the arcology now. What would happen next was none of his concern.

The studio was empty, but there was motion in the rafters overhead, automated cameras sliding aimlessly along their tracks, microphone booms going up and down. Half of the lights were gone, and the gallery swam in shadows, lit by flashes from the main screen. Most of the monitors around the stage were blank and the few still working showed static and distorted colors.

On the great screen, an endless, senseless sequence of frames played over and over; the closeup of a dirty face beneath a helmet, a bullet smashing it to gory pulp; men running out of a burning bunker, jerking and rolling on the ground; a wounded soldier planting a flag on the roof of a tall building.

The soundtrack blared down on him from the stage, marching music blended with explosions and advertising jingles.

He gripped the gallery rail and hauled himself up the steps. Suspended a few feet above, a camera rolled to a halt. The lens tracked and focused upon him. The aperture opened, narrowed, sliced his curved reflection. He grinned at it through the blood, smashed the lens with the butt of his rifle and kept climbing.

His sight wavered in and out like a weak radio signal. The projection room at the top was dark, chairs overturned, desks littered with paper. He lowered himself behind the last row of seats and folded his legs under him. It was harder than he'd expected. Something was wrong with his arms and legs. He sat back against the wall and cradled the rifle. Blood soaked through his uniform shirt, the belt of his trousers. A few of the corpmercs' bullets had gotten through, but he felt no pain, only an emptiness within him, trackless and cold.

The glow from the screen washed over him. A weary face gazed at him with an empty stare and exploded into a mask of blood. Men burned and collapsed, curled into fetal balls, clawed the black dirt. The pictures played again and again, and each face was his own.

A shadow darkened the doorway. Wincing, he leaned the rifle over the edge of the seat and looked down.

Quain walked into the studio, gun pointed into the darkness. He was alone. It had come down to just the two of them now, one dying, the other as good as dead, trapped with nowhere to run.

He braced and took careful aim. Then he remembered the identification tags and unscrewed the smart sights and lined up the shot again. Quain had not moved from the doorway. Black silhouette against a slate of burning light.

Clayton wrapped his finger around the trigger and thought about Josh and Linda, about Prescott and Salvesen and the zone. About Cal and his lost tribe. Searched for guilt, or for meaning, found nothing but savage exhilaration, the animal thrill of destroying an enemy.

He smiled through the blood because he knew this was something that couldn't be taken away from him, something of his own. It was a killing pattern weaved into the eons, the one he shared with the man on the other end of the rifle barrel, with the furious mob surging through the arcology gates, hands clenched on bricks and pipes and metal bars, itching to put them to use.

Even as he fired, he knew that he had missed. Saw the cloned killer go down on one knee, the bullet raise a puff of plaster from the wall, the hand with the sabot pistol come up, guided by reflex wetware.

Saw a starburst of muzzle flash, but no sound.

In the small, unreal stillness, he sensed the impact before it came, and the realization was frightening because it felt like freedom. Something in him opened up, spread wide to embrace it. An all-encompassing comprehension, as wide as the world, compressed into a single point at the center of him. He tried to hold onto it, to face it in its entirety, but it eluded him, unfurled its wings and sailed out beyond the glass and marble and metal.

Solid space began to slip away. Memories took its place, then they too fled. Rapturous, he fled with them, leaving behind the lobby, floating over the river, the grim housing projects, the masses in the streets. He saw, or imagined that he saw, the concrete gates open, the automated guns fall silent, a tide of wrath and desperation burst its dam and flood the gleaming towers. All that was beyond him now.

Above the blue scrim of earth, falling and falling into the great starry night, black emptiness enfolded him from within, twined around him, the silence singing him to sleep.

Thirty-Four

The pilgrims huddled around the fire and watched.

Pale fire split the starfield, a long, blazing spear stabbing down, painting the wasteland in razor-sharp shadows. Thunder poured from the lacerated sky. A flash of radiance in the night, white-hot like the sun at noon, followed by a blast that shook the barren ground. Then silence.

They left the colony before first light and trekked across the desert, guided by the swell of dark smoke against the flat horizon. The youngest among them toted the ancient rifle and the other two carried knives. Neither of them knew what the fire meant but somehow, they sensed it was a turning point, a defining moment after which nothing would be the same. There had been signs. Some of the men and women of the community were believers and they spoke of recent events with a mix of apprehension and hope, looking up at Cal for guidance. The old man did his best to assuage their fears, but in his dark moments he thought about the soldier who had walked out of the burning sand, about the Deacon's disappearance, and his heart was uneasy. Passing traders—there were more of them now—had brought word of violent upheaval in the city, of arcologies attacked and looted, of the conglomerates girding up for war. A bad time was coming, and Cal worried about his colony, of feeding their growing ranks.

It was already hot by the time they reached the impact site and wisps of steam rose from the shores of the lake behind them. They perched on the edge of the crater and looked down. The object was some eight feet in diameter and twenty long, shaped like a cylinder with a tapered end, its scarred surface covered in dust. Its lower part was half buried in the cracked ground. Even at a distance, the cylinder threw off heat like a forge.

None of the three spoke. The only noises were the hiss and creak of cooling metal below, the trickle of yellow dirt down the rim of the crater. Fused glass crackled under their feet, soil blackened by heavenly fire.

They waited. Hours passed. The sun climbed higher and the old man took a tarp out of his pack and they unfolded it for shade. After a while the youngest man laid the rifle down and descended into the crater. The heat had abated.

Carefully, he moved down the length of the cylinder, swept his hand over the pocked metal and shreds of cerametal ablate. The other two joined him. Near the tapered end they found a black glass plate with a sign etched above it. Cal remembered seeing the sign many years ago and something like understanding hovered at the edge of his mind. He ran his callused forefinger over the etching and laid his palm on the glass.

Gears whined under his hand, followed by the hiss of dissipating vacuum. A deep groove under the tapered end widened and latches popped up in the dark interior.

Together the men unscrewed the end off and lowered it to the ground. Four cryogenic containers, their sides inscribed with red symbols, lay nestled one behind the other, surrounded by piles of insulation. Sweating and straining, the men pulled them out into the sunlight.

Cal squatted down on his haunches and studied the symbols. The story they told was a familiar one: he had written part of it himself, in a previous life. Biocultures. Gene-engineered algal strains. A gift of the germ of life for the poisoned desert. His throat tightened with excitement as he tallied the crop yield numbers, subdivided the land into plots. There would be a lot of work to do, tough decisions to be made.

He thought about the necklace of orbitals, the brightest star in the heavens, and dared to hope.

The two younger men were staring at him in silence.

"We'll need the others to help," he said, and started up the side of the crater, the pain in his hips and knees forgotten.

About the Author

Damir's short fiction has been featured in the *Lovecraft Ezine, Dimension6 Magazine,* and in horror and speculative fiction anthologies by Gehenna & Hinnom Books, The Bolthole, Source Point Press, Grinning Skull Press, Ulthar Press and others. He lives in Virginia and earns his living as an auditor, a profession that supplies nightmare material for his stories and plenty of writing time in the form of long-haul flights and interminable layovers.

Website:
https://darkerrealities.wordpress.com
GoodReads:
https://www.goodreads.com/author/show/7224637.
Damir_Salkovic

www.ingramcontent.com/pod-product-compliance
Lightning Source LLC
Chambersburg PA
CBHW030402020726
47493CB00003B/916